It's time for…

Summer Temptations

These two tempting reunion novels will make perfect summer reading!

Casey:

Meet Casey – he's as hot-blooded as they come and he's about to be reunited with the one woman that got away – Emma Clark!

Blame it on Texas:

What's going to happen now that Kate has come home to face her childhood sweetheart Dustin? Rumours are flying fast and furious. And the whole town is watching for what unfolds next…

Summer
Temptations

CASEY
Lori Foster

BLAME IT ON TEXAS
Kristine Rolofson

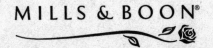

MILLS & BOON®

*MILLS & BOON and MILLS & BOON with the Rose Device
are registered trademarks of the publisher.*

*First published in Great Britain 2004
Harlequin Mills & Boon Limited,
Eton House, 18-24 Paradise Road,
Richmond, Surrey, TW9 1SR*

SUMMER TEMPTATIONS © Harlequin Enterprises II B.V., 2004

The publisher acknowledges the copyright holders of the
individual works as follows:

Casey © Lori Foster 2002
Blame it on Texas © Kristine Rolofson 2001

ISBN 0 263 84108 1

49-0604

*Printed and bound in Spain
by Litografia Rosés S.A., Barcelona*

CASEY

by

Lori Foster

Lori Foster was first published in January 1996 and since then has sold over thirty books with six different houses, including series romance, novellas, online books, special projects and, most recently, single titles.

Lori has brought a sensitivity and sensibility to erotic romances by combining family values and sizzling yet tender love. Though Lori enjoys writing, her first priority will always be her family. Her husband and three sons keep her on her toes. You can find out more about Lori Foster at her website: www.lorifoster.com

Look out for more of Lori Foster's sizzling and sexy novels – coming soon in Sensual Romance™!

You may have met Sawyer, Morgan, Gabe and Jordan in Lori Foster's THE BUCKHORN BROTHERS miniseries. Now it's Casey's turn…and he's really turning up the heat!

This book is dedicated to:

To all my very special friends on the bookjunkies list. You keep me smiling from one book to the next. Sharing with you, knowing you, having your support and friendship, has meant the world to me. Thank you! I'd also like to give a special thanks to these bookjunkies gals: Lois, Ann, Donna and Kristine. It was fun teasing you about Casey, and using your first names. The characters, however, are strictly from my imagination. No pretend characters could ever be as wonderful as each of you. And to Jana Taylor and Cyn Witkus for all the research help on massage therapy. Smooches to both of you!

PROLOGUE

THE FAMILY PICNIC had lasted all day, and Casey had a feeling everything that should have been accomplished had been. In fact, even more had developed than he'd expected—like his present uncomfortable situation.

He hadn't exactly meant to pair up with Emma Clark. She had few friends, none of them female, and Casey had just naturally defended her when the others had started sniping.

So now, with nearly every girl in town chasing after him, he found himself behind the garage at the far end of the house with a girl—the one girl he'd been doing his best to avoid—snuggled up to his side. No one else in the yard could see them. They had complete privacy.

How the hell was a guy supposed to deal with that?

His father and his uncles had been the most eligible bachelors in Buckhorn, Kentucky. It had been fun for Casey growing up in an all-male household and watching his uncles and his dad deal with all that female adoration. Casey had been proud of their popularity and amused by it all. And pleased by the situation, since he'd gained his own share of adoration as he'd matured. He'd learned a lot from watching them—but he hadn't learned how to deal with Emma.

Like his father and his uncles, Casey loved and respected women, most especially his grandmother and his new stepmother and aunts. But then, they were all so different from Emma.

And that thought had him frowning.

Emma was…well, she had a reputation that could rival his Uncle Gabe's, and that said something since Gabe had been a complete and total hedonist when it came to his sexuality. By all accounts, Gabe had started young; from what Casey knew, Emma had started even younger.

At seventeen, she flaunted herself with all the jaded expertise of a woman twice her age. Her bleached-blond hair and overdone makeup advertised her status of being on the make.

Lately she'd been on the make for Casey. For the most part, he'd been able to resist her.

For the most part.

Emma's small soft hand began trailing over Casey's chest. His heart thumped hard, his body hardened. Very gently, doing his best to hide his reaction from her, he eased her away. "We should join the others."

In fact, he thought, all too aware of the heat of her young body so close to his own, he never should have been alone with her in the first place. Thanks to his stepmother and her father, he had a great business opportunity coming up. But before he could take advantage of that, he had several years of college to get through. Emma, with her hard-to-resist curves and open sensuality, would be nothing but trouble.

"No." She stroked down his bare chest, but Casey caught her hand before she reached the fly to his jeans. He liked her more than he should have, and wanted her more than that. Hell, to be truthful, he was crazy nuts with wanting her, not that he'd ever even hinted as much. His plans for the future did not include Emma. They couldn't.

Emma had led a very different life from him. Tangling the two up wouldn't be good for either of them.

His head understood that, but his body did not.

It took more control than he knew he had to turn her away this time.

"Emma," Casey chided, hoping that she couldn't hear the shaking of his voice. He'd only wanted to champion her, but Emma wanted more. She was so blatant about it, so brazen, that it took all his concentration not to give in. Besides, more than anything else, Emma needed a friend not another conquest. And beyond that, Casey didn't share.

"Are you a virgin?" she taunted, not giving a single inch, and Casey laughed outright at her ploy. She was determined, he'd give her that. But then, so was he.

Flicking a finger over her soft cheek, he said, "That's none of your business."

Her incredible brown eyes widened, reflecting the moonlight and a femininity that went bone deep. She shook her head in wonder. "You're the only guy I know who wouldn't have denied it right away."

"I'm not denying or confirming."

"I know," she whispered, still sounding amazed, "but most guys'd lie if they had to, rather than let a girl think—"

"What?" Casey cupped her face and despite his resolve, he kissed her. Damn, it was hard fighting both himself and her. "I don't care what anyone thinks, Emma. You should know that by now. Besides, what I've done or with who isn't the point."

"No," she agreed, her tone suddenly so sad it nearly broke his heart. "It's what I've done, isn't it?"

Thinking about that, about the guys she'd probably been with and the notoriety of her reputation, filled Casey with possessive rage. So many guys had bragged. Too damn many. Ruthlessly, Casey tamped down the urges he refused to acknowledge, and repeated his own thoughts out loud. "I don't share."

"Casey," she said, shyly peeking up at him, her expression tinted with hope, "what if I promised not to—"

"Shh." He couldn't bear for Emma to start pleading, to make promises he doubted she could keep and that wouldn't matter in the long run anyway. He couldn't let them matter. "Don't do that, Emma. Don't make it harder than it already is. Summer break is almost over and I'll be leaving for school. You know that. I won't be around, so there's no point in us even discussing this."

Big tears welled in her eyes, causing his guts to cramp. One of her hands fisted in his shirt. "I'm leaving too, Casey." Her breathing was choppy, the words broken.

Emma leaving? That surprised him. As gently as possible, Casey stroked the tears from her cheeks and then, because he couldn't help himself, he kissed her forehead. "And where do you think to go, Em?" She hadn't finished high school yet, had no real prospects that he knew of, no opportunities. Her home life was crap, and that bothered him too. He wanted...

No, he couldn't even think that way.

"It doesn't matter," she said. "I just wanted you to know."

He didn't like the sound of that, but had no idea what to say. He could see her soft mouth trembling, could smell her hot, sweet scent carried on the evening breeze. Unlike the other girls he knew, Emma didn't wear fragrances. But then, she didn't need to.

Her warm palm touched his jaw. "You're all that matters to me right now, Case. You and the fact that we might not ever see each other again."

Boldly, she took his hand and pressed it to her breast. Casey shuddered. She was so damn soft.

His resolve weakened, then cracked. With a muttered curse, he pulled her closer and kissed her again, this time giving his hunger free rein. Her mouth opened under his, accepted his tongue, gave him her own. It didn't matter, he promised himself, filling his hand with her firm breast, finding her puckered nipple and stroking with his thumb.

She gave a startled, hungry purr of relief, her fingers clenching on his shoulders, her hips snuggling closer to his, stroking his erection, driving him insane.

Casey gave in with a growl of frustration and overwhelming need. He was damned if he did, and damned if he didn't. And sometimes Emma was just too much temptation to resist.

But it wouldn't change anything. He told her so in a muted whisper, and her only reply was a groan.

Two Months Later

CASEY SAT BACK in his seat and watched them all with an indulgent smile. Family gatherings had become a common event now that everyone had married and started families of their own. He missed having everyone so close, but they visited often, and it was obvious his father and uncles had found the perfect women for them.

The girl beside Casey cleared her throat, uncomfortable in the boisterous crowd of his family. It didn't matter because he doubted he'd see her again anyway. Donna was beautiful, sexy and anxious to please him—but she wasn't perfect for him. He knew it was dumb, considering he wasn't quite nineteen yet, but Casey couldn't help wondering if he'd ever meet the perfect girl.

An image of big brown eyes, filled with sexual curiosity, sadness, and finally rejection, formed in his mind. With a niggling dread that wouldn't ease up, Casey wondered if he'd already found the perfect girl—but had sent her away.

Then he heard his aunt talking to Donna, and he pulled himself out of his reverie. No, she wasn't perfect, but she didn't keep him awake nights either. And that was good, because no matter what, no matter how he felt now, he would not let his plans get off track. He decided to forget all about women and the future and simply enjoy the night with his family.

It was late when the family get-together ended and Casey finally got home after dropping off his date. He'd just pulled off his shirt when a fist started pounding on the front door. He and his father, Sawyer, met in the hall, both of them frowning. Sawyer was the town doctor and out of necessity, patients sometimes came this late at night, but as a rule they called first—unless there was an emergency. Casey's stepmother, Honey, pulled on her robe and hustled after them.

When Sawyer got the door open, they found themselves confronted with Emma's father, Dell Clark. Beyond furious, Dell had a tight grip on his daughter's upper arm. His gaunt face was flushed, his eyes red, the tendons in his neck standing out.

Casey's first startled thought was that even though he hadn't seen her in two months, Emma hadn't gone after all. She was right here in Buckhorn.

Then he got a good look at her ravaged face, and he erupted in rage.

He'd been wrong. His plans were changed after all. In a big way.

CHAPTER ONE

ENRAGED AND UNCERTAIN what he planned to do, Casey started forward. Before he reached Dell, Sawyer caught his arm and drew him up short. "Take it easy, Case."

Emma covered her mouth with a shaking hand, crying while trying not to cry, held tight by her father's grip even as she attempted to inch away from him. She wouldn't look at any of them, her narrow shoulders hunched in embarrassment—and possibly pain.

Casey's heart hurt, and his temper roiled. Emma's pretty brown eyes, usually so warm and sexy, were downcast, circled by ruined makeup and swollen from her tears. There was a bruise on her cheek, just visible in the glow of the porch light.

Casey felt tight enough to break as a kind of animal outrage that he'd never before experienced struggled to break free. Every night he'd thought about seeing Emma again, and every night he'd talked himself out of it.

Not once had he considered that he'd see her like this.

His vision nearly blurred as he heard Emma sniff and watched her wipe her eyes with a shaking hand.

With unnecessary roughness, her father shoved her forward and she stumbled across the wide porch before righting herself and turning her back to Casey. Without a word, she held on to the railing, staring out at the moonlit yard. Her broken breathing was audible over the night sounds of wind and crickets and rustling leaves.

"Do you know what your damn son did?" Dell demanded.

Casey felt Sawyer look at him but he ignored the unasked questions and instead went to Emma, taking her arm and pulling her close. It didn't matter why she was here; he wanted to hold her, to tell her it'd be all right.

Drawn into herself, Emma sidled away from him, whispering a broken apology again and again. She hugged her arms around herself. Casey realized the night was cool, and while Dell wore a jacket, Emma wore only a T-shirt and jeans, as if she'd been pulled away without having time to grab her coat. Since he was shirtless, he couldn't offer her anything. He tried to think, to figure out what to do, but he couldn't get his brain to work. He felt glued to the spot, unable to take his gaze off her.

She needed his help.

Honey came to the same realization. "Why don't we all go inside and talk?"

Looking horrified by that proposition, Emma backed up. "No. That's not—"

"Be quiet, girl!" Her father reached for her again, his anger and his intent obvious.

Casey stepped in front of him, bristling, coiled. "Don't even try it." No way in hell would he let Dell touch her again.

Face mottled with rage, her father shouted, "You

think you get some say-so, boy? You think what
you've done to her gives you that right?''

Without moving his gaze from the man in front of
him, Casey said, "Honey, will you take Emma inside?''

Honey looked at her husband, who nodded. Casey
hadn't had a single doubt what his father would do
or say. Not once in his entire life had he ever had to
question his father's support.

Never in his life had he been more grateful for it.

Again, Emma tried to back away, moving into the
far shadows of the big porch. Casey snapped his gaze
to hers, so attuned to her it seemed he felt her every
shuddering breath. "Go inside, Emma."

She bit her lip, big tears spilling over her blotchy
cheeks and clinging to her long lashes. Her mouth
trembled. "Casey, I…''

"It's all right." He struggled to keep his voice soft,
comforting, but it wasn't easy—not while he could
see the hurt in her eyes and feel her very real distress.
"We'll talk in a little bit."

Speaking low and gentle, Honey put her arm
around Emma, and reluctantly, Emma allowed herself
to be led away. The front door closed quietly behind
them.

With his daughter out of sight, Dell seemed more
incensed than ever. He took two aggressive steps forward. "You'll do more than talk. You'll damn well
marry her."

Casey gave him a cool look of disdain. That Dell
could treat a female so callously made him sick to his
stomach, but that he'd treat his own daughter that way
brought out all Casey's protective instincts. More than

anyone else he knew, Emma needed love and under-standing. Yet, her own father was throwing her out, deliberately humiliating her.

"You brought her here," Casey growled. "You've delivered her to my doorstep, to *me*. What she or I do now is no concern of yours. Go home and leave us the hell alone."

Though Casey knew it would only complicate things more, he wanted to tear Dell apart. It wouldn't strain him at all. He was taller, stronger, with raw fury adding to his edge. He deliberately provoked Dell, and waited for his reaction.

It came in a lightning flash of curses and motion. The older man erupted, lunging forward. Smiling with intent, anxious for the confrontation, Casey braced himself.

Unfortunately, Sawyer caught Dell by his jacket collar before Casey could throw his first swing.

At well over six feet tall, solid with muscle, Sawyer wasn't a man to be messed with. He slammed Dell hard into the side of the house, and held him there with his forearm braced across his throat. He leaned close enough that their noses nearly touched.

"You come onto my property," Sawyer snarled, looking meaner than Casey had ever seen him look, "treating your only daughter like garbage and threatening my son?" He slammed Dell again, making his head smack back against the wood siding. "Unless you want me to take you apart right now, which I'm more than willing to do, I suggest you get hold of your goddamn temper."

Dell's face turned red from Sawyer's choking hold, but he managed a weak nod. When Sawyer released him, he sagged down, gulping in air. It took him several moments, and Casey was glad that Emma had gone inside so she didn't hear her father's next words.

Wheezing, Dell eyed both Sawyer and Casey. "You're so worried about Emma, fine. She's yours." He spit as he talked, his face distorted with anger and pain. "You and your son are welcome to her, but don't think you can turn around and send her back home."

"To you?" Casey curled his lip. "Hell no."

Something in the man's eyes didn't make sense. The fury remained, no doubt about that. But Dell also looked…desperate. And a bit relieved. "You swear?"

He should have hit the son of a bitch at least once, Casey thought. He nodded, and forced the next words out from between clenched teeth. "You just make sure you stay the hell away from her."

Glaring one last time, Dell stepped around Sawyer and stomped down off the porch. At the edge of the grass, he stopped, his shoulders stiff, his back expanding with deep breaths, and for a long moment he hesitated. Casey narrowed his eyes, waiting. For Emma's sake, he half hoped her father had a change of heart, that he showed even an ounce of concern or compassion.

Dell looked over his shoulder at Casey. His mouth opened twice but no words were spoken. Finally he shook his head and went to his battered truck. He didn't glance back again. His headlights came on and he left the yard, squealing his tires and spewing gravel.

Casey stood there, breathing hard, his hands curled

into fists, his whole body vibrating with tension. The enormity of the situation, of what he'd just taken on, nearly leveled him. He squeezed his eyes shut, trying to think.

Jesus, what had he done?

Sawyer's hand slipped around the back of his neck, comforting, supportive. A heavy, uncomfortable beat of silence passed.

"What do you want to do first, Case?" Sawyer spoke in a nearly soundless murmur, his voice disappearing in the dark night. "Talk to me, or talk to Emma?"

Casey looked at his dad, a man he loved and respected more than anyone else on earth. He swallowed. "Emma."

Nodding, Sawyer turned them both around and headed for the door. Casey hoped a few answers came to him before the morning light began creeping over the lake. Because, at the moment, he had no idea what the hell was going on.

EMMA HEARD the opening and the closing of the front door. She squeezed her eyes shut, horrified, ashamed, scared spitless.

And oddly relieved.

More tears leaked out, choking her, burning her cheeks and throat. What had she done? What choice had she been given?

Honey touched her arm in a motherly way. "Drink your hot chocolate. And Emma, everything will be okay. You'll see."

Shaking down deep in her soul, Emma wiped at her eyes. She felt like a child, and knew she looked more like a barroom whore. Her makeup had long since been ruined and her nose and eyes were red. Her hair was a wild mess and her T-shirt was dirty.

Though the Hudson household was cozy and warm, she still felt chilled from the inside out. In that moment, she wondered if she'd ever be warm again.

Hugging herself in self-conscious dismay, she wished she could just disappear. She didn't belong in this house with these nice respectable people. But disappearing wasn't an option. She'd gotten herself in this mess and now she had to face them all. She had to explain.

She owed Casey at least that much.

At that moment, barefoot and shirtless, Casey came around the corner into the kitchen. His muscled arms crossed over his chest as he stopped in front of the kitchen table where she sat. His light-brown eyes, filled with compassion and confusion, warmed to glittering amber as he looked her over.

Stomach churning in dread, Emma flicked her gaze away.

Casey's father, Sawyer, stood behind him. Honey sat beside her. She felt surrounded, circled by their concern and curiosity, hemmed in by their kindness.

The damn tears welled up again and she felt herself start to shudder. Oh God, if she bawled like a baby now she'd never forgive herself.

His expression solemn, Casey held out his hand. "Let's me and you talk a little, Emma."

She stared at him through a haze of tears.

Sawyer frowned. "Casey…"

"Just a few minutes, Dad. I promise."

Honey sent Sawyer a pointed look, then patted

Emma's shoulder. "You can use the family room. Sawyer and I will make sandwiches and join you in just a few minutes."

Keeping her head bowed so she wouldn't have to make eye contact with anyone, Emma left her chair. She didn't want to take Casey's hand, and tried to walk around him, but he caught her and his fingers laced into hers. His hand was big and warm, strong and steady. Reassuring.

Normally, just being near him made her feel more secure. But not this time.

To her amazement, when he reached the family room, Casey sat down and tugged her into his lap. She couldn't remember anyone ever holding her like that before. Emma was so shocked she almost bolted upright, but Casey wrapped both arms around her and pulled her so tightly to him, her head just naturally went to his shoulder. Her shaking increased.

Very gently, Casey stroked one hand up and down her back. "Em? Tell me what's going on."

Despite her resolve, she clutched at him. "I'm so sorry, Casey. So, so sorry."

He pushed her hair away from her face, then reached for a box of tissues on the end table and held them in front of her. Emma blew her nose, but it didn't help. The tears kept coming and she couldn't make them stop. "I didn't mean to get you involved, I swear."

Calmly, as if she hadn't just turned his life upside down, he said, "Involved in what?"

That was the thing about Casey. He was always calm, always so mature and sure of himself that, without thinking, she'd used his name and now… Emma grabbed for three more tissues. This was where she had to be careful. "I told my parents that I'm pregnant."

Casey went very still. Silence hung heavy in the air, broken only by her gasping breaths and awful sniffling. Casey sat there, tall and proud and strong, while she fell apart like a deranged child.

In that moment, Emma hated herself.

His hand began stroking her again. "I take it they weren't too happy about it?"

She laughed, but the humor faded into a wail. "I couldn't think of what else to do."

"So you came to me?"

He didn't seem nearly as outraged as she had expected. But then Casey was so different from any other guy she knew, she didn't know what to expect from him. He had a good handle on everything, on his life, his temper, his future.

"It's not…not what you think." This was even harder than she'd imagined. On the silent drive to his house, with her father fuming beside her, she'd tried to prepare herself, tried to make decisions. But this was the worst thing she'd ever done.

"No?" His thumb carefully smoothed over the bruise on her cheek.

God, she wished he'd say something more, maybe yell at her or throw her out. His calm destroyed what little control she'd been able to hold on to. "No." She shook her head and leaned away from the gentleness of his touch. It took one breath, then another, before she could speak convincingly. "I don't need or want anything from you, Case."

The intensity of his dark gaze seeped into her and she tried to look away.

Gently, Casey brought her face back up to his. "Then why are you here, Em?"

"I just…" *I had to escape.* She drew a shaking breath and attempted to gather herself together. The last few hours had seemed endless, and the night was far from over. "I needed to get away and I couldn't think of anything else."

A rap on the door made her jerk, and she looked up to see Sawyer and Honey standing there, each carrying a tray. Sawyer held sandwiches and Honey held mugs of hot chocolate.

Emma started to groan. God, they were like Leave it to freakin' Beaver or something, so homey and together that nothing shook them for long, not even the neighborhood riffraff dropping in with a bombshell that should have disrupted the rest of their lives.

Envy formed a vise around her heart, but she knew she'd never belong to a family like theirs. They'd never want her.

Her own family didn't.

Sawyer's smile appeared strained but kind. "I think we should all do a little talking now."

He set the tray on the coffee table and settled into a chair. Honey did the same. They both seemed to ignore the fact that she'd ended up perched on Casey's lap, held in his strong arms. But the second Emma realized just how that would look, she shot to her feet. Before she could move too far away, Casey leaned forward and caught her wrist. Unlike her father's grip, his was gentle and warm.

Casey's hold offered comfort not restraint.

He came to his feet beside her, and she had the awful suspicion he wanted to provide a united front to his parents. He faced his father squarely, without an ounce of uncertainty or embarrassment. "Emma is pregnant."

Sawyer's jaw locked, and Honey looked down at her clasped hands, but not fast enough to hide her distress. When Emma started to speak, Casey squeezed her hand, silencing her. She understood what he wanted to do, and this time it was love clenching her heart. Not infatuation, not jealousy for all he had.

Real love.

There didn't exist a better man than Casey Hudson. Emma knew in that moment she'd never forget him, no matter what turns her life took in the morning.

Very slowly, her movements deliberate and unmistakable, Emma pulled herself away from Casey. She took one step, then another and another, until she stood several feet away from him.

It wasn't easy, but she managed to face his parents. This time her gaze never wavered. What she had to say was too important to leave any doubts. "Casey has never touched me."

Sawyer sat up a little straighter, and his eyebrows came down in a dark frown of bewilderment. Honey's gaze darted between them.

"Emma…" Casey took a step toward her.

She shot up a hand to ward him off. His nobility, his willingness to sacrifice himself, amazed her and made her love him that much more. She smiled at him, her first genuine smile in weeks. The time for sniffling and crying and being a fool had ended. She owed this family more than that. She owed Casey so damn much. "Casey, when I told my parents I was pregnant, I lied."

"But…"

Feeling stiff and awkward, she rolled one shoulder in a casual shrug. "I'm sorry." Her words trembled, nearly incoherent, and she cleared her throat. She wanted to beg him not to hate her, but that wouldn't be fair. "I know it was wrong. I had to say something to get away and I couldn't think of anything else."

His gaze locked on her, Sawyer rose from his chair. He looked angry, but Emma had the feeling his anger wasn't directed at her. Still, she couldn't stop herself from backing away at his approach. When she caught Casey's frown, she halted and forced herself to remain still.

With a large gentle hand on her chin, Sawyer tipped her face this way and that to examine her bruised cheek, then he carefully looked at the rest of her face. He was an imposing man, and she'd always been in awe of him. Now, with him in front of her and Casey close at her side, she almost felt faint.

"What happened to your face, Emma?" Sawyer's tone left no room for evasions. He expected an answer. He expected the truth.

He couldn't have it.

Emma touched the bruise, and winced. "I…I fell, that's all."

Casey snorted.

She cast him a quick worried look, but couldn't meet his piercing gaze for more than a few seconds. They didn't deserve to be lied to, but neither did they deserve to be drawn into her problems. If they knew, they'd never let her get away. She'd done enough to them. From here on out, she would handle things. Alone. She had to.

Sawyer again tipped up her chin, this time to regain her attention. "We can help if you'll let us."

Did every one of them take nobility in stride? Emma wiped her eyes on her crumpled tissue, wondering how to explain without telling too much. Shame bit into her, and she sighed. "Dr. Hudson, I'm so sorry—"

Casey caught her elbow and whirled her around to face him, his anger barely leashed. "Quit apologizing, damn it. It's not necessary."

Emma pulled back. "I've barged in here—"

"Your father barged in, not you." Casey's light-brown eyes burned nearly gold, and his jaw was set. "You're not responsible for what he does, Emma."

"But…this time I am," she explained gently. She was very aware of his parents' attention. "I told him I was pregnant, and I told him…I told him that you were the father."

She turned to Sawyer and Honey in a rush, stumbling over her words. "Casey hasn't ever touched me, I swear. He wouldn't. He's so much better than that. But I knew if I named any other guy…" She stalled, not sure what else to say. From the time she became a teenager, she'd been with so many boys. And yet, she'd named the only one who hadn't wanted her.

Hands on his hips, Casey dropped his head forward, staring at the floor. He made a rough sound, part growl, part sarcasm. "None of the other guys would have defended you, would have taken you in."

Relief that she hadn't had to explain, after all, made

Emma's knees weak. "I used your integrity against you, and I *am* sorry." Twisting her hands together, she faced Sawyer. "Everyone in Buckhorn knows that you and your brothers are good people. I thought that you might help me, so I used Casey's name to get here. It wasn't right and I can understand if you hate me, but it was the only thing I could think of."

"Emma," Honey murmured, her tone filled with sympathy, "no one hates you."

Impatient, Sawyer shook his head. "Why did you need to get here, Emma? That's what I want to know."

And Honey added, "But of course you're more than welcome to stay—"

"Oh, no." Appalled by the conclusions she'd led them to, Emma shook her head. "No, you're not stuck with me or anything like that." She'd made a real muddle of things, she realized. "I have no intention of imposing on you, I swear."

They met her promises with blank stares.

She started trembling again. She'd never felt more unsophisticated or more trashy than she did right at that moment, standing among them. The comparisons between herself and them made her stomach pitch. She wanted to take off running and never look back.

Soon, she promised herself. Very soon. "I have some money that I've saved up, and I know how to work. I'm going to go to Ohio first thing in the morning."

"What's in Ohio?" Casey asked, and he didn't look so even-tempered now. He looked ready to explode.

A new life, she wanted to tell him, but instead she

lied. Again. "I have a…a cousin there. She offered me a place to stay and a job."

Her expression worried, Honey glanced at Sawyer, then Casey, before tilting her head at Emma. "What kind of job?"

What kind of job? Emma blinked, taken aback by the question. She hadn't expected this. She'd thought they'd be glad to see her gone. Oh, she'd known that they would offer to let her stay the night, that they'd be kind. She wouldn't have come to them otherwise. But she figured once she told them she had a place to go they'd send her on her way with no questions asked.

Think, she told herself, and finally mumbled, "I'm not sure, actually. But she said it'd be perfect for me and I assume it'll be something…reasonable."

The way they all looked at her, they knew she was lying. Emma started backing away toward the phone. "I…I'm going to call a cab now." She dared a quick peek at Casey, then wished she hadn't. In all the time she'd known him, she'd never once seen him so enraged. "When…when I get settled, I'll write to you, okay?"

Casey again crossed his arms over his chest. "That won't be necessary."

Her heart sank and she wanted to crumble in on herself. "I understand." Why would he want to hear from her anyway? She'd offered herself to him plenty of times—and every single time he'd turned her away. And still she'd barged into his life.

"You don't understand a damn thing." Casey began striding toward her. "Emma, you're not going anywhere."

His tone frightened her. She felt locked in his gaze, unable to look away, unable to think. "Of course I am."

"No." Sawyer strode toward her too, his movements easy, nonthreatening, which didn't help Emma's panic one bit. "Casey is right. It's damn near the middle of the night and you look exhausted. You need to get some sleep. In the morning we'll all talk and figure out what's to be done."

"No…" She shook her head, dazed by their reactions.

"Yes." Sawyer took her arm, his expression gentle, his intent implacable. "For now, I want you to eat a sandwich and drink some chocolate, then you can take a warm shower and get some sleep."

In a quandary, Emma found herself reseated on the sofa. They weren't throwing her out? After what she'd done, what she'd just admitted to them?

Her own father, despite everything or maybe because of it, had used the opportunity of her supposed pregnancy to rid himself of her. And her mother… No, she wouldn't, *couldn't*, think about that right now.

Honey smiled at her. "Please don't worry so much, Emma. Everything is okay now."

"Nothing is okay." Why couldn't they understand that?

Honey's gentle smile never slipped. "I felt the same way when I first came here, but they're sincere, I swear. We're *all* sincere. We just don't want you rushing off until we know you'll be all right."

Confusion weighed heavy on her brain. She didn't know how to deal with this.

Casey sat down beside her and shoved a peanut butter and jelly sandwich into her hand. Emma stared at it, knowing she wouldn't be able to swallow a single bite without throwing up. She had to do... something. She had to get out of here before their acceptance and understanding weakened her resolve.

She would not become someone else's burden.

Her mind made up, she put the sandwich aside. "I'd really like to just take a shower if that's okay. I know I look a mess."

Using his fingertips, Casey wiped away a lingering tear she hadn't been aware of. He hesitated, but finally nodded. "All right. You can sleep in my room tonight."

Her eyes widened and her mouth fell open. Casey grinned at her, then pinched her chin. "I'll, of course, sleep on the couch."

Mortification washed over her for her asinine assumption. At her blush, Casey's grin widened. She couldn't believe the way he teased her in front of his parents.

"You could have used Morgan's old room, except that Honey's been painting it and everything is a mess in there."

Morgan was his uncle, the town sheriff. Most people thought he was a big, scary guy. He was enormous, but he'd always been kind to Emma, even when he'd caught her getting into trouble, like breaking curfew or being truant from school. Newly wed, Morgan had recently moved into his own house.

"I'll take the couch." Emma thought that would be easier, but Casey wouldn't hear of it.

"You'll take the bed."

His father and stepmother agreed with him. In the end, Emma knew she was no match for them. Exhaustion won out and she nodded. "All right." It would be strange sleeping in Casey's room, in his bed. A secret part of her already looked forward to it. "Thank you."

Casey took her down the hall to the bathroom, then got her one of his large T-shirts to sleep in. She knew it was selfish, but she accepted the shirt, holding it close to her heart. It was big and soft and it held his indescribable scent. Since she couldn't have Casey, it was the next best thing.

Their bathroom was bigger than her whole bedroom. It was clean and stylish and that damn envy threatened to get hold of her again. Emma swore to herself that someday, she'd have a house as nice as this one. Maybe not as big, but just as clean and warm and filled with happiness. Somehow, she'd make it happen.

Knowing it would take forever for it to dry, she didn't bother washing her long hair. When her opportunity arose, she had to be ready, and she didn't want to run away with wet hair. She did brush out all the tangles and tie it back with a rubber band. The shower did a lot to revive her and make her feel less pathetic.

After she'd dried off and donned the shirt, Emma glared at herself in the mirror, and cursed herself for being such a crybaby. Casey wouldn't be a whiner. If something happened in his life, he'd figure out how to deal with it. He'd do what he had to.

And so would she.

With the makeup washed away, her red nose and eyes looked even worse. The bruise showed up more too. It had all been necessary, she reminded herself, but still the thought of change terrified her—just not as much as staying.

She lifted the neckline of the shirt and brushed it against her nose, breathing deeply of Casey's scent. She closed her swollen eyes a moment to compose herself.

Everyone was waiting for her when she left the bathroom, which made her feel like a spectacle. She was used to being ignored, not drawing attention. In a lot of ways, she preferred being ignored to this coddling. They were all just so…*kind*.

Sawyer gave her a cool compress to put over her puffy eyes, along with two over-the-counter pills that he said would help her relax and get some sleep.

Honey fussed over her, occasionally touching her in that mothering way. She told Emma to help herself if she got hungry during the night and to let her know if she needed anything.

She'd rather die than disturb any of them further. Emma knew she could be very quiet when she needed to be; she'd learned that trick early in life. Like a wraith, she could creep in and out without making a sound. No way would she wake anyone up tonight.

Honey kissed Emma on the forehead before she and Sawyer went down the hall, leaving her alone with Casey so he could say good-night. Emma was amazed anew that they'd trust her enough to leave Casey in the room with her, especially now that they had firsthand evidence of her character. She was a liar and a user.

Then she realized it wasn't a matter of trusting her. They trusted Casey, and with good reason.

Casey sat on the edge of the bed and looked at her. After a moment, he even smiled.

Emma remembered how many times she'd done her best to get Casey this close. That last time at his family's picnic, she'd almost succeeded. But in the end, Casey had been too strong-willed, and too moral to get involved with her. She'd decided that night to leave him alone, and for the most part she'd stuck to that conviction. She hadn't seen him in so long.

Now he was right next to her and she was in his bed, and she could see the awful pity in his gaze. That hurt so much, she almost couldn't bear it. She'd make sure this was the last time he ever looked at her that way.

"Are you all right now, Em?"

"I'm fine," she lied, confident that it would be true soon enough. "I just wish I hadn't put your family through all this." She wished she could have thought of another way.

Rather than reply to that, Casey smoothed his hand over her head. "I've never seen your hair in a po-nytail."

Her heart started thumping too hard and her breath caught. She stared down at her hands. "That's be-cause it looks dumb, but I figured I looked bad enough tonight that nothing could make it worse."

As if she hadn't intruded in the middle of the night, hadn't dragged him into her problems, hadn't dis-rupted his life, Casey chuckled. "It does not look dumb. Actually it looks kinda cute." Then, startling her further, he leaned forward and brushed his mouth over her forehead. "I'll be right out on the couch if you need anything, or if you just want to talk."

Emma said nothing to that.

"Promise me, Em." His expression was stern, with that iron determination that awed her so much in evidence. "If you need me, you'll wake me, okay?"

"Yeah, sure." *Not in a million years.*

Looking unconvinced, Casey straightened. "All right. I know it's not easy, but try not to fret, okay? I'm sure we'll be able to figure everything out."

We. This family kept saying that, as if they each really wanted to help. She'd made herself his problem by using his name, but by tomorrow he wouldn't have to worry about her ever again. "Casey? Thank you for everything."

"I haven't done anything, Em."

She lifted his large, warm hand and kissed his palm. Her heart swelled with love, threatening to break. "You're the finest person I've ever met."

THE RED HAZE OF DAWN streamed through the windows when Honey shook Casey awake early the next morning. He pushed himself up on one elbow and tried to clear away the cobwebs. He'd been in the middle of a dark, intensely erotic dream. About Emma.

His father stood behind Honey and right away Casey knew something was wrong. "What is it?"

"Emma is better than me," Honey said.

Casey frowned at that. "How so?"

"None of us heard her when she left."

Sawyer looked grim. "There's a note on your bed."

Casey threw the sheet aside and bolted upright. He wore only his boxers, but didn't give a damn. His heart threatened to punch out of his chest as he ran to his bedroom. Worry filled him, but also a strange panic.

She couldn't really be gone.

He came to a halt in the middle of his room. The covers had been neatly smoothed over the empty bed, and on the pillow lay a single sheet of paper, folded in half.

Dreading what he would read, Casey dropped onto the mattress and picked up the note. Honey and Sawyer crowded into the doorway, watching, waiting.

Dear Casey,
I know you told me not to say it, but I'm so sorry. For everything. Not just for barging into your life tonight but for trying to corrupt you and trying to interrupt your plans. It was so selfish of me. For a while there, I thought I wanted you more than anything.

Here she had drawn a small smiley face. It nearly choked Casey up, seeing her attempt at humor. He swallowed and firmed his resolve.

But that would have been really unfair to you.
I'm also sorry that I took the money you had on your dresser.

Casey glanced at his dresser. Hell, he'd forgotten all about the money, which, if he remembered right, amounted to about a hundred dollars. Not enough for her to get very far. Emotion swamped him, then tightened like a vise around his chest, making it hard to breathe.

I had some money of my own, too. I've been saving it up for a long time. I promise as soon as I get settled I'll return your money to you. I just needed it to get me away from Buckhorn, and I figured better that I borrow your money and leave tonight than to continue hanging around being a burden.

Damn it, hadn't he told her a dozen times she wasn't a bother? No. He'd told her not to apologize, but he hadn't told her that he wanted her there, that he wanted to help. That he cared about her.

Have a good life, Casey. I'll never, ever forget you.

Love,
Emma Clark

Casey crumpled the letter in his fist. He wanted to punch something, someone. He wanted to rage. It felt as though his chest had just caved in, destroying his heart. For a long moment, he couldn't speak, couldn't get words out around the lump in his throat.

Sawyer sat down beside him with a sigh. ''I'll call Morgan and see if he can track her down.''

As the town sheriff, Morgan had connections and legal avenues that the others didn't have. Casey looked at his father, struggling for control. ''We don't know for sure where she's going.''

"To Ohio, to her cousin, she told us," Honey reminded them.

"She never gave us her cousin's name."

"I'll call Dell." Sawyer clapped Casey on the shoulder, offering reassurance. "He'll know."

But half an hour later, after Sawyer had finished his conversation with Emma's surprisingly rattled father, Casey's worst suspicions were confirmed. Emma didn't have a cousin in Ohio. As far as Dell knew, there was no one in Ohio, no relative, no friend. Dell spewed accusations, blaming Casey for his little girl's problems, for her pregnancy, even going so far as to insist he should be compensated for his loss. He said his wife was sick and now his daughter was missing.

Casey suffered a vague sense of relief that Emma had gotten away from her unfeeling father. If only he knew where she'd gone.

If only he knew how to get her back.

Neither he nor Sawyer bothered to explain the full situation to Dell Clark. If Emma had wanted him to know, she would have told him herself. Eventually Dell would know there had never been a baby, that Emma had only used that as an excuse to be thrown out—to escape.

But from what?

Casey hoped she hadn't gone far, that it wouldn't take too long to find her. Damn it, he *wanted* to take care of her, dumb as that seemed.

But hours after Sawyer put in the request to Morgan, he came outside to give Casey the bad news.

Casey had been standing by a fence post, staring out at the endless stretch of wildflowers in the meadow. He'd bored the horses with his melancholy and they'd wandered away to munch grass elsewhere. The sun was hot, the grass sweet smelling and the sky so blue it could blind you. Casey barely noticed any of it.

"Case?"

At his father's voice, Casey jerked around. One look at Sawyer's expression and fear grabbed him. "What is it?"

Sawyer quickly shook his head. "Nothing's happened to Emma. But Morgan checked with highway patrol… They haven't seen her. There've been no reports of anyone fitting her description. It's like she vanished. I'm sorry, Case."

Casey clenched his hands into fists, and repeated aloud the words that had been echoing in his head all morning. "She'll turn up."

"I hope so, but…something else happened last night." Sawyer propped his hands on his hips and his expression hardened. "Late last night, Ceily's diner caught fire."

Slowly, Casey sank back against the rough wooden post. "Ceily…?"

"She wasn't even there. It was way after hours, during a break-in, apparently." Sawyer hesitated. "Morgan's investigating the fire for arson."

"Arson? But that means…"

"Yeah. Someone might have tried to burn her down."

On top of his worry for Emma, it was almost too much to take in. Ceily was a friend to all of them. Everyone in town adored her, and the diner was practically a landmark.

"It's damn strange," Sawyer continued, "but the

fire was reported with an anonymous call. Morgan doesn't know who, but when he got on the scene the fire was already out of control. Structurally, the diner is okay, but the inside is pretty much gutted. Whatever isn't burned has smoke damage.''

Casey felt numb. Things like arson just didn't happen in Buckhorn.

Of course, girls didn't accuse him of fathering a nonexistent baby very often either. "Morgan's okay?''

"He's raspy from smoke inhalation, but he'll be all right. Ceily's stunned. I told her we'd all help, but it's still going to take a while before she'll be able to get the place all repaired and opened again.''

Barefoot, her long blond hair lifted by the breeze, Honey sidled up next to Sawyer. Automatically his father put his arm around her, kissed her temple and murmured, "I just told him.''

Honey nodded. "I'm so sorry, Casey. Morgan has his hands full with the investigation now.''

"Meaning he doesn't want to waste time looking for Emma?''

Honey didn't take offense at his tone. "You know that's not it.'' She reached out to touch his shoulder. "He's done what he can, but considering the note she left, there's no reason to consider any foul play.''

Sawyer rubbed the back of his neck in agitation. "I know how you feel, Case. I'm not crazy about her being off on her own either. Hell, I've never seen such an emotionally fragile young woman. But Dell doesn't want to file her as a missing minor, so there's nothing more that Morgan can do. She'll come back when she's good and ready, and in the meantime, all we can do is wait.''

Honey patted Casey again. ''Maybe she'll contact you. Like Sawyer said, we'll wait—and hope.''

When Casey turned back to the meadow, both Sawyer and Honey retreated, leaving him alone with his worries. Yes, he thought, she'll contact me. She had to. They shared a special bond, not sexual, yet…still special.

He felt it. So surely she felt it too.

THE DAYS TICKED BY without word from Emma.

The fire at the diner had stolen all the news, and Emma's disappearance was pretty much skipped by most people. After all, she hadn't made any lasting friendships in the area. The boys had used her, the girls had envied her, and the schools had all but given up on her. Not many people missed her now.

In the next few weeks, the town gradually settled back down to normal, but an edgy nervousness remained because whoever had broken into Ceily's diner and started a fire was never found. Casey went through his days by rote, hurt, angry with himself as much as with Emma.

Three months later, he got a fat envelope filled with the money Emma had taken, and a few dollars more. In her brief note, Emma explained that the extra was for interest. There was no return address and she'd signed the note: *Thanks so much for everything. Emma Clark.*

Frustrated, Casey wondered if she always signed her first and last name because she thought he might forget her, just as the rest of the town had.

At least the return of the money proved she was alive and well. Casey tried to tell himself it was enough, that he'd only wanted her safe, that all he'd ever felt for her was sympathy with a little healthy lust thrown in.

But he'd be a complete fraud if he let himself believe it. The truth burned like acid, because nothing had ever hurt as much as knowing Emma had deliberately walked away from him.

He didn't ever want to hurt like that again.

Since she didn't want to return, didn't want to trust him, *didn't want him,* he couldn't help her. But he could get on with his life.

With nothing else to do, he went off to school as planned. And though he knew it hadn't been Emma's intention, she'd changed his life forever. He wanted her back, damn it, when he'd made a point of never having her in the first place.

Forget her? There wasn't a chance in hell that would ever happen.

CHAPTER TWO

Eight Years Later

THOUGH SHE COULDN'T SEE beyond the raised hood, she heard the very distant rumble of the approaching car and gave a sigh of relief. Damon, who had been about to set a flare on the narrow gravel road, walked back to her with the flare unlit. He stuck his head in the driver's-door window. "I'm going to flag this guy down and maybe he'll give us a hand."

Emma smiled at him. "The way this day is going? We'll be lucky if he doesn't speed on by and blow dust in our faces."

B.B. hung his head over her seat and nuzzled her ear. His doggy breath was hot and impatient. Likely, he wanted out of the car worse than she did. The winding gravel roads opened on both sides to endless stretches of overgrown brush that shielded anything from rabbits to snakes. B.B. heeded her call, so she wasn't really worried about him wandering off. But she also didn't want to take the chance that he'd get distracted with a critter on unfamiliar ground.

The day had already been endless with one hitch after another. What should have been a six- or seven-hour drive from Chicago to Buckhorn, had turned into eight and a half, and they hadn't even had a chance to stop for a sit-down meal. Even with the occasional breaks they'd taken and her quick stopover at the hospital, they were all beat. The dog wasn't used to being confined for so long, and neither was she.

Damon patted her hand. "Stay put until I see who it is. This late on a Saturday night, and in a strange town, I don't want to take any chances with you."

Emma rolled her eyes. "Damon, I grew up here, remember? This isn't a strange place. It's Buckhorn and believe me, it's so safe it borders on boring."

"You haven't been here in eight long years, doll. Time changes everything."

She scoffed at that ridiculous notion. "Not Buckhorn. Trust me."

In fact, Emma had been amazed at how little it had changed in the time she'd been away. On their way to the one and only motel Buckhorn had to offer, they'd driven through the town proper. Everything looked the same: pristine, friendly, old-fashioned.

The streets were swept clean, the sidewalks uncluttered. There were two small grocery stores at opposite ends of town, each with varying specialties. The same clothing store that had been there for over a hundred years still stood, but painted a new, brighter color. The hairdresser's building had new landscaping; the pharmacy had a new lighted sign.

Lit by stately lampposts, Emma had gazed down a narrow side street at the sheriff's station, situated across the street from a field of cows. Once a farmhouse, the ornate structure still boasted a wraparound porch, white columns in the front, and black shutters. Emma wondered if Morgan Hudson still reigned supreme. He'd be in his mid-forties by now, but Emma would be willing to bet he remained as large, strong and imposing as ever. Morgan wasn't the type of man ever to let himself go soft.

She also saw Gabe Kasper's handyman shop, now expanded into two buildings and looking very sophisticated. Apparently business was good for Gabe, not that she'd ever had any doubts. Women around Buckhorn broke things on purpose just to get Gabe to do repairs.

Then she'd seen Ceily's diner.

Her stomach knotted at the sight of the familiar building, quiet and closed down for the night but with new security lights on the outside. Everyone in town loved that quaint old diner, making it a favorite hangout.

Her heart gave a poignant twinge at the remembrance of it all.

"For once," Damon said with dramatic frustration, drawing her away from the memories, "will you just do as I say without arguing me into the ground?"

B.B. barked in agreement.

"You guys always gang up on me," Emma accused, then waved Damon off. "Your caution is unnecessary, but if it'll make you feel better, I'll just sit here like a good little helpless woman. Maybe I'll even twiddle my thumbs."

"Your sarcasm is showing, doll." He glanced at the dog. "B.B., see that she stays put."

The dog hung his head over her shoulder, mournful at the enormity of the task.

The approaching car finally maneuvered through all the twists and turns of the stretching road, and drew near. Arms raised, Damon rounded the hood to signal for assistance. It must be a nice vehicle, Emma thought, hearing the nearly melodic purr of the powerful engine. She'd learned a lot about cars while living with the Devaughns.

Unfortunately, she hadn't learned enough to be able to change a water pump without a spare pump on hand.

At first, because of the angle of the road, the swerving headlights slanted partially in through her window, blinding her. When the car stopped right in front of them, the open hood of her Mustang kept her from being able to see the occupants. In a town the size of Buckhorn, the odds weren't too bad that she might recognize their rescuers. Though few people had really befriended her, she'd grown up with them and could still recall many of them clearly.

Beside her, B.B.'s head lifted and he rumbled a low warning growl at the strangers. Emma reached over her shoulder to put her hand on his scruff, calming him, letting him know that everything was okay.

The purring engine turned off, leaving only the night sounds of insects. "Well, hello."

With amusement in his tone, Damon replied, "Good evening."

Emma couldn't see, but she could hear just fine, and the feminine voice responding to Damon was definitely flirtatious. She sighed.

Sometimes Emma thought he was too good-looking for his own good. He wasn't overly tall, maybe an inch shy of six feet, but he had a lean, athletic build and warm, clear blue eyes and the most engaging grin she'd ever witnessed on a grown man.

Everywhere he went, women turned their heads to watch him.

"Can we give you a lift?"

"Actually," Damon's deep voice rumbled, "I'd just like to make a call to Triple A. Do you have a cell phone with you? My battery went dead an hour ago."

A car door opened, gravel crunched beneath someone's feet, and the next voice Emma heard almost stopped her heart. "Sorry, I don't carry one when I'm not working. The ringing is too bothersome. But we can take you into town to make the call."

Stunned, Emma pushed her car door open and slowly climbed out. Damon wouldn't leave her alone to go to town and make the call, especially once he realized that he'd just flagged down the only person in Buckhorn that she had serious reservations about seeing again.

B.B. jumped over the seat and climbed out behind her, sticking close to her side. The big German shepherd moved silently across the grass and gravel, his head lifted to scent the air for danger, his body alert.

Emma paused a moment in the deep shadows, sucking in fresh, dewy air and reminding herself that she was now an adult, not a lovesick schoolgirl with more bravado than brains. There was no reason to act silly. No reason to still feel embarrassed.

Casey was nothing to her now. He'd never really been anything to her except a friend—and an adolescent fantasy. After what she'd done to him, and after eight long years, friendship wasn't even an issue.

She had planned to see him, of course. Just not yet. Not when she looked so… Emma stopped that line of thought. It didn't matter that she wore comfortable jeans and a logo sweatshirt, or that her eyes were shadowed from too little sleep over the past few days.

Smoothing her hair behind her ears and straightening her shoulders, Emma slipped around the front of the Mustang and stepped into the light of the low beams. B.B. stationed himself at her side, well mannered but ready to defend.

Emma took one look at Casey and a strange sort of joy expanded inside her. He looked good. He looked the same, just…more so. With every second of every day, she'd missed him, but she didn't know if he would even remember her.

"Well, I thought I recognized that voice," Emma said, proud that only a slight waver sounded in her words. "Hello, Casey."

Damon twisted around to face her, and Casey's head jerked up in surprise. Emma held herself still while the woman with Casey scooted closer to him, blatantly staking a claim.

Caught between the headlights of both cars, they all stood there. The damp August-evening air drifted over and around them, stirring the leaves and the tension. Moths fluttered into the light and wispy fog hung near the ground, snaking around their feet. Emma heard the chirp of every cricket, the creaking of heavy branches, her own stilted breath.

His body rigid, his thoughts concealed, Casey stared toward Emma. In the darkness, his eyes appeared black as pitch, intensely direct. He explored her face in minute detail, taking his time while Emma did her best not to fidget.

The silence stretched out, painful and taut, until Emma didn't know if she could take it anymore.

Finally, he took a step forward. "Emma?"

Like a warm caress, his familiar deep voice slipped over and around her. He said her name as a question, filled with wonder, surprise, maybe even pleasure. At eighteen, he'd seemed so grown up, but now that he was grown, he could take her breath away.

Her smile felt silly, uncertain. She made an awkward gesture, and shrugged. "That'd be me."

"My God, I'd never have recognized you." He strode forward as if he might embrace her, and Emma automatically drew back. She didn't mean to do it, and she silently cursed herself for the knee-jerk reaction to seeing him again. His physical presence, once so comforting, now seemed as powerful, as dark and turbulent, as a storm. The changes were subtle, but she'd known him so well, been so fixated on him, that they were glaringly obvious to her.

At her retreat, Casey drew to a halt. His smile faltered then became cynical, matching the light in his eyes. He veered his gaze toward Damon, and Emma knew he'd drawn his own conclusions.

When he faced her again, his expression had turned icy. "I'm surprised to see you here, Em."

"My father…he's in the hospital." She hated herself for stammering, but when she'd thought Casey might touch her, her heart, her pulse, even her thoughts had sped up, leaving her a little jumbled. *No, no, no,* she silently swore, wanting to deny the truth. Surely, eight years was long enough. It *had* to be.

But right now, with Casey so close she could feel the beat of his energy and the strength of his presence, it felt as if less than eight days had passed. Long-buried emotions clamored to the surface, and Emma struggled to repress them again.

Oh, it wasn't that she still pined for Casey, or that she carried any fanciful illusions. The time away had been an eternity for her. She'd gone from being an immature, needy girl to a grown, independent woman. She'd learned so much, faced so many realities, and she now considered herself a person to be proud of.

But seeing him, being back in Buckhorn...well, some memories never died and her last ones with Casey were the type that haunted her dreams. She could still blush, remembering that awful night and what she'd put him and his family through. Like old garbage, her father had dumped her on Casey's doorstep—and he'd taken her in.

That wasn't the only thing that made her hot with embarrassment, though. The nights that preceded her eventful departure were worse. She'd thrown herself at Casey again and again, utilizing every female ploy to entice him—and had always been rebuffed. The strongest emotion he'd ever felt for her was pity.

And now he had no reason to feel even that.

"I'd heard your dad was sick. Will he be all right?"

It didn't surprise her that he knew. There were few secrets in Buckhorn, so of course he'd heard.

Renewed worry prodded her, sounding in her tone. "He was asleep when I stopped at the hospital earlier, and I didn't want to disturb him. He needs his rest. But the nurse assures me that he's doing better. They have him out of intensive care, so I guess that's a good sign. I just…I wish I could have talked with him."

"What happened?"

She swallowed hard, still disbelieving how quickly things had changed. The call from her mother had rattled her and she hadn't quite gotten a grip on her emotions yet. She hadn't seen her father in so long, but she'd always known he was there, as cantankerous and hardworking as ever. But now… Emma stared up at Casey and felt the connection of a past lifetime. "He had a stroke."

"Damn, Em. I'm so sorry to hear that."

She nodded.

Casey shifted closer, scrutinizing her as if he couldn't quite believe his eyes. His expression was so probing, she felt stripped bare and strangely raw.

When Casey moved forward, so did the very pretty redhead with him. She plastered herself to his side in a show of possessiveness. "You two have met?"

Casey glanced at her, then draped his arm over her shoulders with negligent regard. There didn't seem to be any real level of intimacy between them.

But then what did Emma know about real intimacy?

"Emma and I practically grew up together." Casey watched her as he said it, his eyes narrowed, taunting. "We were close, real close I thought, but she's been away from town now for…"

"Eight years," Emma supplied, unwilling to hear him say any more. Close? The only closeness had been in her head and in her dreams. Dredging up her manners, Emma held out her hand and prayed the darkness would hide her slight trembling. "I'm

Emma Clark, and this is my friend, Damon De-vaughn.''

With a look of suspicion, the redhead released Ca-sey to shake hands politely with both Emma and Da-mon. "Kristin Swarth."

"It's delightful to meet you," Damon murmured, and Kristin's frown lifted to be replaced by a coy smile. Damon had charisma in spades and the ladies always soaked it up.

Though Damon had no problem warming up to Kristin, he didn't treat Casey with the same courtesy. The second she'd first said Casey's name, Damon had gone rigid and he hadn't relaxed again.

Now, at the introduction, Casey eyed Damon anew, then drew the woman a little closer. "Kristin and I work together."

It wasn't easy, but Emma managed another smile. "I hope we're not interrupting your plans?"

"Not really." Casey gave her a lazy look. "I was just about to take Kristin home."

At the word *home,* B.B. let out a friendly *woof,* and Emma laughed. "I'm sorry, I almost forgot. This is my pal, B.B."

With a wide grin, Casey hunkered down in front of the big dog. "Hello, B.B."

Using noticeable caution, the dog sauntered for-ward, did some sniffing, and then licked Casey's hand. Emma had almost forgotten how good Casey's family was with animals, Casey included. His Uncle Jordan was even a vet, but they all loved animals and were never without a menagerie of pets.

"Where'd you come up with the name B.B.?"

Emma chuckled, her tension easing with the topic.

B.B. was her best friend, her comrade in arms when necessary, her confidant. They'd comforted each other when there was no one else, and now it often seemed B.B. could read her mind. "Big Boy," she explained, and B.B. barked in agreement.

"He's a gorgeous dog." Casey stroked along B.B.'s muscled back, then patted his ribs. "How old is he?"

Damon answered for her, his gaze speculative as he watched man and dog bonding. "We're not sure, but probably about nine or so. He was young when Emma got him, more a ball of fur with nothing big about him, other than his appetite."

Emma quickly elbowed Damon, hard. A history of how she'd gotten the dog was the last thing she wanted discussed. She didn't mean for Casey to witness that prod, but when she glanced down at him, their gazes clashed and held. He didn't say anything, and that was a relief. When she got Damon alone, she'd choke him.

As Casey scratched the dog's head and rubbed his ears, Emma absorbed the sight of him. It seemed impossible, but eight years had only made him better—taller, stronger, more handsome. As a teen, he'd been an unqualified stud. As a grown man—wowza.

The gentle evening breeze ruffled his dark-blond hair, and his brown eyes caught and held the moonlight. He wore dark slacks and a dress shirt that fit his wide shoulders perfectly. Emma forced her gaze away. It was beyond dumb for her to be ogling him.

The car behind him was, amazingly enough, also a Mustang, but surely a much newer, ritzier model.

Emma nodded at the car, trying to see it clearly in the shadows of the night. "Black or blue or green?"

Keeping his hand on B.B.'s head, Casey straightened. "What?"

"Your car."

He swiveled his head around and looked at the car as if he'd never seen it before. "Black."

"Mine is red and in desperate need of a water pump. If you're heading into town, do you think you could direct someone this way? Or is there even road service in the area yet?"

Casey shook his head. "Hell no. If you call Triple A it'll take them at least a couple of hours to get out here to you."

Emma groaned. She was dead on her feet and anxious to get settled. All she wanted to do was shower, eat and sleep, in that order. She'd already stopped at the hospital on the way into town. Damon had kept an eye on B.B., letting him walk about on the grounds while she'd spoken briefly with the nurses before visiting her father.

He'd looked so old and frail, and hadn't registered her visit. She'd wanted to touch him, to reassure herself that he was alive, stable. But she'd held back. Since the doctor was due to see him again in the early morning, she planned to be there so she could get a full update on his prognosis.

Casey moved closer to her again. "The garage is closed for the night, too. That hasn't changed. We still roll up the sidewalks by nine. But I can give you both a ride into town if you want."

Emma looked at Damon. He lounged back against

the car and smiled his sexiest smile. "We'll be staying at the Cross Roads Motel. Is that too far off?"

Casey cocked one eyebrow and gave Emma an assessing look. "You're not staying with your mother?"

"No." Just the thought of seeing her mother again, of being back in the house where her life had been so miserable, made Emma's stomach churn. Because Casey couldn't possibly understand her reserve, she scrambled for reasons to present to him, but her wits had gone begging. It didn't help that Damon was deliberately provoking Casey, suggesting an intimate relationship that didn't exist. "The house is small, and my mother... Well, I, ah, thought it'd be better if..."

Before she could say any more, Damon was there. "We've been driving for hours," he interjected smoothly, "and we're both exhausted. Just let us grab a few things and we can stop holding you up."

Casey frowned. "You're not holding me up."

"*I* need to be going," Kristin said, clearly miffed by the turn of events and the way everyone ignored her. Her tone turned snide and her eyes narrowed on B.B. "But I have my cat in the car and she doesn't like strangers. She especially doesn't like dogs. Casey, you know she'll have a fit if we try to put another animal in there with her. Besides, there's not room for everyone."

Casey turned to Emma with a shrug. "I'm afraid she's right. Kristin treated me to dinner because I agreed to help her move."

Laying a hand on his chest, Kristin turned her face up to his. "You know that wasn't my only reason."

Casey countered her suggestiveness with an inattentive hug. "We've got the last load in the car now. The floor and the back seat are already packed."

Damon brought Emma a little closer, and no one could have missed the protectiveness of his gesture. Emma refrained from rolling her eyes, but it wasn't easy. She was the last woman on earth in need of protection, but Damon refused to believe that.

"No problem." The baring of Damon's teeth in no way resembled a smile. And if Emma didn't miss her guess, he was relieved to send Casey away. She only wished she felt the same. "Perhaps you could call us a cab, then?"

"No cabs in Buckhorn. Sorry." Reflecting Damon's mood, Casey looked anything but sorry by that fact. "And you know, if you don't get to the Cross Roads soon, you'll get locked out."

"Locked out?"

"Yep." Casey transferred his gaze to Emma—and his eyes glittered with a strange satisfaction. "Emma, you remember Mrs. Reider? She refuses to get out of bed to check people in after midnight." He lifted his wrist to see the illuminated dial on his watch. "That gives you less than fifteen minutes to make it there."

The beginning of a headache throbbed in Emma's temples. She rubbed her forehead, trying to decide what to do. "It was difficult enough convincing her that B.B. wouldn't be a problem."

Casey lifted an eyebrow. "I'm surprised you *could* convince her. She's not big on pets."

"Paying a double rate did the trick. And I just know she'll still charge us if we don't make it there on time. Her cancellation policy is no better than her check-in policy."

Casey's eyes twinkled in amusement. "She's the only motel in town. She can afford to be difficult."

"Damn." Damon started to pace, which truly showed his annoyance, since Damon normally remained cool in any situation.

Casey stopped him with a simple question. "Can you drive stick?"

Somewhat affronted, Damon said, "Of course."

"Great." Casey pulled a set of keys from his pocket and tossed them to Damon, who caught them against his chest. "Why don't you take Kristin on home? The Cross Roads Motel is on the way. You can stop and check in, get your room keys, and then after you get Kristin unloaded, you can come back for us."

Damon idly rattled the keys in his palm, looking between Casey and Emma. "Us?"

"I'll stay here with Emma and B.B."

Emma nearly strangled on her own startled breath. Seeing Casey so unexpectedly had unnerved her enough. No way did she want to be alone with him. Not yet. "I can drive a stick."

B.B. looked at her anxiously and took an active stance. His muscles quivered as if he might leap after her if she tried to leave.

"Right." Damon sent her a look. "And you really think he'll stay alone with me on an empty street while you ride off with a stranger? He'll have a fit. Hell, he'd probably chase the car all the way into town. It'd be different if we were at the motel and you left, but out here…"

"Okay, okay." Damon was right. B.B. was so defensive of her, she often wondered if he hadn't been a guard dog in another life.

"Besides," Damon added, further prodding her, "the room is held on my credit card." He stared at Emma hard, undecided, then abruptly shook his head. "Hell no. Let's forget this. It's already late, so what's a few more hours? We can wait for Triple A and then find a motel back on the highway to stay in for the night."

Emma gave that idea quick but serious thought, and knew the only reasonable thing to do was to stop acting like a desperate ninny. She couldn't imagine finding another motel that would allow her to bring B.B. inside. Besides, Damon had driven most of the hours, and despite his suggestion, he looked exhausted. B.B. wasn't in much better shape.

She'd stopped being selfish long ago.

"It's all right, Damon." She gave him a smile to reassure him. "I'm beat and so are you. You go on, and B.B. and I'll wait here."

Kristin crossed her arms and struck a petulant pose. "Don't I get a vote on this?"

Casey spared her a glance. "Not this time." Then he added, "And, honey, don't pout." He walked her to the car, his large hand open on the small of her back, urging her along while he spoke quietly in her ear.

Damon used that moment to pull Emma aside. He practically shoved her behind the open driver's door and then bent close. "Dear God," he muttered, holding his head. "I can understand why he became your adolescent hero, Emma. He's testosterone on legs."

Emma couldn't help but laugh at Damon's look of

distaste. He wasn't into the whole machismo display. Damon was far too refined for that, a man straight out of *GQ*. He also knew exactly how to lighten her mood. Not that he was wrong, of course. If anything, Casey was more ruggedly masculine now than he'd ever been.

Emma decided to tease him right back. "I hate to break it to you, Damon, but he's obviously into women."

Refusing to take the bait, Damon glanced over at Kristin with critical disdain. "*I'm* into women. He's obviously into twits. There *is* a difference."

Casey and Kristin were still in quiet conversation, their bodies outlined by the reaching glow of the car lights. "You really think so?"

"That she's a twit? Absolutely."

"No, I didn't mean that." She swatted at him and stifled a laugh. "I mean, do you think they're a couple?"

"Worried?"

Damon knew better. She wouldn't be in Buckhorn long enough to get worried about Casey and whom he might or might not be involved with. Probably his girlfriends were too many to count, anyway. Until he'd turned sixteen, Casey had been raised in an all-male household. Sawyer and his three brothers had been the most eligible, respected and adored bachelors in Buckhorn. One by one they'd married off, starting with Casey's father. But Casey had inherited a lot of their appeal and long before Emma had left town, the females had been chasing him. "Only curious. I haven't seen him in so long."

Damon's look plainly said *yeah, right*. "I think he

wants to be into her, if you need true accuracy. Whether or not he likes her—who knows?'' Then he added with more seriousness, ''You know to most men, liking and wanting have nothing in common.''

That was Damon's staunchest requirement. He had to genuinely like and respect a woman to decide to sleep with her. Intelligence sat high on his list, as did motivation and kindness. The second a woman got gossipy or catty, he walked away. Unlike many of the men she'd known through the years, Damon wasn't ruled by his libido. Emma respected him for that, even while she knew he'd be a tough man to please.

Again Emma chuckled, but her humor was cut short as Casey called, ''You ready to go?''

Damon ignored him as he cupped Emma's face, forcing her to look him in the eyes. ''Will you be okay?''

''Yes, of course.''

''Too fast, doll. That was nothing more than an automatic answer.''

''But true nonetheless.''

He waggled her head. ''Just be on guard, okay? I don't want to see you hurt.''

''I'm not made of glass,'' she chided.

''No, it's sugar I think.'' He lifted her hand to his mouth, nipped her knuckles and said, ''Yep, sugar.''

Emma was well used to that teasing response— he'd been saying it to her since she was seventeen years old, when they'd first met. She'd been backward, afraid, alone. And he'd treated her like a well-loved kid sister.

Laughing, she turned toward the other car, and

caught the censure on Casey's face. He didn't say a word, but then he didn't have to. She knew exactly what he thought. And none of it was nice.

Worse, none of it was accurate.

CHAPTER THREE

EMMA STOOD in front of her car, watching Damon and Kristin drive away. With their departure, the previously calm evening air suddenly felt charged. She was aware of things she hadn't noticed before, like the warm, subtle scent of Casey's cologne, the nearly tactile touch of his watchfulness. The pulsing rhythm of her own heartbeat resounded everywhere, in her chest, her ears, low in her belly.

B.B. shifted beside her, restless and uncertain with this turn of events and her renewed tension.

Though he didn't make a sound, she knew Casey was now closer behind her. As if he'd touched her, she shivered in reaction, and continued to stare after the car.

"So how've you been, Em?" His voice was low and intimate, a rough whisper of sound somewhere above her right ear.

The twin taillights of the other car faded away, swallowed up by distance and fog, the inky blackness of the night. Left with nothing to stare at, Emma drew a deep breath, took two steps away and turned to him with a bland smile. "Good. And yourself?"

"Good." He visually caressed her face, slowly, thoroughly, as if he'd never seen her before. As if maybe he'd...missed her.

Emma moved to the side of the car, taking herself out of the harsh beams of the headlights. The dog followed and she leaned down to give him a reassuring pat. When she straightened, Casey was even closer than before and he made no attempt to move away. She felt vaguely hunted.

"You look so different, Em."

She wasn't about to back away a second time. Faking a calm that eluded her, she shrugged. "Eight years different."

"It's not your age," he murmured, once again looking her over in that scrutinizing way of his. "Your hair is different."

Emma started to reply, but the words hung in her throat as Casey reached out and caught a shoulder-length tress, rubbing it between fingers and thumb.

Both breathless and a little indignant, she tossed her head so that her hair fell behind her shoulders. That didn't deter Casey. He simply drew it forward again, making her frown. He was bolder than she remembered…. No, that wasn't true. He'd always been bold—with the girls he'd wanted.

He just hadn't ever wanted her.

"I don't bleach it anymore." Despite being annoyed, awareness trembled in her belly, sang through her veins. "This is my real color."

His long fingers tunneled in close to her scalp, warm and gentle, then lifted outward, letting the silky strands drift back into place. "I can't see it that well here in the shadows."

Her breath came too fast. "Light brown."

"I never really understood why you lightened it." He stroked her hair again, totally absorbed in what he did, unmindful or uncaring of her discomfort. "Or why you wore so much makeup."

She refused to apologize for or explain about her past. That was one of the things Damon had taught her—to forget about what she couldn't change and only look forward. "I thought it looked good at the time, but then, I was only seventeen and not overly astute."

Casey stood silent for only a minute. "Why don't we sit in the car? The air is pretty damp tonight."

Being that she was already far too aware of him, she didn't consider that a good idea. But the dog had heard him and, not wanting to be left out, quickly went through the open driver's door and performed an agile leap into the back seat.

Emma gave a mental shrug and scooted inside, leaving Casey to go to the passenger side. The consummate gentleman, he closed her door first before walking around the hood of the car. When he slid into his seat, she had only a moment to appreciate the sharp angles and planes of his face fully lit by the interior light. He closed his door too, and the light clicked off with a sort of symbolic finality that made her senses come alive.

Casey twisted sideways in his seat and spoke in a low vibrating murmur. "Better turn off the headlights, Em, or you'll have a dead battery to go with the busted water pump."

Though Emma knew he was right, she hated to be in utter darkness with him. Her awareness of him as a man defied reason.

He hadn't touched her, but God, she felt as if he had. All over.

"There's a flashlight in the glove box."

Casey opened the small door, moved a few papers aside and pulled out the black-handled utility light. He didn't hand it to her, didn't turn it on, but instead held it in his lap. She turned off the headlights and inky blackness settled in around them. Emma wondered if he could hear the wild pounding of her heart.

Her reactions irritated her as much as they distressed her. No other man had ever affected her this way. She'd had plenty of relationships since she'd grown up, and she'd assumed her tepid reactions had been mostly due to maturing, to wising up, to learning what was best for her. She'd accepted that sex was pleasurable but not vital. It eased an ache, provided comfort, added to the closeness, and nothing more.

Yet, sitting in a dark car next to Casey Hudson, she felt the biting greed of lust in a way that hadn't touched her since…since the last time she'd been this near him.

"So what have you been doing with yourself?" he asked, and Emma started in surprise.

"What?"

"It's been a long time." His voice held the same easy cadence she remembered from long ago, but there was an edge to it now. An edge to him. "You disappeared without a trace, so I'm just wondering what you've been up to."

Emma didn't want to get into this now. He wouldn't understand and she wasn't up to explaining. In truth, it wasn't any of his business what she did or had done while she'd been away from Buckhorn. But telling him so would have been too ballsy, even for her, and would have made her sound defensive.

Keeping her answer vague, she shrugged. "Working, like most people I guess."

She braced herself for the questions that would follow, and wondered at the hesitation she felt in explaining her job to him. Damn it, she loved her job and was proud of herself for doing it so well.

But Casey took her off guard by skipping her occupation and going straight to a more difficult topic. "You and Damon involved?"

Anger flashed through Emma, pushing some of the sexual awareness aside. Regardless of their pasts, she didn't deserve an inquisition.

"Are you and Kristin?" Her voice sounded sharper than she'd intended, but Casey just laughed.

"No." His white teeth gleamed in the darkness. "As I said, she's a co-worker, a friend. No more than that."

Emma shook her head. Men could be so dense. "So you say. My guess is that she wants to be considerably more."

Casey touched her cheek, a casual gesture that felt hotly intimate and made her breath catch. "Yeah, well, I can be stubborn when I want to be."

She almost replied *I remember,* but caught herself in time. His honesty provoked her own. "Damon and I are friends."

"Uh-huh."

She didn't care if he believed her or not. *She didn't.* She turned away to stare out the window, letting Casey know without words that he could think what he wanted.

"If you were homely," Casey teased, "then I could maybe believe it. But Em?" He waited just long enough to make her antsy. "You're far from homely."

She tried to ignore him. The field to her left sounded with a thousand insects: the buzz of mosquitoes, the singing of crickets. Like stars in the sky, fireflies twinkled on and off.

She hadn't forgotten that Buckhorn was beautiful in the summer, but somehow the clarity of it had been blunted. The colors, the smells, the texture of the air and the lush grass and the velvet sky...

Casey stroked one finger over her cheek, down to her throat, then her shoulder. "Hell, if anything, you're more attractive than ever, and you were plenty attractive at seventeen."

Her heart punched painfully against her rib cage. How had the conversation gotten out of hand so quickly? Her laugh sounded more believable this time. "I'm guessing you must have lowered your standards."

Casey stared at her, not comprehending.

Emma rolled her eyes. "I've been in the car all day, Case. I'm dressed in what can only be called my comfortable clothes—and that's if I'm being generous. No makeup, my hair's windblown..."

"You look sexy as hell to me."

The way he growled that pronouncement robbed Emma of clear thought. She searched her brain for something to say, some way to derail him. "How long will it take Damon to get back, do you think?"

Casey didn't take the hint. He didn't stop touching her either. He smoothed her hair behind her ear and curled his fingers around her head. "Men only pretend to be friends with women to get one thing."

Goaded, Emma shifted around to face him. His hand dropped, but his gaze, glittering in the darkness, remained steady.

Even the gearshift between them didn't hinder Casey's movements. He got so close that Emma inhaled the warmth of his masculine smell on every breath.

"Is that right?" Her voice shook, her hands trembled. "Then I guess we're enemies, because there's never been a single thing you wanted from me."

Beneath the fall of her hair, Casey's hand curved around her neck in a gentle restraint that felt far too unbreakable. Trying to be inconspicuous, she pressed into the car door. It didn't help.

With near-tactile intensity, his gaze stroked her face, then rested on her mouth.

"True." There was a heavy, thrumming beat of silence, and Casey whispered, "Until now."

KNOWING HE PUSHED HER, knowing it was unfair, Casey tried to pull back. But damn it, he wanted her. Seeing her again...it hit him like a ton of bricks, throwing him off balance, making him defensive and fractious and keenly alert. Emma had influenced his life when he hadn't thought that possible. Forgetting her hadn't been easy.

In fact, he'd never managed it.

Just the opposite.

At twenty-seven, his solid position within his step-grandfather's company should have been enhanced with a wife on his arm and a couple of kids underfoot, just as he'd always intended. Instead, no woman had ever quite measured up.

The bitch of it was, he had no idea what they

needed to measure up to. He didn't even know what he was looking for.

Until moments ago, when he saw Emma standing there.

As always, her eyes had been huge and soft, and all his senses had quickened with recognition. He hadn't experienced that rush of pure, white-hot intensity since... *No,* he wouldn't do that, wouldn't give her credit she didn't deserve. She'd run out on him and he wasn't quite ready to forgive her for that. But he was more than ready to take what he'd often regretted missing so many years ago.

Her small hands lifted to press against his chest, burning him, heightening the ache. "Casey..."

The way she said his name was familiar. Did she want him to stop or, like him, was she anxious to feel the flash fire of their unique chemistry? Her appearance, her attitude, were different. But her natural sensuality hadn't waned at all. Instead, it had aged and ripened and gotten better, richer. No woman had ever affected him like Emma did, and now, with no effort at all, she'd gotten him hot.

She wasn't a lonely, insecure child anymore.

She wasn't afraid, wasn't mistreated.

He had no reason to hold back, no reason to still feel protective. *Damn it.*

Without thought, Casey let his fingers stroke the nape of her neck. Just as it always had, her softness drew him, the remembered texture of her skin, her hair and her scent... God, he loved her scent. Heady and warm, it mingled with the damp fog and the gentle evening breeze.

He felt alive. He felt challenged.

"Emma?"

Her thick lashes lifted.

"Are you married?"

She shook her head, causing the silky weight of her hair to glide over his arm.

"Engaged?"

"No." She pulled her head back a little and Casey kissed her throat, nuzzling her fragrant skin, breathing her in. A sound of near desperation slipped past her open lips. "Are you…?"

"Hell no. There's no one." He didn't want to talk about that though. "You feel good, Em. You smell even better."

"Casey."

If she kept saying his name like that, he'd lose it. "You know, since you and Damon aren't involved…" If she had no commitments to anyone, then why not? It didn't matter that he rushed things. They were both grown now, both adults, so Emma could damn well make a rational decision now, rather than one based on fear and insecurity.

"Damon and I are friends." A measure of steel laced her declaration.

Had she misunderstood his suggestion?

Casey drew back so he could see her face. Her heavy lashes half covered her eyes as she watched him warily. She remained guarded, but she didn't push him away. He tried a different tack. "You're staying at the Cross Roads tonight."

"Yes."

Adulthood had provided new dimension to her features. Her cheekbones were more noticeable, her mouth wider, fuller, her jaw firm. She was lovely—

and he had to have her. "You'll be sleeping alone?" Which would make it easy for him to join her.

Her gaze flickered away, and his stomach knotted even before she spoke. "That's none of your business, Casey."

Frustration unfurled in his guts, making his tone raw with sarcasm. "Sounds like a *no* to me."

Chin lifted, she faced him squarely and confirmed his suspicions. "No. I won't sleep alone."

Very slowly, doing his best to rein in his seldom-seen temper, Casey released her and moved back to his own seat. The sexual turbulence remained, gnawing at him, testing him, but now other, darker emotions gripped him too. He didn't want to study them too closely. "I see."

He could feel her turmoil. And he could taste her interest, damn her. It was there, shimmering between them. Yet, she'd be with Damon, her *friend*.

Once long ago, Casey had been her friend. Probably her best friend, if not the only one. He'd told her then that he didn't share. That much hadn't changed. He wanted her, but on his terms.

And that's how he'd have her.

Emma slowly straightened in her seat and stared straight ahead. "I seriously doubt that you see anything."

The dog stuck his head over the seat and whined. Emma shifted enough to pat him, then buried her face in his scruff. "It's okay, B.B."

Casey sat in brooding silence for several moments, watching as she comforted the big dog. Slashes of moonlight silhouetted her body and the slow movements of her stroking hands through thick fur. She ignored him as if he didn't exist, not once looking at him. It didn't matter.

Despite any protest Devaughn might make, Casey knew he'd eventually have her.

By her own admission, she wasn't married, wasn't engaged, so no one, Damon included, had any real claim on her. That left Casey free to do as he pleased. And it would please him a hell of a lot to take care of unfinished business so he could get her out of his system and get on with his life. It felt as if he'd been on hold for eight years. Now, finally, he'd discover what he'd missed so many years ago. Finally, he'd appease the ache.

Because he knew he'd lost ground by letting her see his anger, Casey changed his tack. "I got the money you sent."

Startled, she released the dog. "I'm sorry I took it in the first place. It was wrong."

"You know I'd have given it to you if you'd asked." She nodded without recognizing the outright lie. Hell, if Emma had asked him for money, he'd have known her plans and rather than leave her alone that night, he'd have kept close to her. He'd have stayed with her and everything would have turned out different.

He wouldn't have lost her for so long.

Remembering that night still made Casey tense. So many times over the years, he'd replayed it in his head, thinking of things he should have done, should have said. He'd given up on ever seeing her again.

Now she'd returned, and he'd done nothing but paw her. He wanted to tell her that he'd missed her, that she'd left a void in his life. But, damn it, she'd walked out on him without a backward glance. It still pissed him off.

"Where did you go when you left, Em?"

More silence. She turned her head to stare out the window.

Not bothering to hide his exasperation, Casey said, "C'mon, Emma. Hell, it's been damn near a decade. Does it really matter if you tell me?" He couldn't soften his tone, couldn't soften his reaction to her. Emma had always had the ability to make him feel things he didn't want to feel, to feel things he hadn't felt since she'd left him.

He could see her resistance, her reticence. She didn't trust him, never really had, and that bothered him most of all. "You came to me once, Emma. Why can't you talk to me now?"

"People change over time, Casey."

"Me or you?"

"In eight years? I'd say both." Turning from the window, she looked at him and sighed. "I don't even know you anymore."

In so many ways she knew him better than anyone ever had. But he was glad she didn't realize it. "So where you went is a big secret, huh?" He rubbed his upper lip as he considered her. "Must be something scandalous, right? Let me think. Wait, I know. Did you become a spy?"

She rolled her eyes, looking so much like the old teasing girl he used to know.

"No? Well, let's see. Did you join up with a circus or get sent to prison?"

"No, no, and no."

"Then what?" Unable to help himself, he stretched

out his arm and cupped her shoulder. Her nearness made it impossible for him *not* to touch her. The ancient, baggy sweatshirt she wore all but hid her breasts. But Casey knew their softness, their plump weight. How they felt in his palms.

Oh yeah, he remembered that too well.

Emma lifted her face and met his gaze. ''There's no reason to rehash old news.''

''It's not old for me.'' He recalled the many nights he'd lain awake worrying about her, imagining every awful scenario that could happen to a girl all alone. It had made him sick with fear—and blind with rage. ''I offered you help, Emma, and rather than take it you left me a goddamn note that didn't tell me a thing. You ran out on me. You stole money from me.'' *You ripped out my heart.*

She bit her lip, her face awash in guilt. ''I'm sorry.''

Damn it, he didn't want her apology. He thought to take back the words, but instead he drew a deep breath and continued, hoping to cajole her, reassure her. ''I worried about you, Emma, especially when I found out you didn't have a relative in Ohio. I worried and I thought about you and wished like hell I'd done something different. I screwed up that night, and I know it.''

Her eyes were wide and dark, filled with incredulity. ''But...that's nonsense.''

''I don't think so. You came to me, and I let you down.''

''No.'' She leaned forward and her cool fingers caressed his jaw. His muscles clenched with her first tentative touch. ''Don't ever think that, Casey. You

did more than enough. You helped me more than anyone else ever could have.''

"Right."

"Casey…" She hesitated, then she whispered,
"You were the best thing that ever happened to me.
You always made me happy, even after I'd gone
away."

Robbed of breath by her words, Casey closed his
hand over hers and kept her palm flat against his jaw.
It was such a simple touch, and it meant so much to
him. "But I don't deserve an accounting? Or do I
have to go on wondering what happened to you?"

She tugged her hand free and let it drop to the
gearshift. Their gazes were locked together, neither of
them able or willing to look away. The dog laid his
head on the back of the seat between them, watching
closely. He gave a whine of curiosity.

B.B. probably felt Emma's distress, Casey thought,
because he sure as hell felt it. He regretted that he'd
upset her, but he needed to know where she'd gone
and how she'd gotten by. He *had* to know.

"All right." Her whispered words barely reached
him, then she cleared her throat and spoke with new
strength. "But it's a boring story."

"Let me be the judge of that."

With a sigh, she dropped back into her seat and
folded her hands in her lap. Her hair fell forward to
hide her face. Casey wanted to smooth it back so he
could better see her, but he didn't want to take a
chance on interrupting her confession.

"For the first two weeks I lived in a park. There
were plenty of woods so it was easy to hide when
they shut the gates. There were outdoor rest rooms

and stuff there, places for me to clean up and get a drink and…'' She rolled her shoulders. ''I had everything I needed. In a way, it was fun, like an adventure.''

''Jesus, Em. You don't mean…''

''Yeah.'' She dredged up a smile that didn't do a damn thing to convince him. ''I slept on the ground, using my backpack for a pillow. You know, it reminded me of all those nights we used to stay out late on the lake. You remember how we could hear the leaves and see all the stars and the air was so cool and crisp? We'd get mosquito bites, but it was worth it. Well, it was like that. A little scary at times, but also sort of soothing and peaceful. It'd be so quiet I'd stare up at the sky and think about everyone back in Buckhorn.'' Her gaze darted away, and she added on a whisper, ''I'd think about you.''

Pained, his heart aching, Casey closed his eyes. Emma didn't know how her words devastated him, because she wasn't looking at him.

''That's where I found B.B. He was still a puppy, a warm, energetic ball of fur, and when we saw each other, he was so…happy to be with me.'' She laced her fingers together, waited. ''Someone had abandoned him.''

Just as her father had abandoned her?

''I picked ticks off him and used my comb to get snarls out of his fur and he played with me and kept me company.''

This time her smile was genuine, a small, sweet smile, as she talked about the dog. Casey wanted to crowd her close and put his arms around her and protect her forever. The urge was so strong, he sounded gruff as he asked, ''Why did you stay in a park, Emma?''

''There was nowhere else to stay. I used the money I had—and your money—to pay for my bus fare to Chicago, and for food. After I got there, I couldn't get a job because I couldn't give a place of residence, and I couldn't get a place of residence without a job reference. I was afraid if I went to any of the shelters, they'd contact my family and...send me back home.''

Casey scrubbed at his face. Emma was twenty-five now, but he saw her as she'd been when she left— young, bruised, scared and lonely. What she'd gone through was worse than he'd suspected, worse than he'd ever imagined. He'd held on to the belief that she knew someone, that she'd had someone to take care of her. But she'd been all alone. Vulnerable. And it hurt to know that.

''I'm not sure what would have eventually happened. But then one day B.B. got really sick. He'd eaten something bad and he was dehydrated, weak. He could barely walk. I was so afraid that I'd lose him, I chanced going to the vet clinic that I'd seen not far from the park. That's where I met Parker Devaughn and his son, Damon.''

She turned to B.B. and hugged him close. Several seconds passed, and Casey knew she was weighing her words. ''It took almost a week before B.B. was healthy again. I hung out there, staying by his side as much as they'd let me.''

The images flooding his mind were too agonizing to bear. ''What happened?''

''They...figured out my situation when I couldn't pay the bill and offered to let me work it off instead.''

"They realized that you were homeless?" Casey wanted to hear all the details about where she'd slept, how she'd stayed safe. When the dog was sick, she'd been alone more than ever.

But one thought kept overriding all others. How bad had it been for her in Buckhorn that she'd rather sleep alone in a park with no one for company except an abandoned dog? What the hell had happened to make her run away?

Emma gave a small nod. "I couldn't leave B.B. and they wouldn't let me have him without explaining. I was afraid they'd turn me in and send me back home. But when I told them everything, they surprised me."

"Everything?"

She glanced at him, then away. Skipping his question, she said, "They took me in and they've treated me like family ever since. Parker even helped me to get my G.E.D. and to find a job I love. Life now is…great."

She'd left out everything painful, either to spare him or because she couldn't bear to talk about it. Casey didn't know which, and neither was acceptable. He suddenly wanted her to be his friend again, that young girl with the enormous soft eyes always filled with invitation. The girl who always came to him with open admiration and her heart on her sleeve. The girl who'd wanted him—and only him.

His decisions, his feelings for her back then, had seemed so simple and straightforward. He'd liked controlling things, only letting her so close, giving her only as much as he wanted and holding back everything else.

Or so he'd thought.

But somehow Emma had crawled under his skin and into his head, his heart. He hadn't known until she was gone that she'd taken more than he'd ever meant to give her. He hadn't known until she was gone, and a big piece of him was missing. Being apart from her while becoming a man hadn't changed how he felt. It had only complicated it.

Disturbed by his reaction to her, he teased her by tugging on a lock of her hair. "That story is so full of holes I could use it for a sieve."

"No, I've told you everything that's important."

"Em…"

"Thanks to Parker and Damon, I did fine," she insisted. She smiled a little, and her eyes glinted with humor. "In fact, I might owe them even more than I owe you."

Annoyance fought with tenderness, making his voice gruff. "You don't owe me a damn thing and you know it."

"I knew you probably felt that way." She shook her head, still smiling in that small, tantalizing way that made him want to lick her mouth. "That's one of the things that always made you so special, Casey."

Hearing her say such a thing took some of the edge off his urgency. He liked thinking that he'd been special to her, because she'd certainly been special to him. He just hadn't known it until it was too late.

Acting on impulse, he took her hand. "Have breakfast with me tomorrow. We can catch up on old times and you can fill me in on the pieces you're leaving out right now."

She gave a shrug of apology. "I can't. I'm going to the hospital first thing."

He'd almost forgotten about her father and felt like an ass because of it. It surprised him that she'd return to see the man who'd run her off, but he supposed time could heal those wounds. And Dell wasn't in the best of health. "We can make it dinner."

She closed her eyes on a sigh of weariness. "I don't think so, Casey."

Her rejection struck him like a blow. "I'm special," he asked, "but not special enough to share a meal with?"

She swiveled her head toward him. "I'm sorry—"

In an instant, his temper snapped. "Will you quit saying that!"

She flipped her hair back and her eyes flashed. "Don't yell at me."

"Then quit apologizing." And in a mumble, "You always did apologize too much."

B.B. let out a low warning growl, breaking the flow of anger. Emma turned to the big dog and rubbed his muzzle. In a calmer tone, she said, "I can't make any plans because I don't know what my schedule will be, or how much free time I'll have."

And she wasn't sleeping alone.

Casey cursed softly, but he couldn't blame Devaughn. If he had Emma warming his bed, no way would he let her out with another man.

He wouldn't give up, but he would slow it down. He'd been her friend once, maybe her only friend in Buckhorn. He'd build on that. He'd give her time to breathe, to get used to him again.

Until Emma got the water pump fixed, she'd need transportation to the hospital. He'd be happy to oblige, to give her a helping hand.

One thing was certain, before she took off this time he'd have all his questions answered. He'd be damned if he'd let her sneak out on him a second time.

CHAPTER FOUR

AS IF FROM A DISTANCE, Emma heard the knock on the thin motel-room door. She forced her head from the flat, overstarched pillow and glanced at the glowing face of the clock. It was barely six-thirty and her body remained limp with the heaviness of sleep. She'd only been in bed five hours.

After Damon had finally returned and they'd transferred everything from her car to Casey's and gotten to the Cross Roads Motel, it had been well past one o'clock. She hadn't unpacked, had only pulled off her shoes, jeans, bra and sweatshirt, and dropped into the bed in a tee and panties. She'd been so exhausted, both in body and spirit, that thoughts of food or a shower disintegrated beneath tiredness.

Why would anyone be calling on her this early?

B.B. snuffled around and let out a warning *woof*, but Emma patted him and he resettled with a modicum of grumbling and growling. Stretched on his side, he took up more than his fair share of the bed. ''It's okay, boy. I'll be right back.''

Probably Mrs. Reider, she thought, ready with a complaint of some kind, though Emma couldn't imagine what it might be. They'd kept very quiet coming in last night and hadn't disturbed anyone as far as she knew.

B.B. was atop the covers, so Emma grabbed the bedspread that had gotten pushed to the bottom of the bed. She halfheartedly wrapped it around herself and let it drag on the floor.

Without turning on a light, she padded barefoot to the door, turned the cheap lock, and swung it open. The room had been dark with the heavy drapes drawn, but now she had to lift a hand to shield her eyes against the red glow of a rising sun. She blinked twice before her bleary eyes could focus.

And there stood Casey.

His powerful body lounged against the door frame, silhouetted by a golden halo. In the daylight, he looked more devastatingly handsome than ever. Confusion washed over Emma and she stared, starting at Casey's feet and working her way up.

Laced-up, scuffed brown boots showed beneath well-worn jeans that rode low on his lean hips and were faded white in stress spots, like his knees, the pocket where he kept his keys. His fly.

Emma blinked at that, then shook her head and continued upward. With the casual clothing, he'd forgone a belt. In fact, two belt loops were missing from the ancient jeans.

In deference to the heat, he wore a sleeveless, battered white cotton shirt that left his muscular arms and tanned shoulders on display. Mirrored sunglasses shielded his eyes, and his mouth curled in a lopsided, wicked grin. ''Morning, Emma.''

Her tongue stuck to the roof of her mouth, making speech difficult. ''What are you doing here?''

Lifting one hand, which caused all kinds of interesting muscles to flex in his arm, he showed her the smallest of her suitcases. "You forgot this in the trunk of my car. I thought you might need it today."

"Oh." She looked around, not sure what to do next. She did need the case, seeing that it held her toiletries and makeup. But she could hardly invite him in when she wasn't dressed. Loosening her hold on the bedspread, she reached for the case. "Thank you…"

Casey removed the decision from her. Lifting the case out of reach, he stepped inside just in time to see B.B. bound off the bed and lunge forward with a growl. When he recognized Casey, he slowed and the growl turned into a tail-wagging hello. Casey greeted the dog while eyeing the bed he'd vacated. Being a double, it provided just enough room for one woman—and her pet.

He quirked an eyebrow at Emma as realization dawned. She hadn't slept alone, so he couldn't accuse her of lying. But she hadn't slept with a man either, which had been his assumption.

Casey grinned and reached down to pat the dog. "You've sure got the cushy life, don't you, B.B.?"

The dog jumped up, putting his paws on Casey's shoulders. Casey laughed. "Yeah, sleeping with a gorgeous woman would put any guy in a good mood."

Left standing in the open doorway, Emma hadn't quite gathered her wits yet. Too little sleep combined with Casey Hudson in the morning could rattle anyone. She certainly wasn't up to bantering with him. "He's always slept with me. It's one reason I bring him along everywhere I go."

"Gotcha." Casey looked around again, and his grin widened. "So. Where's Damon?"

He tried to sound innocent, but failed. Knowing the jig was up, Emma scowled at him. Would he now consider her fair game, since she wasn't involved? What would she say to dissuade him if he did?

Did she really want to dissuade him?

The connecting door opened and Damon stuck his dark head out. With only one eye opened, he demanded, "What the hell's going on?" Then he saw Casey, and that one eye widened. "Oh, it's you. I should have known."

In his boxers and nothing more, Damon pulled the door wider. Emma wasn't uncomfortable with his lack of dress. More often than not, Damon acted like her brother.

Casey took in the separate rooms with a look of deep satisfaction. "Morning, Devaughn."

"Yeah, whatever." Damon yawned, leaned in the doorway, and crossed his arms over his naked chest. His blue eyes were heavy, his jaw shadowed with stubble, and his silky black hair stuck out in funny disarray. "You country boys like to get up early, I take it?"

"Country boys?" Casey didn't sound amused by that description.

Undisturbed by Casey's pique, Damon lazily eyed him with both eyes this time, taking in the old snug jeans and the muscle shirt. "Brought it up another notch, I see."

Casey's scowl darkened. "What?"

Damon just shook his head and glanced at Emma. "Give me a minute to get dressed."

She didn't want to turn this into a social gathering, and besides, both men were bristling, which didn't bode well. "That's not necessary."

"No?"

"No." Emma saw Damon's surprise and rubbed her forehead. He looked as tired as she felt, so why didn't he just go on back to bed so she could deal with Casey in private? She moderated her tone. "It's fine, Damon. Get some more sleep."

He didn't budge. "You turned willing overnight?"

Her moderation shot to hell, Emma ground her teeth together. "Damon..."

"Was it the macho clothes that turned the trick?"

Casey shifted his stance but Emma growled, causing both B.B. and Damon to watch her warily.

Damon straightened in the doorway with dawning suspicion. "Have you had your coffee?"

Emma slowly looked up at him. A long rope of tangled hair hung over her bloodshot, puffy eyes. She wore only her T-shirt and a bedspread. Curling her lip, she asked, "Do I look to you like I've had coffee?"

"Shit." He turned to Casey with accusation. "So where is it?"

Casey blinked in incomprehension. "Where is what?"

As if speaking to an idiot, Damon enunciated each word. "The coffee?"

Casey shrugged, but offered helpfully, "They keep a pot brewing in the lobby."

"Right. In the lobby. And here I had the impression you knew something about women." Shaking his head at Casey in a pitying way, Damon turned to

Emma. "Just hang on, doll. I'll run down and snag you a cup."

On a normal day Emma would have thanked him and dropped back into bed. But this wasn't a normal day. Today, Casey stood in her temporary bedroom looking and smelling too sexy for a sane woman's health and she wasn't properly dressed. "It's okay. B.B. needs to go out too, so I might as well get the coffee myself." And then she wouldn't be left closed up in the motel room with Casey.

Apparently stunned, Damon blinked at her. "Are you sure?"

"I'm sure I'm going to smack you if you don't stop pushing me."

"All right, all right." Damon held up both hands, which should have been comical given that he wore only print boxers. "Hey, what do I know about a woman's needs? They're ever shifting and changing, right? One day coffee is a necessity before she can open her eyes. The next, no problem, she'll get it herself."

Emma turned away and stomped to the dresser to snatch up her jeans. Ignoring both men, she trailed into the bathroom and shut the door. She didn't exactly slam it, but her irritation definitely showed.

She heard Casey whistle low. "Wow. Is she always like that in the morning?"

"Be warned—*yes*."

Casey chuckled, but Damon, clearly disgruntled, said, "I wouldn't if I was you. What you just saw is nothing compared to how grouchy she'll get if she doesn't get a cup of coffee real soon."

"I'll keep that in mind."

"You do that."

Emma brushed her teeth while praying that Damon would now go back to bed. He did, but not without a parting shot.

"I usually fetch her a cup before I wake her up, especially when she hasn't had enough sleep. But since you did the deed this morning, and at such an ungodly hour at that, you can deal with the consequences all alone."

She heard Damon's door close, then heard Casey mutter to B.B., "You won't let her hurt me, will you, buddy?"

B.B. whined.

Emma exited the bathroom. She slipped her feet into her sneakers, latched B.B.'s leash to his collar and stepped around Casey to head out the door. Obedient whenever it suited him, B.B. followed, and, without a word, Casey fell into step behind him. She'd only gone down three steps, her destination the lobby where fresh coffee waited, when she heard Casey begin humming some tune that she didn't recognize.

He knew she slept without a man. Emma wondered what he intended to do with that knowledge, because she knew Casey too well to mistake him now. He was up to something, and she dreaded the coming battle.

It was herself she'd have to fight, of course. She'd never been able to resist Casey, not then, and not now. Damn.

BEFORE SHE COULD HEAD for the lobby, Casey caught Emma's arm. "Take B.B. to the bushes, then park yourself at the picnic table. I'll get the coffee."

She looked ready to argue, so Casey reasoned with her. "You can't take the dog inside, and he's starting to look desperate. Really, fetching you a cup of coffee won't tax me. I'll even get one for myself. Okay?"

She glanced at the dog, who did indeed appear urgent, then nodded. "All right. Lots of sugar and a smidgen of cream."

"Got it." Casey sauntered away with a smile on his face. He'd spent the night thinking about Emma, and being sexually frustrated as a result. He couldn't say what he'd expected this morning when he'd knocked on her door, but the picture she'd presented had taken him by surprise.

Soft. That was the word that most often came to mind when he thought of Emma. Soft eyes, soft heart, soft breasts and hips and thighs…

This morning, still sleepy and wrapped in a bedspread, she'd been so soft she'd damn near melted his heart on the spot, along with all the plans he'd so meticulously devised throughout the long night. He'd taken one look at her and wanted to lead her right back to bed.

It had been doubly hard to give up that idea once he knew Damon had a separate room.

Seeing her sleek, silky hair tangled around her shoulders, her cheeks flushed, her eyes a little dazed had made him think of a woman's expression right before she came. Emma's very kissable mouth had been slightly puffy, and her lips had parted in surprise when she saw him at the door, adding to the fantasy.

Her legs…well, Emma had always had a killer ass and gorgeous legs. That hadn't changed. As a perpetually horny teen, resisting her had been his biggest struggle. As an adult, it wasn't much easier. In fact, he had no intention of resisting her now.

Unfortunately, she'd pulled on jeans rather than the ultrashort shorts he remembered in their youth, and her legs were now well hidden. But she hadn't bothered with a bra yet. With each step she took, her breasts moved gently beneath the cotton of her T-shirt, and the faintest outline of her nipples showed through.

Casey's muscles tightened in anticipation of seeing her again and he snapped lids on three disposable cups of coffee then plucked up several packets of sugar, two stirrers and some little tubs of creamer. He stuffed them in his pockets. Balancing the hot cups between his hands, he shouldered the door open and started back to Emma.

In limp exhaustion, she rested at one of the aged wooden picnic tables that had always served as part of Mrs. Reider's small lot. Guests used the tables often, but this early in the day no one else intruded. Casey didn't make a sound as he approached, and Emma remained unaware of him.

She'd kicked off her shoes, and her legs were stretched out in front of her with her bare toes wiggling. Sunlight through elm leaves, shifting and changing with the careless breeze, dappled her upturned face.

The air this time of morning remained heavy with dew, rich with scents of the earth and trees. Emma sighed and her expression bespoke a peacefulness that made Casey smile from the inside out. He liked seeing Emma at peace. When she'd been younger, so often what he'd seen in her eyes was uncertainty, loneliness, even fear.

She spoke a moment to B.B., who sprawled out in the lush grass at her feet, then she reached up and lifted her hair off her nape. Casey stalled in appreciation of her feminine gesture. Even from her early teens, Emma had displayed an innate sensuality that drove every guy around her wild. She stretched her arms high, and her hair drifted free to resettle over her shoulders.

Damn. He absolutely could not get a boner in Mrs. Reider's motel lot.

Neither could he allow Emma to affect him this strongly. He had to remember that despite her appeal and everything he'd once felt—still felt—she'd walked out on him and hadn't bothered to get in touch in eight long years. And she hadn't come back for him now. If her father wasn't so sick, she wouldn't be here.

"Here's your coffee." His emotions in check, Casey took the last few remaining steps to her and set the cups on the tabletop. "I hope you haven't chewed off any tree bark or anything." He scattered the sugar packets and creamer beside the cups.

Eyes scrunched up because of the sun, Emma turned to him with a frown. "Damon exaggerated. I'm not that bad."

"If you say so." He smiled at her. "But remember, I witnessed you firsthand. For a minute there I expected to see smoke come out of your ears."

She looked ready to growl again, but restrained herself. "I hadn't had much sleep."

"I'm sorry I woke you."

"You don't look sorry."

Casey shrugged and continued to smile.

Emma considered him a long moment, then took the coffee and quickly doctored it to her specifications. The second she tipped the cup to her mouth, she moaned in bliss. "Oh God, I needed that." She took another long drink. "Perfect. Thank you."

Casey sipped his own coffee, prepared much like hers. "Not a morning person, huh?"

She shook her head. "I'm barely civil in the morning. I've always been more a night owl."

He remembered that—and a whole lot more.

She didn't say anything else, made no effort toward casual conversation, which annoyed him. She sat with him, drank the coffee he'd brought to her, but kept him shut out.

To regain her attention, he touched the back of her hand with one fingertip. "I still think waking up with you would be fun."

Surprised by that comment, Emma froze for a good five seconds. Abruptly, she drained the rest of her cup and stood. She didn't look at him. "Thanks again...for everything." She started to step away.

Casey moved so fast, she gasped. In less than a heartbeat he'd reached over the table and snatched her narrow wrists, shackling them in his hands. He stared into her mesmerizing, antagonistic brown eyes until the air around them fairly crackled.

"Don't go." Two simple words, but his heart pounded as he waited.

She looked undecided.

"I brought you another cup." Casey stroked the

insides of her wrists with his thumbs, kept his tone easy, persuasive. "Sit with me, Emma. Talk to me."

He ignored the rise of her breasts as she slowly inhaled. Her hesitation was palpable, forcing him to think of more arguments, other stratagems, until she said, "Why?"

Sensing that she'd just relented, Casey relaxed. "Sit down and I'll tell you why."

With enough grumbling to wake the squirrels, she dropped into the seat. This time she slid her legs under the table and faced him with both elbows propped on the tabletop to hold her chin. "I'm waiting."

Casey took in her belligerent expression and swallowed his amusement. Not once in all the time he'd known her had Emma ever shown him disgruntlement. She'd shown him adolescent lust, feminine need, a few flirting smiles and occasionally her vulnerability.

It didn't make any sense, but he felt as if he'd just gained three giant steps forward. "Yeah. You know, I think I'll feel more secure if you drink the other cup of coffee first." He prepared it as he spoke, and handed it to her with a flourish.

She slanted him a look through her thick lashes. "With the way you've acted so far, you're probably right." She accepted the coffee and sipped. "You've been deliberately provoking."

Casey waited until she swallowed before he spoke. "There's still something between us, Emma."

She promptly choked, then glared at him before searching in vain for a napkin. Casey offered her his clean hankie. "You okay?"

She brushed away his concern. "Something, huh?"

Her voice was still raspy as she wheezed for air. "Well, I can tell you exactly what that *something* is."

Casey tilted back. "That right?"

"Sure." She finally regained her breath. "I'm not dead. I felt it too."

Her mood was so uncertain, he couldn't decide how to handle her. "You know, you're a lot more candid when you're crabby."

Without another word, she dropped her head to her folded arms. He didn't know if she was laughing, but he was certain she wasn't crying.

Casey wanted to touch her, wanted to feel the warmth of her skin. Her light-brown hair lay fanned out around her, spilling onto the table. The sun had kissed it near her temples, along her forehead, framing her face with natural golden streaks. Her hair looked heavy and soft and shiny. The length of her spine was graceful, feminine. Her wrists, crisscrossed under her head, were narrow, delicate.

Everything about her turned him on. At the first hint of her scent, the natural perfume of warm woman fresh from her bed, he got excited. Around her, he felt things more acutely than he had for years.

Making an abrupt decision, he stroked one large hand over her head, down to her nape. "I want you, Emma."

Her silent laughter morphed into a groan.

Casey waited, content to smooth her hair and rub her shoulder. Content just to touch her in this innocent way. For now.

When she lifted her head, she was smiling and her eyes twinkled with teasing devilment.

Dazzled, Casey let his hand drop to the table. He

couldn't pull his gaze away from her. "You are so pretty when you smile."

That made her laugh again. "Casey Hudson, you're as shameless as your uncles ever were, and God knows they were nigh infamous for their ways with women."

"Until they married, maybe." Her infectious smile soon had him grinning too. "Now they've taken to family life with as much gusto as they relished bachelorhood. I have a passel of nieces and nephews to prove it."

"Yeah, well, they were bachelors long enough for you to pick up their habits, I see. I've barely been in town a single night."

"But it feels like old times, doesn't it?" To him, it was as if she'd never gone away, they'd fallen into such an easy familiarity.

"Maybe, but it's still only one night, and already you're hitting on me."

"Tell me you don't want me."

Her smile disappeared, replaced with chagrin. "I wish I could."

His heart swelled and thumped. "Then…"

"No." The shake of her head seemed all too final. "Based on our pasts, I can understand why you think I'd just jump into bed with you. We both know I tried hard enough to get you there before I left. And I won't claim I've been a nun since leaving."

That made him wince. The thought of her with other men shouldn't have mattered, but it did. It always had.

"I'm only going to be in town for a short while

and having a brief fling for old time's sake isn't on the agenda.''

"Why not?'' Though he didn't like what he wanted called a fling, he'd take what he could get for now. He wanted her that much.

She wrinkled her nose at him. "C'mon, Case. We're both older and wiser and more mature.''

"Which only means we can damn well take advantage of the chemistry.'' He tipped his head, studying her. "The second I recognized you, Emma, I felt it. Again.'' Hell, it had nearly knocked him on his ass.

She stared at him a moment, then turned to look out over the street. "You know, I'd forgotten how wonderful it was to be in Buckhorn in the morning. In my apartment in Chicago, I don't hear birds first thing or see black squirrels running up a tree. The air I breathe isn't so fresh it has almost the same kick as my coffee. I'd forgotten the scents and the sights.''

As hard as he'd tried, he hadn't forgotten a damn thing. He felt nettled—until she spoke again.

"I'd almost forgotten your effect on me.'' Emma's smile was a little sad, her dark eyes a little wistful. She picked a fat clover blossom from the ground and twirled it between her fingers. "I kept your shirt, did you know that?''

Watching Emma enjoy her surroundings, hearing the catch in her voice stirred him as much as being stroked by another woman would have. Casey felt primed enough that he would happily take her deeper into the trees and skim off her jeans right now—if she'd been at all willing.

But she wasn't.

Her old vulnerability, which had kept his baser instincts at bay as a teenager, was now gone. But in its place was something just as compelling to his heart. He took her hand. "What shirt?"

"The one you gave me the night I left."

"The night you snuck away."

"Semantics." Her crooked smile charmed him. "It smelled of you, so even when you weren't with me, you were. Do you know what I mean?"

He nodded. "It was something familiar."

"It was you. I still have it, though after all this time the scent is gone."

The idea of her hugging his shirt to her body night after night burned him. "Spend the night with me," he offered in a low rasp, "and you can have my whole damn wardrobe."

Her mouth curled, but the humor didn't spread to her eyes. "If I spent the night with you, Casey, I'm afraid I wouldn't want to go."

Her honesty surprised him, and it must have showed. She squeezed his hand and then pulled away.

"I don't mean to put you on the spot, I really don't. I'm not asking you for anything, because I don't need anything. I got my life together and I'm happy with it. But you were always my ultimate fantasy, and I have a feeling that indulging a real-life fantasy wouldn't be a good idea."

He discounted all that fantasy nonsense to ask, "Why?" A little indulgence sounded like a hell of an idea to him.

"It'd complicate things, when I won't be around long enough to deal with anything complicated."

Most of what she said seemed too difficult to understand. Her fantasy? He didn't want to be anyone's fantasy, but he did want to be her reality. In bed.

Anything more than that…well, he doubted he could ever trust Emma again. He'd wanted to be her savior, her protector, and instead she'd walked. And hadn't contacted him even once through all the long, lonely days that had followed. He'd gone from worried sick to angry to bitter.

Now she was back and all the other emotions faded behind the sexual greed, because that at least was easy enough to understand. "You just got here and you're already talking about leaving. How long do you plan to stay?"

She shrugged. "Damon's on a self-assigned sabbatical. He's rethinking his life, so he's able to stay as long as I want."

"A sabbatical from what?" Damon Devaughn seemed like a very real complication. He was close to Emma, no two ways about that. How close—that's what Casey wanted to find out.

"He's an architect, but he's tired of commercial design…you know, putting up shopping centers and parking lots. He wants to go into residential design and do single-family housing instead, because it's more personal. The thing is, starting over will mean realigning his life along with a huge cut in pay. Not that he can't afford it, but he's thinking things through."

It surprised Casey that he and Damon might have something in common—discontent with their current careers. For months, Casey had been rethinking his future plans, and wondering if he'd made a mistake in being lured by his stepgrandfather into a position of money and influence. The job provided a challenge and drew a lot of respect, but because his office was in Cincinnati, it also took him away from his home. At first his big corner office had seemed impressive, but he'd quickly realized that he didn't like sitting behind a desk and answering to others, working for strangers instead of neighbors and friends. Dealing with computers and electronic programs was so impersonal, it left Casey feeling empty.

Unlike Damon, he hadn't yet made up his mind to do anything about it. He wanted a change, but instigating it would stir things up a lot.

"What about you, Emma? How much time do you have off work?" She hesitated so long, Casey's irritation resurfaced. "Is it such a big deal telling me one little thing about your life?"

She pushed her hair off her forehead, thoughtful for a moment before she smiled and shrugged. "I've already spilled my guts, so what difference does it make?"

Another cryptic comment that he couldn't understand. "It doesn't."

"All right." She made up her mind and nodded. "I suppose I can stay as long as I like too. I have my own business. It's small, but I like it that way, and since I'm the boss, I don't have to answer to anyone. But, unlike Damon, I can't afford to stay off indefinitely. How long I stay depends on how my father does, but I'm thinking that if I want to have a business to go back to, I shouldn't stay more than a few weeks."

Her obvious enthusiasm added to his curiosity, and he asked, "What kind of business is it?"

She chewed on her smile, then rolled her eyes. "I'm a massage therapist."

"A...?"

"Yeah, a massage therapist. And I'm good." She went on in a rush, as if to convince him. "My shop is called The Soothing Touch and I've got a really dedicated clientele. When I told them all I'd be gone for a while, they wished me well and told me they'd be waiting for me when I got back."

Casey stared. Not a single intelligent comment came to mind.

At his continued silence, Emma's smile faded and she gave him a defiant look. "I started by working in the Tremont Hotel fitness center, then branched out on my own. Now I work from my own shop throughout the week, but I also do house or office calls over the weekend and in the evening. And once a month I teach sensual-massage classes to couples."

The images that leaped to Casey's mind left him numb: Emma rubbing oil over a man's naked back, his thighs. Emma visiting some corporate asshole in his office. Emma *enjoying* her damn job.

Doing his best to keep the cynicism out of his tone, Casey repeated, "Office calls, huh?"

She nodded. "A lot of executives have high-stress jobs. They'll pay big bucks to have me come to the office and relax them during their lunch hour or before a big meeting."

He absolutely hated the way she put that.

"I have portable equipment that I use. It's not the same as coming to the shop, but I carry special music and oils with me. Sometimes, if it's allowed in the offices, I'll light candles too."

"Candles?"

"Mmm." She looked displeased with his continued, short questions. "You surround the client with soothing ambience. Incense or scented candles, soft music, low lights. I can make a body go boneless in a one-hour session."

Casey's eyebrows pulled down in a suspicious frown. "I just bet you can."

She frowned right back. "You can stop right there, Casey Hudson. I know assumptions run wild and believe me, I've heard every stupid joke there is, so don't bother. Massage therapist is not a euphemism for call girl, you know. I'm not ashamed of what I do. In fact, I'm proud that I do it so well."

This new facet to Emma's personality fascinated Casey. He liked the way she stood up to him, how she defended herself. And because he knew he had jumped to some hasty conclusions, he relaxed enough to tease. "And here I was going to ask what you charge."

Her nose lifted. "Thirty-five an hour at my shop, fifty if it's a house or office call."

Casey considered her, and then had to ask, "I bet most of your clients are men, right?"

"What do you want to bet?"

Keeping the grin off his face wasn't easy. "A kiss?"

"Doesn't matter because you lose. Most are women in their mid-forties, early fifties."

"Really?" That relieved him, until she continued.

"But like I said, some are execs—male and female—with seventy-hour-a-week jobs. And some are athletes with sports injuries that still bother them."

"Athletes?"

"I treated one of the Chicago Cubs for a while early in the season."

New jealousy flared. "What the hell for?"

"He was in a slump and so every time he went to bat, he got tense." She spoke candidly and knowledgeably, using her hands to emphasize. "Massage can help loosen contracted, shortened muscles and at the same time, stimulate flaccid muscles."

Casey grunted at that. "With you touching him, I find it hard to believe there was anything flaccid on the guy." Sure as hell wasn't anything flaccid on him, and he was just *thinking* about her touch, not experiencing it. But he would. Oh yeah, he most definitely would.

Rather than get angry, she got exasperated. "Now you're just being nasty."

"I want you," he reiterated, as if it explained everything. And to his mind, it did.

Her mouth fell open. "I can't believe how pushy you've gotten. You know, you're the only man ever to say such a thing to me."

Casey examined her face, from her sexy mouth and stubborn chin, up to her hair gently teased by the morning breeze. When he locked onto her dark bedroom eyes, she fidgeted in a way that had Casey's insides clenching. "Sorry, Em, but no way in hell can I believe that."

She smirked. "Hey, I've heard other, more crude come-ons. But not an outright statement like *I want you.*"

Never in his life had Casey sat with a woman and had such a discussion. In the normal way of things, if he wanted to get intimate, he made a move and she either reciprocated or not. He didn't spell out his intent and give her a chance to rebuff him. This was unique, exhilarating—and so was Emma. "Well, I do. Want you, I mean. So why shouldn't I be honest about it?"

"Oh, by all means, be honest. Just know that it's not going anywhere."

He didn't like hearing that, and he sure wouldn't accept it, so he changed the subject. "When can I get a massage?"

Her eyes widened. "Never."

"Why not?"

"Because…" She got flustered, and a blush rose all the way to her eyebrows. "I just know you too well. I'd be uncomfortable."

With his eyes holding hers, his body warm with memories, he said, "You've touched me before, Em. Plenty of times, in fact."

"That was a long time ago."

"You don't like touching anymore?"

She groaned and covered her face. "It's not that."

So she did like touching? Anyone, or him specifically? It made Casey nuts wondering what she'd done and who she'd been with…and how much she might have enjoyed it. "Then what, Em?"

She dropped her hands. Her gaze landed first on his face, then dipped to his chest, shoulders. She looked away to the parking lot. "I'll, um, give it some thought, okay? That's all I'll promise for now."

"Yeah, you do that." In the meantime, Casey knew damn good and well that he'd think of little else.

CHAPTER FIVE

THE IDEA OF GETTING her hands on Casey's bare flesh left Emma jittery. She'd given too many massages to count, and she'd always been friendly, talkative, but detached. She could never be detached with Casey.

She decided it was past time to go. Standing, she slipped her feet back into her shoes and avoided his astute gaze. "The coffee's gone and I've got a full day ahead. I should get on my way."

Casey stood with her and to her extreme relief, he dropped the topic of a massage. "What's on the agenda?"

"I have to get the car fixed first, then I want to take Damon into town so he can explore while I make the drive to the hospital." Both Casey and B.B. fell into step behind her when she started back toward the room.

"Several questions come to mind."

The day was already warming, and Emma knew that by ten o'clock, it would be sticky with humidity and heat. "Yeah? Like?"

"How're you going to get your car fixed when you're here, the car is on the road, and the garage is in town?"

"I figured I'd call a tow truck." She stopped right outside her door. She didn't want Casey in her room again. "I can do the work myself, but it's not easy without my tools."

"No kidding? You really know how to work on cars?"

Her feminist core insulted, Emma glared at him. "Do you know how to change a water pump?"

"Sure. But that's because I helped Gabe work on our cars and trucks often enough. I learned, but I wouldn't say it's something I'd choose to do."

Casey's uncle, Gabe Kasper, was known as a handy-man extraordinaire. He could build, repair or remodel just about anything. It made sense that Casey would have learned alongside him. "I helped Damon and his father work on cars, and they helped me with my Mustang. I like it. Besides, I've done all the restoration myself, so I don't trust many other people to touch it."

The smile he gave her looked almost…proud. Emma shook her head to clear it, refusing to disillusion herself.

"You baby your car."

Emma's chin lifted. "She's a seventy Boss in cherry condition. I rebuilt the 429 engine. Front and rear took me four years. After all that, of course I baby her."

"Damn." Casey laughed, but his expression was warm, amused. "Massage therapist, mechanic and beautiful to boot. A woman to steal a man's heart." He touched her nose with a dose of playfulness. "It was so dark, I didn't see your car that well last night, so I didn't notice…" He stopped, touched her cheek and sighed. "Okay, truth is, it wasn't your car that held my attention."

Emma had no idea what to say to that, so she just watched him and waited.

"Of course, now that I know it's a classic Boss, I can understand why you'd want to oversee the work. One problem, though."

"What?"

"It's the weekend and the garage won't open till Monday."

Eyes closed, Emma dropped back against the door. "Damn. I forgot about that."

"Around here, almost all the trade businesses still close on the weekends. Only the grocery stores and restaurants stay open. Buckhorn never changes, Emma. No one really wants it to."

"I told Damon as much when we drove in." Now what could she do? Wait another day to see her father? She might not have any choice.

"Can I offer a solution?"

Emma opened one eye. "What?"

"I'll give Gabe a call. He's got a tow truck and he can replace your water pump—I promise you can trust him. He'll treat your car with kid gloves. While he does that, I'll drive you to the hospital."

"No."

Casey crowded closer, blocking the sun with his wide hard shoulders, lowering his head closer to hers. "Why not?"

With him invading her space, Emma found it difficult to speak, but more difficult to move away. "I might be at the hospital for a while. I don't want you to have to wait."

"I've nothing else planned for the day."

She widened her eyes in disbelief. "It's Saturday

and you have nothing to do?'' *No dates with beautiful women?*

''Nothing important.''

She found that very hard to swallow, knowing first-hand of Casey's popularity. ''Then you should just relax, not spend your time hanging out in a hospital.''

''You can pay me back by going boating with me. Do you still remember how to ski?''

Longing swelled up inside her. She missed being on the lake, missed the peacefulness of the water, the joy of skiing, the fresh air and sunshine. As a kid, she'd often escaped to the water, staying there late until it was safe to go home again. Sometimes Casey would hang out with her and they'd listen to the frogs croaking and the splash of gentle waves on the shore.

She'd also met plenty of other boys on the lake, and none of them had been interested in the frogs. In those days, sex in a quiet cove had been as much of an escape for Emma as anything else. ''I haven't skied since I left here.''

''No kidding? The Devaughns weren't much for water?''

''It's not that. I was just…busy.''

Casey looked very unconvinced. ''It's like riding a bike—you never forget how. And I bet B.B. will love being in the boat too. I haven't met a dog yet who doesn't.''

''What about Damon?''

Casey lowered his lashes, hiding his expression. ''I thought he wanted to explore the town a little.''

''He might, but I'm not going to abandon him on his first day in town.''

Rubbing the back of his neck, Casey muttered, ''So

he'll come along—'' he narrowed his eyes at her ''—if you insist.''

It was so tempting to give in to him, on all counts. She had missed the exhilaration of boating, the wind in her hair, the sun on her face. And accepting Casey's assistance would save her from the hassle of finding another ride to the hospital. ''Gabe doesn't mind working on a Saturday?''

''He wouldn't schedule work, no. But this is different. He's always willing to help out. I doubt it'll take him that long.''

''Why would he want to help me out?''

Casey's voice gentled in reproach. ''You've forgotten how my family is if you have to ask that.''

She gave a short laugh. ''No one in her right mind would ever forget your family. I half wondered if Buckhorn would have sainted the bunch of them by now.''

Casey's unselfconscious smile made him more handsome than ever. ''We like to lend a helping hand. Most everyone in Buckhorn does.''

Emma didn't reply to that. She remembered all too well how most of the locals felt about her. She'd been shunned at best, a pariah at worst. But his family had been wonderful.

''Let me be helpful, Em.''

Oh, she could imagine that husky voice seducing any number of women. That is, if they needed to be seduced. She'd be willing to bet the women had been chasing Casey most diligently. ''It'll take me a little time to get ready. I haven't even showered yet.''

His gaze warmed, then moved over her with slow deliberation. ''Take your time. While you do that, I'll come in and give Gabe a call. We can grab a bite to eat on the way to the hospital. How's that sound?''

B.B. scratched at the door, indicating he'd had enough of idle conversation. He wasn't much of a morning creature either. ''All right.'' She opened the door and watched B.B. head straight for the bed. With one agile leap he hit the mattress, circled once, twice, then dropped with a doggy sigh, his nose tucked close to his tail.

As she entered, she realized just how small and crowded the room was. The second Casey stepped in and closed the door behind him, it became even smaller. Emma laced her fingers together. ''Promise me that if Gabe has other plans, you won't push him. I'm sure I could figure something else out.''

''Absolutely.''

She wasn't sure if she believed him or not. Resigned, she went to the connecting door and tapped on it, then stuck her head inside. Damon was on his stomach, his face turned toward her, snoring. Ignoring Casey for the moment, she crept in and touched Damon's bare shoulder.

Immediately his eyes opened, but otherwise he didn't move. ''Hey, doll,'' he said in a rumbling, still half-asleep voice.

''You awake enough to catch an explanation?''

''Depends.'' He stretched, then pushed up to his elbows. ''Is Romeo gone?''

From his hovering position in the doorway, Casey said, ''If you mean me, no.''

Damon dropped his head forward. ''Persistent, isn't he?''

Casey showed his teeth in a false smile. "Afraid so."

"All right. I'm awake." Damon pushed into a sitting position on the side of the bed and ran his hand through his hair. "What's up?"

"The garage is closed on weekends. Casey's uncle is a handyman and we're going to see if he'll fix the car while I go to the hospital."

"Wait." Damon held up a hand, got sidetracked by a huge yawn, then eyed her. "You're saying you'll let someone else touch your car?"

"I know Gabe, or at least his reputation with cars. He's good."

"Yeah, yeah. I remember the stories. All the holy men of Buckhorn—"

Emma felt like throttling him, especially when she heard Casey chuckle rather than take offense. Through her teeth, she said, "You can either sleep in—"

"Nope, I'm awake now."

"—join us—"

He laughed and spared a glance for Casey. "Does *he* get a vote on that one?"

"—or go exploring."

"So many options. Let's see." He slapped his knees. "I choose C. That is, unless you want me to go to the hospital with you." His voice dropped and he caught her hand. "How do you feel about seeing your dad? You okay?"

Emma glanced at Casey and found him listening intently. Though her stomach was in knots at the idea of facing her father after so many years, she mustered a smile to relieve both men of worry. "I'll be fine, really."

"It's been a long time, doll."

"Exactly. Past time I visited."

Damon didn't look convinced, but he knew her well enough to let it go. "What about B.B.?"

"He'll be happy to sleep until I get back. Then I'm going to take him boating with me."

"Boating?"

Without turning to face Casey, Emma flapped a hand toward him. "He, uh, he has a boat."

"Of course he does."

Casey spoke up, his tone dry. "We have several boats, actually. A speedboat for skiing, a pontoon, couple of fishing boats. The biggest recreational draw for Buckhorn is the three-hundred-and-five-acre water reservoir."

"A man-made lake?"

"Exactly. Around here, everyone considers a boat as important as a car."

Emma cleared her throat and tried to sound enthusiastic. "I thought you might like to go along, Damon."

"Not I, thank you. I can already hear the awkward squeaking of that third wheel."

By his very silence, Casey agreed, but Emma rushed to convince him otherwise. "You wouldn't be a third wheel! And I'd love to show you the lake, Damon. It's beautiful and so peaceful. You could see some of the vacation homes built along there."

"I remember everything you've told me about it." He yawned again, stood, and scratched his belly. "How about we go check it out after the car is fixed

and you've had a chance to visit and get reacquainted? Maybe in a day or two?''

"Are you sure?''

"Most positive.'' Damon strolled to his open suitcase resting on the dresser. He pulled out chinos, a
black polo shirt and clean boxers. "I'm heading to
the shower. I'll be ready in half an hour.''

The second the bathroom door closed, Casey
walked over to Emma and took her arm. "Why don't
you go ahead and get ready too while I call Gabe?
You don't want to miss the doctor at the hospital.''

The town's small hospital, Buckhorn Memorial,
was efficient and well run, but it wasn't equipped for
anything life or death. She'd been reassured when she
found out her father was staying there, rather than at
one of the larger neighboring hospitals in the next
city. It told her that a full recovery was expected.

Still, the idea of seeing him left her nervous, anxious and wary. She'd spoken to him regularly over
the years, but because of how they'd parted, the mutual ruse they'd pulled off, their conversations always
felt superficial. Despite everything, despite how she'd
left him—how he'd *helped* her to leave—Emma knew
he loved her.

Just not enough.

"All right.'' Putting off going wouldn't make it
easier. She'd made her decision and now she'd follow
through. "I won't be long.''

Casey watched her as she riffled through her suitcase to locate a sundress, panties and sandals. The
dress, a fitted chambray sheath with embroidered scal-
lop edging, was casual and cool enough for the summer sun, but also dressy enough for the hospital. It

always packed well, but the white cotton blouse she'd brought along as a jacket was wrinkled. Hopefully the steam from her shower would help. As she headed for the bathroom, Casey stretched out on the bed with B.B., propping his back on the headboard and reaching for the only phone, situated on the nightstand.

Emma's mouth went dry, not only because he was in her bed, where she'd slept, and he looked right at home there. But because B.B. rolled to his back and waited for Casey to scratch his chest—and Casey did, as if they'd been longtime friends. B.B. was always polite unless provoked, but he didn't warm up to strangers easily. Yet he already treated Casey like a pal.

Emma sighed and went on into the bathroom before she did something stupid, like join Casey on the bed. She felt melancholy, and with good reason. Like her, it seemed her dog had a fondness for Buckhorn's golden son. Well, they'd both just have to get over it, because once her business was finished in Buckhorn, Emma fully intended to return to her old life, the life where she'd found contentment.

Her life—without Casey Hudson.

OF COURSE, Gabe agreed to help out, just as Casey had known he would. He hadn't yet told his uncle who he was helping, just a lady friend. Casey wondered if Gabe would recognize Emma. The others had known her better. His father because of Emma's trip to their house. His Uncle Morgan because, as sheriff, he'd had occasion to check up on Emma for skipping school and breaking curfew. And his Uncle Jordan would probably recall her from the hospital, the night

Georgia's mother had taken ill and he and Emma had dropped in to help out. Granted, Jordan had been mightily distracted with Georgia and her two children. Casey was convinced that Jordan had fallen in love with Georgia that night. But he'd surely at least noticed Emma.

His youngest uncle, Gabe, had only met her a few times, interspersed with all the other girls that Casey had dated. Casey didn't want any of his relatives looking at him with speculation, wondering about his feelings. It was better that Gabe be the only one to know about Emma. At least for now.

Still idly rubbing the dog's neck, Casey listened as B.B.'s breathing drifted into a doggy snore. He grinned. B.B. was a beautiful, well-groomed, healthy animal, testament to the care Emma had given him. He obviously had a regular sleeping spot in the bed, too.

Lucky dog.

Casey wouldn't have minded a little of Emma's care directed his way, yet she seemed determined to keep their involvement platonic. He'd have her alone this afternoon and he'd begin working on her.

Knowing Gabe would be there soon, Casey got up to stroll the room, peeking out the window to the parking lot every so often. As he paced, he noted Emma's open suitcase, stuffed mostly with casual clothes. He also saw her bra on the only chair in the room, strung over the arm. He stopped to stare, impressed with her feminine choice.

He absolutely loved lingerie, the sexier the better.

The discarded bra, likely removed the night before, appealed in a big way. Made of ice-blue transparent lace, it looked sheer, but had an underwire. The reason she would require an underwire tormented his libido with visions of her full breasts free, or held only by his hands. Casey picked up the bra, rubbing the delicate material between his fingers.

"That surely has to be illegal."

Disgusted at being caught, Casey dropped the bra and turned to face Damon Devaughn. "What's that?"

"Molesting a woman's clothing." Devaughn lazily moved into the room, propped his hip on the dresser and crossed his ankles. He wore pressed tan chinos, a black designer polo and casual loafers. "Does Emma know that you have these kinky tendencies?"

Casey narrowed his eyes. Around Emma, Damon acted casual but proprietary, intimate yet not sexual. Casey couldn't quite figure him out. Then he decided *what the hell?* and just blurted out his biggest question. "Are you gay?"

Damon blinked at him and a smile twitched on his mouth. Somewhat demure, he said, "Why do you ask?"

Stumped as to how to reply, Casey scowled. "It seemed pertinent to the situation."

"Ah, let me guess. It's my fashion sense, isn't it?" He smoothed his hands over his shirt. "No? My neatly trimmed hair?"

When Casey didn't bother to reply, Damon's eyes narrowed. He crossed his arms over his chest, and Casey couldn't help but notice that muscles bulged. He didn't understand Devaughn, but he had to admit that the man was no wimp.

"Or," Damon asked, dragging out the word until

Casey wanted to throttle him, "is it because I like Emma, even though I'm not screwing her?"

Casey took an aggressive step forward before he could stop himself. He felt like smashing Damon and wasn't even sure why. No, that was a lie. He knew he disliked Damon because the man was close to Emma. "It was a simple question, Devaughn."

"No."

"No *what?*"

"No, I'm not gay." Damon shrugged. "A simple answer."

Striving for control, Casey drew a slow deep breath, then another. They both heard the shower stop, and the telltale sounds of Emma moving around in the bathroom. Naked.

Casey swallowed, distracted by images of her toweling off. Staring toward the bathroom door, he muttered, "I didn't mean to offend you, Devaughn. I have nothing against—"

"Yeah, yeah, whatever. No offense taken." Suddenly the bathroom door squeaked open and Damon, too, turned to stare.

Emma, her hair wrapped in a towel, stuck her head out. She looked startled to find that she already had both men's attention. She glanced first at Casey, then at Damon. "I need a blow-dryer. Who has a motel without blow-dryers in the bathroom?"

She sounded very disgruntled, then answered her own question. "Obviously Mrs. Reider, which I should have guessed, but I stupidly assumed that she'd gotten a little with the times over the past decade."

Damon laughed. "I'll get mine. Hang on."

Casey mouthed silently, *I'll get mine,* then realized Emma was watching him. He pasted on a leering smile. "You need any help?"

Eyes wide, Emma asked, "With what?"

"Drying off?"

"Uh, no." She looked toward the connecting door as if willing Damon to reappear. He did, curse him.

"Here you go. Don't electrocute yourself."

Emma snatched the dryer out of his hand, cast another quick look at Casey, and shut the door. Seconds later, a loud hum reverberated throughout the room, ensuring Damon and Casey some privacy.

Damon took immediate advantage. Steely-eyed, he advanced on Casey until he stood a mere foot in front of him. "I haven't had many occasions to issue these hairy-chested, testosterone-drowned warnings, but I hope you'll listen despite my inexperience in these things, because I'm dead serious."

Casey drew back and it took him a moment to figure out what the hell Damon had just said. When his meaning sunk in, Casey shook his head. Damon was about the oddest damn duck he'd ever run across. "Yeah, I'm listening, Devaughn. Wouldn't miss it, in fact."

"I love Emma like a sister—a younger sister whom I feel very protective of."

That suited Casey just fine. As long as Damon didn't lust after her, he could love her all he wanted. "I'm glad to hear it."

"You crushed her once."

Casey scowled. How much had Emma told him? *What* had she told him? "If that's true, it wasn't on purpose.'' Hell, Emma had run out on him, not the other way around.

"Yeah, well, you were a kid." Damon's voice dropped to a harsh whisper when the blow-dryer got turned off. "But you're not a kid anymore. Don't hurt her."

Nettled at being chastised, Casey turned away to the window. "I wasn't planning on it." No, he planned on making love to her until they were both exhausted.

Damon followed. "Bullshit. You're on the prowl and we all three know it."

"All three?"

"Emma isn't a stupid woman and she's well acquainted with come-ons. In case you've failed to notice, she's got this natural sexuality about her that turns normal men into wildebeests in heat."

Casey's hands curled into fists. Was it his imagination, or was Damon getting stranger by the moment? "I noticed."

Damon's expression lightened, and he even grinned. "It was a facetious statement, man. Believe me, I noticed you noticing."

"Is there a point to this, Devaughn?"

"Yeah. If you're half as honorable as Emma claimed, you'll leave her alone."

Half as honorable? He again wondered exactly what Emma might have said about him. "I can't do that."

Angered, Damon stepped toward him—and Emma came out of the bathroom. She looked…astounding.

Casey immediately forgot all about Damon and his half-baked warnings. Emma's hair, loose and soft and feminine, bounced gently around her shoulders and caught the reflection of every light. She wore only a touch of makeup, which made her eyes even larger, darker. But it was the gloss on her lips that really got to Casey. Damn, he wanted to lick it off her mouth, then taste her, only her. Her mouth drove him nuts it was so sexy.

The chambray dress fit her and emphasized every womanly curve without seeming too obvious. She carried a blouse in one hand, her sandals in the other. Without looking at him, she bent and slipped on one sandal, then the other. Enthralled, both he and Damon watched in silence until she was ready.

"Is Gabe here yet?"

Casey shook himself out of his stupor. He moved the utilitarian curtain aside and looked out the window. "Just pulled in. I told him I'd watch for him, so we should go on down."

She nodded and went to sit on the side of the bed next to B.B. The big dog raised up in silent query. "I'll be back soon, bud. You sleep."

The dog's tail smacked hard against the mattress in agreement, and Casey could have sworn he grinned. Then he resettled his head and went back to sleep.

"He understands you?"

"He knows a lot of phrases, and he's smarter than most people I know." Emma picked up her purse. "Besides, he's used to dozing the day away when I work. He'll be fine."

Damon held the door open and they all went out to the parking lot together. Gabe stood lounging against the side of his tow truck in dark sunglasses, a backward ball cap, ragged cutoffs and an unbuttoned shirt that showed his tanned chest. All in all, typical weekend wear for Gabe.

Emma smiled when she saw him and said in an aside to Casey, "He hasn't changed a bit." Then Gabe's youngest daughter, five-year-old Briana, stepped out from behind him and Emma laughed. "Well now, that's new!"

Casey grinned. "We wondered if there'd be any girl babies born into the family since the dominant gene appears to be male. But Gabe surprised everyone, including his wife, by fathering not one, but three daughters. They're five, seven and nine years old. All with blond hair and blue eyes. This is Briana, the youngest."

With twinkling eyes, the little girl scooted to Casey and held up her arms, obliging Casey to lift her. He hefted her to his hip, kissed her golden head, and gave her a fierce hug. "Hey, squirt."

"She's beautiful," Emma said, and stroked Briana's little shoulder. Briana beamed at her for the compliment.

"All three of his daughters are."

Emma laughed again. "Actually, she looks like a small feminine version of Gabe."

"Exactly. Makes him nuts, too."

Damon stepped forward with an outstretched hand. "Damon Devaughn. Thank you for coming out on a weekend."

Gabe, always jovial, shrugged off the remark. "Not a problem. Casey said you have a Mustang Boss. Can't very well leave a sweet car like that on the side of the road, not even here in Buckhorn."

"It's not my car. It's Emma's."

"Emma?" His uncle didn't seem to remember her at all, until he went to shake her hand, which caused him to look at her more closely. "You look familiar." He glanced at Casey. "Have we been introduced before?"

Casey wanted to groan. He sent Gabe a look, but his uncle was distracted trying to recall where and when he'd met Emma.

"I'm from here originally," Emma said. "And really, Mr. Kasper, we do appreciate the help."

"Good God, girl, no one calls me mister. Gabe will do, if you don't want to make me feel old." Gabe stared at her a moment more while attempting to recall her. A smile appeared. "That's right, I remember now. You're that girl who…"

He drew up short on his verbal faux pas, and Casey hurried to fill in the awkward silence. "Emma's been away for eight years."

"S'that right?" Gabe lifted the cap from his head, scratched his right ear and then replaced his hat, all the while grinning. "Welcome home, Emma."

Scrupulously polite, Emma said, "I'm just here for a visit."

Gabe took his daughter from Casey. "Don't be silly. You don't *visit* home, because you can't ever really leave it." Before anyone could argue that point, Gabe turned to Damon. "You're coming with me, right?"

Damon pulled his concerned gaze from Emma. "Yes. I have the keys to the Mustang. I was hoping to explore the town while you repaired the car."

"Have you had breakfast?"

"Not yet."

"Then I'll drop you at Ceily's diner. You'll get the best ham and eggs in three counties."

Damon and Emma shared a look of mutual wariness. Not understanding, Casey took Emma's arm. "You remember Ceily, don't you, Em?"

She looked stricken only a moment, and in the next instant her face was blank of any expression. She pulled sunglasses from her purse and slipped them on. Casey noted that her hand shook and her tone was clipped when she finally said, "Yes. I remember her." Her smile appeared forced. "You'll enjoy the food, Damon."

Casey didn't know what had upset her, but he decided it was past time to get on the road. "Damon, we'll see you later." Much, much later. "Gabe, thanks again." He waved to Briana. "Be good to Damon, sweetie."

When Damon slid into the seat next to her, Briana beamed at him and said, "You smell good."

"Why, thank you," Damon said with a chuckle.

Gabe groaned. "This is the penance I pay for my misspent youth. Three flirting daughters will definitely be the death of me."

Emma smiled at the exchange as Casey led her to his car. Her moods changed quicker than the breeze, but eventually he'd understand her. Once they finished the visit to the hospital, he'd have her alone on the lake. He'd get some answers, make some headway—and reestablish old bonds.

He could hardly wait.

CHAPTER SIX

DAMON FELT as if he'd stepped into another world, or at least taken a step back in time. "We're not in Kansas anymore, Toto," he murmured to himself.

Gabe Kasper, a very friendly, laid-back fellow with the absolute worst fashion sense Damon had ever witnessed firsthand, had dropped him off in the middle of the town—if you could call such a small, old-fashioned gathering of buildings a town. But the architecture was impressive, ornate yet sturdy, able to withstand the passing of time.

Prior to letting him out of the truck, Gabe had pointed in the direction of the diner and admonished Damon to stay out of the sun.

True enough, he wasn't much for tanning, and a ball cap, especially one worn backward as Gabe preferred, was out of the question. While looking around, Damon noticed that nearly every person he saw was dressed in a similar fashion. It was like being at Palm Beach during spring break. He wondered how many people constituted the local denizens and how many were vacationers visiting the lake.

Women paraded up and down the sidewalks in shorts and bathing-suit tops. Adolescent boys were shirtless. Some children were barefoot. Every doorway spawned several loiterers and damned if there weren't two grizzled old men in coveralls playing checkers under the shade of the barbershop awning. It was like landing in Mayberry, but with color. Lots and lots of color.

Enormous, lush oak trees lined the side of the road and provided some shade to most of the storefronts. The sky was so blue it dazzled. Flowers grew from every nook and cranny, and birds of every size and song flitted about.

Damon drew a deep breath and felt his lungs expand with fresh, humid air. Jesus, he liked it. A lot.

He strolled along the sidewalk, soaking in the atmosphere and acclimating himself. A few minutes later, he smelled the luscious scents from the diner even before he saw it.

When they'd driven through the night before, Emma had pointed the place out, but other than noting the location, he'd paid little attention. He'd been too worried about Emma, watching her to see how she took her return to Buckhorn.

As an architect, he now studied the simple but unique lines of each structure. The diner was spacious, in the same design as the other buildings around it, but modern windows and roofing materials had been added, making it somewhat unique. He knew that eight years ago it had been gutted by fire, which probably accounted for the improvements. Damon shook his head. Emma had retold the story so many times that he knew it by heart.

He continued along, nodding to the people who gave him cautious looks until he reached the diner. Up close, the modern materials were even more noticeable. Still, the reconstruction was a quality job, nicely executed.

The walkway had been swept clean, the windows were spotless, and the ornate oak front door stood propped open by a large clay flowerpot filled to over-flowing with purple, yellow and red flowers. The quiet buzz of conversation mingled with the sounds of dishes clacking, food sizzling on the grill and a jukebox playing.

Damon peered inside, making note of the tidy rows of booths and tables, the immaculate floor, the utili-zation of every available space. Apparently Ceily did an efficient job of running the diner, and in hiring good help. He wondered if he'd be able to meet her. Based on everything Emma had told him about her, he was curious. He'd already formed an image of her in his mind and he wondered if she'd look as he pic-tured her—work-worn, tired, frumpy. As he was glancing around, a waitress moved into his view, drawing his attention.

The second Damon's gaze landed on her, every-thing and everyone else faded into the background. Lord have mercy, they grew the girls healthy in Buck-horn. He leaned into the doorway to watch her, and felt intrigued.

Damon had always considered Emma to be a lus-cious woman, healthy and earthy and sensual. The woman now bent to a booth picking up dishes was just as luscious, maybe more so because, damn, he didn't view her in any familial way.

He did a visual sweep of her body, taking in every detail and noting the lack of a ring on her left hand, as well as the delicate bracelet circling her slim ankle.

He also noted that she appeared busy but happy, rushed but energized.

Tight, faded jean shorts made her rump look especially round—a deliberate effort on her part, no doubt. A red cotton crop top hugged her breasts and showed off her trim, lightly tanned midriff. A sturdy utility apron with only a few spots on it had been tied loosely around her hips, looking more like decoration than protection against stains. Sun-streaked, sandy-brown hair hung to the middle of her back, contained in a loose ponytail that added to the country-girl charm. She wore snowy-white canvas sneakers on her feet. Cute.

He'd known, admired and sexually enjoyed a lot of polished, sophisticated women. Not once had he ever gotten involved with a country bumpkin. The idea appealed to his sense of adventure and variety. Would she romp with him in the hay? Make him biscuits and gravy the morning after? He grinned to himself, wondering at the possibilities and feeling a tad whimsical.

Someone at the table behind her spoke, and she laughed as she turned—and caught Damon's speculative stare. As if the meeting of their eyes snared her physically, she went still. Her wide smile faded but her green eyes remained bright. Damon estimated her to be in her early thirties. Their gazes locked for a long moment before the customers regained her attention. She dismissed Damon with a quick, curious smile and got back to work.

Miss Ceily had done all right in hiring that one, Damon decided. Not only was she a conscientious worker, but she provided some very nice scenery.

Propelled forward by his own curiosity, Damon stepped inside. He watched her a moment more to judge which tables were hers then he seated himself. And he waited. He didn't stare at her again; that would have been too obvious. But his awareness of her was so keen he always knew just where she was within the diner. He listened to her as she visited with the other customers, and decided her laugh was nice. Her voice had the same pleasant country twang he'd noticed the first time he'd met Emma.

Satisfaction oozed through him as he sensed her approach. It'd be interesting to see if she suited him. And if she did, well, this visit might turn out more stimulating than he'd anticipated.

She set a glass of ice water in front of him. "Hi there." Without blinking, she leaned her hip on the edge of his booth and met his bold gaze.

Damon allowed a small smile. Checking for her name, he glanced at her breasts, but she wore no name tag, so he couldn't look as long—or as thoroughly— as he'd have liked. Glancing back at her face, he kept his gaze fixed, his voice low and heavy in a way that he knew would indicate his interest. "Hello."

The second he spoke, her slim eyebrows lifted. "A visitor, huh?"

Her easy, friendly familiarity pleased him. "Guilty. My lack of accent gave me away?"

"That it did, but don't worry. You won't stand out too much. This time of year we have a lot of vacationers around." She looked him over, then asked, "You staying at the lake?"

"No." Damon continued to smile without offering

further explanations. He waited to see if she'd push him or back off.

She did neither. "I didn't think so. You don't look much like a fisherman."

Startled by that disclosure—and a little relieved, because, really, who would *want* to look like a fisherman?—he said, "No?"

Her smile quirked. "Too tidy."

"You have sloppy fishermen in the area, do you?"

"Not sloppy. Relaxed." She straightened away from the table. "Fishing requires a lot of patience and time spent in the weather. You don't look all that patient, and you don't look like you hang outdoors much."

Now *that* sounded vaguely like an insult, causing him to frown. So he didn't have a tan. Hadn't she heard that too much exposure to the sun wasn't healthy for you?

With a look of innocence, as if she hadn't just deliberately riled him, she tapped the menu. "You had a chance to decide what you want, yet?"

Oh, he knew exactly what he wanted. Damon pushed the plastic printed menu aside without interest. "What do you recommend?"

Her smile widened and her lashes lowered in a coy, rather effective manner. "That'd depend. Whatcha in the mood for?"

Damn, her flirting stirred him. It had been far too long since he'd had the relief of sex. "I somehow doubt it's listed on the menu."

"We're not that backward." She shifted, and deftly managed to draw his attention to her legs again. "Why don't you give us a try?"

"All right." He eyed her shapely hips, not lingeringly, but with enough intent that she couldn't miss it. "How about something…hearty."

Suddenly she laughed in delight, tipping her head back and showing a seductive length of throat. She had a husky laugh, and it turned him on. But then, at that particular moment, everything appeared to be turning him on.

"Hearty, huh?"

"That's right."

Smoothing a wisp of tawny hair behind her ear, she said, "All right. We have a sinful egg and ham casserole that'll stick to your ribs till dinnertime."

"Sinful, you say? Interesting. And who prepared it?"

She looked at him beneath her lashes. "Me."

"Ah." He tilted his head to study her. Her lashes were long and thick, her eyes smoky, with small crinkles at the corners that showed her to be a woman used to laughing, a woman who lived her life with enthusiasm. Her nose turned up slightly on the end, giving her an elfin appearance in direct contrast to her earthy sensuality. And her body…he'd love to see her naked. He was fair sick of skinny women on a perpetual diet, honed so tightly that nothing ever jiggled. With a long, leisurely ride, this woman would jiggle—her breasts, her behind…

Feeling the heat expand inside him, Damon stuck out his hand, anxious to touch her. "I'm Damon Devaughn, by the way. I'll be in the area for a little while."

"S'that so?" She took his hand, but didn't perform

the customary shake. Instead, she just held on to him, giving her own brazen show of interest. "I'm Ceily."

Surprise momentarily made him mute. Damn, he hadn't seen that coming. To be sure, he asked, "Ceily, as in the owner of the diner?"

"One and the same." She smiled down at their clasped hands, one eyebrow raised, but she didn't pull away from him. And Damon didn't release her. She had a firm hold, her hand slim, warm, a little rough from work.

For whatever reason, he'd expected Ceily to be older, more timeworn, tired. Emma's memories of her had been of a grown woman, yet Ceily must have had responsibility for the diner at an early age because by his count, she was still young.

Beyond his sexual interest, Damon felt... impressed.

Knowing who she was slanted things though, made them a tad more difficult, but not impossible. He decided to test her before he got any more involved. "I'm here with a friend."

Disappointment made her green eyes darken. "Female friend?"

"Yes." He released her hand and leaned back in his seat, watching for her reaction. "You might remember her. Emma Clark?"

A brief moment of confusion crossed her features, then she brightened. "No kidding? I remember Emma. She's Casey Hudson's age, right?"

Damon scowled. Why the hell would she mention Casey? "That's right. In fact, she's with Casey today, visiting her father in the hospital."

Ceily turned and hollered toward the kitchen.

"Hey, I need a casserole and—" She looked back at Damon. "What do you want to drink?"

"Do you have sweet tea?"

Nodding, she yelled, "And an iced tea."

A dark-haired man in a hair net poked his face into an opening visible behind the bar that led into the kitchen. "Be ready in a sec."

"Thanks." Without being invited, Ceily sat down in the booth opposite Damon. "So Casey's already hooked up with her, huh?" Dimples showed in her cheeks when she grinned. "Doesn't surprise me much. From what I remember, she always did like him. And he's just like his uncles, meaning he's not one to waste time."

"How…reassuring."

Ceily laughed, then crossed her arms on the table-top and leaned toward him. It was a toss-up what fascinated him more—her mouth or her cleavage. "You with her, or just friends?"

"Friends." She wasn't wearing any lipstick, but her naked mouth looked very appealing. Her bottom lip was plump, her upper lip well defined. "If it was more, I wouldn't be flirting with you."

That sexy mouth tilted up. "So you are flirting, huh?"

"Of course." He stared into her eyes without smiling. "And you're flirting back."

She shrugged. "Around here, that might mean something—and then again, it might mean nothing."

"Around here?"

"We're all real sociable and quick to tease."

"I see. So which is it this time?"

She pondered her reply before answering. "I

reckon it means I wouldn't mind showing you around the area, if you're interested.''

Uncertainty made her offer casual, yet Damon noted her anticipation, the way she held herself hopeful. Oh yes, the trip had become quite intriguing.

''My interest has already been established.'' His body hummed with that interest as he began considering what the night might bring. The irony of it amused him. Emma might not like it, but then there was no reason she had to know right off.

He reached across the table and took her hand again. ''So tell me, Ceily. What time do you get off work, and how late do you want to stay out?''

CASEY WATCHED EMMA grow increasingly subdued the farther they got from town. The ride to the hospital took her back along the way she'd come in, to the outskirts of the city proper. The twenty-minute trip had been mostly silent, yet not uncomfortable. From the drive-through, they'd picked up two bottles of orange juice and breakfast sandwiches to eat along the way. Emma had also downed another cup of coffee.

After gathering the sandwich wrappers and empty bottles together, Emma had spent the remainder of the ride looking around with a mixture of awe, recollection and melancholy. She'd missed Buckhorn, that much was plain.

So why had she waited so long to return?

Casey didn't mind her silence as she reacquainted herself with the area. But the closer they got to the hospital, the more she retreated until he could feel her agitation. Was she worried about seeing her father again?

Old habits were indeed hard to break, and Casey found himself wishing he could shield her from the unknown. Would her father be happy to see her again? Or would he treat her with the same callous disregard he'd shown so long ago?

For the rest of his life, Casey knew he'd remember the look on her bruised, tear-streaked face the night her father had jerked her forward, presenting her as a problem, ridding himself of her.

It still infuriated him, so how must it make *her* feel to face Dell again?

The roads here were smooth, open, with no need to shift from fifth gear. Though the temperature had reached eighty already, with high humidity, Emma had been all for skipping the air-conditioning in favor of leaving the convertible top down. Casey glanced toward her, watching her hair dance behind her, seeing the concentrated, determined expression on her face.

He tightened his hands on the steering wheel, fighting the urge to reach for her. "Hey."

She started, then glanced at him. "What?"

"You okay?"

"Sure, I'm fine." She clutched at her purse in her lap, giving away her unease. "Just thinking."

"About what?"

"I don't know. Everything. Nothing." She turned toward him, folding one leg onto the seat. She had to hold her hair out of her face with her hand. "Buckhorn hasn't changed at all."

Her position exposed more of her thigh—something Casey made immediate note of. As a teenager, she'd kept a golden tan. Now she looked fair, with only a faint kiss from the sun. He had to clear his throat. "Not much, no."

"Everything seems exactly the same, maybe aged a little more. But still…the same."

"That bothers you?"

She leaned back in her seat and stared up at the sky. "No." She spoke so low her voice almost got carried away on the wind. Casey strained to hear her. "It's just that I've changed so much, and yet I still feel like I don't belong here."

A vague panic took Casey by surprise. "This is your home." He sounded far too gruff, almost angry. "Of course you belong."

Silence hung between them, pressing down on him, until she swiveled her head toward him. "If you have anything you need to do today, you can just drop me at the hospital."

It bugged the hell out of him how she kept trying to shove him away. "I'll wait for you."

"Dad's probably not up to a long visit, but it still might be an hour."

"I'll wait."

She stared at him, so Casey gave her a smile to counter his insistent tone and then, because he *had* to touch her, he opened his hand over the gearshift in invitation. She hesitated only a moment before reaching across and lacing her fingers in his. Like old times.

Now, that felt right—Emma reaching for him, accepting him. The touch of her hand to his, palm to palm, fingers intertwined, filled him with a sense of well-being.

Two minutes later, he parked in the crowded visitors' section of the hospital lot. Emma, now utterly silent, flipped down her visor to quickly comb her hair and reapply lip gloss. He'd seen the feminine routine performed by numerous women. But this was Emma, and she fascinated him.

He went around to her side of the car and held her door open. "You look beautiful, Emma."

She sent him a look of tolerance. "I'll settle for passable, thank you."

"Very passable, then." Casey took her arm as they crossed the scorching lot. Damp heat lifted off the pavement in waves. "Do you remember the last time we were here together?"

Nodding, she said, "With your Uncle Jordan and his wife. But that was before they'd gotten married."

"The night they met, actually. Georgia's mother, Ruth, was sick, and Jordan had brought them, along with Georgia's two kids, to the hospital." While driving to the hospital to lend a helping hand, Casey had found Emma walking on the side of the road. As if the picture had been painted on his brain, he recalled exactly how she'd looked that night in ultrashort shorts, a hot-pink halter, and her skin dewy from the humidity as she'd sashayed down the roadway. *All alone.*

He'd been worried about her, as usual, and had insisted on giving her a ride. She'd climbed into his car, then made him sweat even more with wanting her.

Shaking his head, Casey wondered why the hell he

hadn't taken what she'd offered. If he had, maybe he wouldn't feel as he did now. And maybe he wouldn't have felt this way for most of his adult life.

Putting himself back on track, he continued with the family discussion. "Ruth still has some problems with her lungs, but now she's hooked up with Misty and Honey's dad, and he pampers her. She's doing pretty good."

"Do you mean your grandfather? Do you work for him now?"

"Stepgrandfather officially, but yeah. I've been working with him since I finished college. I'm the executive vice president of sales and marketing."

"Wow." Emma sounded genuinely impressed. "That sounds like an important position."

Self-conscious about the rapid and consistent promotions, Casey grumbled, "My grandfather has shoved me right up the ladder. He takes every opportunity to give me a bigger office, a better parking spot, more perks. It's his goal that I'll eventually run the company for him."

"What exactly is his company?"

"Electronics, computer hardware. You know, very high-tech, state-of-the-art stuff for businesses. Boring stuff." He laughed at himself. "Very boring."

"I see." Her look was filled with comprehension in a way exclusive to Emma. She understood him, which made long explanations unnecessary. "So you don't like your job, or is it your grandfather you don't like?"

He avoided giving her a direct answer by saying, "I like him fine. He's loosened up a lot, especially since he and Ruth married."

That disclosure diverted her. "Wow, everyone is getting married."

Casey stared ahead, strangely annoyed. "Nope, not everyone."

Emma did a double take, probably trying to judge his mood. When she saw his sour expression, she went a little quiet. "Like everyone else, Casey, you'll eventually find the right woman and swear love everlasting."

She didn't sound overly thrilled with that prospect, which pretty much mirrored his own feelings on the matter. Marriage? Just the thought of it left him tight and uncertain in a way he refused to accept. "We'll see."

Emma bit her lip, feeling the new tension just as he did. In an obvious effort to lighten the mood, she said, "Georgia had two really cute little kids, right?"

"Yeah, but they're not so little anymore. Lisa is fifteen and a real heartbreaker, though she doesn't know it, or else doesn't care." He glanced down at Emma, saw her pensive frown, and regretted adding to her uneasiness. She had her hands full with the coming confrontation. "Lisa's more into her studies than boys, and she's so smart she scares me."

Emma relaxed enough to grin at that. "As I recall, nothing scares you—especially a female."

That was far from the truth, but Casey just shook his head. "Adam's thirteen, a helluva football player and real interested in becoming a vet like Jordan. He's even got the soothing voice down pat. They're great kids."

She gave a wistful sigh. "You've got a lot of nieces and nephews now, don't you?"

He shrugged. To Emma, it probably seemed like a lot. She had only her mother and father, and had been estranged from them for a long time. "Jordan has those two; Morgan has Amber, now eleven, and Garrett who's nine. And Gabe has the three daughters." Casey grinned. "By the way, they not only look like Gabe, but they all take after him, too."

"Natural-born flirts, huh?"

"Yep. And it makes him crazy. Gabe's about the most doting father you'll ever meet, and he shakes whenever he talks about his girls growing old enough to date."

Emma snorted. "He's probably remembering his own unrestrained youth."

"Gabe was rather unrestrained, wasn't he? Not that any of the women complained."

"'Course not."

Casey admired the way her eyes glowed, her cheeks dimpled when she was amused. Hearing Emma laugh was a treat. "I have a little brother too, you know. Shohn, who's almost ten now. He's a hyper little pug, never still, and he knows no fear." Knowing he bragged and not caring, Casey added, "He learned to water-ski when he was only five. Now he's like a damn pro out there."

"Uh-huh. And who taught him to ski?"

Casey pushed the glass doors open and ushered her inside. "Me."

Air-conditioning rolled over them as they stepped into the hospital and headed for the elevator. Casey transferred his hand to the small of Emma's back, and just that simple touch stirred him. Her waist dipped in, taut and graceful, then flared out to her hips.

Standing next to her emphasized the differences in their sizes. He told himself that was why he felt protective. Then. Now.

Always.

Naturally, he cared about her. They'd been friends for a long time, and that, combined with the sexual chemistry, heightened his awareness of her. It wasn't anything more complicated than that.

But even he had to admit that talking with Emma came pretty easy. He couldn't remember the last time he'd shared stories about his family. When he was with a woman, he remained polite, attentive, but everything felt very…surface. There wasn't room for personal stuff. Yet with Emma, he'd just run down his whole damn lineage—and enjoyed it too much.

He was disturbed with his own realizations on that, when he heard someone say his name. He looked down the hallway and saw Ms. Potter, the librarian, being pushed in a wheelchair by a nurse, followed by her daughter, Ann. Casey drew Emma to a halt. "Just a second, okay?"

He went to Ms. Potter and bent to kiss her cheek, which warmed her with a blush. "Getting out today, huh?"

"Finally."

"You were only here two days," the nurse teased, then added, "And you were a wonderful patient."

Ms. Potter fussed with the elaborate bouquet of spring flowers in her lap. "Even so, these will look much better on my desk than on the windowsill here."

Casey gave her a mock frown. "Your desk? Now don't tell me you're rushing right back to work."

"Monday morning, and it's none too soon. I can just imagine what a mess my books are in. No one ever puts them away properly."

Ann stepped up to the side of the wheelchair. Her brown eyes twinkled and her dark hair fell in a soft wave to her shoulders when she nodded down at her mother. "The flowers are gorgeous, Casey. Thanks for bringing them to her."

"My pleasure." He saw Ann look beyond him to Emma, so he drew her forward. "Ann, Ms. Potter, do you remember Emma Clark?"

Ms. Potter, always sharp as a tack, said, "I do. It was a rare thing for you to come to the library, young lady."

Embarrassed, Emma stammered, "I—I've never been much of a reader."

"You only need to find the right books for you. Come and see me next week and we'll get you set up."

Emma blushed. "Yes, ma'am."

Casey did his best not to laugh. Ms. Potter had a way of putting everyone on the spot, but always with good intentions. She genuinely cared about people and it showed.

Ann stared hard at Emma before her eyes widened with recognition. "Now I remember. You went to school with me, didn't you?"

"A long time ago, yes. I think we were in the same English class."

"That's right. Didn't you move away before your senior year?"

"Yes." To avoid going into details, Emma grinned

down at Ms. Potter. "That's a doozy of a cast you have on your leg. And very art deco, too."

Ms. Potter reached out and patted Casey's hand. "You can blame this rascal right here. I was all set to keep it snowy white, as is appropriate for a librarian and a widow my age. But Casey showed up with colored markers." She pointed to the awkward rendition of a flower vine twining around her ankle in bright colors of red and blue and yellow. "Before I could find something to smack him with, Casey had flowers drawn all over me. After that, everyone else had to take a turn."

The nurse shook her head. "She loved it. She wouldn't let me move those markers and she made sure everyone who came in left their signature behind."

"Tattletale," Ms. Potter muttered with a smile.

Emma bent to look more closely and laughed. Casey had signed his name to his artwork with a flourish. Others had added a sun and birds and even a rainbow. "It looks lovely."

"I think so—now that I'm used to it."

Laughing, Ann said, "Mom is insisting on going back to work, but she'll only be there part-time and with limited duties. Your dad is stopping in later today to see her, to make sure it'll be okay, and he'll keep tabs on her."

Casey shook his finger at Ms. Potter. "I know Dad won't want you overdoing it."

Ann said, "That's what I told her, which is why I got two student employees to promise to stay with her and follow her directions. They'll be doing most of the lifting and storing of books." Ann winked at

Casey. "Mom'll have the library back in order in no time."

"I'll be checking in on you with Dad," Casey warned, "so you better follow doctor's orders. That was a nasty break you had." He took Ann's hand. "If you need anything, let me know."

Ann pulled him toward her for a hug. "We'll be fine, but thank you. And, please, thank Morgan again for us. If he hadn't found her car that night..."

Casey explained to Emma, "Ms. Potter ran her car off the road, and because of the broken leg, she couldn't get out to flag anyone down. Morgan was doing his nightly check and noticed the skid marks in the road. He found her over the berm and halfway down the hill."

"If you're going to tell it, tell it right. The deer ran me off the road." Ms. Potter sniffed. "The silly thing jumped out right in front of me. Of course, he escaped without a scratch."

"Thank God for Morgan. I thought she was at bingo and wouldn't have worried until she didn't come home. She might have been there for hours if it hadn't been for him."

"It's his job," Casey commented.

Ann turned to Emma, and her dark eyes were sincere but cautious. "I should get Mom home. Emma, it was nice to see you again."

Casey slipped his arm around Emma as she said, "Thank you. You too."

"Have you moved back home?" Ann asked.

"No, just visiting my father."

"He's here at the hospital too," Casey explained. But because he didn't want Ms. Potter or Ann to ask

Emma too many questions, he gave their farewells. Ann had been as nice as always, but anyone could blunder onto uncomfortable ground. He kissed Ms. Potter on the cheek again, and drew Emma away.

They moved inside the elevator and Emma pressed the button for the fifth floor. "Is Ann married?"

She asked that casually, but she looked and sounded stiff. Casey wanted to hug her close, but he had no idea why. "Not yet, but she and Nate—you remember Morgan's deputy?—are getting real friendly, especially since this happened with her mom. On top of the broken leg, she had more scrapes and bruises than I can count. Nate was the one who went to get Ann while Morgan took Ms. Potter to the hospital."

"They seem nice."

"Ms. Potter's a sweetheart, and Ann's just like her."

"Pretty too."

Casey shrugged. Ann had dark hair and eyes, and a gentle smile. He supposed she was an attractive woman. What he noticed most about her though was that she didn't judge others. She had a generous heart, and he liked that about her. "She's thanked Morgan about a dozen times now. She and her mom are really close."

Emma actually winced. If he hadn't been watching her so closely, he wouldn't have seen it. Emma quickly tried to cover up her reaction. "As big and bulky as he is, Morgan can be really gentle. He's a perfect sheriff."

Casey wasn't fooled. "I think so."

"Your dad's the same way." She spoke fast, almost chattered. "I remember when most every female in Buckhorn mooned over him and your uncles. Even the girls my age used to eye them and fantasize."

Casey put his hands in his pockets and leaned against the elevator wall. "You too?"

She cast him a quick, flustered look. "No. Of course not."

"How come?"

"I had my sights set on a different target." Her attempt at humor fell flat, even though she lightly elbowed him. "I was embarrassingly obvious."

Something in her tone got to Casey. Nothing new in that. Emma had always touched him in ways no one else could. "You never embarrassed me, Em."

She appeared rattled by the seriousness he'd injected, and quickly turned her attention to the advancing floor numbers. Casey crowded closer to her and inhaled the subtle aroma of her hair and skin. It was the same as and yet different from what he remembered. Would she taste the same?

The elevator door hissed open and Emma all but leaped out. He had to take big steps to keep up with her headlong flight down the hallway toward her father's room. Her nervousness had returned in a crushing wave. He could feel it, but was helpless as to how to help her.

When she reached the right door, she gave Casey an uncertain look. "There's a waiting room at the end of the hall if you want to watch a little television or get some coffee." She pushed her hair behind her ear with a trembling hand.

He glanced down the hall. It was empty. Not that it mattered. In that particular moment, he had to hold her. He pulled Emma against his chest and gently enfolded her in his arms. She resisted him for a moment before giving up and relaxing into him.

God, it felt good, having her so close again. He lowered his mouth to her ear, felt her warmth and the silk of her hair against his jaw. "I'll be waiting if you need me."

She lifted her head to stare up at him, embarrassed, confused, a little flushed. "I'm fine, Casey. Really."

The softness of her cheek drew his hand. He wanted to stroke her all over, find all her soft spots. Her hot spots.

Taking her—and himself—by surprise, he bent and kissed her. Her lips parted on a gasp, an unconscious invitation that was hard to resist. But Casey kept the kiss light, contenting himself with one small stroke of his tongue just inside her bottom lip. He leaned back, hazy with need, not just lust but so many roiling emotions he nearly groaned.

Using just her fingertips, Emma touched her mouth, drew a breath, and then laughed shakily. "Well, okay then." Bemused, she shook her head, turned and opened her father's door to peer inside.

Casey watched as she entered the room. Damn it, he'd rattled her when all he'd meant to do was offer comfort.

He heard her whisper, "Dad?" with a lot of uncertainty and something more, some deep yearning that came from her soul. Then the door shut and he couldn't hear anything else.

Humming with frustration, Casey stalked into the waiting room. There was no one else there, yet empty foam cups were left everywhere and magazines had been scattered about. He occupied himself by picking up the garbage, rearranging the magazines and generally tidying things up.

It didn't help. Pent-up energy kept him pacing. All he really wanted to do was barge into that room with Emma to make sure her father didn't do or say anything to hurt her. Again.

He hated feeling this way—helpless, at loose ends. Emma was a grown woman now, independent, strong. She neither wanted nor needed his help. There was no reason for him to want to shield her, not anymore.

Moving around didn't help his mood, not when his imagination kept dredging up the sight of her bruised face eight years ago.

After about ten minutes, he gave up. Telling himself that he had every right to check on her, Casey strode across the hallway and silently opened the door to Dell Clark's room. The first bed, made up with stiff sheets and folded back at one corner, was empty. A separation curtain had been drawn next to it so that he couldn't see the second bed where Dell rested. But he could hear Emma softly speaking and he drew up short at the sound of her pleading voice.

Without a single speck of guilt, Casey took a muted step in and listened.

CHAPTER SEVEN

DELL'S VOICE sounded weak and somewhat slurred, from the stroke or the medication, Casey wasn't sure which. But he could understand him, and he heard his determination. "See yer mama."

"Dad." Weariness, and a vague acceptance, tinged Emma's soft denial, making Casey want to march to her side. "You know I can't do that. Besides, I doubt she even wants to see me. And if I did go, we'd just fight."

Casey realized that Emma hadn't yet seen her mother. She hadn't even been to her home, choosing instead to stay in a motel. He frowned with confusion and doubt.

"She'szer mother."

"Dad, please don't upset yourself. You need your rest."

Shaken by the desolation in Emma's words, Casey didn't dare even breathe. Their conversation didn't make sense to him. Why would Emma make a point of coming to see her father, the man who'd run her off, but not want to visit her mother?

"Damn it." Dell managed to curse clearly enough, but before he spoke further, he began wheezing and thrashing around. Casey heard the rustling of fast movement, heard Emma shushing him, soothing him.

"Calm down, Dad, please. You'll pull your IV out."

In his upset, his words became even more slurred, almost incomprehensible. "Hate this...damn arm..."

"The nurse says you'll get control of your arm again soon. It's just a temporary side effect of the stroke. You've already made so much progress—"

"'*Mnot a baby.*"

A moment of silence. "I know you're not. I'm sorry that I'm upsetting you. It's just that I want to help."

"Go 'way."

There was so much tension in the small room, Casey couldn't breathe. Then Emma whispered, "Maybe this was a bad idea, maybe I shouldn't have come home..."

Casey's heart skipped a beat, then dropped like a stone to the bottom of his stomach. If she hadn't come home, he wouldn't have ever gotten the chance to see her again.

Dell didn't relent, but a new weariness softened his words. "She neez you."

As Emma reseated herself in the creaky plastic chair, she brushed the curtain, causing it to rustle. "Dad, she doesn't even like me. She never has. When she called to tell me about you, she made it clear that nothing's changed. I've tried to help her, and it's only made things worse."

"Can't help 'erself," Dell insisted.

Even before she spoke, Casey could feel Emma's pain. It sounded in her words, weary and hoarse and bordering on desperate. "You have to stop making excuses for her—for her sake, as well as your own."

"Love 'er."

Sounding so sad, Emma murmured, "I know you do." Then softly, she added, "More than anything."

"Emma…"

Images from the past whirled through Casey's mind. Emma hurt. Emma wandering the streets at night. Emma with no money for new clothes or schoolbooks.

Emma needy for love.

He fisted his hands until his knuckles turned white. *I know you do,* she'd said. *More than anything.*

Or anyone?

With sudden clarity, Casey knew that Emma wasn't estranged from her father.

No, as he remembered it, Dell Clark had been genuinely worried when Emma had run off. He'd blustered and grumped and cast blame, yet there'd been no mistaking the fear and regret in his eyes.

But her mother…not once had she asked about Emma, or shown any concern at all. Casey had all but forgotten about the woman because folks scarcely saw her anymore. She stayed hidden away, seldom going out.

Now Emma was in town, but staying at a motel rather than her home. And despite her father's pleas, she resisted even a visit with her mother.

In rapid order, Casey rearranged the things he knew, the things he'd always believed, and decided he'd come to some very wrong assumptions. Just as Emma had fled to his house for protection, perhaps Dell had gone along with that plan for the same reason.

Because she needed a way out.

Jesus. He propped his hands on his hips and dropped his head forward, trying to decide what to do, what to believe.

The door swung open behind him, making him jump out of the way, and Dell's doctor entered, trailed by a nurse. Recognizing Casey from his association with Sawyer, the doctor bellowed a jovial greeting. "Casey! Well, this is a surprise."

In good humor, he thwacked Casey on the shoulder. There was nothing Casey could do now but take his hand. "Dr. Wagner. Good to see you again."

"But what are you doing here?" Concern replaced Dr. Wagner's smile. "The family's okay?"

Emma stepped around the curtain, rigid, appalled, her attention glued to Casey. Her big dark eyes were accusing, her mouth pinched.

Casey got his first look at Dell and realized that he looked like death. His face was white, his eyes red-rimmed and vague from medication, one more open than the other. His mouth was a grim line, drooping on one side, and his graying hair stuck out around an oxygen tube that hooked over his ears and ran across his cheeks to his nostrils. More tubes fed into his arm through an IV. Machinery hummed around him.

Aw hell. Casey watched Emma for a moment, hoping to make her understand that everything would be okay now, that it didn't matter what he'd heard or what had happened in the past. But she turned away from him.

"The family's fine," Casey said without looking away from her. "I'm here with Emma."

The doc apparently sensed the heavy unease in the

room and glanced from one person to the next. "I take it you two know each other then?"

"Yeah." Accepting that everything had changed—the past, his feelings, his motivations—Casey moved toward her. "Emma and I go way back." His attention shifted to Dell. Damn it, the man was too sick to deal with Casey's anger right now. He drew a breath and collected himself. "Hello, Mr. Clark."

Dell gripped the sheet with one gnarled hand while the other flailed before resting at his side. "Sneakin' 'round."

"Of course I wasn't." He reached Emma and looped his arm around her stiff shoulders. She didn't look at him and, if anything, her expression was more shuttered now that he touched her. "I just stepped in to check on Emma."

Emma ducked away from him. "Dr. Wagner, I'd like to speak to you privately."

"Yes, yes, of course." The good doctor looked stymied.

Casey nodded to him. "We'll wait outside until you finish your checkup with Dell."

"Use the waiting room. I'll come for you there."

Emma shoved the door open and strode out. She'd only made it three steps when Casey caught her. His long fingers wrapped around her upper arm in a secure yet gentle hold. "Oh no you don't."

She whirled on him, equal parts furious, indignant and, if Casey didn't miss his bet, afraid. "*You had no right.*"

Still holding her with one hand, Casey brushed the backs of his knuckles over her cheek with the other. "Now there's where you're wrong, sweetheart. You gave me the right eight years ago when you came to me. And this time, it won't be so easy for you to run off. This time you're going to tell me the truth.'' He touched the corner of her mouth. ''You can count on it.''

EMMA STRUGGLED to get enough air into her starved lungs, but the panic set in quickly. Nothing had really changed, she knew that now. Her reaction to Casey, his protective instincts, her smothering fear…it was all still there. It had only taken one day back in Buckhorn to make it all resurface.

Just like his father and uncles, Casey had a soft spot for anyone in need. She hadn't wanted him to see her that way. Not this time. Not now. But given what he'd just overheard, she knew damn well he'd be doling out the pity again. God, she couldn't bear it.

She licked dry lips and cautiously tried to free her arm. He didn't let go.

''Why are you doing this, Casey?''

All his attention remained on her mouth, unnerving her further. ''Doing what?''

She rolled her shoulder to indicate his hold. ''This…overwhelming bombardment. You insist on coffee, insist on giving me a ride, insist you have to know everything even though it's none of your business. Why nose in where I don't want you?''

''Where is it you don't want me, sweetheart?''

Oh, that soft, coaxing voice. She couldn't let him do this to her. She'd come home because she had to, and all along she'd expected to see Casey again. This time, however, she'd wanted his respect. "What's between me and my father doesn't concern you."

Filled with conviction, Casey started to lead her into the waiting room.

"Casey!"

They both looked up to see the young nurse who'd accompanied the doctor into her father's room. She'd slipped out the door and she had her sights set on Casey. As she bore down on them with a proprietary air, Emma tried to retreat.

She heard Casey's annoyed sigh as he tugged her closer and draped his arm over her shoulders. Emma didn't know if he did it as a sign of support, or to make damn sure she couldn't slip away. Whatever his purpose, it didn't matter. She couldn't let it matter.

But being tucked that close to him shook her on every level. He was so hard, so tall and strong and masculine. Heat and a wonderful deep scent seemed a part of him, encompassing her and filling her up in places she'd forgotten were empty. With every pore of her being, she was aware of him. He was her living, breathing fantasy, and he kept touching her in that man/woman way, just as she used to dream of him doing.

Only the timing was all wrong now. Or she wasn't right for him—and never would be.

She had to get away.

The nurse halted in front of them, her smile bold, her posturing plain. Unlike Ann, who had been cordial, not by so much as a flicker of an eyelash did this woman acknowledge Emma. "Casey, I had such a nice time last weekend." She spoke with a heavy dose of suggestion. "I sort of expected you to call."

While Emma went stiff enough to crackle, Casey was loose and casual and relaxed, as if he didn't hold Emma prisoner at his side, forcing her through this awkward come-on.

"I've been busy." And then to Emma, "Lois and I were both at the same party last weekend."

Lois? Forgetting her own discomfort for a moment, Emma took in the bouncing brown hair and heavy hazel eyes. Recognition dawned. "Lois Banker?"

With an effort, Lois pulled her gaze from Casey. She lifted perfectly plucked eyebrows. "That's right. And you are…?"

Unbelievable, Emma thought in wonder. At least the maturity had shown on Ann. Her dark hair was shorter now, and there'd been a few laugh lines around her eyes. But Lois…she looked just as she had in high school. She was still pretty, perky, stacked.

She still had a thing for Casey.

Emma dredged up a smile even as she lifted her chin, preparing for the worst. "You don't remember me, but we went to school together." She held out a hand. "Emma Clark."

Lois scowled as she scrutinized Emma, and then slowly, with the jogging of her memory, her lip curled. "Emma Clark. Yes, I remember you." She shifted away from Emma's hand as if fearing contamination.

Emma found the petty attitude ridiculous, but not unexpected. Lois had never hid her dislike of her. But Casey pulled Emma a little closer and his fingers on her shoulder contracted, gently massaging her in a manner far too familiar. Of course, Lois made note of it, and her expression darkened even more.

Casey said, "Emma is back for a visit."

"A brief visit?"

You wish, Emma thought, and then was appalled at herself. Good God, she had no claim on Casey, and Lois certainly had no reason to be jealous of her. "Until my father is well."

Lois's eyes narrowed. "I hadn't made the connection." She glanced at Casey's hand on Emma. "Mr. Clark… He's the one who was drunk when he had a stroke, isn't he?"

Emma took the well-planned words like a punch on the chin. They dazed her. And they hurt.

"My father doesn't drink." Defensive and a little numb, Emma retreated. "Excuse me, please."

Casey released her as she pushed away. "Emma?"

On wobbly legs, Emma wandered into the waiting room and headed for a plastic padded seat, praying she wouldn't embarrass herself by tearing up.

Why would Lois say her father had been drinking? Emma knew for a fact that he never touched alcohol. Like her, he'd made other choices.

In order to find answers, would she have to go see her mother, after all? Memories fell over her in a suffocating wave.

Then Lois's voice reached her, offering a much-needed distraction.

"Casey, what in the world are you doing with that nasty girl?"

In response to the slur, Casey became terse. "Nasty girl, Lois? Just what the hell does that mean?"

"Oh come on, Case." Lois's laugh of disbelief

grated along Emma's nerves until she shivered. "She was the biggest slut around and everyone knows it. Besides, from what I've heard, you certainly had first-hand knowledge about—"

"Shut up."

Lois gasped, but otherwise remained silent. Emma squeezed her eyes shut. Firsthand knowledge? Is that what people thought, that Casey had given in to her relentless pursuit? What a laugh.

Then a worse theory occurred to Emma and she curled her arms around her stomach. Oh no. Surely no one had heard her outrageous claims of being pregnant. Her father wouldn't have told a soul, and Casey's family wasn't the type to gossip. Yet Lois had inferred something…

"You need to grow up, Lois, and learn some manners."

"*I* need to learn manners?" Her outrage was clear. "I'm not the one who slept with every guy in Buck-horn."

Casey snorted. "As I recall, not that many guys were asking."

"Casey!"

"See ya around, Lois."

The sound of Lois's angry, retreating footfalls couldn't be missed. Emma sighed, aware of Casey's approach but unsure what she should say to him. Already she'd caused him problems, but he didn't want to hear her apologies, he'd been plain about that.

She felt steadier now, but still swamped in confusion. Her father didn't drink—never had—and she knew in her heart he never would. What had Lois meant by her comment?

Emma expected Casey to seat himself. Instead, he crouched down beside her. "Em?"

Startled, Emma stared at him.

With concern darkening his brown eyes, he said, "Hey. You okay?"

Casey came from a long line of caregivers. As a doctor, his father tended everyone from infants to the elderly. Being the town sheriff, Morgan set out to protect the innocent, and Jordan was the perfect vet with a voice that soothed and a manner that reassured. Even Gabe, the resident handyman, made a point of lending a helping hand to anyone who needed it.

She understood Casey's nature, but did he think she was made of fluff? "Why wouldn't I be?"

"Lois is a bitch."

Emma couldn't help but chuckle at that. "No, she's just hung up on you. She saw your arm around me and misunderstood."

"She understood." He put his rough palm on her knee with his long fingers curling around her. She hadn't realized the back of her knee could be so sensitive until Casey's fingertips brushed there. "I'm sorry she said what she did."

Trying to ignore his touch, Emma put her hand over his. "It's not the first time, Casey. If you go around alienating your friends over me, you're going to find yourself pretty lonely."

He ignored her warning to ask, "She's called you names before?" As he spoke, he clasped both her knees and Emma had the flashing thought of him pushing her legs open and settling between them. The image had an instantaneous effect on her body: her breath hitched, her belly tingled, her flesh heated. She didn't have the time or concentration for this.

In a rush, she shoved to her feet and stepped away. "Of course she did. Most of the boys from here—men now, I suppose—wanted to get me in bed and most of the girls hated me because of it."

Very slowly, Casey came to his feet. "She's jealous."

How ridiculous. "Hardly. Everyone always knew that I wanted you, but that you always turned me down."

Casey looked pained. "I'm sorry, Em."

"What did she mean when she said you had first-hand knowledge about me?"

He hesitated.

"Casey?"

With a shrug in his tone, he said, "For a while, people thought you ran off because of me." His eyes narrowed. "No one knew about that night, how your father brought you to me. No one knew that I asked you to stay—but you left anyway."

Startled, Emma could have sworn she heard resentment in his tone. But that didn't make any sense. "I'm glad that's all it is."

Sounding almost lethal, Casey repeated, "You're glad?"

He couldn't understand. "I didn't want you insulted, but I don't care what she says about me—I never have."

Casey watched her with brooding intensity. "I don't believe that."

The day had been too tumultuous for her to hold on to her temper. "And I don't care if you don't believe it. I made my choices and I've lived with them.''

''Em…''

''I slept around. So what?'' Bitterness that had simmered for years suddenly boiled over. ''Just because I'm female it's a huge sin to enjoy sex, to enjoy being touched? How many females have you slept with, Casey?''

His jaw tightened.

''Ah. Should I take that blank expression to mean there are too many to count? What about Lois's reference to last weekend? Did you sleep with her then?''

''No.''

She found that hard to believe and let him know it with a look. ''But because you're male, that's just fine, right? Better than fine. What makes you a stud makes me a whore.''

''Stop it, Em.''

The furious rasp of his voice didn't register. ''No one's ever talked about all the guys who bed hop, the guys who came to me. But a woman…''

''*Stop it.*''

Emma went slack-jawed at his raised voice. Never in her life had she heard that particular tone from Casey. With her, he'd been cajoling, teasing, concerned, sometimes firmly insistent. Always gentle. But never outraged.

Of course, she'd known him only as a boy. Now he was a man.

She blinked at him, a little awed by the level of his anger. It showed in every taut, bunched line of his muscled body. His jaw was clenched, his hands curled into fists. Oh boy.

Emma pulled herself together. She hadn't intended to ever have this discussion with Casey, but since it had begun, she wished she'd chosen a better place than a hospital waiting room.

More in control of herself, and her voice lower now, Emma sighed. "Casey, I'm not ashamed of my past. At least, not that part of it." There were other things, things her family had done, things she'd covered up, the way she'd always pressured him, that still made her hot with regret. But not her sexuality. "I was young and healthy and I enjoyed sex. I still enjoy sex."

A low savage sound escaped him, similar to a snarl. He locked his hands behind his head and paced away.

His reaction stunned her. It almost looked as if he was restraining himself—and had a devil of a time doing so. "If you can't deal with that then you should head on home now. I'll find a ride back to the motel."

Casey turned and stalked to the waiting-room door. For one heart-stopping moment, Emma assumed he was going to storm out in a rage. He was leaving her and her heart hurt so badly she nearly doubled over with the crushing pain. She knew Casey would never love her, but she'd already started hoping that they could be friends.

Instead, he belatedly snapped the door shut to afford them some privacy. When he turned to face her, he still looked livid but he, too, had lowered his voice.

"I don't give a royal fuck how many boys you slept with, Emma."

Despite herself, his wording made her mouth fall open.

Very slowly, with intimidating deliberation, Casey stalked her. "But I do care that you were too young to be making those decisions."

Her chin lifted. "You're telling me you waited?"

"Apparently longer than you did." He pointed a finger at her. "And before you say it, before you assume that being in an all-male household gave me encouragement to screw any female who offered, you should know that I got a lot of lectures on responsibility. Dad, Morgan, Jordan—hell, even Gabe—they all endlessly harped on about ramifications. What might be meaningless sex to me could mean a whole lot more to a girl, especially if she got pregnant, or her folks found out. So, no, I didn't indiscriminately indulge in opportunities."

"And it bothers you that I didn't show that same restraint?" She kept her chin high, but the idea that he'd start judging her now hurt.

"What bothers me is that you did a hell of a lot of stuff because you were always lost and alone." His expression hardened, his jaw drew tight. "And I didn't do enough to help you."

"*No—*"

He gave her a warning look that made her swallow her automatic denial. "It's my turn, Emma, so you just be quiet and listen."

Emma snapped her mouth shut and began backing up as he kept advancing. Never had he looked so big, so imposing. So irritated with her.

She bumped into the wall and was annoyed with herself for retreating. She wasn't afraid of Casey. Out of all the things she'd ever felt for him, not once had fear ever been an issue.

Casey crowded into her, caging her in with his body. When she started to sidle away, he gripped her shoulders and held her firm. They stared at each other in silence until Emma gave up and held still.

"I care that you've been lying to me from the start."

"But..."

"I care that I let you get away."

Her eyes widened. *Let her get away?* Far as she knew, Casey hadn't wanted her to stay. Oh, he'd offered her help because Casey was the type of man who could do nothing else. But he'd made it clear many times that she didn't factor into his future. Well, this *was* his future, and just because she'd materialized didn't mean...

His hands kneaded her shoulders absently, while his gaze burned. "And you can bet your sweet ass I care that *I've* never had you." He leaned closer and his voice dropped to a guttural whisper. "I care about that a lot."

Her heart thundered, and her pulse went wild. Unable to maintain eye contact with him so close, Emma looked away. But Casey wasn't allowing that. He put a fist under her chin and brought her face back around, forcing her to meet his burning gaze. His eyes had narrowed with intent, starting a trembling deep inside her. "You quote double standards to me, but you wanna know what's really unfair?"

"No."

He pressed into her until she felt his hard flat abdomen against her belly. Oh God. Her whole body came alive, quivering with primal awareness.

"It's unfair for a gorgeous young woman to keep throwing herself at a guy until he can't sleep nights for wanting her too much. And then she runs off and no other woman will do because he has a taste for her—a goddamned hunger—yet, damn it, she's gone."

"Casey…" She gave the breathless complaint automatically. She couldn't allow herself to believe him. Always, he'd rejected her, wanting no more than friendship. Time apart couldn't have changed that.

His fingers tunneled into her hair, holding her head still. He lowered his forehead to hers and his eyes closed, his voice going rough and deep. "It's unfair because now that you're here again, all grown up and sexier than ever, you no longer want me."

She felt his warm breath on her lips, felt the heat of his frustration, his urgency, which sparked her own. Her body was melting into his, her nerve endings tingling and alive. Not want him? She was dying for him.

"I'm sorry, sweetheart," he murmured against her mouth, "but I don't intend to let you get away with it."

He said that so simply, sort of slipping it in there on her, it took a second for his statement to sink in. When his meaning dawned on her, Emma became alert with a start, only to have any thoughts of rejecting him quelled beneath a ravaging kiss. He didn't ease into the kiss. No, he took her mouth with ruthless domination.

Emma loved it.

All objections scattered, as insubstantial as a hot summer breeze. Aware of her surrender, Casey groaned low in his throat and tilted his head, fitting his mouth to hers more securely. He continued to hold her immobile, pressing her to the wall. She felt the muscled hardness, the vitality of his body against her breasts, her belly and thighs. She tried to squirm, to get closer, but his grip didn't allow it.

The kiss was an onslaught, never broken, always going deeper, taking and giving, and Emma forgot they were in a hospital with people milling around outside the room.

Casey didn't forget. Slowly, reluctantly, he pulled back. His thumbs brushed the corners of her swollen mouth. Emma fought to get her eyes open.

"I love your mouth, Em. So damn sexy." He nipped her bottom lip, licked her upper, took her mouth again. He sank his tongue in, soft and deep.

Emma groaned.

"I used to imagine your mouth on me," he whispered, "and it made me nuts."

Hearing him say it made her imagine it now. *"Yes."* She would love to taste Casey—everywhere. "Yes." She reached for him again.

Casey stepped them both away from the wall and urged her head to his shoulder, then wrapped his arms around her to hold her tight. He took several long, unsteady breaths, which allowed her to do the same. Emma was so shaken that if Casey hadn't supported her, she thought she might have melted into a puddle on the floor.

"I'm going to give you time, Emma."

She flattened her hands against the firm wall of his

chest, relishing the feel of him. Time? She didn't need time. At the moment, she didn't want time. Unless it was time enough to explore him, to kiss him everywhere, to feel him deep inside her. Oh God, she *would* melt.

"I'm going to wait so you won't feel rushed."

She couldn't stop shaking. "I won't."

He went still, cursed softly, then turned his face in and kissed her ear. "Shh. Not yet. First you're going to get comfortable with me again. Then we're going to talk, and I want the truth this time, Emma."

Her heart, which had only just begun to calm, kicked into a furious gallop again. "No…"

"And then." His tongue touched her earlobe, licked lightly inside to make her shiver. "*Then* I'm going to lay you down, strip you naked and sate myself on you." He groaned as if being tortured. "I've got nearly a decade of lust to make up for, sweetheart, so it's going to take me a really long time to get my fill. I hope you're up for it."

Emma shuddered. She had no idea what to do, what to say. But in that single moment, she made a decision. She wouldn't leave Buckhorn again without having Casey first.

If that made her feelings for him harder to deal with, so be it. She wasn't a weak woman with silly illusions. She knew from past experience that Casey wouldn't want her as a permanent fixture in his life. She knew she'd never fit into Buckhorn. She never had.

When she'd left, there'd been a lot of things she wanted. Security, respectability, a close family…and

Casey Hudson. But of all those things, it was only Casey who had kept her awake at night.

She had the security and respectability that came with a good job, an attitude adjustment, maturity. She had a family; not her own, but the Devaughns were very special to her and she loved them. She'd attained things of value, but she'd also learned that they weren't enough. She hadn't admitted to herself what was still missing in her life until Casey made it clear that he wanted her.

She'd never be close with her own family; seeing her father again had proven that. But she could have this—she could have her memories of Casey. With everything combined, she'd make that be enough for a lifetime.

She looked into his mellow golden eyes, glittering with excitement. His sharp cheekbones were flushed with arousal. For her. Emma whispered, ''All right.''

The heat in his eyes flared, but was quickly banked. ''God, Emma.'' He took several deep breaths, leaned back and finally managed a smile. ''The minutes are going to seem like hours until I can get you alone.''

Emma nodded.

''Until then, let's talk about your dad—and what really happened the night he dropped you on my doorstep.''

CHAPTER EIGHT

CASEY SAW the shuttered way Emma guarded herself. Well, too bad. Sometimes the truth proved painful but, damn it, he deserved that much.

He couldn't stop touching her, smoothing her warm cheek, relishing the feel of her. He could barely wait until she was naked so he could rub his hands, his face, over her whole body. He wanted to stroke her breasts, her belly. Between her thighs.

The second she'd agreed with him, he'd gotten semihard and he had a feeling he'd be that way until he got her alone. Heat snaked through him, adding to the sexual tension and making his voice gruff. ''Come on, Em. You know you can tell me anything.''

She closed her eyes tightly. ''People don't just fall into old relationships that easily, Case.''

''You and I do.'' Spending the day with her had reaffirmed that much. Emma looked different, and her attitudes were wiser, more confident. But the closeness between them existed as strong as ever. No other woman had ever touched him so easily. ''Regardless of what you ever thought, Em, you've always had a special place in my heart.''

''Casey.'' She sounded strained and covered her face with her hands.

He couldn't keep from kissing her again, but he

contented himself by pulling her hands away and brushing his mouth over her forehead. "I care about you—I always have. In all the time you were gone, that hasn't changed."

"No? You want to sleep with me now. That's sure not how I remember it."

Something else that was different—her lippy come-backs. They amused him. "I always wanted you and you know it." He leaned down to see her face. "I think you enjoyed tormenting me, sending me home with a boner, knowing I'd be miserable all night long." The fact that he could tease even when he was this aroused said a lot about Emma and how relaxed he was in her company.

She denied his accusation with a quick shake of her head. "You didn't have to be miserable. I would have taken care of you."

Casey's moan turned into a laugh. "You're still tormenting me. Now, enough with the distractions. What happened that night, Emma? Why were you so desperate to get out of Buckhorn?"

"You don't really want to know."

"Of course I do."

"Then you don't really *need* to know. Casey, I don't want to involve you. It wouldn't be fair."

She looked truly set in her decision, and Casey knew she wouldn't tell him a thing. He was contemplating ways to get around her stubbornness, when the waiting-room door opened and Dr. Wagner stuck his head in. "Am I interrupting?"

Casey stepped back from Emma. To keep her from ushering him out of the room, he said, "Not at all. We're anxious to hear how Dell's doing."

Emma made a sound, clearly aghast at his audacity in including himself. Casey pretended not to hear. She wanted to shut him out again, but he wasn't about to budge. She'd agreed to sleep with him, to accept him as a lover. She could damn well accept him as a friend and confidant too. Whatever Dr. Wagner had to tell her, he could share it with them both.

Lois, peeved and hostile, stepped in behind the doctor. The way she watched Emma was so malicious, it should have been illegal.

Casey had never paid that much attention to Lois before now. He'd thought her cute, a little silly. He'd been out with her once or twice, casual dates that didn't amount to much and definitely didn't go beyond a few kisses. But he hadn't known how catty she could be. Poor Emma, to have put up with her and the other women like her.

He had new insight into what Emma's teen years must have been like in Buckhorn, and it was decidedly worse than he'd thought.

"Let's sit down," Dr. Wagner suggested.

Emma went to a chair and Casey stood behind her, his hands on her shoulders, making it clear to the doctor and to Lois that he was there for her.

Many times in the past, he'd stood in front of her, trying to shield her. He knew now that she was stronger than he'd ever suspected. She had to be to have survived with her naturally generous nature still intact. Standing behind her, offering her support in what she chose to face, and respecting her strength to do it, seemed more appropriate.

The doctor pulled up his own chair facing Emma, and Lois sat beside him. Dr. Wagner pasted on his patented reassuring physician's smile. "Ms. Clark, your father is doing much better today. I see improvement not only in his mental capacity in identifying objects, but also in his mind/eye coordination." The doctor turned grave. "But, to be truthful, for a little while there I thought we might lose him."

"Lose him?" Emma stiffened in alarm. "But I thought…"

"You're seeing him now, with much improvement. For three days he had no clear recognition of most things. He knew what he was seeing, but he couldn't find the word in his memory to identify it."

Emma bit her bottom lip. "I came as soon as I was told, but I had to pack up and I didn't arrive in Buckhorn until late last night. I stopped here first. My father was asleep, so I just looked in on him." She twisted her hands together. "The nurse said he'd be okay."

"And she's correct. But I anticipate quite a bit of therapy not only to help him deal with what he's suffered and his diminished capacity—which should be only temporary—but to help rebuild his coordination. We'll get his meds regulated—blood thinner and blood pressure medicine to keep him from having another stroke."

For several minutes, the doctor explained the causes and effects of a stroke, and Emma listened in fretful silence.

"He'll need to be monitored for TIAs—or mini strokes."

Emma nodded. "The nurse said that he also fell?"

Dr. Wagner's eyebrows rose in surprise. "Your mother didn't tell you he fell off the porch steps when she called you? She said she found him unconscious, which is why she called the paramedics. And good thing too, as I've already said.''

Lois made a face. ''He'd been drinking, so his wife thought he'd just passed out.''

Scowling, Dr. Wagner twisted around to face the nurse. ''Incorrect, Ms. Banker. Alcohol had been spilled on him, but he had not consumed any noticeable amount.''

When he turned back to Emma, his expression gentled and he reached out to pat her hand. ''It's my guess that he was carrying a bottle of whisky when he had the stroke. It spilled all over him and, yes, we could smell it. I had thought to question his wife about it, but haven't seen her yet.''

Emma stammered, ''Mom d-doesn't get out much.''

Casey wanted to roll his eyes at her understatement. Her mother was a recluse. She was seldom seen around town, and apparently she hadn't even ventured out to visit her husband.

''I see.'' The doctor gave her a long look, then referred to his notes. ''Well, he did some further damage with his fall. We got the MRI back on his ankle, and luckily it isn't broken, though it is still severely swollen and I'm certain it's causing him some pain. Add to that the bruising on his ribs and shoulder…well, he took a very nasty spill. I'm relieved he didn't break his neck.''

Emma nodded. ''Me too.''

''You say you're from out of town. Will you be able to stay around to attend him, and if not, is your mother capable of the task?''

"I…" She glanced at Casey, who squeezed her shoulder, then back at the doctor. "What kind of care will he need?"

Appearing to be a little uncomfortable, Dr. Wagner explained, "I don't anticipate he'll go home for a while yet. But when he does, he'll need help with everyday tasks until he regains control of lost motor skills. He'll need transportation back and forth to the hospital for therapy. He may even need help feeding himself, dressing…at least for a while. As I said, his improvement so far is quite promising, but we can't make any guarantees."

"I understand." She waited only a moment before giving a firm nod. "I can be here as long as I'm needed."

Casey wondered if she could stay indefinitely. She'd made a life in Chicago…by all accounts, a happy life that suited her. But her roots were in Buckhorn. Whatever had driven her away the first time, he'd be here with her now, offering her support in whatever way she needed. Maybe it'd be enough.

Emma dropped back in her seat, and Casey noted the weariness in her face. She looked beautiful to him, so he hadn't at first noticed. But now that he did, he felt guilty. She'd been given worrisome news, spent several hours on the road yesterday with only a few hours' sleep to recoup, and then faced her father.

And he'd been bulldozing her straight into an affair. He suddenly felt like a bastard. No, he wouldn't change his mind. He couldn't. But he would treat her gently, give her plenty of time.

"I hope I've relieved your mind," Dr. Wagner said.

"You have. I'm sure I can handle things, as long as you tell me everything I need to know."

"Yes, of course. When he's ready to be discharged, we'll give you a list of his prescriptions, along with instructions on his general care. He'll have regular checkups and you can always reach someone here at the hospital or at my office if you have questions. Thanks to his injured ankle and ribs, he'll spend a good deal of time in bed, so you'll also need to rotate his position until he's back on his feet. He's going to be very sore for a while."

Wearing a half smile, Emma admitted, "I'm a massage therapist, so I know about sore muscles."

"A massage therapist?" Lois asked, looking down her nose.

"Excellent," Dr. Wagner said at almost the same time. "It's too bad you don't live here. I could have used your services last week after a day spent fishing." He chuckled as he rubbed the small of his back. "I'm getting too old to sit on the hard bench of a fishing boat for hours on end. I was stiff for two days. But the wife had no sympathy. None at all."

Emma laughed with him. "I'll be glad to help you out while I'm here. Just give me a call. The desk has my number."

Dr. Wagner brightened. "Careful now. I'll hold you to it."

"It'll be my pleasure. A thank-you for all the good care you're giving Dad."

Casey wasn't at all sure he liked the sound of that, and then he caught himself. Dr. Wagner was a grandpa, for crying out loud. A kind old man who'd known his father forever. Yet…Lois had the same damn thought, given her spiteful expression. She smiled, but it was a smile of malicious intent.

Casey wondered how much Emma would let him help. Considering what he'd learned, he knew it wouldn't be easy for her to be home with both her parents. Yet her father's health dictated that she do just that.

He wanted to do what was best for her, and if that meant helping her with Dell… He and her father were not on great terms—not since the night Dell accused him of getting Emma pregnant—but Emma would have cleared that up with her father by now. Dell would certainly have realized that he wasn't a grandfather, and Casey wasn't a father.

Not that he didn't want to be. Someday. With the right woman.

He looked at Emma again and felt a strange warmth spread through his chest. Emma was such a gentle, affectionate, sensitive woman, she'd make a wonderful mother.

And if she knew your thoughts, Casey told himself, *she'd probably head directly back to Chicago.* Hell, he scared himself, so he could only imagine how Emma would react.

"You'll be hearing from me." Dr. Wagner shook her hand, then clapped Casey on the shoulder. "I'm off to see the rest of my patients."

He went out, yet Lois lingered. She looked Emma up and down with a sullen sneer. "A massage therapist? Is that what they're calling it these days?"

Casey felt like strangling the little witch for her insinuation, yet Emma only smiled. "Far as I know, Lois, that's what they've always called it. You didn't know that? I'm surprised, since the field of massage therapy has become an integral part of health care, and you *are* a nurse, after all.''

Stung, Lois pursed her mouth. ''It sounds like a shady front to me. I remember you too well. I can just imagine what you do while *massaging* someone.''

Emma leaned toward her, taunting, egging her on. ''It is scandalous. Why, I light scented candles and play erotic, relaxing music. But I'm good, Lois, so good, that I get a lot of repeat customers.'' She held up her hands. ''I'm told I have magic fingers and that I can work the tension out of any muscle.''

Red-faced, Lois said, ''It's an excuse to get naked and get…rubbed.''

''You make that sound so dirty!'' Emma laughed. ''Actually, people with real physical ailments come to me. Strained muscles, stress, rehab after an injury…''

Lois sputtered in outrage. ''You should encourage people to see real professionals.''

''Oh? You mean like the massage therapists employed by the hospital? I noticed their offices downstairs. They're not quite as well equipped as I am, but they're still adequate.''

''They're accredited.''

''Me too.'' Emma fashioned a look of haughtiness. ''I'm certified with the AMTA and licensed by the city of Chicago. You know, you look so puckered up, you should really try a little massage. All that frowning ages a person and gives her wrinkles.''

''I do see a few frown lines, Lois,'' Casey managed to say with a straight face. It was strange, but seeing

Emma so confident, even cocky, turned him on. "Maybe the folks downstairs will give you an employee discount."

Clearly knowing she'd lost that round, Lois stalked out in a snit.

Unwilling to let Emma leave the same way, Casey caught her elbow. She'd put up a good front for Lois, but he could see that she was miffed over his interference with the doctor. "Do you want to visit with your father some more before we head off?"

She considered it, and finally nodded. "Maybe just to smooth things over before I leave."

Casey hated for her to face him alone again, but he already knew he wasn't welcome. "Hey." He touched her chin and resisted the urge to kiss her. "Don't let him get you down, okay? He's bound to be a little grouchy, all things considered."

"It's not that." She started out of the room. "There are some things my father and I will never agree on, that's all. But I don't want to argue with him here, not while he's hurt and sick."

This time Casey waited for her in the hall, but he could hear them speaking. The words were indistinct, but the tone was clear: Emma calmly insistent, Dell complaining, even whining. Casey winced for her. Under the circumstances, being Dell's caretaker wasn't going to be easy.

When she emerged ten minutes later, looking more agitated than ever, he slipped his arm around her waist. They walked down the hallway to the elevator in silence, but once inside, Casey pulled her into a hug. "Ms. Clark, I'm noticing a few frown lines on you, too."

A reluctant smile curled her lips, but her eyes remained dark with worry. "Is that right? Think I should stop for a massage?"

"What I think is that you should talk me through it. Maybe I have magic fingers too."

The smile turned into a grin. "I never doubted it for a second."

"But first, a day on the lake with the sun in your face will work wonders."

To his surprise, Emma sighed. "Oh, that does sound like heaven."

Aware of a slow, heated thrumming in his blood, Casey urged her off the elevator and through the lobby. Already he visualized her in a bikini, her skin warmed by the sun, dewy with the humidity… He had to swallow his groan to keep from alerting her to his intent. He'd have her alone in the boat, on the lake, with no way to escape. Touching her, kissing her, was a priority.

But first he intended to discover all her secrets. Something had happened to her, something bad enough to make her leave her home. Bad enough to make her leave him.

He wasn't letting her off the boat until he knew it all.

CHAPTER NINE

B.B.'S HOT BREATH pelted Casey's right ear as he drove. The dog, like Emma, enjoyed having the top down, his face in the wind.

Emma's long hair whipped out behind her and she constantly had to shove it from her face. In something akin to awe, she breathed, "It's so beautiful out here."

Glancing at her, Casey agreed. Now that they'd hit the back roads leading toward the lake, the foliage was thicker, greener, lush. Blue cornflowers mixed with black-eyed Susans all along the roadway. Cows bawled in sprawling pastures, goats chewed on tall weeds grown along crooked fence posts. Blue-black crows as fat as ducks spread their wings and cawed as the car went past.

The narrow roads forced Casey to slow his speed, but he didn't mind. Watching Emma reacquaint herself with her hometown made every second enjoyable. She waved to farmers in coveralls who tipped their straw hats to her and then lazily waved back. She strained to see tobacco huts and tomato stands and moss-covered ponds. She embraced the wind in her face and the sun in her eyes.

She laughed with the sheer joy of it all.

And Casey felt positively frenetic with lust. It

burned his stomach and tightened his throat and kept him uncomfortably edgy.

If, as he'd first assumed, he had only lust to deal with, he'd have already pulled over to the side of the road and taken Emma beneath a tree on the sweet grass. She claimed to be willing and there was plenty of privacy here once you got far enough from the road that no cars would notice you. Making love to Emma with the hot sun on his back and the birds overhead would be downright decadent, something straight out of his dreams.

But he was afraid what he felt for her was more than mere lust. He wasn't sure how much more and he wasn't sure how hard it'd be to convince her of it. Emma seemed hell-bent on remembering how he'd once rejected her, instead of giving them both a chance to get reacquainted as adults. Not that he blamed her. Looking at her now, he couldn't understand how he'd ever turned her down.

Emma was as earthy and sexual and appealing as a woman could be. And she was in her element here.

She belonged in Buckhorn. Did she belong with him?

They'd stopped at the motel where Emma had changed into her suit and a zippered terry-cloth cover-up. Snowy-white and sleeveless, it hung to midthigh, showing off the shapely length of her legs. She'd raised the zipper high enough to rest between her breasts. Casey could see the top of her beige, crocheted bathing-suit bra, which made him nuts wanting to know if it was a bikini or a one-piece.

She wore dark sunglasses and brown slip-on sandals, and she had a large cotton satchel stuffed with a colorful beach towel, sunscreen, a bottle of water and her cell phone. She commented that she wanted the hospital to be able to reach her if they needed to.

Before they'd left the motel she'd also taken the time to call Damon on his phone, and discovered that the car was repaired and he was touring the area. Emma had promised him that she'd be back for dinner. Luckily, to Casey's way of thinking, Damon had explained that he had a date, so Emma should take her time visiting.

Emma hadn't seemed at all surprised or concerned with how fast Damon had gotten acquainted. Apparently he had a way with women, given the fond smile Emma wore while rolling her eyes.

Casey had no idea what Damon had planned, and he didn't much care. As long as Damon stayed busy, he couldn't interfere with Casey's pursuit of Emma.

He turned the car down the long driveway to his family's home. The property here was lined with a tidy split-rail fence to contain the few farm animals they kept. Their menagerie often varied, since some of his father's patients paid for medical services with livestock, which they in turn often donated to the needier local families.

At present, they had several horses, an enormous hog, a fat, ornery heifer and two timid lambs. They'd keep the horses, and Honey had grown partial to the lambs. But the hog and heifer had to go. They terrorized Honey every chance they got. Whenever Honey was around, the damn cow dredged up the most threatening look a big-eyed, black-spotted bovine could manage.

Casey adored Honey, and a day didn't go by that

he didn't appreciate her and all she gave to them, to his father. Because Sawyer's first marriage had been such a public fiasco, no one had ever expected him to remarry.

Casey had enjoyed being raised in an all-male household, but having Honey around had been even better. Softer. Over the years, she'd planted numerous flowers along the outside of the fence: enormous white peonies, tall irises and abundant daisies. Something was always in bloom, making the area colorful and fragrant.

Holding her hair from her face, Emma glanced around at the familiar stretch of land. "I thought we were going to the lake?"

"We are." He kept his gaze on the road and off the sight of her creamy skin. "But I want to stop at the house first. I need to change and grab the boat keys."

"You live at home?"

"In the apartment over the garage. I lived in Cincy for a while, just because I thought it'd be more convenient. But it didn't take me long to decide I prefer the forty-minute drive to and from work every day." Now, more than ever, Casey was glad he hadn't moved out of the area.

The sprawling log house came into view. Built on a rise and surrounded by mature trees and numerous outbuildings, it looked impressive indeed. In his younger days, Casey had lived there with his father and his uncles. Morgan now had a house farther up the hill, but not more than a ten-minute walk away. Jordan had moved into Georgia's house with her and the kids after they married, and Gabe bought a place in town with Elizabeth.

Morgan's newest official vehicle was in the yard. Because so many people in Buckhorn lived off the beaten path or in the hills, Morgan drove a rugged four-wheel-drive Bronco. Misty, his wife, had convinced him to trade from black to white last year. Actually, she'd wanted red, but Morgan had refused that. He said the sheriff's emblem painted on the side would clash.

Casey saw Emma take in the crowd in front of the house. With the dark glasses on, he couldn't see her eyes. But he watched the tilt of her head, the lack of a smile on her pretty mouth.

It appeared Morgan and Misty were dropping off the kids, Amber and Garrett. They stood on the steps, Morgan wearing his tan uniform and Misty in a casual dress. Sawyer and Honey were beneath the shade on the porch, drinking tall glasses of iced tea. Shohn was there, too, with Morgan's dog, Godzilla. All in all, they made an intimidating crowd of people.

When they saw Casey pull up and park beneath an oak tree, the kids raced to the car to greet him. The boys were shirtless and in sneakers; Amber wore a T-shirt and cutoffs and was barefoot.

B.B. twitched his ears, alert to the activity but not overly concerned. When he spotted the kids, his tail started thumping in earnest. Casey hadn't known they'd all be there. He waited, worried that Emma would be upset to be dropped into the middle of his overwhelming family.

Instead, she sat back in her seat with a sound of

wonder. "It's incredible, but they look almost the same."

Relieved, Casey reached over and smoothed a long lock of hair behind her ear. "Dad has gray at his temples now, but Honey says it makes him look distinguished."

"She's right. He's still so handsome it's almost unfair. And Shohn looks just like him. But, if anything, Morgan's gotten even bigger."

"Misty calls him a brick wall." Casey looked at his imposing uncle in time to see Morgan pat Misty on the rump. She swatted at him and he laughed.

Shaking his head, Casey said, "I swear, they still act like newlyweds."

"Yeah, and it's wonderful." Emma sighed. The kids had almost reached them. They were making a clatter, laughing and calling out. "You can see which kids are his. That shiny black hair, and just look at those blue eyes."

Emma opened her door, not waiting for Casey. B.B. jumped out beside her and whined in excitement, practically pleading to be released so he could play with Godzilla. The kids skidded to a halt in front of Emma and then stared.

Shohn squinted up at her. His dark hair was mussed and he had dirt on his knees. "Does your dog bite?"

"Only on bones." She grinned as she said it. "But not leg bones. Just steak bones."

Garrett held out a hand and B.B. licked it. "Can we play with him?"

The dog whined again with the most pitifully pleading expression, amusing the kids.

Because they had plenty of land for running, Casey

unhooked the dog's leash. "You guys go easy on him, okay? He doesn't know you yet."

Amber stroked his muzzle and giggled when his tail started furiously pounding the ground. "We'll watch him for ya, okay?"

Casey left it up to Emma.

"Honey won't mind having him loose?"

"'Course not." Luckily, Honey loved animals as much as they all did. Except for big cows and snarling hogs.

"All right." Emma scratched B.B.'s ear, then patted his side and released him by saying, "Go play."

B.B. bounded forward, leaping this way and that in his exuberance at seeing another dog. Godzilla went berserk with his own joy, which prompted the kids to do the same. Amber and Garrett ran off after the dogs, but Shohn hung back, still squinting. "You Casey's girlfriend?"

Casey started to reply, but Emma beat him to it. "I'm a friend and I'm a girl, so I guess you can call me a girlfriend."

"He's got a lot of girlfriends."

Emma's mouth curled. "I never doubted it for a second."

Shohn laughed, but in the next second Casey threw him over his shoulder and held him upside down. "Brat. Quit trying to scare her off or I'll have to hang you by your toes."

Casey pretended to drop him and Shohn roared with laughter. When Casey finally set him back on his feet, Shohn moved a safe distance away, posed to run, and gave a cocky smile. "If she turns you down, Case, I'll take her. She's real pretty."

Fighting a laugh, Casey feigned an attack and, like a flash, Shohn ran off to join the other kids. Casey looked at Emma and saw she wore an ear-to-ear grin, which prompted his own. So she liked kids, did she? A good thing, since there were quite a few in the family. "You're not going to turn me down, are you, sweetheart?"

Rather than answer, she said, "Gee, he reminds me of someone else I know. Now, who could it be?"

Every moment Casey spent with her canceled out the time they'd been apart. He pulled her into his side. "I was shy."

"Ha!"

"Shohn's only ten, but I swear he's girl crazy already. The little rat flirts with every female, regardless of her age. Makes Honey nuts. Dad just shakes his head." He gave Emma a squeeze. "And of course, my grandmother says he reminds her of Gabe."

Emma laughed. "Where is your grandmother?"

"She and Gabe's father, Brett, live in Florida, but they get up this way every couple of months to visit."

Because Casey was lingering in the yard, giving Emma a chance to brace herself for his family, Sawyer left the porch and headed toward them. It seemed he'd been seeing patients, given that he wore dark slacks and an open-necked button-down shirt with the sleeves rolled up. He smiled at Emma without recognition. "Hello."

He held out his hand and Emma took it. "Hello, Dr. Hudson. It's been a long time."

Cocking one eyebrow, Sawyer looked to Casey for an introduction. Casey stared at his father hard, trying to prepare him. "Dad, you remember Emma Clark."

The other eyebrow lifted to join the first. Sawyer still held her hand and now he enclosed it in both of his. If he'd been surprised, he quickly covered it up. "Emma, of course I remember you. It has been a long time. How've you been?"

"Just great." B.B. charged up next to her, with Godzilla in hot pursuit. "Casey said it was okay to let him run."

Sawyer admired the dog for a moment, then nodded. "He's fine, and obviously he doesn't mind the children."

"B.B. loves kids. He's very careful with them."

"He's a beautiful animal." Sawyer released Emma and gestured to the porch. "We were just taking a break. Would you like something to drink?"

She glanced at Casey. "We were going out on the boat…"

"There's time. I need to change anyway."

She pushed her sunglasses to the top of her head and nodded. "Then yes, thank you. I'd love to visit for a few minutes."

Casey was amazed at her. He'd expected her to be uncomfortable, maybe embarrassed. Instead, she waved to Honey, strolled right up to the porch and began greeting everyone with a new confidence that was both surprising and appealing. Any awkwardness she'd felt as a youth was long gone.

Sawyer shot Casey a look filled with questions.

"She's in town to see her father."

"The hell you say? After all this time? It's been…what? Over eight years."

"Dell's had a stroke."

"I heard." In a small town, news traveled fast. "He'll be okay?"

"Doc Wagner seemed to think so." They were still in the yard, out of earshot from the others. Casey rubbed the back of his neck, struggling with how much he wanted to say. But he'd always been able to talk to his dad and now more than ever he wanted to share his thoughts. "About when she left…"

Sawyer clasped Casey's shoulder. "I didn't think we'd ever see her again. I worried about that girl for a long time." He searched Casey's face. "I know you did too."

There was no denying that. Though he'd tried to hide it, his father knew him too well to be fooled. "You know…" He glanced up at Sawyer. "We all assumed the same things back then, with how Dell dropped her off here, and her bruised face, the way she was crying."

"But?"

"But seeing her with him today, I realized we assumed too much."

Sawyer gazed toward the porch where the women and Morgan gathered. "How's that?"

"I took her to the hospital today to visit him."

Again, Sawyer lifted his dark eyebrows. "When did she get to town?"

"Last night."

"And you're already chauffeuring her around?"

"It's not like that. We're…"

Sawyer waited.

"Hell, I don't know." He could just faintly hear Emma speaking on the porch, her tone friendly and natural. He watched her, saw the easy way she held herself, how she greeted Morgan and Misty. He shook his head. "I had a time of it, convincing her to let me hang around. She's different now, but how I feel about her is the same."

"How do you feel about her?"

Casey scowled. "I'm not sure, all right? I just... Seeing her again made me realize how much I'd missed her." He was starting to feel sixteen again, waiting for his father to give him another lecture on the importance of rubbers.

"Nothing wrong with that."

Casey shifted uncomfortably. "Her car broke down on the way into town last night. Gabe fixed it for her this morning, but she needed to visit her dad early so she could catch Dr. Wagner. I drove her, then waited around. And damn, listening to her with her father, well, things aren't as they always seemed."

"Honey is waving at us. Maybe you better catch me up later." They started toward the porch, but halfway there Sawyer asked, "Do you know what you're doing, Case?"

"Yeah." He frowned. "At least I think I do."

"Will Emma be moving back home?"

He shook his head. "She says not. She has her own business in Chicago, and some very close friends there."

"So she's only here for a spell?"

Not if he could help it. "I don't know."

"But you want her to stay?" Sawyer didn't wait for an answer. "Maybe we can help. As for her father, I'd planned to pay her folks a visit anyway, to see if there was any way I could help."

"I'll go with you when you do."

Morgan eyed them both when they finally started up the wooden porch steps. Because he'd spent some time hunting for Emma after she'd run away, Casey had no doubt he was bursting with questions. But Morgan would never deliberately make a woman uncomfortable.

Emma had already been seated in a rattan rocker across from Honey. She'd slipped her feet out of her sandals and had her toes curled against the sun-bleached boards of the porch.

Morgan said, "Why don't you take my boat. It hasn't been out in a while."

"All right." He peered at Emma, trying to read her expression. "Maybe I can talk Emma into skiing."

Emma held up her hands. "Oh no. I need to get used to the boat first before I try anything out of the boat."

Misty crossed her arms over the railing. "I finally learned how to ski, but I look pathetic when I do."

Morgan bit her ear. "You look sexy."

Rolling her eyes, Misty said, "Morgan is starting to drool, so I guess we better get going."

"A date with my wife," Morgan rumbled. "That doesn't happen very often."

Hands clasped together, forehead puckered, Emma came out of her seat. "Before you go, could I talk to you just a minute? I mean, all of you?"

Everyone stared. Casey held his breath.

Making a face, Emma said, "I'm sorry to hold you up, but since you're all here, I figured it'd be a good time to apologize." She sneaked a quick look at Casey. "And don't tell me it's not necessary, because it is to me."

"Damn it, Em..." He took a step up the porch stairs toward her.

Morgan laced his arms around Misty and pulled her back into his chest. "Well now, I suppose we've got a few minutes to spare."

Misty snorted. "And the curiosity is probably killing him."

"Casey's right." Honey leaned forward in her chair. "You don't owe us anything at all. But if you want to talk..."

With his hand on the back of Honey's chair, Sawyer said, "I'm curious too. Where'd you go the night you ran off?"

Casey glowered at his family. He thought about just flinging Emma over his shoulder, as he'd done to Shohn, and carrying her off. But that'd probably shoot any chance he had of getting on her good side. He could tell this was important to her, so he locked his jaw and waited.

Emma turned to Morgan first. "My father told me that you looked for me after I took off. I'm sorry that I put you to that trouble by not explaining better when I left, and I'm especially sorry that any of you worried about me. Kids do dumb things, and that night it didn't occur to me that any of you might worry."

Because no one had ever worried about her before? Casey didn't like that probability, but he knew it was likely true.

She turned to Sawyer next. "I never dreamed that you'd actually look for me."

"We just wanted to know for certain that you were okay."

Honey agreed with her husband. "You were awfully young to go off on your own."

"I know. And I appreciate your concern." Her cheeks dimpled with her smile. "It's why I came here that night, because I knew you'd be nice and that you'd understand. I'm sorry I took advantage of you."

"Enough apologies," Misty said. "Morgan likes to fret—it's why he's a sheriff—and Sawyer's no better. They're both mother hens. Obviously you and Casey have made up now, so all's well that ends well."

Casey took that as his cue to move to her side. Without confirming or denying Misty's statement, Emma said, "Thank you."

But Morgan wasn't ready to let it go. "So where'd you disappear to?"

Misty gave him a frown, which he ignored.

"Chicago. I met some very nice people who helped me figure out what I wanted to do. I finished up school and started my own business. Things have been great."

Bemused, Casey could only stare at her. If he hadn't heard the full story—or rather, a less condensed version—he would have believed her life to be a bed of roses. Damn, she was good at covering up. He'd have to remember that.

"What kind of business do you have?" Honey asked.

"Massage therapy. I have my own small studio."

"Ohmigod," Misty enthused. "I know women in town who drive weekly into Florence for a massage. They'll be all over you if they find out."

"Not that Misty needs to leave home for that sort of thing," Morgan stated, while rubbing her shoulders. Misty just smiled.

"Are you going to be in town long?" Honey asked.

"I'm not sure yet."

Casey caught her hand and laced his fingers with hers. He didn't want to hear about her leaving when she'd only just come home. "We have to get going."

"I thought you wanted to change."

"I will, but I figured we'd swing into the apartment on our way down to the lake." The house overlooked the lake, and from the back, it wasn't too far to walk to reach the shore. Casey's apartment above the garage was on the way, so he decided to just drag Emma along with him. The quicker he got her alone, the better.

"All right." Emma finished off her glass of tea. After slipping her sandals back on, she thanked Honey again.

"Will you be back in time for lunch?" Honey wanted to know.

If things worked out as he hoped, they'd spend the rest of the day together. "We'll grab something on the lake, but thanks." Casey hugged the women, said farewell to the men, and led Emma back to the car so she could get her satchel. They went around the side of the house to the garage apartment. Before Emma could call B.B., he fell into step beside her, along with all the kids. The dog almost looked to be laughing, he'd had such a good time.

"Where ya going?" Garrett asked.

Ruffling his hair, Emma said, "Casey is taking me boating."

Shohn perked up. "How about tubin' us, Case?"

Emma looked at Casey in question. She remembered tubing, Casey was sure. At one time or another, just about everyone on the lake had been bounced around on a fat black inner tube, tied with a ski rope and pulled behind the boat. It proved a bruising ride, one guaranteed to get water up your nose and make your body ache. Kids loved it, but most adults had more sense.

Likely Emma's questioning look meant it was up to him whether or not to include the kids.

He voted *not*. Casey wanted to grab Emma and run like hell. Instead, he told Shohn, "How about we save that for another day? Emma hasn't been home in a long time and I want to let her enjoy the ride, not scare her to death with your daredevil antics."

The boys looked downcast, making Casey feel guilty. Then Amber, the oldest of the bunch at a not-quite-mature eleven, elbowed them both. "You can go tubing anytime, dummy. Case has a date."

Shohn slanted a leering look at Casey and grinned like a possum, but Garrett shrugged. "So?"

"So he wants to kiss her. Don't ya, Case?" Shohn made smooching noises while pretending to hold a swooning female.

Emma surprised him yet again by snatching Shohn up close and kissing his cheek and neck until he screamed uncle. Everyone was laughing, Garrett pointing at Shohn, and B.B. jumping around in glee. Amber looked up at Casey, her dark-blue eyes twinkling with enjoyment. He hugged his niece, unable to stop smiling. Damn, having Emma around was nice.

Without even trying, she fit in—into Buckhorn, into his family. Into his heart.

Emma sat down on the bottom step leading up to the rooms over the garage. Casey smoothed his hand over her head. "I'll go change and be right back."

Panting, Shohn sprawled backward across her lap like a sacrifice, his arms spread out, his head almost touching the ground. "Take your time, brother. Take your time."

Emma laughed too hard to answer Casey, but Amber followed him up the steps and through the front door. She helped herself to a drink of water, then flounced onto his sofa while Casey went into the bedroom to change into his trunks.

"I like her," Amber announced, saying it loud so Casey would be sure to hear.

"Me too," Casey called out to her.

"You gonna keep this one?"

Inside his room, Casey chuckled. He remained endlessly amazed at how different his nieces were from the boys. The girls got together and planned, while the boys got together and scuffled. Occasionally the differences were less noticeable, like on holidays when they were all wild little monkeys, but overall the girls were more mature. "She has some say-so in that, you know."

"Daddy doesn't give Mom much say-so. He just picks her up and totes her wherever he wants her to go."

That picture brought about a laugh. Morgan did seem fond of hauling Misty around. 'Course, he'd seen his father toting Honey a time or two as well— whenever she'd fallen asleep on the couch, and sev-

eral times when his dad had that certain look, which
prompted Casey to give them immediate privacy. In
Gabe's case, it was as often as not Elizabeth who was
dragging Gabe off to bed. Jordan, however, was more
subtle. He and Georgia connected with scorching
looks that no one could misunderstand.

Casey finished changing into cutoff jeans, an unbuttoned, short-sleeve shirt and ratty sneakers. He
snagged a beach towel and rejoined Amber. "Your
mom lets Morgan get away with that because she
likes it."

Amber sighed theatrically. "I know. Daddy says
Mom has him wrapped around her little finger."

"Your mom and you both." Casey held his hand
out for her and said, "Let's go before she runs off
with Shohn instead."

"Yeah right." Amber slipped her small hand into
his. "She's probably already in love with you. All the
women act stupid around you."

Casey's heart jumped at that "L" word, but he said
only, "You think Emma acts stupid?"

"No, silly. That's why I think you should keep
her."

When they went back down the steps, they found
Emma doing tricks with B.B. She threw a stick and
he caught it in midair, then brought it back to her.
She told him to roll over, to speak, to shake hands.
The boys were suitably impressed with his every feat.

Without even thinking about it, Casey looped his
arms around Emma from behind and kissed her ear.
The kids all stared wide-eyed. "If you think her dog
is neat, you should see her car."

That refocused the boys' attention.

"Is it as cool as your car?"

"What color is it?"

Teasing, Emma said, "It's better than his car."

Casey raised an eyebrow, but agreed. "Definitely. We both have Mustangs, but Emma's is a cherry-red classic. You know what that means?"

Garrett nodded. "It's old."

"But in great condition."

Frowning, Garrett said, "I'd rather have a new one."

"That's only because you haven't seen it yet," Emma assured him.

Casey gave her a squeeze. "How about we bring the car by here tomorrow and you rats can look it over?"

"Will you stay for dinner?" Amber asked, and even to Casey, who knew her private agenda, Amber looked like innocence personified.

Shohn aimed a thumb at his chest. "You could go out in the boat with us so I can show you how good I ski."

Emma stiffened with alarm, though why the idea of spending time with his family bothered her, he had no clue. She liked the kids, he could tell that much. And she'd been totally at ease even while apologizing and explaining to Morgan, Misty, Honey and his dad.

He let her push out of his hold and move a few steps away.

She turned to face him, saying, "I might already have plans…" But the words trailed off as she got a look at his naked chest. When a breeze blew by, parting the shirt a little more, Emma's mouth fell open, her eyes flared.

Satisfaction built within him.

Well now, that was nice. He was comfortable in his own skin, so casual around the lake he hadn't really thought about her seeing him when he yanked on the shirt. But Emma seemed to appreciate it. Once he got her on the boat, he'd lose the shirt and encourage her to lose the cover-up. He'd get her in the cove and hold her close, skin to skin…

Like perfect little strategists, the kids started begging Emma to return for dinner. Casey decided he would take them tubing—and soon. They deserved it.

He reached out and tugged on a lock of Emma's hair, then mimicked the kids. "Please?"

She swallowed, closed her mouth, and raised her eyes to his. "I'll try." Her smile was staged. "But I'll probably have to bring Damon along."

Casey groaned, grabbed his heart as if he'd been shot, and stumbled into Amber, who laughed while trying to hold him up.

"Who," she demanded around her smile, "is this Damon person?"

Casey straightened. He hugged Amber, then kissed her little turned-up nose. "He's no one important, sweetheart. Just Emma's friend. And if he comes to dinner with us, why then you can all show him how to catch tadpoles and crawdads on the shore, okay?"

Amber's small face brightened in understanding, and she gave Casey a conspiratorial wink. "Okay, Casey. That sounds like fun." She encompassed the boys in a look, and added, "It'll probably take him a long time to get the hang of it, but we'll be patient—even if it takes hours."

CHAPTER TEN

EMMA TRAILED her fingers in the cold water. She loved the sights, sounds and smells of being on the lake, but it all faded away with Casey so near. It wasn't easy keeping her gaze off him. In fact, it proved impossible.

But Lord have mercy, he looked good. He now wore only low-riding cutoffs and he was perched on the driver's seat at the back of the boat, steering one-handed while the wind blew his dark-blond hair and the sun reflected off his smooth, tanned shoulders and the firm expanse of his broad back. He had one muscular, hairy leg braced on the deck of the boat, the other in the seat. She let her eyes follow the line of his spine all the way to the waistband of those shorts…

She jerked her gaze away. Staring at Casey's muscled backside would not help her get it together. The air was hot, but it didn't compare to what she felt on the inside. Casey had matured in ways she hadn't counted on. His body had always been lean and strong, but now he had filled out and his strength was obvious in the flex of muscles in his upper arms, across his chest and shoulders. He wasn't a hulk like Morgan, just nicely defined and very macho.

He was hairier than she remembered too. Not too

much, but there was a sexy sprinkling of dark-brown hair on his chest that faded to a thin line toward his navel, then a silkier line still down his belly—and behind his fly.

Emma breathed too deeply, imagined too much, but she wanted to touch him, kiss him.

When they'd first gotten in the boat, B.B. had demanded all her attention. He'd tottered back and forth, looking out one side of the boat then the other, constantly whining. He didn't like the way the boat moved and kept him unsteady. But within ten minutes, he'd settled down and now he watched out the back, his body braced against the casing for the inboard motor. His tongue hung out the side of his mouth and his furry face held an expression of excitement.

Emma had been smiling over that when Casey casually pulled off his shirt and stowed it in the side of the boat. While she ogled him, he suggested she remove her cover-up. She'd declined, and had been trying not to stare at him, without much success, ever since.

The lake was crowded with boats everywhere, more so than she remembered it being in the past. At first Casey had driven at breakneck speed, cutting across the wakes of other boats, bouncing over choppy waves, causing the water to spray into the boat and making her laugh. He'd gradually slowed and moved closer to the shoreline so that now they glided through the water, watchful of skiers and swimmers and noisy Jet Skis.

A flashy cabin cruiser filled with sun worshipers zipped up alongside them. Lounged around the boat, three men and three women waved, prompting Casey to return the greeting. Emma saw his friendly smile, the way his raised arm showed a tuft of dark hair beneath, how his biceps bulged. She also saw how the women coveted Casey with open admiration, while the men leered at her. She didn't know if anyone recognized her, and she didn't stare back long enough to recognize anyone herself, but before the day was over, his friends would be talking. She hated that, but had no idea how to avoid it. Whether it was fair or not, she *did* have a reputation, and yet Casey was determined to be seen with her.

Her thoughts scattered as he steered the boat into a deep cove at the far end of the long lake, away from the congestion. He didn't bother to speak over the roar of the motor, but every so often she felt the intensity of his gaze settle on her. Little by little he slowed until the motor only purred and the ride was easy and smooth, just gliding through the water.

By the time they were out of sight from prying eyes, she couldn't hold back any longer and moved to the seat behind him.

Casey twisted his head toward her. He wore dark reflective sunglasses, but she could tell by the set of his mouth, the slight flare of his nostrils, that his mind had centered on the very same thoughts.

Without saying a word, Emma knelt on the seat and settled both palms on his bare shoulders, smoothing her hands down to his shoulder blades, then to his sides in a deep, sensual massage. Hot. Taut. Silky-smooth flesh over hard muscle.

Casey went still except for the expanding of his chest and back with each deep breath he took. She loved touching him, stroking him. "Emma…" he said, half in pleasure, half in warning. "Damn, you are good."

She leaned forward and pressed her open mouth to the spot where his shoulder melded into his neck. She breathed his heated scent while rubbing deeply at muscles, relaxing him and exciting him at the same time. "You're the most beautiful man I've ever seen."

He shuddered and reached back for her hand, then drew it forward to his mouth to kiss her knuckles. He held her that way, with one arm draped around his neck, her breasts flattened on his back. She put her cheek on his shoulder and hugged him. Strangely enough, she felt both content and turbulent.

"I want to show you something, okay?"

So overwhelmed with sensation, Emma could barely speak. She nodded.

He slowed the boat even more to drift into dark green, shallow water riddled with sunken tree limbs and covered with moss. This finger of the cove was narrow, barely big enough for a boat to turn around. Emma worried for the boat's prop, but figured Casey knew what he was doing.

That thought was confirmed when she spotted a skinny weathered dock with uneven boards at the very tip of the cove. It had old tires nailed to the side to protect the boat, with grommets for a tie-up. Casey brought the boat up alongside it, turned off the engine and secured it with the ease of long practice.

Enormous elms grew along all sides of the shoreline, with branches reaching far out across the water to form a canopy over the cove. She could hear the

croak of frogs, the splash of carp, the chirp of katy-
dids. The air smelled thick with all the greenery.

Casey brought her around next to him. Every line
of his body was drawn tight. "You like it?"

"It's incredible."

"I bought it. There're two acres, and the little cabin
up the hill." He didn't look away from her as he
explained that. "More like a shack, really. But it's
secluded and peaceful."

Emma slipped off her sunglasses to peer into the
surrounding woods. Sure enough, halfway up the hill
a small house was just barely visible through the thick
trees and scrubby shrubs. Like the dock, it was con-
structed of weathered wooden planks and consisted
mostly of a sloping screened-in front porch. A skinny
dirt path led down to the dock.

She gazed up at the tall trees, blocking all but a
few rays of sunshine, then she listened to the quiet.
Her tone low in near reverence, she whispered, "It's
almost magical."

B.B. whined, then leaped nimbly from the boat to
the dock. He started sniffing, working his way to the
shore.

Still staring at her, Casey asked, "Will he be
okay?"

Emma nodded. "He won't take off. He just wants
to explore the area."

"If he goes too far, he'll find a few cows on the
adjoining farm. But that's it. For all intents and pur-
poses, we're alone here."

He touched the zipper of her cover-up, right between her breasts, with one finger. His dark glasses

still in place, his voice a low murmur, he said, "Let's lose this now, okay?"

Trembling from the inside out, Emma nodded. "All right." Uncertainty made her feel clumsy. She wasn't shy, really, but it had been a long time since she'd experienced the freedom of the lake. Everyone everywhere wore little more than a suit, some skimpier than others. In comparison, hers was modest, concealing as much as a regular bra and panties might.

But that wasn't the point. She knew Casey would touch her, knew he wanted to have sex with her, and the very idea of it had her near to moaning. She kept her attention on Casey's chest, instead of his face, and dragged the zipper all the way down. She stood in front of him, while he sat in the driver's seat, his face level with her breasts, his knees open around her legs.

With an absorption that shook her, Casey set his sunglasses aside, reached out and caught the top of the terry cloth and tugged it slowly down her arms. Amber eyes took in the sight of her body as he dropped the cover-up on the seat behind her.

Leaves rustled overhead. Water lapped at the shore. A bird chirped. Neither of them spoke.

Casey wrapped his hands around the backs of her thighs, making Emma quiver. He stroked her, sliding his palms slowly and deliberately up over her hips to her waist where his thumbs dipped in near her navel, back and forth across her belly. He watched the movement of his fingers, then leaned forward and pressed an openmouthed kiss to the rise of one breast, another in her cleavage, lower, on her ribs.

Shaking under the sensual onslaught, Emma braced her hands against his shoulders. "Casey…"

"It seemed like you were gone forever, but now that you're back, it's like you never left." He licked her navel, took a gentle love bite of her belly. In a gravelly voice, he rasped, "This has been a long time coming."

Closing her eyes, Emma tunneled her fingers through his thick, warm hair. She stroked his nape, then pulled him closer. "Yes."

His hands moved back down her body to her bottom. He kneaded her, groaned, closed his mouth around her nipple through the bathing-suit bra. She felt the press of his hot tongue.

"Casey."

In the next instant, he stood and Emma found herself flush against him, his mouth on hers, his tongue sinking deep. He pressed his rigid erection into her belly, his breathing labored, his hands trembling as he touched her everywhere with a gentleness that bordered on awe.

He lifted his mouth and looked at her. The heat in his eyes stole her breath, then he kissed her again, easy, slow. Against her mouth, he said, "Emma, honey, as gorgeous as you are in that suit, all I can think about now is getting you out of it."

Emma looked around the area, which was deserted but still out in the open. "It…it's been a long time since I made out in a cove…"

"Don't." Casey's hands tightened on her and he squeezed his eyes shut. Three deep breaths later, he got control of himself. Despite his obvious turmoil, he cradled her close and spoke quietly near her ear. "I'm talking about making love, not making out. And I thought we'd go up to the cabin. It's clean, and no one ever comes here.'' He opened his mouth on her neck, pressed his tongue to her wildly thrumming pulse. He groaned again. ''I need a long time, Emma. Hours. Days.'' Her heart thundered, and she heard him barely whisper, ''A lifetime.''

Her knees nearly buckled. But men often said things they didn't mean when they were aroused. She had to remember that so she didn't set herself up for disappointment.

Flattening her hands on Casey's chest, she levered him back, smiled and said with absolute certainty, ''Yes.''

B.B. FOLLOWED THEM up the hill and into the enclosed front porch. The dark screening kept bugs out and shaded the room, but let in the fresh air. With the small house buried in the dense woods, it was cool and smelled a little earthy.

The dog did a quick reconnaissance of the area, sniffing everything, pushing his nose into every corner. He decided it bored him, and went back out through the screen door into the yard. They watched him as he wandered down to the dock, found a heated spot beneath a ray of sun. He turned around, circled and dropped.

Emma smiled. ''He's so lazy,'' she said, her voice sounding thick.

Suffering the most raging case of lust he'd ever known, Casey seated himself on the side of the twin-size bed. The white cotton sheets were rumpled and the pillows still bore the imprint of his head from his last retreat three days ago. Then, he'd been considering his life, his future, what he wanted to do. There'd been many decisions to make.

Now all other concerns were pushed aside in his need to have Emma. Again, he clasped her hips and looked at her adorable belly, the way her bra lifted her breasts, how the waistband of the bottoms stretched across her hipbones. The bikini was nearly the same color as her skin, but nowhere near as soft.

"I put the bed in here when I bought the place. It's great for napping, and I like to come here and think."

As bold as ever, Emma straddled his lap, then settled onto him, groin to groin, belly to belly, breasts to chest. Her eyes were heavy, her face flushed, her lips parted. She touched his jaw with her fingertips while staring at his mouth. "What do you think about, Casey?"

You, he started to say, but caught himself. Damn, she looked ready. But he wanted to go slow, to make it last. He pushed his hands into her bottoms, cuddled her firm cheeks and rested his face against her breasts. "Work. Life. Hell, I dunno." He'd often thought about her, wondering where she was and what she was doing. "I just like kicking back here, getting away from everyone."

Emma nuzzled against his ear. "Do you bring women here for sex?"

He jerked back, offended and annoyed. "Only you, Emma."

Her big brown eyes darkened, and turned velvet with emotion.

Without even trying, she twisted him inside out. "Kiss me, Em."

She did, and damn, she knew how to kiss. Her enthusiasm singed him and left him so primed it was a wonder he didn't slide her beneath him right now.

Patience, he reminded himself. He wanted more than one quick fuck. He wanted… Hell, he didn't know everything he wanted. But he wanted more. Of her. Of this.

Her bra ties slid free easily enough, yet the closeness of their bodies kept it in place. Casey clasped her shoulders and held her away from him. The cups dropped away from her breasts and Emma, while smiling at him, removed the top completely.

Beautiful. Casey held her steady as he leaned forward and closed his mouth around her left nipple. Her body flexed the tiniest bit in reaction and she made a sound between a groan and a purr.

He locked his arms around the small of her back to keep her from retreating as he feasted upon her. He took his time, loving the taste and texture of her, the small sounds she made. When her nipple was tightly beaded, he switched to her other breast.

At first, the gentle rocking of her body didn't register. When it did, Casey had to look at her. With her head tipped back, her lips parted, her fingers caught in his hair, she epitomized female abandon.

Using his teeth with devastating effect, he further taunted her nipple, until she whispered, "Casey, *please…*"

He shuddered in reaction. "I love hearing you say my name." He couldn't wait any longer. Lifting her to her feet, he quickly finished stripping her. She didn't say a word when he hooked his fingers in the waistband of her bottoms and skimmed them down her legs. She stepped out of the material, he set them aside, and they both went silent.

So often in his dreams, he'd imagined having Emma just like this.

She stood there with her belly pulled tight, her nipples wet from his mouth. His to take. Casey drew a heated breath—and knew he was falling hard all over again.

It should have bothered him. Emma had walked out on him once; she kept secrets from him still. She'd only been back in town for a day and had definite plans for taking off again. But, at the moment, none of that mattered.

Keeping his eyes on the neat triangle of pubic hair between her legs, he unsnapped his shorts and shoved them down, removing his boxers at the same time. He kicked them aside on the dusty porch floor. He knew Emma was staring at his erection. He locked his knees and let her look her fill, but it wasn't easy when his every muscle strained against the need to hold her again.

In a breathless whisper, she said, "I hope I'm not dreaming."

That made him smile and relieved some of his tension. "Come here, and I'll make sure you're awake." The words were barely out of his mouth and Emma was there, her small hands sliding up and over his chest to twine around his neck, her belly pressing into his groin, her mouth turned up for his. She showed no reserve, no hesitation. And the kiss she gave him left him shaking.

Hoping to slow her down, he lowered them both to the bed and moved to her side. The urge to climb on top of her and sink deep into her body was already strong. With her encouraging murmurs and touches, holding back was hell. But he'd been waiting for over eight years so what did a few more minutes matter?

And he had been waiting, he knew that now. The dissatisfaction he'd felt with every female since Emma now made sense. They'd been lacking simply because they weren't Emma. She was special in ways he hadn't realized.

Propping himself up on his elbow, Casey stared down at her.

She shifted, trying to bring him back to her, flesh to flesh. "Casey?"

"Shh." Fingers spread wide, he settled his hand on her belly and felt her muscles contract. "I love just looking at you, Emma."

Her velvety brown eyes, so hungry, so hot, held his as she caught his wrist and urged his hand lower, between her parted thighs. She started at the first touch of his fingers there, moaning softly, her breath hitching.

Watching her face, Casey gently opened her with his fingertips, stroked over her swollen vulva, her clitoris. She was wet, hot. His own heartbeat roared in his ears.

As he teased, her back arched off the mattress, making her breasts an offering. He dipped down to gently suck on her nipples at the same time he sank his middle finger deep. Her reaction was startling— and damn exciting. Inner muscles clenched tight around his finger, her body shivered, her legs stiffened.

"Casey." So much pleading in one small word.

Hell yes, he loved hearing his name, especially the way she said it now, with all the same need he felt.

A rosy flush covered her body, warming her skin and intensifying her luscious scent. Casey took his time suckling her, fingering her, enjoying her. Perversely, the more frantic Emma became, the more she moaned and writhed and pleaded, the more determined he was to take his time, to leisurely make her crazy with lust. And to prove to her that she couldn't feel this with any man other than him.

She was so easy to read, not because her hands clenched fitfully in his hair and her broken moans were so explicit. Not because her hips rocked against his hand, faster, harder. But because he knew this one particular woman better than any other. It seemed he always had. And he knew he always would.

He felt her begin to tremble, felt the stillness that signaled the onset of her release, and he surged up from her breasts to take her mouth in a voracious, claiming kiss.

Goddammit, she was his. She'd always been his. She...

The clench of her nails on his shoulders shattered his thoughts and warned of her release. Heart ready to explode, he rode out the climax with her, kissing her face, murmuring to her, maintaining the steady press and stroke of his rough fingertips between her thighs until she finally pulled her mouth away to gulp frantically for air. She took her pleasure as naturally as a woman should—relishing it, giving in to it.

"Oh God," she groaned as she slumped back into the mattress, still breathing too hard, still shivering. Her eyes were slumberous, heated. Damp with tears.

He wanted more.

He needed it all.

Casey came to his knees to look over her temporarily sated body—temporary, because no way in hell was he done with her. He touched her everywhere, parting her legs wider, stroking her with both hands, catching her already sensitive nipples. He luxuriated in the feel of her warm, soft flesh in places that he'd once considered forbidden to him.

"You care about me, Emma. It's still there—whatever it is between us."

Her eyes were closed, her face turned slightly away. She nodded, sniffed, and more tears seeped out around her thick lashes.

Frowning, Casey trailed his fingers down her body, over her belly, through her pubic hair and between her lips. She was creamy wet now, swollen, throbbing. He watched her eyes open…and thrust three fingers into her hard.

She cried out softly, twisting on the sheets.

"Admit it, Em. Say it." He waited, but she stared at him with that lost expression that had the ability to rip him apart. His teeth clenched. "Tell me it's still there. *Tell me you care about me.*"

She swallowed hard and offered up a small, shaky smile. Looking more vulnerable than any woman ever should, she whispered, "Always, Casey." Her voice broke, and she laid one palm over his heart. "Always."

A tidal wave of feelings took his breath. He couldn't wait a second more. He snagged the condom from his shorts pocket and rolled it on in record time. Emma waited until he started to settle over her, then she rose up and pushed him to his back. Eyes still glistening with tears, that small secret smile still in place, she stared into his eyes. "It's my turn."

Casey groaned. That husky purr of hers would be the death of him. His muscles cramped when she wrapped both hands around his erection and stroked, slow, easy. Again and again.

He was still trying to get himself under control when she lifted herself over him, positioned him against her tender sex, and sank down so languidly he nearly lost it there and then.

"Emma…" His awareness of her was so heightened, he felt everything, every tiny movement and touch. Like the press of her smooth legs around his hips, and her buttocks on his thighs. The way her hands contracted on his chest and how her body squeezed him with each retreat, then softened around him as she sank down again.

Her breasts swayed, drawing his hands, then his mouth. Much as he enjoyed seeing her astride him, she was too far away. Craving the touch of her body to his, Casey sat up and pulled her closer so he could reach all of her, her slim back, the luscious flare of her hips and the firm resilience of her ass cheeks. He kissed her, keeping her mouth under his even as he felt his testicles tightening with his climax.

As she wrapped her legs completely around him, Emma never missed a beat, rising and falling, rising again. She didn't let him hold back, didn't give him a chance to regain control. When he came, she took his harsh groans into her mouth and gave back her own sweet sounds of release. Their bodies strained, clung, and then shuddered roughly. Her arms wrapped around his neck, Emma leaned into him.

Casey felt her heartbeat rioting against his jaw and he pressed a kiss to her breast. Emma's fingers stroked idly through his hair, petting him, hugging him tight every couple of seconds. The contentment lasted for long minutes. He felt at peace, whole in a way that had eluded him until now.

But with the edge taken off his hunger, Casey knew he had to tend to other things. He mentally braced himself, then carefully stretched out on the bed with Emma resting over his chest.

He was still inside her when he kissed her temple and said, "Now we talk."

"Mmm." She toyed with his chest hair, and Casey could hear the sleepiness in her voice, reminding him once again that she was short on rest, heavy on worries. "About what?"

Staring at the warped boards in the ceiling, Casey tightened his arms around her back so she couldn't run from him. "About you." He kept his tone calm, firm. "About what happened that night you came to my house."

She stiffened in alarm, but he couldn't relent. This was too important. She tried to struggle away from him but he stroked her, hoping to soothe her, to offer reassurance.

"Casey…"

He held her close to his heart. "I want to talk about your mother."

"No."

"Yes."

She lifted her face so he could see her disgruntled

frown. Casey smoothed her tangled hair back and studied her taut expression. He touched the corner of her mouth with his thumb, and said, "She's a drunk, isn't she, Emma?"

DAMON SMILED at the picture Ceily made in her sundress and sandals. Given the understated outfit, she should have looked innocent. Instead, she looked hot. Tantalizing. Like a wet dream.

He knew women well enough to know she'd spent extra time preparing for him. It showed in the carefully applied makeup, the subtle sexiness of her clothes.

She'd spent the last hour showing him around Buckhorn, not that there was that much to see other than the beautiful scenery. They'd had ice cream, and watching Ceily lick a cone was a special form of foreplay he wasn't likely to forget anytime soon. Damon was sure it had been deliberate. And it had worked.

He'd barely been able to take his gaze off her as they'd waved to a hundred of her "close friends" and browsed the one and only gift shop.

After showing him all the landmarks, she'd driven her small compact to the outskirts of town, parked near a pasture and gotten out. Carrying a small cooler of drinks and with a plaid blanket over his arm, Damon followed her. He had to be careful of cowpatties, a unique concern that.

He wasn't quite sure where Ceily was leading him, but he gladly followed. Walking behind her, taking in the sway of her lush hips, certainly wasn't a hardship.

The humid breeze ruffled her hair and played with

her skirt when she twisted to look at him over her shoulder. "There's a beautiful creek right down here."

The entire area looked splendid—the perfect place to build some small vacation cabins or retirement homes. "Is this your property?"

"No, it belongs to my grandpa."

He wondered if her grandpa would be willing to sell. "You've lived here your whole life?"

"Yep." She stopped in front of a crystal-clear creek filled with churning water. The sound alone could mesmerize, but with the wildflowers here and there, birds circling and Ceily close by, it was outright magnificent.

Damon spread the blanket and watched her settle onto it. Ceily wasn't an introverted or uncertain woman. She had a teasing, confident presence that aroused him.

He dropped next to her and slanted her a teasing look. "If I get too hot, do you intend to throw me into the creek?"

Utilizing considerable thought, she plucked a long blade of grass. "I thought we might both cool off when the sun sets."

Damon arched an eyebrow. "Skinny-dipping?"

Her mouth curled while she positioned the blade of grass between her thumbs. "I bet you're a virgin, huh?"

"Was it my uncommon restraint that led you to that conclusion?"

Laughing, she said, "I mean a virgin to skinny-dipping. Somehow I can't see you frolicking outdoors in the buff."

Damon rested back on one elbow. "I'm always up for new experiences, especially when they're initiated by a beautiful woman."

He jumped when she raised both hands to her mouth, the blade of grass somehow caught between, and gave an earsplitting whistle. When she looked at him for approval, he asked, "Is that how country girls whistle?"

Pushing her hair behind her ear, Ceily nodded. She didn't quite look at him when she idly tossed out, "Wanna see how country girls kiss?"

Feeling a curl of heat, Damon murmured, "That's a dumb question for such a smart girl."

She laughed and came down over his chest, knocking him flat. "I like you, Damon."

"Is that so?" He smiled, enjoying her silly banter. "Show me."

"All right." Her eyebrows lowered. "But I should warn you first that I don't sleep with a guy on the first date."

"Pity." Did she expect him to start complaining? He held his grin back with an effort, ready to disappoint her. He liked Ceily, and he appreciated her honesty. He held her hair away from her face and brushed his lips over her chin, her throat.

"You're not mad?"

"That you've been teasing me? No. I happen to be enjoying your efforts."

"Unbelievable."

Feeling smug, he grinned at her, knowing he had just surprised her. "So how many dates will it take me?"

She stared deep into his eyes, lowered her mouth to his and groaned. "Let's play it by ear."

The second her mouth touched his, Damon was lost. Damn, she was sweet, and yet she was also brazen. A delicious combination.

Slowly the kiss ended. Ceily licked her lips, sighed and rested her head on his chest. "Want me to teach you how to whistle like that?"

Damon was in the most powerful throes of lust he'd felt in years, and she wanted to teach him how to whistle. He laughed, liking the novelty of it, liking her more by the moment. "That's exactly what I was thinking about. Whistling. And with a blade of grass, no less."

She poked him in the ribs. "Liar."

He tightened his arms around her so she couldn't prod him again. "At the risk of sounding trite, what's a smart girl like you doing in Buckhorn?" Damon could easily picture her in the city, charming one and all.

She pushed up to see his face. "This is home. Where else would I be?"

The way she said it, he felt foolish for asking. Though he'd come with a distinct sense of contempt for the town that had ostracized Emma, Buckhorn had managed to charm him as well. The relaxed air, the openness, the sense of being where you belonged, fed something in his soul. The idea of settling here teased at him. "Your grandfather own a lot of land?"

Her sigh held a wealth of melancholy. "He does, but soon he'll have to sell a major portion of it, including this spot, which is one reason I brought you here. I don't know how much longer I'll get to enjoy it.''

"Is he selling to developers?"

"He doesn't want to. But he needs the money, so…'' She shrugged.

A variety of emotions clamored for attention. Damon hated that Ceily would lose something important to her, but at the same time his mind already churned with the possibilities. It would be an insult to the land to clutter it with shopping centers or parking lots, but a few cozy cabins spaced out along the creek…well, it'd be lovely. And lucrative.

He couldn't think about purchasing the land without thinking about Ceily as well. She was in her mid-thirties, single, which prompted another question. "Okay, so why isn't a warm, sexy woman like you married?''

Her cheeks dimpled with a smile. "I suppose I have high standards, and all the best men were taken.''

"And those standards are…?''

"Mmm. Let's see.'' Somehow, her hand on his chest just happened to be over his left nipple. If she stroked him one more time, he was going to have to jump into the icy creek on his own volition. "He'd need to be caring, like Sawyer Hudson.''

A dark cloud intruded on his contentment. "Case Hudson's father?''

"Yep. Sawyer is a local doctor and everyone in these parts loves him. He's almost perfect, but I'd want someone to be bold and vigilant too, like his brother, Morgan. He's the sheriff.''

Damon saw a definite pattern beginning. "For crying out—"

"And gentle like his brother Jordan, handy like Gabe…"

"Enough." Damon rolled her beneath him. In a growl, he said, "I think you're teasing me again."

She laughed up at him, proving him right. "Maybe. But I've always been a *little* in love with each of them." Her gaze moved over his mouth and she added gently, "No one else ever quite measures up."

Damon's eyebrows lifted. "By God, that sounds like a challenge."

She looped her arms around his neck. "Does it?"

Damon had the feeling she knew exactly what she was doing. Never in his life had he felt the need to compete for a woman, and he wasn't about to start the barbaric ritual now. Despite those assurances to himself, he tangled his hand in her hair, tipped her mouth up to his and said, "I don't want to hear you say their names again."

"But—"

He kissed her, not just a kiss, but full-body contact, heartbeat to heartbeat, and long minutes later when he felt her thigh slide up along the outside of his, he lifted his head. Her lips were wet, her eyes smoky.

Satisfied, Damon pried himself away from her and stood. "Now," he said, while trying to subtly readjust himself, "about that dip in the creek…"

CHAPTER ELEVEN

EMMA GAVE UP TRYING to get away from Casey. Oh, if she flat out told him to release her, he would. But then he'd wonder at her overreaction, especially in light of what they'd just shared. She didn't want to give away more than necessary.

She settled back against him—a most comfortable place to be—and made her tone as unaffected as possible. Despite her wariness in discussing her problems with him, she felt mellow and sated and emotionally full.

She kissed his chest and asked, "Why do you want to know?"

"I want to know everything about you. When we were younger I was so busy trying to resist you, I never thought to ask some important questions." He patted her behind. "It took all my willpower and concentration to say no."

She smiled.

Casey relaxed his hold to stroke her back. "I always assumed that your dad mistreated you. Did you know that?"

A logical assumption, she supposed, but mostly untrue. "No, my dad never physically hurt me."

"Okay, not physically." He'd caught her small clarification and asked for one of his own. "But he did hurt you, didn't he, by not putting you first, as all parents should?''

Perhaps, Emma was thinking, she should tell him some of it. It would help to show the broad contrasts in their lives and make him understand why she couldn't stay in Buckhorn. It wouldn't be easy for him to understand because Casey had always known love, always had security. Could he even comprehend what her life had been like?

But she'd taken too long to answer him. He turned to his side so that Emma faced him. With a tenderness that felt *almost* like love, he tipped up her chin and kissed her nose. ''Trust me, Em.''

''I do. I was just trying to figure out how to say it, where to begin.''

''Your mother is a drunk?''

''For as far back as I can remember. All our holidays and special occasions were tainted because she'd drink too much, and once she started, she'd keep drinking for days, and then need more days to recover.'' Somehow, telling Casey about her darkest secrets wasn't as bad as she'd anticipated. He held her, warm and strong, and it made it so much easier. ''She got to where she didn't need a reason to drink. She'd just decide to and the times between episodes narrowed until she was drinking almost as often as not.'' Emma took comfort in the steady thumping of his heart and admitted, ''She's not a nice drunk.''

Casey's eyes were steady on her face, not giving her a chance to retreat emotionally or hold anything back. ''She got violent?''

''Sometimes.'' That was so awful to admit, Emma immediately tried to explain. ''Her judgment was off when she drank. She'd take everything wrong, no matter what you said or what you did. And she'd get furious.''

Casey muttered a low curse and gathered her closer.

''It's all right.'' Emma gave him one truth that she'd learned long ago. ''Being hit wasn't the worst part of it.''

''No?'' He drew a shuddering breath, and his voice sounded raw. ''What was the worst part?''

She shrugged. ''Being afraid. Not knowing when it would happen, not knowing what to expect or when. I hated walking on eggshells, always being so uncertain.''

She'd never talked about her mother with anyone, and now she found there were things about her mother's illness that she wanted to say. ''You know what? It was strange, but I got to where I could figure out when she'd drink just from the anticipation in her voice. Or her tone. Something about her mannerisms. I could even talk to her on the phone and I'd hear it and…I didn't want to go home.''

Breathing too hard, Casey kissed her temple, her ear. She felt his grim resolve to hear it all, so she continued.

''It might have been a week or a month. It might have been only a few days. But I knew if she started to drink, she'd get drunk.'' Emma sighed and turned onto her back to stare up at the roof. ''Those were the nights I'd stay out.''

''So she couldn't touch you?''

''That, and because she's so…ugly when she's

drunk. Mean and nasty and hateful. She made me feel ugly, too.''

"Oh, Em." He squeezed her tight.

"By the morning, she'd be in a near stupor and much easier to deal with. When she'd finally sober up, she'd be sorry. Really, really sorry. And she'd be sick for days.''

"Jesus." He gave a long, disgusted sigh.

She shrugged as if it didn't really matter—when really it mattered too much. It always had. "Dad tried to run interference—he really did. But he's always worked two jobs and he…'' Emma squeezed her eyes shut. "He loves her. He'd tell her not to drink, threaten to leave her. And once he even refused to buy her any alcohol. But…that didn't stop her either." Emma hated remembering that night. It still had the power to make her stomach pitch in fear.

She shrugged, shaking off the sensations of old. "Dad loves her too much to ever really enforce any consequences.''

"Hey." Casey's big hand opened on the side of her face. "You deserve love too, you know.''

"I know." God, her voice sounded far too small. She hated that, hated her pathetic childish weakness when it came to this one topic. She'd grown strong through the years, but it seemed she'd never outgrown her childhood hurt. "That's why being with the Devaughns was so great. They do love me. Damon and I are close. I had a…a normal life with them and it was wonderful.''

Only they weren't her real family, just good people. They'd felt sorry for her at first, but that pity had turned to love. She knew it, felt it whenever she was around them. And she loved them in return.

"That's why Damon came with you?"

"He worries," she admitted. "I told him I'd be fine, but he didn't want me to be alone. He hadn't counted on you though." She turned her head toward him and had to smile. He was rumpled from their lovemaking, a little sweaty, his eyes still smoldering. And, for the moment, all hers.

"Damon knew about you, of course. I told him how I'd come to your house that night and he naturally had questions. I was prepared to see you again, Casey, but neither of us expected you to..."

Casey cupped her breast. "Reclaim you?"

"Casey Hudson, there's no way you can reclaim something you never had and never wanted in the first place."

His long fingers continued to caress her, shaping her breast in his palm, gently, easily, as if he now had the right. And she supposed he did.

"I was young too, Emma. I didn't know what I wanted until it was too late. I thought I had to stick to my grand plans and—"

"And I wasn't part of those plans. How could I be? I understand all that, Casey. And I'm so proud of you."

He wasn't looking at her, but rather at her breast. Now he leaned forward and briefly suckled her nipple, making her close her eyes on a moan. She was still sensitive from their recent lovemaking and just that easily her body softened for him again.

He released her only to blow a warm breath over her damp flesh. "I want a chance with you, Emma."

His eyes shifted to hers and the moment their gazes collided, she felt pinned in place. "I want you to give us a chance while you're here."

Oh God, that hurt, to even think of something permanent with Casey. She spoke the words aloud, not just for his benefit, but for her own so she didn't start reaching for things she couldn't have. "I have a life in Chicago."

Casey nodded. "I used to think I wanted a life in Cincinnati. But the more entrenched I've gotten there, the more I've realized that I hate the job with my grandfather, am sick of the damn commute and resent my time away from my home." He stared down at her with a thoughtful frown. "Haven't you ever felt that way?"

"No. There were things about Buckhorn that I missed." She tugged on his chest hair and teased, "You, of course. And the water, the air and the…freedom. But you have tons of friends here, and family who love you. I don't. You can't know what it's like to be the outsider, for your own mother to despise you and for your father to care more about her than anything else, including what she does to you. You can't—"

Casey sat up and swung his legs over the side of the bed. Startled, Emma visually traced the long line of his back down to his buttocks. Her throat felt thick.

He turned back to her as suddenly again, his expression devoid of emotion. "You know about my mother, Emma?"

She nodded. Most everyone in Buckhorn knew that Sawyer wasn't really Casey's father. Casey's mother got caught cheating and Sawyer started divorce proceedings. When she birthed Casey, she planned to adopt him out. Instead, Sawyer had been at the hospital with her because she had no one else, and once he held Casey, he'd immediately claimed him as his own. After some nasty gossip—spread mostly by Casey's mother—she took off. No one had heard from her since. But Sawyer, along with Morgan, Jordan and Gabe, had raised Casey, and there wasn't a soul who knew them who would question that Casey had been well loved.

"I looked her up once." His eyes lit with cynicism. "Bet you didn't know that."

"No." Emma, too, sat up and tugged the sheet over her lap.

"Not one of my better ideas. I don't know what I expected, but she wanted nothing to do with me. She was pretty damn plain about that." He rubbed a hand over his face. "I haven't told anyone else, not even Dad."

"I won't ever say a word." Stupid woman, Emma thought, then added out loud, "She doesn't deserve you, Casey."

His smile now was chagrined. "Like your parents don't deserve you? It's true. You're a beautiful person and pretty damn special. I hope you know that."

Such a lavish compliment made her blush.

"I wasn't looking for pity, though, any more than you were. I only told you because I wanted you to see that we do have some similarities."

Emma laughed. "Right."

"We both love Mustangs."

She gave him that one.

"And we both love the water." Casey bent and

kissed her throat. "And sex." He nuzzled her breast. "I'd say that's enough to build on."

"You're the only person I know who'd think so, which just goes to prove how extraordinary you are."

That had him raising his head and frowning. "I'm just me, Emma, prone to making lots of mistakes. Taking the job with my stepgrandfather was one of them, though now I'm not quite sure how the hell to get out of it."

"You don't think he'd understand?"

Casey grunted. "I don't know. He's made me the damn heir apparent, and while I hate the job, I'm rather fond of him. I don't want to disappoint him."

"What is it you want to do?"

"Something here. Something simple. Like you— which is another similarity—I want to have my own small business rather than help run a gigantic organization."

Prodding him, she said, "Like…?"

He laughed. "I don't know for sure, nosy. But I'm thinking maybe I'd try being an accountant and financial planner. I already have a BBA in accounting and an MBA in accounting and taxation. I could get a CFP certification…" He finally noticed the comical confusion on Emma's face and drew to a halt. "Sorry. A lot of mumbo jumbo, huh?"

She couldn't hold back her grin. "Since the closest I got to a college was driving past in my car, and the idea of crunching numbers makes my brain throb, yeah. But I take it you're already qualified?"

He laughed. "For the most part. And I *do* enjoy crunching numbers, especially if I can help people plan better. You know, a lot of folks around here are selling land and not getting what they should. Some of the older people are retiring without enough to live on." He shook his head. "As I said, I'm still thinking on it. And thinking right now, with you sitting there looking like that, isn't easy."

Emma grinned, and hiked the sheet a little higher. "Better?"

"Hey now, I didn't mean you should…"

Emma swatted at him when he reached for the sheet and they both laughed. "Okay," she said when he retreated again, albeit with a big grin, "so that's one mistake you've made. And not even really a mistake because it sounds to me like you've already got it figured out. You know what you want to do—you're just dragging your heels about doing it. I say go for it. What have you got to lose?"

"A great job? Financial security?"

She snorted. "You'll be an overnight success."

He stared at her intently, then suddenly sounding too serious again, he said, "You know your faith in me is downright scary. Always has been."

Her faith was well deserved, but he didn't look open to hearing that.

He put his hand on her thigh and squeezed. "I'm not perfect, honey, and I don't even want to be. I've made more mistakes than I can count." His hand slid higher, under the sheet and up to the inside of her thigh. "But losing you was the worst of the lot."

He kept saying things like that, confusing her so much.

"The night you left me—you and your mother had been fighting?"

"I didn't leave you." Good God, where did he get these notions? "I left Buckhorn."

Casey just waited.

Her calm now shot to hell, Emma said, "Yes." But then she shook her head, trying to pick and choose her words. "Not really fighting, but she was drunk and Dad couldn't reason with her and things just got out of control…" *Boy, was that an understatement.* "I didn't want to stay for that anymore. I decided it was past time to go."

"If your dad hadn't had the stroke, you wouldn't have come back." He made it a statement rather than a question.

"No." This was the hard part, where she had to be really careful. "I'd talked to them a few times, but nothing had changed. They knew how to reach me, and though Dad called every so often, like on my birthday and holidays, Mom only called four times, and two of those times she was drunk."

Casey lowered them both to lie on the mattress. His hands held her face still for the soft press of his mouth to her forehead, chin and cheeks. "Don't let them continue to influence your life."

"I don't!"

"When you avoid Buckhorn because of them?" Put that way, she had no more denials to offer. "You're here now, and who knows for how long? Your dad may need you for months, maybe longer. He might never fully recover. Is your mother capable of taking care of him, considering she has a drinking problem?"

Surely that wouldn't be the case. She hadn't even

had the opportunity to consider such an eventuality. Things were happening too fast...

"Give us a chance, Emma. That's all I'm asking. Quit shutting me out and let's see how it goes." He moved against her and added, "Do you think you can do that?"

From breasts to thighs, his hard, naked body covered her. She could feel his erection against her belly, his warm, fast breath. Pushing all probable consequences aside, she reached for him. "Yes."

THEY'D FALLEN ASLEEP. Exhausted, Emma slept like the dead and woke with Casey propped on an elbow beside her, smiling. B.B. was splayed over their legs.

"He snuck in about a half hour ago."

Emma stretched up to peer at the dog. As if he felt her awareness, he rolled to his back and looked at her upside down. Casey chuckled and reached down to scratch his throat.

"I can see this might turn tricky. Maybe I should get another cot and set it up at the other end of the porch."

"Wouldn't work," Emma informed him. "He'd still crawl up here. He's too used to sleeping with me."

"He got dirt and leaves in the bed, but at least he's dry. And he didn't complain at having me here."

"He likes you." Emma stroked Casey's shoulder. "I like you, too."

"Yeah?" His slow smile warmed her heart. "Well, I'll have to remember this combination, huh?"

"What combination?"

"Great sex and a little rest."

Laughing, Emma stretched and said, ''The sex was incredible, and I did need the rest.'' She peeked at him. ''But do you think you can add food in there somewhere?''

''Whatever it takes to keep you happy.''

If this was a dream, Emma thought, she didn't want to wake up. Casey was so attentive, constantly touching her, kissing her. Sharing details of her mother's sickness hadn't been nearly as painful as she'd feared, because Casey had shared some of himself in return. And best of all, he had no complaints about her dog. Every other man she'd dated had resented B.B.'s interference—which had made them very dispensable. But not Casey. Rather than scold the dog, he'd made room for him and even given him affectionate pats. But then when had Casey ever been like other guys?

After they got dressed, she finally got a tour of the little run-down cabin. It needed some repairs, no doubt about that, but it was still quaint, boasting a stone fireplace currently blackened from use, a minuscule bathroom—which she made use of—and a tiny kitchenette that even had running water. Other than the bathroom being sectioned off, it was all one open room.

Casey showed her where he'd like to erect a gazebo, where he'd clear an area for a picnic table and perhaps a shelter. The charm of the cabin would definitely be the seclusion and the surrounding nature. Casey promised to bring her there often, and Emma already looked forward to the return.

A few minutes later, after Casey insisted on covering her in sunscreen with excruciating, and exciting, attention to detail, they took the boat out again in search of food. First, Casey pulled in to the boat dock with the intention of getting hot dogs and chips. He changed his mind when, seconds after they'd docked, Lois and Kristin, along with a contingent of friends, converged on him. They'd docked their own boat and had been in the process of restocking their drinks and snacks.

It wasn't unusual to run into people on the lake. As Casey had told Damon, people used their boats almost as much as their cars. But to see the two women together...well, that boggled Emma's mind. Her luck couldn't be that bad. She caught Casey's apologetic shrug, prompting her to ask, "They're friends?"

"Everyone knows everyone else around here, babe, you know that."

"But...they both want you!"

That made him laugh, and shake his head at her. "I told you I work with Kristin, and Lois is—or rather was—a friend."

Apparently, he was still annoyed with Lois for her sniping remarks at the hospital. Emma tried to ignore both women as they sent her baleful looks while moving in on Casey. It wasn't easy. They wore tiny bikinis, gorgeous tans, and they were all too ready to play touchy-feely with Casey.

Because of the men who'd accompanied Lois and Kristin, Emma was grateful that she'd put her cover-up back on. They were being nice enough about it, only barely looking, but judging by their curious attention, she assumed Lois had already clued them in to her identity.

Casually polite, Casey spoke with the women while

gassing up the boat. Two of the men, dressed only in snug trunks, walked around the dock to Emma's side. B.B. gave a low growl of warning, alerting Casey to their approach.

One of the young men knelt down, which brought him closer to eye level with Emma. He grinned at her with what looked to be real pleasure. "Emma, I'd heard you were back. It's good to see you again."

Her dark glasses shielded her eyes and gave her a false sense of privacy. "Thanks. I'm sorry...do I know you?"

Chagrin added color to his already tanned face. "You don't remember me?"

"Should I?"

He ribbed his friend and they both laughed. "Naw, I guess not. It was a long time ago."

His friend added, "And you have lost some hair."

They laughed, and the first man held out his hand. "Gary Wilham."

The name jogged her memory, causing Emma to look closer. True, he had a bit of a receding hairline, but he was still quite handsome. And still built like a linebacker... "I remember now. You played football for the school."

"That'd be me."

"Sorry about that. I'm not real good with faces anymore." She and Gary had had a short-lived... thing. She wouldn't call him a boyfriend, and they hadn't officially dated. But if he expected her to be embarrassed, he'd be disappointed.

He kept the handshake brief and merely polite, surprising her. "So." He gave her the once-over. "You look terrific. How've you been?"

Relaxing, Emma said, "Good. And yourself?"

"Real good. You in town for long?"

"A few weeks maybe." Or months. She just didn't know yet.

"That's great." He glanced at Casey, then back to her with casual interest. "Catching up with old friends?" At her nod, he said, "Perfect. We're all going waterskiing. Want to join us? It'll give you a chance to get reacquainted with everyone."

Emma barely had her mouth open to make her excuses when Casey started the boat's powerful motor, making conversation more difficult. The men backed up. Emma turned and saw that Casey, too, wore his glasses—and a very false smile.

"Sorry, Gary. We've already got plans. Maybe some other time?" And he put the boat in reverse before Gary could offer any alternatives.

A little stunned at their hasty retreat, Emma waved to the men bidding her a fast farewell. Once they were several yards out in the lake, she said, "That was rather abrupt."

"He was about to ask you out. As to that, if he finds out where you're staying, he'll probably call."

Suffering faint disappointment at Casey's attitude, Emma raised an eyebrow. "You mean he'll expect to jump back into…old times."

Though his glasses hid his eyes, there was no mistaking Casey's annoyance. "No, damn it. I meant he and every other guy who looks at you will notice what an attractive woman you are and hope to get closer. Reacquainting himself is just an excuse."

"Oh." Emma felt small for projecting her own thoughts onto him. "Sorry."

"As to that, I'd appreciate it if you'd quit putting words into my mouth, okay?"

To give him his due, she winced theatrically. "Okay, I'll try."

"And while we're on the subject, I'd like us to come to an understanding."

That he was heading back toward Morgan's dock didn't escape her notice. "Two questions. One, is our day at the lake over?"

He stared straight ahead. "You're starting to look a little pink, despite the sunscreen. I think you've had enough sun, but I thought we'd head back to the house to eat. If Honey doesn't have anything ready, then we'll grab a bite at Ceily's."

Just hearing Ceily's name made her stomach clench. She swallowed hard, prayed Honey had dinner going, and nodded. "Question two, what understanding?"

His mouth flattened before he huffed out a long breath. In rapid order, he slowed the boat and reached for her hand, then pulled her up and into his side. Still looking severe, he drew her close for a brief kiss. "I have to get back to work tomorrow, but I'll cut my hours short and be home by five all week. That'll give us most of the evening to be together."

Amazed at the plans he made, at the way he wanted to adjust his routine to suit her, Emma could only stare at him.

"I have no right to ask you this," he went on, "but I was hoping you'd spend all your free time with me—and only me."

"My free time?"

He glanced ahead as another boat going at breakneck speed came around the bend. "Yeah. I realize you'll need to be with your father a lot, and I'm willing to do that with you too, whenever I'm around. But I...damn it, Em, I don't want you going out with other guys." He'd sounded belligerent, but just as quickly went tender with a self-conscious laugh. "I swear, it'd make me nuts."

It would take her time to get used to Casey wanting her. "I'd like that."

"Making me nuts?"

She laughed. "No, spending more time with you. But you're right that I need to see my dad often. It's why I'm here, after all. And since it looks like I'll be here awhile, I might need to drive back home to get more clothes..."

"We'll get it all worked out."

We. She really liked the sound of that. But would Casey still feel the same when he found out the truth of why she'd left? He'd asked her to tell him the whole truth, but through lies of omission, she'd denied him that. He'd also asked her to trust him, yet how could she? She knew Casey, knew what a good person he was. He'd been very understanding so far, but he wouldn't be able to understand everything she'd done.

When she'd only planned to be in town for a week or so, she'd thought she might be able to avoid confronting past transgressions. If she needed to stay a month or more, the chances of being haunted by her past increased.

Yet what else could she do?

She'd start by simply enjoying what time she could have with him. And she'd face demons as they arose, not a second before. If it all fell apart in the end…well, it was no more than she'd ever expected.

Probably no more than she deserved.

In the meantime, she'd take what she could—and wait for it all to come crashing down.

CHAPTER TWELVE

BY THE TIME Casey walked her to the motel-room door, it was past midnight. Exhaustion pulled at him, but he hated for the day to end. It had been a unique pleasure, watching Emma interact with his family. She'd helped Honey with dinner, fallen naturally into the routine of serving the kids, and when Gabe showed up with Elizabeth, she'd spent over an hour discussing car motors with him.

Casey knew everyone was curious about her, but they'd also enjoyed her company. Emma was very easy to be with, in a hundred different ways. Maybe if he brought her around them more often, she'd realize what he already knew—that she fit into his life with ease.

Emma turned at the door to smile at him, and Casey had to kiss her again. And once he kissed her, he wanted so much more. Making love to her this afternoon had been deeply satisfying...but not nearly enough. He wanted her again, right now. If she hadn't looked so weary, he might have invited himself in.

He consoled himself with the fact that she'd agreed to see him every day. He had no doubt that at least part of their time together would be spent in bed.

After a full day in the sun and water, and after the rambunctious attention from all the kids, B.B. was tired as well. While Casey feasted on Emma's sweet mouth, the dog collapsed in a heap at their feet.

Though he told himself merely to kiss her goodnight, Casey couldn't resist taking a little more. He flattened his hands on the door at either side of her head, angled his hips in, and relished the feel of her soft, accommodating body flush against his. Emma clung to his neck, taking his tongue, giving him her own. They both groaned at about the same time.

"You're hard again," she whispered against his mouth with what sounded like awe.

"And you're so damn soft," he growled, rubbing his nose against her cheek, her throat, her chin.

She stared into his eyes, slowly licked her lips, then offered, "If you'd like to—"

The door opened behind her.

With a yelp, Emma, who'd been leaning on the door with Casey's full weight against her, lost her balance and fell inward. Because his hands had been flat on the door, Casey couldn't stop himself from falling in too. He tried to brace himself, but his feet got tangled over the dog.

Damon said, "What the hell!" just before the three of them landed hard on the floor in a welter of arms and legs. Damon cursed again, Emma gave an *umph* as she got squashed, and Casey quickly tried to lever himself off her. But B.B. had been jerked awake with a start and found it all great fun. He jumped on Casey's back and knocked him flat against Emma again.

Everyone froze.

Into the silence, Damon, who was on the bottom of the heap, murmured dryly, "Well. My first ménage à trois, but somehow I never figured I'd be on the bottom.''

Emma started snickering, while it was Casey's turn to curse.

''I'm being quite crushed,'' Damon added. ''So, Emma, doll, if you wouldn't mind…?''

''I'm trying,'' she claimed around her giggles. She realized her legs were open to Casey, cradling him. ''But Casey—''

Flustered, Casey again felt B.B.'s paws on his back, then a wet tongue—the dog's—drag over the back of his neck. ''No, B.B., *down.*''

The dog retreated, but stayed close, bouncing here and there, ready to leap in again if anyone looked willing. Casey shoved himself into a sitting position then assisted Emma off of Damon.

Damon, the idiot, just lay there, his hairy legs sprawled out, wearing no more than his underwear. ''I'm flattened.''

Casey wouldn't mind flattening him. But Emma laughed and poked him in the abdomen. ''Get up, you big faker. You're not hurt.''

He did, but he groaned and groused in the process.

Casey eyed him. ''Do you live in your damn drawers?''

''I was ready for bed, I'll have you know, because unlike the two of you, I returned at a respectable hour.''

''Yeah?'' Emma grinned. ''And when was that?''

''About twenty minutes ago,'' he admitted with a smile. ''And I expected to find you in bed.''

''I just bet you did,'' Casey grumbled.

''But,'' Damon said, dragging out the word, ''you

stayed out rather late. So I was listening for you and worrying, as any self-respecting, pseudo–big brother would. When I heard the muted noise at the door, but no one came in, I got curious—and found myself sexually compromised.''

Emma apparently thought the guy was hilarious, given how she laughed. That earned her a tender smile from Damon, leaving Casey to feel like a damn outsider. He didn't like it, not at all. But he supposed he'd have to work on tolerating Damon, given Emma seemed so fond of him.

And he had called himself a big brother to her.

It dawned on them all at once that they were seated on the floor. Almost as one they stood, both men assisting Emma.

''Your nose is pink.'' Damon flicked her cheek with a finger. ''Too much time frolicking in the sun?''

''We were on the lake a good part of the day. And it was wonderful. I can't wait to show it to you.''

''I look forward to it. I've already explored a bit of the countryside—and you're right, doll, it's spectacular.''

Emma brushed herself off, then allowed Casey to draw her into his side. Around Damon, more than anyone else, he felt the constant need to display possessiveness.

''So who gave you the tour, Devaughn?''

Damon went very still while clapping his gaze on Emma. He replied to Casey, but it was Emma who held all his attention. ''A friend of yours, actually. Ceily Brown.''

Emma gave a tiny jerk. ''You were with Ceily?''

He rubbed the back of his neck. ''Yes. I met her

while having lunch. I thought she was a waitress and didn't realize she was the owner of the place until we'd already been flirting back and forth a bit and things were…in progress.''

Startled, Casey asked, ''Ceily was flirting with *you?*''

''So?''

Uncomfortable with the idea, Casey shrugged. ''So she doesn't…that is, she normally…''

''I know.'' Damon grinned. ''She's discriminating. She told me so.''

Emma suddenly turned to Casey. ''Well, I suppose we should call it a night.'' She attempted to usher him—inconspicuously—toward the door.

Casey refused to budge. ''What's wrong?''

''Nothing.'' Her smile didn't touch her eyes. ''It's just that it's way past my bedtime and it has been a busy day. I'm ready to drop.''

B.B. agreed with that and headed for the bed. Casey decided he'd pressed her enough for one day. He'd made enormous headway already. ''All right.'' He went to the door, but brought Emma with him.

Damon didn't move, he just crossed his arms and watched them. In his underwear. Casey really didn't like him much at all.

''I'll see you tomorrow when I get home. Will you have your cell phone on you so I can find you?''

''Yes. I should be done visiting the hospital by then, but I'll need to think about a run back home.''

Damon asked, ''We're leaving already?''

Casey scowled at him, but Emma said over her shoulder, ''I'll explain in a minute.'' Then to Casey, she said a firm, ''Good night.''

He smiled. Then he laughed. His timid little Emma was long gone, and in her place was a woman more exciting than he'd ever known. "Good night, sweetheart." He bent and kissed her, but kept it quick and light with Damon looking on. "Sweet dreams."

EMMA SHUT THE DOOR behind Casey. She apparently heard Damon approaching, because she pretended to faint, falling back against him. "Oh Lord, what a day," she said.

Damon caught her under her arms and laughed. "Made your knees weak, did he?" Seeing her so happy made him happy too. From the second he'd gotten a good look at her, he could see she positively glowed, and not just from too much sunshine. Casey had a startling effect on her, and that told him all he needed to know.

Groaning, Emma straightened, but went to the bed to flop down. "It's too incredible." She stared at Damon in what he could only call wonder. "He wants to see me."

Damon pretended to gasp as he followed her over to the bed. "No! He wants to see a gorgeous, sexy woman? How strange. What do you suppose is wrong with that man?"

Fighting a smile, Emma smacked at him. "It's more complicated than that, and well you know it. And he doesn't just want to see me a little. For as long as I'm here, he asked that we be exclusive."

"He's a possessive ape. I picked up on that right off."

"He is *not* an ape."

Damon noted she didn't challenge the possessive part.

"And Damon, we might be here a lot longer than
we'd first planned. Or at least, I'll be. That's what I
meant about making a run home. I'll probably need
more clothes. But there's no reason for you to stay."

Damon could think of several reasons to hang
around, and first and foremost was his astounding reaction to a certain small-business proprietor. Then
there was the stretch of land Ceily's grandfather was
supposedly going to sell. And his own dissatisfaction
with his life...

Emma spent several minutes explaining her father's
condition to him, and Damon, as usual, did his best
to be a good listener. He had such wonderful, caring
parents himself, he couldn't imagine the emptiness
she had to feel, knowing hers cared so little for her.
Yet, she still suffered with her own sense of responsibility toward them. It was another mark of Emma's
generous spirit, and one of the reasons she was so
easy to love.

"What are you going to do?"

Propping her elbows on her knees, Emma buried
her face in her hands. "I don't know," she wailed
with only slightly exaggerated frustration. "I want to
be with him. God, to be truthful, I still have feelings
for him."

He'd assumed that much all along, of course, which
was one reason he'd insisted on accompanying her on
this trip. Emma didn't love easily, but when she spoke
of Casey, the love she felt for him was more than
apparent. "And how does he feel?"

She shook her head and straightened. "At first, it

was almost like he thought he'd been slighted…
because he hadn't gotten to…uh…''

''Make love to you?'' Yeah, Damon could see that.
Hudson might consider her the one that got away.
He'd been controlling things, keeping Emma at arm's
length—right where he wanted her, not too close but
within reach. Then suddenly she wasn't around at all
and he'd likely floundered with mixed feelings. Far
as Damon was concerned, it served him right.

But the way Emma avoided his gaze when she nodded, Damon wondered if the sex issue had already
been seen to. It would explain her glow and the heat
he'd witnessed in Hudson's eyes. He almost grinned.
''I take it once isn't enough?''

She punched him in the arm. ''You know me too
well.''

''I was talking about him, actually but, yeah, I
know you too well. And there's no reason to blush.
If you're happy I'm happy.''

Absently, she began to stroke B.B., and the big dog
gleefully dozed off. Emma was good with her hands
and she loved touching. If you sat by her, you could
expect to get as many pets as the dog. She made a
perfect massage therapist—and she'd make an even
better lover.

''I know getting involved with him, even temporarily, is beyond stupid.'' She winced. ''When I leave,
it's going to make it so much harder. But I just can't
resist grabbing this opportunity.''

Watching her closely, Damon asked, ''So who says
it has to be temporary?''

She blinked at him, laughed a little nervously. ''Because it's just sex.''

"Did *he* say as much?"

With an uncertain look, she shook her head. "No."

Damon squeezed her knee. "Then I think you need to stop making assumptions and give the guy a chance. If he just wanted sex, seems to me his little co-worker Kristin was more than willing."

She thought about that, then nodded. "True."

"And you definitely need to shake off that dark cloud. You're in Buckhorn two days and already you're reverting to that silly girl I first met."

"I wasn't silly."

He grunted. "You had no clue who or what you were. You kept trying to fade into the background, to disappear completely, which was very silly because a woman like you is always noticed."

Her eyebrow lifted this time. "A woman like me?"

"Smart, sexy, warm and sincere. Men have built-in homing devices for women like you. You can't be in the vicinity without males perking up—and I don't just mean their attention." He bobbed his eyebrows so she wouldn't misunderstand. "You're around, and men know it."

That had her laughing. "You are so absurd sometimes."

"No more absurd than you. Forget the past, doll. Forget the girl you used to be and the boy you always thought he was. Just take it day by day and see what happens. If Casey Hudson possesses even half the sterling qualities you always attributed to him, I'll be shocked if he doesn't fall madly in love with you." In fact, Damon thought the poor guy was already halfway there. He looked at Emma as if he wanted to eat her up, and he didn't even try to hide it.

"Now—" Damon stood to stare down at her

"—it's time to hit the sack. I'm seeing Ceily again tomorrow."

"You are?"

"Indeed. She's a charming little minx, I'll say that for her."

"If you say that *to* her, she's liable to clobber you."

Damon grinned. "I can handle her, don't worry. But she suggested I be ready early, and I'm beginning to realize that, around here, that means crawling out of bed before the sun comes up."

Emma gave him a long look, no doubt wondering how involved he planned to get with Ceily. He could understand her surprise. Hell, he was still reeling himself. Of all the women in Buckhorn, she was probably the last woman he should be spending extra time with, all things considered.

But as usual, Emma didn't pry except to ask, "So you're going to be staying too?"

He sauntered toward his own room, but when he reached the doorway, he looked back at her with a smile. "The infamous Casey Hudson sees me as competition, despite my assurances to the contrary, and I'm finding that amuses me a lot. So, yes, doll, I'm staying. In fact, wild horses couldn't drag me away." Damon couldn't wait to see how the town's golden boy worked this one out.

In the meantime, he'd be working on buying some land—and seducing Miss Ceily. Things looked promising.

And here he'd feared Buckhorn, Kentucky, might be boring. It was anything but.

MORGAN STOOD at the grill, turning burgers, rolling wieners and brats, and seasoning pork ribs. As the official cook for the day, he'd opted for a wide variety to please all the family who'd turned out for the impromptu get-together. All around him, the kids were playing and the animals were running about. Up on the porch, he could hear the wives chatting and laughing. Life was good.

He glanced over to where Casey and Emma sat beneath a tall elm tree, practically glued together. It was just like old times, except that two of Gabe's fair-haired daughters were with them, watching as Emma taught them how to weave clover buds together for ankle bracelets. The girls loved them, and when Casey made a larger one and placed it on Emma's head like a tiara, they giggled.

Sawyer walked up to him. It was his day off so he wore jeans and a tan T-shirt. "Out of the ten days she's been in town, this is the fifth time Case has had her over for dinner."

Morgan raised an eyebrow. "I knew they were getting tight. But that's sounding pretty serious considering he doesn't usually bring his dates around that often."

"Hell, the days he hasn't brought her here, he's spent with her somewhere else. Everyone in town and on the lake has noticed, which I think might have been his intent. I've never seen him chase a woman like this."

Shrugging, Morgan said, "Usually they're chasing him." He expertly flipped a burger, then stepped back as flames shot upward from the grease. "Misty told me that the gossip among the young ladies is getting

kinda nasty. With Emma around, they're all out of
the running, and apparently they're not too happy
about that.''

''What kind of gossip?''

''Oh, that Case feels sorry for her. That he's using
her. That she's using him.'' He shrugged. ''Typical
catty stuff. Misty was fit to be tied when she got
home.''

Sawyer smiled. ''I take it she straightened them
out?''

''That she did. But stop grinning, cuz your wife
was right there with her and just as adamant about
stopping rumors.''

''You're on fire,'' Sawyer told him, then waited
while Morgan retrieved a slightly charred hot dog and
moved it to another part of the grill. ''You know
Honey dotes on him. If Emma makes him happy, then
she's all for it.''

''She does appear to keep him smiling.''

''True. And if she's around, he's by her. Or watching her. Or watching that no one else is watching her.
It's bound to cause talk.''

Grinning, Morgan said, ''Reminds me a bit of me
back in my day.''

''Reminds me a bit of any guy in love.''

Nodding thoughtfully, Morgan said, ''Yep. That's
about it, I suppose.''

Jordan strolled up with three frosty colas, one already opened and half gone, the other two for his
brothers. Gabe followed along behind him. ''What
has you two over here gossiping like old women?''

Shoeless and in a sleeveless shirt, Gabe leaned

against a tree. "We could see your frowns from the porch."

Accepting his drink and taking a healthy swig, Morgan nodded toward Casey. "Think he's in love with her?"

Gabe snorted. "That's what has you all puckered up? Well, let me set you straight—yes. He loves her."

Jordan used his wrist to wipe the sweat from his forehead. "Hear, hear."

Sawyer said, "Hmm."

"You like her, don't you?" Gabe glanced over toward Emma in time to see his youngest daughter climb into her lap and give her a hug. "Because I like her fine. She's a pretty little thing. And she's damn good with cars. Almost as good as me." He shook his head. "Gotta admire that."

"She's damn good at neck rubs too."

Gabe squinted his eyes. "Do tell."

Grinning, Sawyer said, "Morgan helped Howard dig out a tree stump. And by 'helped,' I mean he did it himself. He seems to forget he's an old man now."

"I'm in my prime, damn it." Then Morgan raised his nose. "Just ask Misty."

"Yeah, well, prime or not, he pulled more than a few muscles showing off. Emma happened to be here when he started complaining and within minutes she had him blissfully relaxed and half-asleep."

Gabe stared over toward Emma. "Wonder if I could get her to show me how to do that."

"She showed Misty."

"And Honey." The two brothers grinned at each other.

"Needing help with Elizabeth, are you?" Jordan taunted Gabe.

"Naw, but the woman is insatiable. I figured if I could get her to sleep a little more…"

After everyone stopped chuckling, Gabe said, "You're fretting for nothing. Because if I know women—and you know I do—Emma is as much stung as Casey is. It's almost embarrassing, the way she looks at him."

Jordan elbowed him. "Like anything could embarrass you."

"Hey, I'm an old married man, completely oblivious to lecherous looks." He grinned sinfully as he said it.

"We all like her," Morgan pointed out. "But isn't she here only temporarily?"

Sawyer nodded. "That's what concerns me the most. Yet she's the only female Casey has brought around the family this much."

"That oughta tell ya something, I suppose."

Morgan rolled his eyes at Gabe. "Yeah, it tells us that he loves his adoring uncles and values our approval."

"She has mine."

"Mine too."

Sawyer shifted, running a hand through his hair and sighing. "She left here because she didn't like it, or because she had some mighty big personal problems. Whichever, I'd hate to see Case hurt."

"He's smart. He knows what he's doing." Jordan clapped Sawyer on the shoulder. "Of course, a man's finer senses tend to warp a little when he's getting his heart drop-kicked by love."

Morgan nodded. "It's cruel the way a woman can lay you low."

Gabe said, "As long as she's laying me...." The others lifted their drinks in a salute.

Just then, Misty yelled from the porch, "You got the meat ready for me?"

Morgan smiled while the others quickly turned their backs to snicker. "Always, sweetheart, always." Then under his breath to his brothers, "She can't get enough."

Jordan raised his eyebrows. "Yeah, well, your wieners are on fire."

Morgan hurried to move things around on the grill. Gabe glanced up, saw that Elizabeth had joined Misty in setting out side dishes, and yelled, "You ladies getting...*hungry?*"

She smiled back with a look guaranteed to knock the wind out of him. "Ravenous."

Gabe clutched his heart. "Oh God, I asked for that, didn't I?"

Sawyer called to Honey, "Be right there, sweetie." And he blew her a kiss.

Jordan said, "I like Emma's friend, Damon."

"He loosened right up, didn't he? When I first met him, he was such a starched shirt. Nice enough fellow, but so...precise." Gabe said that as though it were a dirty word. "Put my teeth on edge. Never thought he'd be the type to hang around here this long."

"He's still starched, but it's just his way." Sawyer nudged his brothers as he saw Damon come around the corner of the house, led by Amber and looking far from starched at the moment. Judging by his bare wet feet and wind-tossed hair, Amber had taken him along the bank hunting crawfish and minnows again—a pastime Damon apparently enjoyed, much to everyone's surprise.

Amber had insisted on his first such adventure, but since then he'd gone along willingly and they'd fallen into a routine of sorts. Whenever Damon came to the house with Emma, Ceily usually accompanied them, and they'd go to the shore with Amber and any of the other kids who were in attendance that day.

Sawyer also noted that Damon had his pant legs rolled up, his shirt mostly unbuttoned, and Ceily tucked close at his side. "Ceily sure likes him."

"Likes him?" Gabe grunted. "She's totally besotted, always sashaying around in front of him, batting her eyelashes and whispering in his ear. And he enjoys it—you can tell that much."

"Good for her." Morgan pointed a metal spatula at Gabe. "'Bout time she found someone."

"Hey, I got no problem with her being happy," Gabe groused. "It's just that I always figured it'd be someone local. I hope like hell he doesn't break her heart, or worse, talk her into moving away."

"Moving away would be worse than a broken heart?"

Jordan scowled at Morgan, then asked Gabe, "Why would she move away?"

"I understand he's a well-respected architect back in Chicago." Sawyer shrugged. "Can't see him giving that up."

The men all looked up as a scuffle started between Garrett and Shohn, who were a little too close in age at nine and ten not to compete at every turn. Adam, only slightly more subdued at thirteen, stood to the side shaking his head until Honey raced into the yard and said quite loudly, "That's enough!"

The boys broke apart, grumbled a little and, with Honey prodding them along, headed to the porch.

Morgan shoved a platter of hamburgers at Jordan. "Here, carry this. We better feed the savages before they turn on each other."

Laughing, Jordan took the food. "I can remember Mom saying the same thing back in the old days."

Gabe snickered. "Yeah, but usually she was saying it about Morgan."

"Last time I talked to her, she said she'd be coming to town soon. Seems Casey spoke with her yesterday when she called. He mentioned Emma a few dozen times, and now she's more than a little curious."

Sawyer laughed at Jordan. "Nosy is a better description." The brothers all agreed with fond smiles. "I expect she'll be here before too long."

Their mother lived in Florida with Gabe's father, Brett. After losing her first husband and divorcing her second, she'd found true love. It made them all glad to see her so happy, and since she got to Kentucky at least six times a year, they didn't mind that Brett had talked her into retiring in Florida.

Later, after the food had been devoured and everyone, except the kids, was feeling a little more lethargic, Sawyer seated himself near Emma. She and Casey were on the porch swing, their hands entwined, talking quietly.

"So, Emma, I hear you've been busy."

Her brown eyes warmed with a gentle smile. "Dr.

Wagner has scheduled several massages, and so has Ms. Potter. They're both very nice."

"I hear the wives have been in line as well."

She laughed. "Morgan too. But I enjoy it."

Sawyer nodded, having noticed that she was indeed a "toucher." If Emma was near someone, she touched—rubbing a shoulder, hugging the kids, stroking the animals. She was very sweet, very open and friendly, and Sawyer liked her, yet still he worried. "How's your dad doing? Any word on when he might get to come home?"

"They tell me it's still too early to know for sure." Her expression grew troubled. "He had shown so much improvement at first, but this past week there's been no real progress. If anything, he seems more sluggish. They're adjusting his medicine, trying different therapy, but…I just don't know."

Casey kissed her knuckles. "I went with her last night, and she saw him again this morning. He's still talking, not real clear though."

Emma looked away. "He was crying this morning."

Damn. Sawyer glanced at his son and shared his look of concern. But he was a doctor, not just a father, not just a friend, so he put on his best professional face and tried to reassure her. "That's not uncommon with stroke victims. I'm sure the doctor explained it to you?"

She nodded. "Emotional lability, he called it. He said depression is common. I just wish there was some way I could help."

"Hey." Casey put his arm around her. "You're

helping a lot. You're here with him. You've rear-ranged your life. I'd say that's plenty.''

"I'd say so too," Sawyer agreed.

She didn't look convinced. "He's lost so much weight."

That wasn't uncommon either. Sawyer asked, "They still have him strictly on IVs?"

"Yes. They're not sure yet how well he can swallow. I forget what they called it…"

"Dysphagia." Sawyer knew one side of Dell's mouth was weak, so they likely had to be careful of the increased risk of choking. "Emma, it hasn't been that long. Try not to worry too much, okay? He's talking, and he recognizes you. That's pretty mirac-ulous and a good indicator right there." He patted her hand, but he didn't promise her that everything would be all right, because he really didn't know.

A loud beeping broke the quiet, which had Morgan and Damon both reaching for their cell phones, then coming up with frowns because it wasn't theirs. Honey pointed to Emma's purse. "I think it's yours, Emma."

She came off the swing in a rush and fairly dived off the porch to reach the bag she'd left at the picnic table in the yard. Casey stood to watch her, Sawyer beside him. It was the first call that she'd gotten to Sawyer's knowledge and, naturally, it alarmed every-one.

After Emma said a tentative "Hello" into the phone, her lips parted and she slowly sank onto the bench seat at the wooden table.

Casey bounded off the porch steps in one leap and was at her side before she could say, a bit shakily, "I see.'' He stood behind her and put his hands on her shoulders. Damon sat down beside her. Everyone waited, alert.

Avoiding all the curious gazes, Emma said, ''I'm so sorry, Mrs. Reider. Yes, of course, I'll be right there.'' She closed her eyes. ''Yes, I understand.''

Mrs. Reider? Sawyer thought. He'd presumed it was the hospital, that her father had taken a turn for the worse. But instead…

Emma pushed the disconnect button on her small phone, tucked it back into her purse and stood. ''I'm sorry to rush off, but I need to go.'' At the word *go*, B.B. hurried to her side.

''I'll take you,'' Casey said.

She looked horrified by that idea. ''No—''

''I'll take you.'' He wasn't about to be dissuaded, and Sawyer understood why.

Emma looked to Damon, received his nod, and finally agreed. ''All right. I suppose you might as well.''

He might as well? What the hell did that mean? Sawyer wondered. And why did she look as if the rug had just been pulled out from under her?

Reaching for his shoes and socks, Damon said, ''I'm coming too.''

''But…'' With everyone watching the poor girl, she gave up. ''Fine. But I do need to hurry.''

Honey worried her bottom lip. ''Your father is okay?''

''Yes—that is, he hasn't had a change.'' She patted the dog, but her smile was a bit self-conscious. ''That wasn't the hospital.''

Ceily sidled up next to Damon and asked, "Then what's wrong?"

Emma hesitated a long moment before admitting, "It's my mother. She's at the motel where Damon and I are staying. She wants to see me."

Damon looked far too grim, leading everyone else to wonder why a visit from her mother mattered so much. "You ride with Casey," he told her. "I'll drive your car."

Since that was how they'd arrived, she merely nodded.

"Emma?" At Sawyer's query, she turned. For a young woman who'd been smiling moments before, she now looked far too world-weary. It didn't make sense, and filled Sawyer with compassion. "Let us know if there's any way we can help." And he thought to add, "With anything."

She stared at him a long minute before nodding. "Thank you. Dinner was wonderful. Everything was wonderful. I... Thank you."

And then Casey led her away. Sawyer watched until she and B.B. had gotten into his son's car before turning to his wife. Honey hugged his waist. "I'm worried about him, Sawyer."

Sawyer knew exactly how she felt, but he repeated his brothers' reassurances, saying, "He knows what he's doing."

Honey nodded. "I know. But does he know what *she's* doing?"

CHAPTER THIRTEEN

THE PAST WEEK and a half had been wonderful, but now it was over. All the secrets, all the pretending. She didn't know how or why her mother had sought her out, but she knew their reunion was bound to be difficult—just as her relationship with her mother had always been.

"I don't want you to come up with me."

Casey didn't bother to glance at her. "Why?" His hands were tight on the steering wheel, his expression dark.

What could she tell him? That she didn't want everything to end with such an unpleasant scene? "She's my mother and I'll deal with her."

"You think I would interfere?"

"No, but..." She drew a breath and gave him part of the truth. "It embarrasses me."

Casey pulled the Mustang into the gravel lot. He put it in Park, started to say something to Emma, but then stalled as his gaze lit on something. "I'd say it's too late to worry about that."

Emma followed his line of vision and saw her mother. She was half slumped at one of the picnic tables, holding her head with one hand, a lit cigarette with the other.

Emma's heart got caught in her throat. Regardless

of anything else, of the past and the hurt feelings and the dread, she was seeing her mother again for the first time in years. And she was choking on her hurt.

Her mother's brown hair, like Emma's only shorter, was caught back in a blunt ponytail. She wore dark jeans, a short-sleeved white blouse and sandals. Seeing her like that, she could have been anyone's mother. She could have been a regular mother.

She could have been a mother who cared.

Emma knew better though. Ignoring Casey, she opened her door and stepped out. Her mother noticed her then and stood. She swayed, unsteady on her feet, and had to prop herself with one hand on the tabletop.

Of course, she was drunk, just as Emma had expected.

"Where the hell have you been, young lady?"

The slurred words were flung at Emma without regard for the quietness of the lot or the spectators close at hand. Somewhere in the back of her awareness, Emma knew Damon and Ceily had arrived. She knew Casey was close behind her, leading the dog. She knew Mrs. Reider and a few guests watched from the motel-lobby door.

It's not me, Emma told herself. *What she does, who she is, doesn't project on me.* She knew it, had lived with that truism all these years past, but still her shame bit so deep she could barely see as she made her way to the picnic table.

Her voice sounded wooden as she said, "Mother."

"Don't you call me that," her mother sneered, and Emma saw that familiar ugliness in her brown eyes, in the dark shadows beneath, in the pasty sheen of her skin and the spittle at the side of her mouth.

"All right." Sick dread churned in her belly. She knew her mother would humiliate them both. What she didn't know was how to deal with it. As a child, she'd begged, hidden, run away. But she wasn't a child any longer, and her mother was now her responsibility.

"A daughter would have come to see me by now. You know I'm all alone. You know I needed you. But no. You're too good for that, aren't you?"

"You have my number," Emma reasoned. "You could have—" No. Emma stopped herself. She knew from long experience that there was no reasoning with her mother in this condition. It would be a waste of breath to even try, and would only prolong the uncomfortable confrontation. "Why don't I take you home?"

"Oh no, missy. I don't damn well wanna go home now." She took an unsteady step forward. "I want you to take me to the store, and then we're goin' to the hospital to see Dell."

Emma's heart nearly stopped. Take her mother to the hospital? Not while she was drunk. "I won't buy you alcohol." She didn't bother to reply to her other request.

Her mother looked stunned at that direct refusal. Her eyes widened, her mouth moved. Finally, she yelled, "You just get me there and I'll buy it myself. I'm worried about your father and sick at heart and God knows my only daughter doesn't give a damn." As she spoke, she tottered around the table toward Emma. Ashes fell from the cigarette, which was now little more than a butt.

Just as she'd done so many times in the past, Emma

braced herself, emotionally, physically. Even so, she had a hard time staying upright when her mother's free hand knotted in the front of her shirt and she stumbled into her. "You'll take me," she hissed, her breath tainted with the sickly sweet scent of booze and the thickness of smoke, "or I'll tell everyone what you did."

A layer of ice fell over Emma's heart. It was now or never, and she simply couldn't take it anymore. "What *you* did, you mean."

The shock at her defiance only lasted a moment. "No one will believe that." Her mother laughed, and tugged harder on Emma's shirt. "You, with your damn reputation. You don't have any friends around here. Even that nosy sheriff was always checking up on you. He'll believe whatever I tell him. And you'll go to jail—"

"I'll take my chances."

Enraged, her mother drew back to strike Emma, but her hand was still in the air when Casey pulled Emma back and into his side. Her mother's swing, which would have left a bruise, given the force she'd put behind it, missed the mark by over a foot and threw her off balance. She turned a half circle and landed hard on her hands and knees in the rough gravel. Her cigarette fell to the side, still smoldering.

Emma had automatically reached out to break her fall, but she pulled back. She could feel Casey breathing hard beside her, knew he was disgusted and shocked at the scene—a scene he'd probably never witnessed in his entire life, but that was all too familiar to Emma.

B.B. went berserk, barking and snarling, and

Emma, feeling numb, caught his collar to restrain him. She whispered to the dog, soothing him while staring down at the woman who'd birthed her. She waited to see what else she'd do. Her mother could be so unpredictable at times like this.

But she stayed there, her head drooping forward while she gathered herself. Eight years had apparently taken a toll on her too. When she twisted around to look up at Casey, it was with confusion and anger. "Who the hell are you?"

Thinking to protect Casey, Emma said, "He's the sheriff's nephew."

"And," Casey added, his own anger barely under control, "I heard everything you just said."

Slumping back on her behind, slack-jawed, her mother stared from Casey to Emma and back again. Slowly, her lips curled and she pointed at Emma. "Did she tell you what she did? Do you know?" She hunted for her cigarette, picking it up and using it to light another that she fetched from her pocket. She took a long draw, looking at Casey through a stream of smoke. "She tried to burn down the diner."

Emma closed her eyes on a wave of stark pain. She'd held a faint, ridiculous hope that her mother wouldn't take it that far, that she'd only been blustering. That somehow she'd care just a little about her only child.

Barely aware of Casey taking her hand, Emma sorted through her hurt, pushing aside what she could to deal with the situation at hand. Mrs. Reider didn't deserve this scene. She ran a respectable business in a dry county. Having a drunken argument in her lot would probably go down as one of the worst things imaginable.

Slowly, Ceily came up to Emma's other side. She wasn't looking at Mrs. Clark, but at Emma. "You're the one who called and reported the fire that night, aren't you?"

It was so damn difficult, but Emma forced herself to face Ceily. When she spoke, she was pleased that she sounded strong, despite her suffocating guilt. "Yes. I'm sorry. It's all very complicated and I didn't mean for any of it to happen..."

"Your mother started it?"

Amazed that Ceily had come to that conclusion without further explanation, it took Emma a few moments to finally nod.

"That's a lie!"

Ceily ignored her mother's loud denials, speaking only to Emma. "Why? I barely knew your folks."

It would help, Emma thought, if she had a good solid reason to give, some explanation that would make sense. She didn't have one. "You weren't a target, Ceily. The diner is just the first place she came to where she thought she might find either a drink or money to go get a drink."

Ceily shook her head. "But I don't serve alcohol, and I cash out every night before closing up."

"I know. And if she'd been thinking straight, she might have realized it too. But alcoholism...it's a sickness and when you want to drink, nothing else matters..."

Her mother began protesting again, her every word scraping along Emma's nerves until she wanted to cover her ears, run away again. But she no longer had that luxury. She had to deal with this. "She broke in, and things went from bad to worse... I didn't know what to do."

Damon stepped up and looped his arms around Ceily so that she leaned into his chest. It dawned on Emma that Ceily didn't look accusatory as much as curious. Of course, her reaction would have been vastly different eight years ago, the night it had all happened. The shock, the anger and hurt had likely been blunted by time.

"How did you find her?" Ominous overtones clouded Casey's softly asked question.

Emma winced. Because the fire and Emma's visit to his house had happened on the same night, Casey had a right to his suspicions. "Earlier that day, I'd convinced my father that we had to stand together, to get her help. It was the worst argument we'd ever had. She was furious, and...I couldn't take it. So I went out. But I always cut through town coming home." Here Emma gave an apologetic shrug to Casey. "Your uncle had warned me that he'd run me into juvenile if he caught me out so late again."

"He worried about you," Casey told her with a frown.

"I know." Emma smiled, though she felt very sad that only a stranger had worried, and only because it had been his job. "I came home behind the businesses, as usual, because that way I was less likely to be seen from the street. I found my mom coming out of the back of the diner, and I realized what she was doing. Then I smelled the smoke."

"She'd already started the fire?"

"Not on purpose. It was her cigarette, but..."

Wanting to finish it, Emma rushed through the rest of her words. "The fire was small at first and I tried to put it out. But she kept fighting me, wanting us to leave before we got caught."

"Dear God," Casey muttered, and he glared at her mother, who gave him a mutinous look back.

Emma spoke to Ceily. "I knew I couldn't do that. I told her she needed help and that I thought you might let her just pay for the damages if she agreed to go to the hospital for treatment. But she didn't believe me and when I finally got the call through, she…"

"She threatened to blame you?" Casey asked.

Emma turned to him. "Yes. She said she'd tell everyone that I did it. I was…scared. I wasn't sure who might believe her."

"No one would have."

"You might not have blamed me, but—"

"I wouldn't have either," Ceily said.

Damon leaned around to look at Ceily, slowly smiled at her, then gave her a tight squeeze.

Emma couldn't believe they were being so nice. In so many ways, it might have been easier for her if they'd hated her and what she'd done. "I'm doubly sorry then, because I was a coward. The fire was already out of control. I made the call anonymously, went home with my mother and…things got out of control."

"That's how you got beat up that night, isn't it?"

He sounded furious and pained and…hurt? Because she'd been hurt? She glanced at him, but didn't reply because she didn't want to involve him further. "I made plans to leave."

"You came to me."

She shook her head at Casey. He couldn't seem to get beyond that, and she was beginning to think he put far too much emphasis on that one small fact. "With the intent of only staying one night."

"If I'd known that, you never would have gotten away."

"I had to leave. If I'd stayed until morning when everyone started talking about the fire, well, someone would have figured it out. Then I wouldn't have had the option to go."

He scowled, crossing his arms over his chest and appearing very displeased with her assessment. "How the hell did you get out of town so fast anyway?"

Knowing he wouldn't like the answer, Emma winced again. "I hitchhiked once I got on the main road. Neither Morgan nor his deputy saw me, of course, because they were still busy with the fire. With a lift from two different drivers, I got as far as Cincinnati, then caught a bus the rest of the way into Chicago."

Ceily stared at her in horror. "Dear God. You could have been—"

Damon interrupted Ceily. "But she wasn't. Instead, she found my family and she's now a part of us." He reached out and touched Emma's chin. "And she's suffered a lot over this."

"Damon, don't make excuses for me, please. I should have told the truth long ago. I should never have lied in the first place."

Damon, still holding Ceily at his side, addressed both her and Casey. "It took her a few years to get her life in order. After that, she thought about coming home and confessing all—she honestly did. But her father would beg her not to, and with so much time already passed…''

Emma laced her hands together. "I couldn't bear the thought of my mother going to jail."

Her mother shoved to her feet, outraged by the mere suggestion. "No one is taking me anywhere! I didn't do anything. It was you."

Casey shared a look with Ceily, then received her nod. "No, you won't be going to jail. It was an accident, not arson. And even with the breaking and entering, well, it's been eight years. I'm sure the limitations on that have run out."

Emma was agog, her mother smug.

"But…won't the insurance company want their money back? I know there was a lot of internal damage."

Her mother grabbed Emma's arm in a viselike grip. "Shut your mouth, girl."

Casey stepped forward, but Emma stopped him with one look. She had avoided dealing with her mother for too long. When she'd been a child, she'd had an excuse. But as an adult… It was past time she took responsibility for what she'd done, and forced her mother to do the same. "You're going to get help."

"I don't need any help."

For the very first time in over a decade, Emma felt nothing. Not hurt, not need, not even compassion. "It's possible that legal charges might not apply anymore. But there are other things to consider now. Daddy's stroke is serious. If and when he's able to leave the hospital, I'm taking him with me."

"Whaddya mean, 'with you'? He's my husband!''

"And he's my father. He needs someone who can take care of him, not the other way around. He'll need therapy and supervision and encouragement. You're not capable of any of that, so until you get help, get sober, and stay that way, you're on your own.''

The fingers on her arm grew slack, then fell away. "You can't do that." Her whisper was rough with shock.

"Of course I can." Emma swept her arm around the lot. "Thanks to this visit, there are more than enough people who now know that you're incapable of taking care of yourself, much less someone in need of medical attention.''

Damon, Ceily and Casey, along with Mrs. Reider and a half-dozen motel guests made up an audience. Two cars had stopped on the road, having also noticed the spectacle unfolding in the motel lot. In a town as quiet as Buckhorn, it didn't take too much to get the gossip going. She wouldn't be surprised to see the whole thing written up as front-page news in the Buckhorn press tomorrow morning. In the past, that would have devastated her, leaving her curled up with shame. Now, she just wanted things resolved.

"Emma?" Ceily smiled at her. "There was never an insurance claim made. I didn't want my premium to go up, and I'd been planning to renovate anyway, after Granddad turned the place over to me completely. So I used the money I'd saved and fixed it up with a lot of help from Gabe and volunteers from the town.''

Nodding, Emma said, "I'll reimburse you."

"No, you won't." She turned to Mrs. Clark, who

stared blankly down at her feet. "But your mother can pay me one fourth of the money I spent, since there were some things I wouldn't have replaced if it hadn't been for the smoke and fire damage."

"I don't have that kind of money," her mother whispered, looking very lost and confused by it all.

Ceily shrugged. "So get a job. I'll let you make installments."

Her mother's look of horror was almost comical.

"They have a drug abuse and alcohol treatment facility at the hospital," Casey offered, speaking to Emma, not her mother. "We can take her there now." He looked as though he wanted to rid himself of her as fast as possible.

Sadly, Emma now felt the same. Years ago, she'd have done anything to help forge a normal relationship with her mother. She'd begged her, during her sober moments, to get professional assistance. But whenever she was sober, her mother always thought she had control over her drinking. She'd agree to quit, and mean it. But her resolve never lasted and Emma had long since grown tired of her mother's refusal to admit to her sickness.

However, what Emma had said was true—this time she would take her father away if her mother didn't get help. "Mother? What do you say? And before you agree or disagree, you should know I'm either taking you to the rehab facility, or leaving you here. Those are your options. If you stay, I have no doubt Mrs. Reider will give the sheriff a call, and you may well end up with court-ordered rehab anyway."

Her mother stared at her, looking much like a lost child. She was breathing hard, fighting tears, but

Emma also knew an excess of emotion came with alcoholism, so she stiffened her spine and waited. Finally her mother nodded, surprising Emma, giving her hope.

"Listen, doll," Damon said quietly, "she's nothing to you now."

Emma knew that wasn't true. A parent was a parent, good or bad, and she would make the best of this. She turned to Damon and offered him a slight smile. "She's my mother." Then she added with a sigh, "And she got us kicked out of here. Mrs. Reider wants us gone as soon as possible."

Damon groaned. Her mother looked away. Mrs. Reider hovered in the doorway, appearing impatient—and curious since she couldn't hear what was being said.

Ceily and Casey spoke at the same time. "You can stay with me." Then they both blinked, and Casey added, "Ceily, honey, you're more than welcome to Damon. By all means, take him. But Emma and B.B. are coming with me."

Ceily hugged onto Damon's arm. "Works for me."

Emma looked at Damon, who grinned and shrugged. "Sounds like it's all planned out, doll. That is, if you're okay with it."

Casey waited with a sort of tense anticipation they could all feel. But Emma had few choices, and she wanted to be with him. So she nodded. "Thank you."

EMMA WAS SO QUIET Casey couldn't help but worry. Getting her mother to the rehab center had taken far longer, and been more complicated, than he'd anticipated. But throughout it all, Emma had kept her shoulders squared, her emotions in check, and her determination at the fore. She was amazing.

After her mother had willingly signed herself in, Emma made plans to bring some of her things to her. She'd be at the facility for an undetermined length of time, but she'd start dependency counseling right away. Because leaving meant she'd likely lose her husband, she looked resigned to staying. She'd also asked, in a small, fretful voice, if Emma would visit her.

Emma had agreed, but there'd been no embrace between mother and daughter. For her part, Emma appeared motivated by pity for the woman who'd never been a real mother to her. She'd also been so distant, not touching Casey, hardly even looking at him. Casey didn't push her. She needed some private time to come to grips with everything, but under the circumstances that was tough to find. Mrs. Reider's was the only motel in Buckhorn, and any other lodging would put her too far away from her father. Though he wished this were easier on her, Casey was glad she'd be with him, even if it wasn't by choice.

It hadn't taken them long to pack her and Damon's things. While Emma stood by without saying a word, Casey had called ahead to his father to fill him in on the situation. Emma's silence hurt him, because he knew she was hurting. Dealing with her troubles was hard enough, but broadcasting those troubles to the whole town would be nearly impossible to take. Casey feared he'd just lost a lot of headway in convincing her to stay in Buckhorn.

Damon and Ceily were there when Casey pulled down the long driveway. Damon had used the excuse of bringing Emma's car to her, but Casey suspected he also wanted to see her settled. Thankfully, the kids were out of sight, but Sawyer and Morgan, Misty and Honey all waited for them. When Casey stopped the car at the side of the house, his relatives moseyed inside to give them some privacy.

Casey turned off the engine. "You okay?"

It took her a moment, then she said, "It's strange, but mostly what I feel is relief that it's all out in the open. At least now I can deal with it."

Casey nodded. He could understand that. "It'll be okay."

Her laugh sounded a little watery, too close to tears, before she rubbed her face and drew herself together. "Looks like I'll be spending even more time visiting hospitals, huh?"

Jaw locked, Casey reached for her hand. "You owe her nothing." Far as he could tell, all her mother had ever given her was grief.

"I owe this town. I owe Ceily."

"You didn't cause the damage."

"No, but I kept quiet about it. That's a crime in itself."

"You were a kid, damn it."

She raised a hand. "No, Casey. Don't coddle me by making excuses. I'm fine really. Just... exhausted."

Christ, she'd been seventeen years old, burdened with more than most adults could handle. He had no intention of letting her wallow in guilt, but he let it go for now. "We'll go to bed early," he promised her.

That had her laughing again. "*We* will, huh? Does

it bother you that your whole family will know I'm with you?''

Casey gave her a long look before stepping out of the car. B.B. jumped out with him and followed him as he circled the hood. Emma had already opened her own door before they could reach her. With Casey and Emma both carrying bags, they started toward the garage apartment. B.B., now very familiar with the Hudson household, followed along.

Finally Casey couldn't keep his mouth shut, and he said, ''It's been a long day for me too, Emma. Don't piss me off.''

She abruptly stopped, but since he and the dog didn't, she hurried to catch up. ''What are you talking about?''

He'd kept his turbulent emotions tamped down all day—not an easy feat when he damn well loved her and it killed him to see her hurt. Now it felt as if he was imploding, his anger shot up so fast. Dropping her luggage, he whirled on her and gripped her shoulders. ''I damn well want everyone to know you're with me, Emma. The whole town, preferably.''

Eyes huge, she asked, ''There's going to be so much talk. You have to know that Lois and Kristin and probably a dozen of their friends are saying awful things—''

Casey gave her a tiny shake. ''I remember being behind the garage with you eight years ago. You were tempting me, driving me nuts, and you even accused me of being a virgin, then had the nerve to act surprised when I didn't deny it.''

Her eyes softened. ''Any other guy would have, especially since it wasn't true.''

"I told you then that I didn't give a damn what people thought. So, why should I care now, especially when the alternative is not having you nearby? I'm not going to suffer a single moment of discomfort over it."

Some of the tension eased out of her and she gave him a genuine smile.

He pulled her into his chest. "Hell, Emma. I'm so proud of you. Don't you know that?"

"Proud?"

"God, yes." He held her back a little. "Look at you, at everything you've dealt with, all that you've accomplished. I don't know another person who could have handled that scene at Mrs. Reider's with so much grace and dignity."

"It was all I could do not to cry."

"Even if you had, so what? You sure had reason enough. But you didn't. You didn't cave in either. You've taken every rotten thing that's been thrown at you and somehow…" His own eyes grew damp, making him curse, making his voice hoarse. "Somehow you've stayed one of the most beautiful people I've ever known."

Breathing a little shakily, Emma moved back into his embrace. They stood there like that a long time, until Emma finally whispered, "Thank you."

Laughing with exasperation at the way she was forever thanking him for one thing or another, Casey locked his arms around her and hugged her right off her feet. "Baby, it wouldn't matter to me if your mother had burned down three buildings. She's not you." He nuzzled her ear. "I'm just glad that you're home."

Once he said it, Casey was afraid she'd again deny that Buckhorn was her home, so he kissed her, making any rebuttals impossible. It wasn't a lusty kiss, though he was more than ready for one of those too. Instead, he tried to kiss her with all the love he felt. It had been a day of emotional upheavals. She wasn't ready to have him start an overflow of declarations. Soon, he'd let her know how he felt. For now, touching her, holding her, having her close, would be enough.

"Come on," he said against her mouth. "We'll get you settled so you can get some rest."

Emma didn't argue, but when they turned around, they saw that B.B. had run off. They located him quickly enough, on the porch with Sawyer and Shohn. Both Hudson males wore wide, satisfied smiles.

Sawyer yelled out, "He was scratching at the door. Seems he wants to come in."

Emma started to apologize, but Casey cut her off. "He can visit with you for a while if he wants."

Shohn gave a whoop. "Can he sleep with me tonight? I'll take good care of him."

Casey said, "Dad?"

"Sure." Sawyer put one hand on Shohn's shoulder. "Fine by me if Emma doesn't mind."

Emma laughed. "He likes to hog the middle of the bed."

"That's okay." Shohn hung on the dog like a long-lost friend.

"He's liable to want to find me before the night is through," Emma warned.

Sawyer rubbed the dog's ears. "If he does, I'll

walk him over to you. But you never know, so we might as well let him try it.''

Since Casey wanted Emma to himself without the dog in the middle of them, he wrapped up the discussion and hurried Emma on her way. Once they were in the garage apartment, Emma dropped her luggage. ''I can unpack tomorrow.''

Casey glanced up at her. She'd gone straight through to the bedroom and stood next to his bed, her arms at her sides, her expression watchful. ''All right.'' He smiled. ''Are you hungry?''

She shook her head, then licked her lips. ''I'd just like to take a quick shower.''

Visions of her naked, wet, teased through his mind. ''Yeah.'' He cleared his throat. ''Let me get you a towel.''

Ten minutes later, he was stretched out on the bed with his back propped against the headboard. He'd removed his shoes and socks and unbuttoned his shirt, but he was still uncomfortably hot. And uncomfortably aroused.

Yet, he knew sex wasn't what she needed right now.

He tried turning on the television, but he couldn't block the sounds of running water in the bathroom. He felt tortured. Even after the sexual excesses of the past week where they'd spent several hours a day at the cabin making love, the need he felt for her hadn't diminished. Hell, if anything, he wanted her more now than ever.

When the water stopped, that only heightened his awareness. But when Emma stepped out with her hair pinned atop her head and her sweet body wrapped only in a towel, he nearly groaned. She was home. She was with him. She was his.

In the face of so much progress in their relationship, he would be patient.

"Don't get up," she told him as she strolled toward the bed and seated herself on the side of the mattress, near his hip.

Casey stared at her, unsure what she wanted at that particular moment, unwilling to do anything that might make her ill at ease with him.

"Your apartment is fabulous." She stared at his abdomen as she spoke. "I knew Jordan used to live here, but I didn't know it was so nice."

Casey nodded absently while noticing the water droplets that clung to her shoulders. The apartment was open and spacious, located directly over the three-car garage. The kitchen, breakfast nook and living room all flowed into each other, with only the bedroom and bath private. "It suits me."

She rested one slim hand on his naked abdomen. "Will your folks expect to see us tonight?"

Casey almost choked on his indrawn breath. She had to have noticed his erection, given that his cock strained against his jeans, leaving a long ridge beneath the material. But the little tease said nothing. "No. That is, they'll understand if we wait till morning."

"They don't object to me being here?"

His dad had probably already figured out that Emma was special to him. As to that, everyone might know, since he hadn't exactly tried to keep it secret. "No, they're glad to have you here."

Using just her fingertips, she traced the line of hair

from his navel down to the waistband of his jeans, making him shudder. "Did you lock the front door?"

With Shohn used to visiting whenever he chose, and all his young cousins forever underfoot, he'd taken care of that first thing. "Yeah."

"Good." She unsnapped his jeans and slipped her soft, cool hand inside.

Casey groaned. "Emma…"

Without a single reply, she freed his erection from the restriction of his jeans. Casey shifted, then groaned again when she leaned forward and brushed her cheek against him. He put one hand on her head, racked with mixed sensations. Lust was prominent because he could feel her breath on the head of his cock. But he also felt tenderness, because this was Emma, and with every second came the realization that she was his other half, the one woman meant for him.

She made a small hungry sound, and licked him from the base of his shaft to the very tip.

His hand clenched in her hair, his control fast evaporating. "Babe, wait."

Lifting her head, her dark eyes soft and heavy, Emma said, "Mmm?"

Could a woman possibly be more appealing than Emma was at that moment? He'd never get used to the way she looked at him with so much love in her eyes.

Love? God, he hoped so.

Casey closed his eyes and struggled for a deep enough breath so he could be coherent. "Let me get out of these jeans, okay?"

"All right." She agreed readily enough, stood—and then dropped the towel.

Casey lost it.

"Ah, damn, Em." Catching her about the waist, he tumbled her down into the bed and moved over her. The touch of her naked breasts on his chest, her belly on his abdomen, had him in a frenzy of need.

"Your jeans."

"In a second." Hell, if he shucked his jeans off now, he'd be inside her in the next second. He took her mouth, long and leisurely and deep until they were both panting, then slowly worked his way down her body. Kissing wasn't enough, and he indulged in a few gentle yet hungry love bites that had her gasping and squirming under him. She smelled of his soap, and strangely enough even that enticed him. He suckled her nipples until they were tight and straining, put small kisses on her ribs, dipped his tongue in her navel...

"Casey."

Where seconds before he'd been desperate to sink into her, to feel the clasp of her body tight around his shaft, now he wanted her to be desperate. Kneeling between her thighs, he growled, "I want to taste you."

Offering a soft moan for reply, Emma braced herself, legs stiffening, hands knotted in the sheets. Smiling, Casey bent and nuzzled through the springy curls, breathed in her rich scent, and after carefully opening her with his thumbs, covered her with his mouth.

They both groaned, Emma with a sinuous twisting of her body, Casey with the need to take more and more. He moved her legs to brace her feet against his shoulders, cupped her hips in his hands, and held her still for the thrust of his tongue, the careful nipping of his teeth. He found her small, swollen clitoris and drew it gently into his mouth for the softest suckling, the demanding rasp of his tongue.

Within minutes she was ready to come, but like him, she wanted more. "Casey, wait."

Her breathless plea barely reached him with the taste and scent of her pushing him over the edge. He felt her silky thigh on his jaw, felt her heels pressing into his shoulders...

Her fingers tangled in his hair. "Casey, *wait*. I want you inside me. Please."

Breathing hard, he looked up the length of her body. Their eyes met, his glittering, hers dark and vague.

He took one last, lingering taste of her, then lunged to his feet. After hurriedly stripping off his jeans, he found a condom in the bedside drawer and rolled it on. All the while, he watched her, appreciating the sight she made sprawled in his bed, how right she looked there.

Emma came up to her elbows, but fell flat to the mattress again when he moved over her, hooked her thighs in his arms to spread her legs wide, and slid smoothly inside her body. He felt her tightening with that first stroke and pushed her legs higher so that he was deep, so damn deep. She couldn't choose the rhythm, couldn't alter the depth of his thrusts or change the angle. He was in control.

He heard her broken cry on the second stroke, and shuddered at the sharp bite of her nails on his shoulders as she tried to urge him even closer. On the third stroke, harder, deeper, he relished the start of her release. "That's it, Em. Come for me, sweetheart. Come for me."

Her body arched beautifully, her breasts shivered with the strength of her orgasm, her expression was arrested, her breath low and guttural.

Teeth clenched, muscles straining as he held himself deep, Casey joined her, and as they both went boneless, he found the strength to murmur, "You're mine, Emma. Now…and always."

To his relief, she didn't deny it.

But then Emma was already sound asleep.

CHAPTER FOURTEEN

DAMON HAD BECOME as much a regular fixture around the Hudson household as Emma. For two weeks now, he and Ceily had been almost inseparable, which meant when Damon stopped in to visit, Ceily was there too. And more often than not, their visits seemed to be at dinnertime.

It was the first time Emma could remember seeing Damon so taken with a woman. That he should be taken with Ceily was nothing short of supreme irony. But she was happy for him, and for Ceily.

Honey and Misty had grown up with an austere father, which meant their dinners had always been rather subdued events. Now they both relished the boisterous, busy meals spent with friends and family. Since they lived so close, with Morgan and Misty just up the hill, and were best friends as well as sisters, they were often together. They claimed to enjoy the extra *rational* female company in Ceily and Emma, which Emma took to mean a woman not mooning over the brothers or Casey.

Certainly, Ceily was too straightforward to moon, but Emma? She merely hid her mooning. Truth was, she couldn't go five minutes without thinking about Casey—and smiling in absolute happiness. He occupied her every waking moment. The past month spent

with him had been, well, the stuff of dreams…
because she loved Casey with all her heart.

The more time she spent with him, the more she
accepted that she'd actually fallen in love with him
as a teenager, and never really stopped. Neither time
nor distance apart had lessened the emotion one bit.

But being with him, making love to him every
night, waking with him every morning, had strength-
ened that love until she couldn't imagine how she'd
survive when she had to leave him.

Yet she knew that eventually she'd have to do just
that.

While Casey was at work, Emma visited her parents at the hospital. Her father was now much improved, and her mother was, if not pleasant, at least
sober. Dell had been thrilled to find out his wife had
willingly gone into rehab for help. As far as Emma
was concerned, that, more than anything, had helped
revive his spirit. Her mother was allowed to visit him,
and they'd talk for hours. Most of their conversations
centered around her mother's complaints, but in his
commiseration, Dell's speech had gotten much better,
as had his motor control.

Her mother was determined to be there for him. It
wasn't easy, and she had a lot of difficult times, but
she was trying. Losing her daughter hadn't done the
trick, but the possibility of losing her husband was
too much.

They were both healing and, for once, Emma
thought she might be able to be part of her own family. It would never be the ideal—it would never be
the Hudson household—but it was an improvement.

She'd spoken with them about the future, and because they both relied on her now, they were willing to adjust.

Casey had gotten home a half hour ago and, after greeting Emma with a kiss, went straight to the apartment for a shower. With Damon and Ceily visiting again, he knew they'd have dinner with the family, rather than slipping off to the cabin with sandwiches, as they often preferred.

He'd just stepped back into the kitchen, hair still damp, casual clothes now in place of his suit, when Honey announced the fried chicken was ready. Morgan stood to call in the kids, but Casey said, ''I wanted to tell you all something first.''

Into that breaking silence, Emma's phone rang. She jumped, considered ignoring it, but Casey gave her a crooked smile. ''Go ahead. This'll wait.''

A little embarrassed, she made her apologies and answered the wireless phone while stepping out of the kitchen for privacy. With so many people in for dinner, the buzz of conversation still reached her.

Her first reaction to hearing Dr. Wagner's voice was alarm. Because she visited the hospital each day to be apprised of improvements, he had never found it necessary to call her. But at his jovial greeting, she relaxed…until he announced that he'd be sending her father home in the morning.

It was the signal of the end, her last remaining excuse for lingering in Buckhorn. She'd already contacted a Chicago hospital about her father's physical therapy once he left the hospital. It was located close to her home and could provide everything he needed. She'd also made plans with a rehab facility for her mother.

Unaware of her melancholy, Dr. Wagner continued. "You can take a copy of his chart with you, but I've already faxed one to the hospital you specified. Take a day or two to get him settled, then set up routine appointments."

"Thank you, I will." Emma squeezed her eyes shut, but couldn't resist asking, "You're sure he's ready to come home?"

"He's shown marked improvement over the last week. Yes, I'd say he's ready—and anxious. Everyone tires of the hospital in a very short time. And being home with his family is a good therapy in its own way, too."

The quiet drone of conversation in the kitchen had died and Emma wondered if everyone had paused to listen to her. "Thanks, Dr. Wagner. Is there a specific time I should be there in the morning?"

They made arrangements, and while Emma made mental note of all things pertinent, her heart ached. She didn't want to go, didn't want to leave Casey. Didn't want to leave her home.

But how impossible would it be for her to tend her parents here where everyone now knew of her mother's transgressions—and her own. She had to be reasonable, not emotional. She had a thriving business, which had been neglected for almost a month. She had a life, friends, family in Chicago. All she had in Buckhorn was a reputation, and some bad history.

With an invisible vise on her heart, and a lump in her throat, she reentered the kitchen and managed to dredge up a smile. Everyone looked up from the dinner table. "My dad is getting out of the hospital tomorrow."

The expressions varied from surprise, concern, to expectation. Casey merely looked detached, and that confused her.

Emma folded her hands together over her waist. "I'm taking him, and my mother, of course, home to Chicago with me."

Sawyer tossed down his napkin. Unlike his son, he looked far from indifferent. "You're what?"

Honey's eyes were wide. "Oh, but…" She glanced at everyone else, as if seeking help.

Morgan rubbed his forehead and muttered something under his breath. Misty fretted.

But Damon, damn him, looked at Casey with one eyebrow raised. "Well?"

Casey, sighing with long-suffering forbearance, left his seat to stand beside her. "I suppose I'll be going to Chicago too."

"What?" Sawyer pushed back his chair.

Morgan snorted. "Since when?"

"You can't be serious," Honey and Misty said in unison.

Emma gaped at him. "You're not moving to Chicago!"

"Why not?" Casey shrugged, disregarding her shock. "I'd already decided that I wanted to switch jobs—which is what I was about to announce when you got your call."

Everyone started to protest at once, but Casey didn't let it stop him. He held up a hand, silencing one and all. "No, just hear me out. I enjoyed what I was doing up to a point, but now it just isn't enough." He winked at Emma. "Having Emma around helped me to realize what I really want to do."

All eyes turned to Emma, making her gulp.

"Just what is that?" Sawyer finally asked.

"Financial planning. I had thought to open something up here, but..." He shrugged again. "Looks like it'll have to be in Chicago."

Emma's mouth fell open.

Ceily pushed back her chair and joined those who were already standing, which was just about everyone. "I'm going to Chicago too."

Damon dropped his fork and leaned back in his seat. "What the hell for?"

She blinked down at him. "Why, to be with you."

"But I'm staying here."

Emma and Ceily said at the same time, "You are?"

He scowled. "Yes, I am. I like it here." He cleared his throat and, though Emma had rarely seen him this way, he looked uncertain. "I spoke to Jesse about buying his land. We're working out a deal."

Ceily's eyes narrowed. "You spoke to *my* grandfather without telling me?" And then, with her eyes popping wide, added, "He agreed to sell to *you?*"

Damon joined the ranks of those standing. "Well, how else could we keep the land around and not have some city slicker throw a damn water park up?"

"You," Ceily pointed out, "are a city slicker."

"Not anymore," he told her with satisfaction. "I was thinking along the lines of some nice tidy little rental cabins that would blend with the woods. Maybe ten or twelve of them. They'd be unobtrusive but lucrative."

Everyone seemed to be holding their breath. Ceily

crossed her arms over her chest. "If you stay here, I'm going to fall in love with you."

Very slowly, Damon smiled. "Yeah?"

She gave a brisk nod. "And when I do, I'll damn well expect you to marry me."

His look so intimate, Emma blushed, Damon pulled Ceily close and kissed her. "It's a deal."

Casey threw up his arms. "Well, since that's settled... Emma, how soon do we need to leave?"

Emma rubbed her ear, utterly befuddled. "Casey..." She looked around at his family, but none of them appeared willing to help. "You can't leave here."

"Why not?"

Logic remained just out of reach. She shook her head. "This is your home."

"It's your home too. But what the hell? We can make a home anywhere, right?"

Sawyer covered his mouth and, Emma suspected, a smile. She groped behind her for a chair. Honey rushed to scoot one beneath her before she dropped. Morgan gave her an encouraging nod.

They were all nuts. When she finally found her voice, it emerged as a squeak. "Uh, *we?*"

Eyes intent on her face, his sensual mouth tipping in a slight smile, Casey nodded. "Me and you."

"But...it's not just me." He had to understand that. "It's my mother and father and..."

"And me," Damon said. He grinned. "I'm like a brother figure, don't you know."

Casey laughed. "And I'm not just me. Hell, Emma, this lunatic crowd—" he indicated the rapt faces of his family members ''—is only a small part of the group.''

Morgan scowled at him. ''I changed your diapers, boy, so don't give me any lip.''

Sawyer choked on a laugh. ''Are you hinting that you want some privacy, Case?''

He rolled his shoulders, trying to look indifferent—and failing. ''Not particularly. I just want Emma to admit that she loves me.''

Her mouth fell open again. At this rate, she'd end up with a broken jaw.

Misty leaned over to put her arm around Emma. ''Put him out of his misery, hon. Men hate to suffer, this bunch more than most.''

Putting her head in her hands, Emma laughed, or maybe she was crying, or a little of both.

Honey wrung her hands. ''I really would hate to see Casey move away. But more than that, I'd hate to see him brokenhearted.''

They were all nuts. ''Well, of course I love him.''

Casey beamed at her. ''Way to drag out the suspense, Em. Naturally, I love you too. So, where do you want to live?''

There was a time, Emma thought while she fought her smile, when this situation would have totally disconcerted her. She'd have felt out of place, conspicuous. But now she reveled in the open love exchanged between Casey and his family. She wanted to be with all of them. She wanted to have kids who would join the others in the yard, running and playing, happy and carefree and secure in a way she'd never been able to be. They were a good family to be around—a better family to be a part of.

Tears filled her eyes and clogged her throat, making her voice thick. "I'd like to stay here."

Until Sawyer and Morgan both slumped in relief, Emma hadn't known they were so tense waiting for her answer. But to her surprise, Casey didn't seem any more relieved with staying than he had seemed worried about leaving. He walked over to her and took her hand. "Now we could use some privacy. Feel like a boat ride?"

"Yes."

"But you haven't eaten!"

Casey kissed Honey on the top of the head. "Mind if we take it with us?"

Sawyer had already turned and begun packing food into a basket. "'Course she doesn't." He grinned at his son. "Leave B.B. here since he's still playing with the kids. I'll make sure he gets fed. And while you're gone, Honey and Misty can start planning the wedding."

Casey raised an eyebrow at Emma, and Emma laughed. They were overwhelming, wonderfully so. "Thank you."

Rolling his eyes, Casey said, "You say thanks more than anyone I know."

A mere half hour later, Emma found herself in the small cabin Casey owned, naked, beneath him, and thoroughly loved. Casey continued to nibble on her lips, her ear, her chin. The day was so warm, their flesh had melded together. Casey was still inside her.

"You will marry me, won't you, Em?"

She scoffed. "Like you ever had a doubt."

Raising himself up, Casey stared at her with such a serious expression she got worried. "Doubts?

You've filled me with more doubts than any man should ever have to suffer. You left here, when I never thought you would, leaving me to doubt if I'd ever see you again. You came back more wonderful than I thought possible, making me doubt I'd even still have a chance.''

"Casey." How could he have been so silly? She'd been his for as long as she could remember.

"Damn, Emma, I love you so much it's scary."

"I love you too. I always have."

"You did a very good job of hiding it." He kissed her, sweet and gentle, then deeper until he had to tear himself away. He cupped her face, rubbed her temples with his thumbs. "I am so proud of you, Emma, but, God, it's unsettling to know you built this happy life somewhere else, and damned if you didn't constantly talk about running back to it. I kept wondering how long I could keep you here, if it'd be long enough to get you to fall in love with me again." He gave her another hard kiss and pressed his forehead to hers. "Believe me, Em, I've had doubts."

Emma squeezed him tight.

"Are you sure you're okay with staying here in Buckhorn?"

She grinned. More doubts? "Yes. I love it here. I'd just convinced myself it didn't matter because I thought I couldn't stay." Then she felt compelled to ask, "Aren't you happy to be staying here?"

"I'm happy to be with you. That's what matters most."

"But," she said, insisting on the truth, "you'd rather be here, wouldn't you?"

"Yes, I'd rather be here."

"It won't be easy, you know. Kristin and Lois have spread a lot of gossip…"

Casey grinned. "Everyone already assumes they're just jealous—and understandably."

"Because I have you?"

He laughed, squeezed her, shook his head. "No, goose. Because you're so remarkable, beautiful inside and out."

Emma lowered her gaze to his tanned shoulders. "There's my mother and father to deal with."

"And your possessive dog and dumb-ass Damon and—"

She slugged him. "Hey!"

Laughing, Casey rolled so she was atop him. "Just teasing. I like your dog just fine."

She gave him a fierce scowl. "And Damon?"

Casey pretended to consider that, until Emma tweaked his chest hair. "Okay, okay! He's a good guy. I like him, now that I've gotten used to him."

"Really?"

"He loves you, and he's in love with Ceily, so he's okay in my book." His teasing over, Casey pressed her cheek to his heart and held her there. "No family is ever perfect, Emma. We'll make do with your folks, and you'll work at putting up with mine, and we'll have each other. Everything else will work itself out."

EPILOGUE

Two Months Later

CASEY PUSHED the recently repaired cabin door open and was nearly knocked off his feet by B.B.'s greeting. With his keen ears, the dog heard Casey's approach before his car had rounded the last bend. By the time he reached the porch, B.B. was always waiting.

"Hey, boy. Where's my better half?"

B.B. woofed, accepted a few more vigorous rubs, then ran outside to chase a squirrel. He seemed to enjoy the isolated surroundings as much as Emma.

Casey listened to the sound of running water and knew Emma was in the tiny shower. Since marrying her a week ago, he'd been about as happy as a man could get.

At her insistence, they'd moved into the remote cabin after renovating it a bit. Spotlessly clean, with walls, windows and roof repaired, it made cozy temporary quarters until Damon finished directing the builders on their modest house on the lake.

To Sawyer and Honey's delight, they'd been convinced to move nearby, only a few acres away from the main house on the land the family owned. With

Misty up the hill and Emma down, Honey claimed she had the perfect female company close by.

Casey tossed his suit coat aside, pulled his tie free and loosened his collar as he heard the shower shut off, replaced with the sounds of Emma humming. Seconds later she emerged from the bathroom in a long pink T-shirt, her hair wrapped in a towel. The second she saw him, her beautiful dark eyes lit up and she came to him for a kiss.

"I didn't hear you come in," she said, going on tiptoe to hug him.

It was the type of greeting he'd never tire of. Casey took her mouth in a long, deep kiss before slipping his hands beneath the bottom of the shirt and cuddling her bottom. "Mmm…" he said. But before he carried her off, they needed to talk. "How'd it go today?"

"Actually, it was great." She stepped away to the refrigerator and poured two glasses of iced tea. In silent agreement they wandered out to the screened porch and sat in the new pair of rattan rockers bought for just that purpose. B.B. took a leap off the dock— something he'd begun doing only days after they'd moved in, then waded up on the shore, shook himself off and plopped down in the sun to dry.

"The nurse is terrific and Dad really likes her. She's firm but friendly. Even Mom is grateful to her for the help. I think she still worries about Dad, even though he's doing better."

With Sawyer's help, they'd located a home health-care aide to take over Dell's physical therapy and keep him on a healthy diet by supplying both break-fast and dinner. Her presence freed up Emma's time, a necessity since she'd opened a massage therapy salon in Buckhorn, and found herself booked solid almost every day.

Emma's mother had stayed sober since that eventful day in Mrs. Reider's parking lot, much to Emma's relief. They were both trying to get along, though Casey doubted they'd ever be close. But now they were civil, and little by little they were building a tenuous relationship. It was a start.

Casey looked at her profile then set his tea aside. "Come here," he told her, catching her hand and pulling her into his lap. "You were too far away."

She smiled up at him. "Quit stalling. Tell me how things went with your grandfather."

He winced, but ended it with a grin. "We negotiated. I agreed to stay on as a consultant for the new hires in my department, and he agreed he wouldn't ask more than four days a month from me."

"Sounds doable. And like it might appease him. I know you didn't want any hurt feelings."

"He was so set on making me his heir."

Emma curled into him. "And you tried."

There was no refuting that. But he wasn't cut out for the corporate life, not when his roots were so entrenched in Buckhorn. "I think he's refocusing on Shohn." Casey laughed. "And if I know my little brother, he'll be running the business by the time he's twenty."

"I don't doubt he could if he set his mind to it."

Shohn had been the best man at their small wedding, and he'd also danced at the reception with every female in attendance. For a ten-year-old, he was an outrageous flirt and bursting with confidence. The women doted on him, calling him cute and audacious and adorable—a chip off the old block. Shohn just grinned throughout it all.

"You'll set your business up soon?"

"Yes." Since leaving Chicago, her life had been constant turmoil. Between the issues with her parents, relocating her home and work, the wedding, she'd barely had time to relax. More than anything, Casey wanted things to settle down into a calm routine. "I'll finish up two more weeks with Granddad so my replacement can make a smooth transition. My new office ought to be ready by then and all the advertisements will have been distributed. By the time the house is built we should be all set."

Resting her head on his shoulder, Emma said, "You don't need to make promises to me, Casey. The new house, the new jobs…they're a nice start, and I'm happy about them. But I'll always be happy, no matter what, as long as I have you."

Casey turned her face up to his so he could see her beautiful dark eyes. They were filled with love, all for him. Though Emma thought his life had always been blessed, he knew he'd just been passing time without her.

His grin started slow, but spread. "You know, sweetheart, though it's usually your line, I have to say thank you."

Tilting her head, she laughed. "What are you thanking me for?"

"You came back home to me, Em. You gave me a second chance to have the only woman I want. You gave me back *me,* because without you I was only half-alive."

Her eyes were enormous, sexy, shining with love. "Casey."

"I love you so damn much. Just as you are, just as you've always been, and however you'll be in the future. You're mine. Now and forever."

Kristine Rolofson lives in Rhode Island, USA. Married and the mother of six, she began writing when two of her children were only in nappies. She also worked as a secretary, seamstress and waitress, but her passions have also been writing and travel. Known for her Western heroes, sense of humour and strong female characters, this talented author gathers readers wherever she goes.

Kristine enjoyed creating the fictional town of Beauville and the host of characters who play out their lives there. You might have met some of the characters in Kristine's earlier titles *Blame it on Cowboys* and *Blame it on Babies* published in Sensual Romance™.

BLAME IT ON TEXAS

by

Kristine Rolofson

CHAPTER ONE

"BIG NEWS," MARTHA announced into the phone. She cradled the receiver between her shoulder and her chin and hoped her daughter appreciated the effort. Kate never seemed to be overly interested in the goings-on in her hometown now that she lived in New York City, but Martha continued to keep her up with the news. Since the girl had spent more than a few hours at the drive-in with her friends when they were all growing up in Beauville, Martha knew Kate might find this worth listening to.

"Good news or bad news?" her daughter asked, sounding cautious.

"I've got the paper ready right here," Martha said. "I'll read it to you."

"Why don't you just tell me?"

Martha ignored the request. She was better at reading than telling and maybe this way Kate wouldn't ask questions her mother couldn't answer. "The former site of the Good Night Drive-

In will soon become a senior citizens' residence,'' Martha McIntosh read aloud.

"What? The drive-in's *gone?*"

"It sure is.'' And good riddance, too, Martha added silently. She'd watched the digging with more trepidation than most, but now that the concrete was poured she'd decided this was for the best. Her daughter's complete attention caught at last, Martha repeated the article's first sentence and added a few more details. The article was on the front page of the *Beauville Times,* but tucked down at the bottom, on the left, beneath the weather predictions and beside an article about the town council passing the school board's budget. "There's a nice drawing here, too. It's going to be real nice. They started construction this week and they're moving right along.''

"That's so sad,'' Kate said.

"That old place was an eyesore, honey. And we could use something nice to look at, like the Good Night Villas. I thought Gran might move into town and into one of the apartments.''

"Why?''

"Why?'' Martha echoed, running out of patience. You'd think a twenty-seven-year-old woman would understand that an elderly woman shouldn't live twenty miles outside of town. "She's almost ninety, Kate. She needs taking care of.''

"Does she want to move?"

"She's thinking about it," Martha hedged. If Gert Knepper had wanted to move off the Lazy K, she would have packed up her things and driven her truck to town. It didn't matter that she'd lost her driver's license twelve years ago or that she could have all the help she needed by picking up the telephone and asking for it, Gert did things on her own. When she decided to move, she'd appear on the doorstep with her suitcase.

"Right," Kate laughed. "I can't picture her anywhere but on the ranch."

"These apartments or condos or whatever they're called are going to be very nice. Carl said—"

"I guess I can't picture retirement 'villas' in Beauville."

Martha thought they sounded lovely, with everything new and clean and on one level. Carl Jackson was building them, on land he'd inherited from his father. Old Man Jackson had owned most everything in town once upon a time. He'd roll over in his freshly dug grave if he knew his son had become a land developer. "I'm thinking of buying one."

"Why?"

"Because I might be ready for a change." She could picture Kate frowning into her coffee cup. She'd heard the beep of the microwave a few seconds before. Kate was a caffeine addict, and these Sunday morning phone calls were usually punctuated by the sounds of Kate grinding beans, pouring coffee or reheating cups of the stuff. Always on the move, that one. Couldn't even sit still long enough to talk to her mother without reaching for some stimulation. Martha worried about her, wondered what she did for fun, wondered why she liked the city and her big important television job. Wondered if she'd find a nice man and have babies and bring them home to Texas on holidays so Martha could fuss and cuddle.

"That would be a pretty big change," she said. "What does Gran think of all of this? How is she feeling?"

"You'll see for yourself at the party. You're still coming, aren't you? They're not going to make you work on your vacation again?"

"No," Kate said, but there was some hesitation in her voice that made Martha nervous. She knew all too well how Kate's fancy New York City boss expected her to be on call. "Are you sure Gran's okay?"

"That old gal is as stubborn as ever," Martha said, wondering how on earth Gert could live out on the ranch much longer. Sometimes Martha had nightmares about her mother falling down the stairs or tripping over a cat. Gert looked tough, but at that age she had to be fragile. She should be pampered, should sell the ranch that no one in the family wanted to live on but Gert and use the money to take care of herself. ''I tell her all the time she could live like a queen here in town if she'd just sell out.''

''I'm not sure that's what she wants.''

''The Foresters left and went back to New Mexico.''

''She told me. She said she put an ad in the paper to get more help. Did she find someone?''

''She did, but I have my doubts.''

''Why?''

''Do you remember the Jones family? You went to school with some of the boys, didn't you?'' Martha didn't wait for an answer. Of course Kate remembered the Jones boys. Everyone knew that family and the trouble they'd gotten into. One of the boys was in prison. ''They were a wild group of kids.''

''What about them?''

''She hired one of them to help her out. He and his son moved in last week.''

''Which one?''

''What?'' Martha tore her gaze away from the front window. She could have sworn she saw Carl's white Cadillac pass by the house. She wondered if he would stop in and say hello, maybe take her for a drive the way he had last Sunday after church.

"Which one?" Kate sounded as if she was gritting her teeth.

"Not the oldest, but the other one. Dustin."

"Damn."

"What?"

"Nothing. Just a spill."

"Run cold water over it. Are you burned?"

"Not really. It mostly went on my robe." She laughed softly. "You'd think I'd learn not to do ten things at once."

"You and your grandmother are so much alike, always busy," Martha said. She watched as Carl put his Cadillac in reverse and guided it into a parking spot in front of her house. "I'd better get going," she added. "I've lots to do today."

"But Mother," her daughter said, "we haven't talked about Gran's birthday party."

"Later," Martha told her. "I'll call you later." With that, she hung up. He'd promised to take her to see the latest developments on the condos. He'd also promised frozen margaritas and more than a little flirtation.

Martha loved being retired.

"YOU COULD HAVE warned me," Kate said, sipping a cup of freshly brewed coffee. She pushed aside the *New York Times,* all eighty pounds of it, in order to have more room on the table. "Mom started talking about the Good Night Drive-In and all I could think of was what we were doing there with our boyfriends when we should have been watching the movies.''

Emily's Texas drawl was still as strong as ever, even through the phone. "I meant to," she said. "I was gonna mail you the newspaper, but I was afraid you'd think you were growing old and get all depressed and lose your fancy job and become one of those New York City bag ladies.''

"Very funny. Don't you think it's depressing?''

"Honey, depressing is being pregnant for the fourth time in nine years. Sex at the drive-in with Dusty Jones was a hundred years ago.''

Kate didn't want to think about sex. Or having babies. Or Dustin Jones, the one boy her parents had forbidden her to date. The one her grandmother had hired to take care of the Lazy K. "My grandmother just hired him.''

"Hired who? I mean, whom?''

"Dustin.''

"No kidding?''

"He and his son are living out on the ranch.''

"I didn't know he got married.''

"He got Lisa Gallagher pregnant that summer before college.'' The summer from heaven, Kate remembered. The summer she'd made love to Dustin Jones in the back seat of his '72 Buick. "I don't think they ever got married.''

"No, they didn't, but I'll ask George. He'll

know. I wonder what happened to Lisa. I always thought she moved to Dallas.''

"It doesn't matter," Kate lied. Of course it mattered. After all these years she damn well wanted to know what happened after she left town.

"I thought he was working for Bobby Calhoun out at the Dead Horse Ranch. But I never heard he had a boy with him."

"My mother seemed pretty sure. I can call my grandmother and find out if it's true. If she answers the phone." Gert generally disliked having to stop what she was doing to talk to ''some darn salesman.''

"I'll see you in two weeks, right? You're coming home to help blow out the candles?"

"I wouldn't miss it," Kate declared, though she wondered if she could stay the entire two weeks as she had originally promised. There was a whole team of scriptwriters for the show, but that didn't make her workload any lighter.

"What's going to happen next on *Loves of Our Lives?* Is Harley pregnant with Dan's baby or Christian's?''

Kate laughed. "You know I can't tell you."

"I'm afraid I'll have the baby and miss finding out."

"When are you due?"

"In two weeks. Right now. Yesterday."

"And?"

"Not an ache or a pain anywhere, Kate. Plan to spend some time over here, will you? You and George can gripe about progress and teenaged memories. He doesn't like the idea of his drive-in destroyed for a nursing home either. He says it makes him feel like an old man." Emily and George had dated since they were fifteen, married at twenty and become parents at twenty-two.

"At least someone understands."

"Honey, the minute we all ran out and bought VCRs, the days of the drive-in were numbered. The Good Night lasted longer than most, I think, just because Mr. Jackson never cared if it made money or not."

"I suppose. But it's still sad." She took another sip of coffee before continuing. "My mother said she's thinking of moving into one of the apartments."

"Give him the truck, Jennie, and quit teasing," Emily scolded, then apologized. "Sorry, Kate. They're little devils this morning."

"Where's George?"

"At the grocery store. He figures this is all Carl's fault."

"What is?"

"The Good Night Villas. Every single woman— over sixty, that is—figures the way to Carl's very single heart is to buy one of those apartments.

George's mother wants to put her house up for sale.''

. "I think mine does, too." Now she had to worry about her mother being taken advantage of by a real estate Romeo? "Do you think we'll be like that in thirty years?"

"Alone and running after Carl Jackson? I hope not."

"At least thirty years from now you won't be pregnant," Kate teased. "That's something."

"Come home soon, honey. We'll sit in front of the air conditioner and talk about boys, just like we used to."

I could do that, Kate wanted to say. *I could pretend I was eighteen and in love and letting a certain young cowhand unbutton my blouse while* Last of the Mohicans *played on the distant screen.*

"What's New York have that Texas doesn't?" It was the way Emily ended every phone call, and Kate usually replied by telling her friend about her latest date or Manhattan meal or Broadway show. Emily loved all of the advantages of city life, but this time Kate didn't answer the question.

"I wonder if my mother is serious about moving," Kate muttered. "She even wants my grandmother to move in there with her."

"You'll be here soon. You can find out for yourself. Hey, you can even see how Dustin Jones turned out."

I might not have a choice, Kate wanted to say. Even though I'd rather be run over by a speeding taxi and dragged down Broadway with my skirt up over my head.

"IF THAT'S MARTHA again, tell her I'm not home." Gert carried her bowl of oatmeal over to the kitchen table and sat down to eat it. The boy hurried over to the east wall and grabbed the phone off the hook.

"Hello?" A smile turned up his mouth. "Oh, hi."

"Who is it?" she asked.

"It's my dad."

Well, that was all right, Gert figured, giving Danny a nod before she turned back to her oatmeal. She should have put chocolate chips in it, the way she did for the boy. She didn't bother trying to listen to the conversation and instead looked through the stack of last week's mail for something to read. The *Beauville Times* sat there taking up room, so Gert checked through it for the obituaries before she read the headlines.

The Jackson boy was still determined to build those fancy apartments, she noted. Cattle prices had gone up, but not much. The weather was going to be good. Good and hot, she saw, but heat was the least of her worries. The heat didn't bother her much, not like that darn air-conditioning folks stuck everywhere. Give her a good fan. Now there was a healthy invention for you.

"I remember that summer in '22," she said aloud. "Now there was a heat wave," she told Danny, who had hung up the phone and approached the table. "It was so hot my daddy swore we'd all just dry up and blow to Oklahoma."

The boy slid into the chair across from hers and smiled. He sure had a sweet smile, Gert thought. Not like his daddy at all that way, but then boys didn't always take after their fathers. Sometimes they got lucky and forged their own paths.

"Did I ever tell you I had a boy like you once?"

He nodded. "Yes, ma'am."

"Always in trouble, Hank was." Gert figured he'd gotten it from his father's side of the family, of course. Back in the twenties, the Johnson boys had been hell on wheels. Her father had just about had apoplexy when she'd run off with one of them.

"Where does he live now?"

"Oh, he's been gone a long time. He could never stay in one place for too long." She tilted her head at him. "I'll bet you've never even been to a drive-in movie, have you?"

He shook his head. "I don't think so."

"You don't even know what it is. That's too bad." Gert worked on her oatmeal for a moment, then peeled a banana, broke it in half and offered a section to Danny. Another morning ritual, they shared a piece of fruit before the day really got started, before chores. Sometimes she fixed coffee mixed with heavy cream and lots of sugar for the two of them. Sometimes the boy's father would come in and pretend to complain that his eight-year-old son was too young to be drinking coffee.

"I saw some women on television the other day," Gert continued, knowing Danny liked the sound of her voice. He was a funny little guy, this boy. "They'd written a book about the 'old days,' Katie Couric said. Now they're rich and on the bestseller list and everyone's buying their book."

"Cool."

"I could use the extra money," Gert mused. "Why don't you get us some orange juice?" The boy did as he was told, as he usually did. He got stubborn about taking a shower and sometimes she could hear him yelling about it. That yelp always made Gert smile to herself and remember Hank when he was little and still lovable. And still all hers.

"Thank you very much," she said, when he delivered the glasses of juice. It was important to teach the young people manners. Seemed like not too many folks thought of that these days, but folks should learn them just the same.

"I've got some money," Danny said. "Twenty-one dollars."

"Ooh-wee, that's a lot of money," Gert told him. "How'd you get all that?"

"I worked for my dad. A lot."

"Good for you. That's how folks are supposed to get money. By earning it, just the way you did." She watched him beam with pride. He was going to be a handsome boy, probably on the small side, though his father was tall and lean. They both shared dark straight hair and brown eyes. Handsome devils, the two of them, with identical dimples in the center of their chins. That Dustin could have his pick of the women in the county, she was sure, but he didn't mind her teasing him about it.

Gert liked teasing. Her Edwin never minded a good joke, laughed even harder when the joke was on him. That was a good quality in a man.

"I should write a book," she said, taking a sip of the juice when the boy did. "Those other old ladies did real well with theirs. Maybe there's a market for memoirs."

"Memoirs," the child repeated, trying out the unfamiliar word.

"Memoirs. That's like memories," she said. "The story of somebody's life. I've had a pretty interesting life, I think." Or maybe not. Maybe nothing special to anyone else, but she was partial to it.

"I could spice it up a bit," she thought aloud. "Add some old lady wisdom, too. Folks like that, at least in books." But not in person. Martha didn't take too kindly to advice lately, despite her carrying on with the Jackson fella and talking about "villas" and "central vacuuming," whatever that was. Meant you didn't have to sweep anymore, Gert supposed.

"Sweeping's good exercise," she told the boy, who didn't seem to mind the change in subject.

"You want me to get the broom?"

"No, thank you. Not on Sunday. We're not doing chores on Sunday."

"Oh." He looked down at his juice glass, then back at her. "Dad's doing chores."

"Well, that's because your daddy's a hard worker and likes to get things done."

"Yep."

"What'd he want on the phone?"

"Just to check to see if we were okay."

"Well," Gert said, looking around her old kitchen with its worn linoleum and scarred cabinets, "I think we're doing just fine, don't you?"

Danny's dark eyebrows rose. "That's what daddy says all the time." He lowered his voice and repeated, imitating his young, serious father. "I think we're doin' just fine."

Gert couldn't help chuckling. "Well, we are. I don't know why everybody worries so much."

The boy shrugged. "Me neither. You want some more juice?"

"No, thanks. But you help yourself. And there's more biscuits in the bread box over there."

"Okay."

Gert watched him, just for the pleasure of it. It was sure nice to have a youngster around to talk to. To have anyone to talk to, though Danny's father wasn't much for chitchat. She squinted at the clock over the refrigerator. Kate would call today, and she'd be coming home soon for the party.

Maybe she would start writing that book this week so she could surprise her granddaughter with Chapter One.

CHAPTER TWO

"MY DAUGHTER WANTS me to move in to one of those things with her," Gert declared as they drove past the sign announcing the site of the Good Night Villas.

"I guess no one can force you," Dustin said, slowing down the truck so Mrs. Knepper could get a good look. She'd insisted on coming here first, to see for herself the latest change in the town. "Can they?"

"I sure hope not."

"You want me to stop?"

"I sure do."

"Cool," Danny said, tucked in the narrow length of seat behind them. "I like this."

"I'm glad you're having a good time." Dustin wasn't at all sure why he was driving around Beauville on a Monday morning when there was all sorts of work to be done on the ranch, but she was the boss and so here he was on the north edge of town looking at a drive-in where he'd spent a lot of nights panting after Kate McIntosh. Maybe the fascination with drive-ins ran in the family.

He pulled into a dirt area alongside the road, but kept the motor running for the air-conditioning. He didn't want this nice little old lady passing out from heatstroke. "There. How's this?"

"Just fine." She rolled down the window and stuck her head out as if she was going to yell at the construction workers. Not that anyone would've heard, with a dozer moving dirt around behind the foundation. A blast of dusty hot air wafted into the truck, but the elderly woman seemed oblivious to it as she watched the construction crew of five men erecting framework. "They don't move too fast, do they."

"It's the hottest part of the day," he pointed out, hoping she'd close that window before she expired from the heat and the dust. It scared him, how old she was. "Maybe you should—"

"They can take their time, for all I care. I'm in no hurry to die in one of those silly villas." She sighed. "I'll bet you spent a few nights in this place. Or are you too young to remember the drive-in movies on weekend nights?"

"I remember." Darkness. Kissing Kate. Pressing her down on the back seat, the one with the rips in the vinyl he'd taken great pains to repair. To this day duct tape made him think of making love to a brown-haired teenaged girl.

"My family used to keep cattle here, back before the railroad came through. Did you know that?"

"No, ma'am."

She pressed the button on the door and the window rolled up. "My, that's easy."

"Yes." He waited a moment. "Are you ready to head back to town, Mrs. Knepper?"

"I think you'd better call me Gert. We should be on a first-name basis since we live together."

"And me?" the boy said, leaning forward so that his chin touched Gert's shoulder for a brief moment. "What can *I* call you, Mrs. Knepper?"

"Mrs. Knepper," his father replied.

"Well, now, most of the children I know call me Grandma Gert, so you sure can, too, Danny," Gert declared. "If that's okay with your daddy."

Dustin nodded and put the truck in reverse. "Where to now, Gert?"

"The library, I think. I have some books to get and then we'll get groceries after we go to the bank."

"Sure."

"Danny can go to the library with me and help me carry the books," Gert said. "You must have errands of your own to do without dragging an old lady around with you."

"I'm worried about the heat, Gert. You want to get a cold drink at the café first?"

"I wouldn't mind. The boy and I might have one of those chocolate milk shakes."

Danny got a kick out of that idea. "Oh, boy," he said, leaning forward again. "I never had one of those before."

"Well, my goodness." Gert was clearly speechless. She frowned at Dustin. "Does he have one of them milk allergies or something?"

"Not that I know of." He didn't know much, that was certain.

"What's that?" the boy asked.

"It means you get sick when you drink milk or eat ice cream, things like that," Dustin explained, hoping he was right. No one had warned him that becoming a father meant you were supposed to be right about everything.

"I'm okay," Danny insisted. "Grandma Gert and me've been drinking milk all week."

"We sure have," the old woman agreed. "So I guess a chocolate milk shake will go down real good—with some French fries and maybe a hamburger, too."

"Wow," the child whispered under his breath. Dustin winced, wondering what in hell Lisa had done to this kid besides the crap he already knew about. Too thin and too quiet, Danny still had that scared look in his eyes, like someone was going to yell at him or worse. Dustin felt sick to his stomach and his hands clenched the steering wheel.

Gert gave him a sharp look. "You'd rather be back at the ranch working, wouldn't you?"

"Well, ma'am, there's a lot that needs doing." Not that any of it would matter if Gert decided she'd lived out there for too long. He could always go back to the Dead Horse and work for Bobby Calhoun, but what would he do with the boy? Growing up in a bunkhouse was no place for a kid, and it was long past time to get started on making some kind of home for the child. And for himself.

"I thought maybe I should be running more cattle."

"You've got the grass," he agreed.

"Well, see to it, Dustin. Maybe we'll try to make some money this year."

He nodded. "Yes, ma'am. We sure could, though it might take me more than a year. I've come up with a plan for the cattle and the grass but it's not short-term."

"A plan is good," Gert agreed. "Making some changes is good, too. You grew up around here, didn't you?"

"Yes, ma'am. Outside of Marysville."

"But you know my granddaughter, Kate."

"Yes." Intimately.

Unfortunately.

KATE WAS LATE. And there would be hell to pay, along with the possibility of missing seeing her grandmother blow out the candles on her birthday cake. Kate could do without the crowds and the fruit punch and the photographer from the *Beauville Times,* but she hated to disappoint her mother and grandmother, especially when they looked forward to her visits so much. And she looked forward to the peace and quiet of her hometown.

She hurried through the airport toward the car rental booths. Already hot and uncomfortable, she was ready for the arctic temperatures of her rental car. She'd brought her suitcase to the office, just in case, but there hadn't been time to change into something less businesslike than a black suit and shell-pink camisole. It had been another hellish week on *Loves of Our Lives,* which made getting home even more difficult.

Everyone in town would be at the party. The grange hall would be filled. She wondered for the hundredth time if Dustin would be present or back at the ranch taking care of things there. Odd that Dustin Jones would end up on the Lazy K, along with his son, who must be eight now. Seeing Dustin wouldn't bother her, she decided, signing the papers to rent the biggest, fastest Lincoln available. She would be polite, of course. She scooped up the keys and the directions to the Alamo lot and hurried toward the wide doors that fronted the sidewalk. She would pretend that nothing had ever happened between them, that he hadn't broken her heart and made her feel like the biggest fool in Texas.

"THERE SHE IS," Gert declared, pointing to the door. "You can rest easy now, Martha. Our girl is home."

"Thank goodness." She hadn't realized she'd been so tense and worried, but she worried when she knew Kate was flying. She always listened to the hourly news reports on the radio just to make sure there hadn't been a plane crash, even though she knew Kate would call her when she was safe in her apartment or hotel room. There was always that span of time when she didn't know if Kate was safe, that span of time when she prayed a lot. Maybe that was the trouble with having only one child. You couldn't spread the worry around. "I wonder what happened."

Gert shrugged. "Doesn't matter, Martha, as long as the child gets here safe and sound."

"She's not a child," she said, watching her beautiful daughter make her way toward them. Her hair was streaked gold and fell in fashionably tousled lengths to her shoulders, her elegant black pantsuit made her look like a movie star, or like those women in the magazines with perfect lipstick and jewelry and fingernails. "She's too thin."

"You always say that."

"It's always true. She works too hard."

"We'll fatten her up," Gert promised. "I made cinnamon rolls this morning."

Martha frowned at her mother. "In this heat?"

"I got up early. Couldn't sleep."

"Too much excitement," Martha declared, leaning down to make sure her mother didn't look too tired. No, Gert looked pleased, a woman who had reached the age of ninety and lived to tell about it. The blue-flowered dress with the pearl necklace looked good on her and the pink lipstick had been a nice touch. Too bad her mother wouldn't agree to getting her hair done yesterday.

"Go rescue her," the older woman said. "Joey will talk her ear off."

"He always liked her. I don't know why she didn't give him a chance. Now he built that nice house south of here and—"

"The feeling wasn't mutual," Gert said, giving Martha a little push. "I'd do it myself but it'll take me too long to get out of this chair. This crowd's got me blocked in."

"All right," Martha said, needing little encouragement to greet her child. "Joey doesn't look as if he's making much progress."

"Ha," Gert sniffed. "It'll take a stronger man than—oh, hi, Esther. Thank you for coming."

Martha left her mother talking to one of her longtime friends from church and, careful not to get any punch spilled on her as she walked through the crowd of Beauville residents, went to her daughter.

"Mom!" Kate waved and said something to Joey, probably promising to stop by his store this week. As if Kate wouldn't prefer to buy her fancy jewelry in New York.

"Kate, I'm so glad you're finally here. I was so worried," she said, giving her daughter a quick hug. "You've lost more weight."

"You always say that," she said, sounding exactly like her grandmother.

"Well, it's true."

"I'm sorry I'm late. We had a problem with the show and I had to fix it before I could leave, and then my flight out of Kennedy was delayed two hours because of rain and—"

"They work you too hard," Martha said, leading her toward Gert, who was presently surrounded by well-wishers and unable to be seen through the crowd. "You need this vacation."

"I can't wait," she said. "I'm so glad to be home and—"

"Martha? You look terrific, as always." She turned to see Carl beaming at her. Not a tall man like her Ian, Carl was at eye-level. It was somehow comforting, not to have to look up to see into a man's eyes.

"Thank you," she said, trying not to sound flustered. "You know my daughter, don't you?"

He shook Kate's hand. "Of course. Kate. Your mother tells me all about your TV show and your life in the big city."

"Oh?" Her eyebrows rose, but Kate was as polite as she always was. Not many people could tell what Kate was thinking behind those calm hazel eyes. "I've heard about your plans for the drive-in, too."

"Not plans anymore, Kate. *Reality*. We've poured the foundation." Carl moved closer to Martha, which thrilled her more than a little, though she didn't want Kate to get the wrong idea.

"If you'll excuse me," Kate said, "I need to wish my grandmother a happy birthday."

"You just arrived?" Carl asked, standing so close to Martha that their arms touched.

"Yes." Kate gave her mother a questioning look. "Are you coming, Mother?"

"Of course. We'll see you later, Carl," she said, patting his arm just a little bit before she followed her daughter to see Gert.

"Welcome home," he called after them.

Kate paused. "Mother, is that man—"

"Here, honey," Martha interrupted, not about to discuss her personal life in a hall filled with everyone in town. And Kate used "Mother" when she had something serious to discuss, another reason to hurry her along. She nudged her daughter through the crowd of senior citizens that surrounded Gert.

"Grandma," Kate said, smiling down at her grandmother, whose face lit up with matching happiness.

"Well, well, come give me a hug," Gert said, struggling to rise out of her chair. Several people hurried to help her, so for a moment there was some confusion until Kate was in her grandmother's arms and embracing her. Martha blinked back tears. It was so good to have her daughter home again. If anyone could talk sense into Gert, it would be Kate. After all, she was the smartest person in the family, the most successful and the one with all the answers. If Kate said, "It's time to move to town," then that's what Gert would do. She and Martha could have side-by-side suites at the Good Night complex.

"Did I miss the birthday cake?" Kate asked.

"You think I'd blow out ninety candles without my favorite granddaughter here to help me?" She motioned to Martha. "What do you think? Can we do it now?"

"I'll get it started, but it's going to take a few minutes to light."

Kate moved toward her. "I'll help."

"No." Martha shooed her away. "See if you can find Jake. I saw him a little while ago, but his wife looks like she's going to have that baby any time now, so I imagine she's sitting down.'' Martha scanned the room, then pointed to the west corner of the building. ''I see him.'' She tried to catch his attention, but her nephew, deep in conversation with a group of men, didn't see her wave. Well, Kate would take care of it. The cousins—half-cousins, actually—always seemed glad to see each other, and Gert's other grandchild needed to be in on the birthday cake presentation.

Martha hurried toward the kitchen, picking up volunteers along the way, along with compliments about Kate's appearance. Her girl had done well. And gotten what she'd wanted. Martha missed her, but that was the way life was. Children grew up and moved away, and mothers made their own lives.

Their *new* lives.

CHAPTER THREE

SHE WAS HOME. Turning cartwheels in the middle of the grange wasn't an option, though tempting. Her black pantsuit, with its fashionable amount of spandex fabric, could withstand the exercise but she didn't know if her mother's heart would tolerate the shock. As a child, she'd been notorious for turning cartwheels any time that joy overtook her and she could no longer keep all the happiness inside. As an adult, she had to be content with smiling. She was home, in Beauville, where everything was safe and familiar. Including her handsome cousin who turned, waved and headed over to meet her in the middle of the room.

"What are you smiling about?" Jake put his arm around her shoulders and hugged her against his side. "Are you that glad to be back home?"

"Of course. And I'm happy to see you," she said, planting a kiss on his cheek. "I hear you're going to be a father very, very soon."

"Any day now." He beamed and glanced back

at his wife, who saw Kate and waved. Elizabeth seemed to glow, though she looked about to burst.

"It's too hot in here, Jake. Take her home."

"Soon," he said. "Neither one of us wanted to miss seeing a cake with ninety candles on it. I guess we're doing it now?"

"I came to get you, for the pictures."

"Sure, but I have to get Beth. I don't dare let her out of shouting range these days."

Kate followed him, wishing she knew Elizabeth better. They'd married last summer, but Kate hadn't met her until Christmas, and even then there hadn't been much time to really get to know each other. All Kate knew about her cousin's wife was that she was from Rhode Island, she had no family of her own except a grown niece, and had offered Kate the use of her east coast beach house anytime she wanted to use it.

"You know Dusty Jones, don't you?" Jake asked, as a lean dark-haired man stood on the other side of Elizabeth and helped Jake get her to her feet.

"Yes," Kate said, intending to glance at him only briefly. He was taller than she remembered, though the wide shoulders and lean build were the same. She avoided meeting his gaze, sensing he wasn't any more pleased to see her than she was to see him. She would have thought that nine years would have made them both immune to bad memories, but maybe there were some things that just stuck, no matter how much time had passed.

"Hello, Kate," Dustin said, but he looked at the pregnant woman beside him. "There, Elizabeth. I guess we got you on your feet okay."

"I knew I shouldn't have sat down," the woman chuckled. She reached for Kate's hand. "Kate. It's so good to see you again."

"And I'm glad to see you," Kate said, "but are you sure you should be in the middle of all of this right now?" Elizabeth looked as if she was expecting triplets, and she looked flushed. Kate made a mental note to turn up the air-conditioning.

"Don't worry." Elizabeth smiled and patted her enormous belly. She wore a mint green sundress and, despite her rosy cheeks and damp bangs, looked like a model for elegance during pregnancy. "I've promised Jake I'd let him know when the first twinge begins. I didn't want to have to leave before Gert saw her cake, though, but so far so good. Oh, I almost forgot," she added. "Emily wasn't feeling well this morning and thought she'd better skip the party. She asked me to tell you she would call you tomorrow."

"Do you think she's going to have the baby today?"

Elizabeth shook her head. "I don't know, but if she beats me to the delivery room I'm going to be very, very jealous."

"I didn't know you two knew each other so well," Kate said, realizing that the two women had more in common with each other than they did with her. She fought another twinge of envy for Elizabeth's pregnant glow.

"Yes. And I want you to meet Emily's neighbor, Lorna Sheridan." Elizabeth tapped a petite blond woman on the shoulder. When she turned, Kate saw that the woman held a baby in her arms. Both had light yellow curls and blue eyes, and both were beautiful. The baby wore a cute blue-and-white striped sunsuit, so Kate assumed he was a boy. "Lorna, I'd like you to meet Jake's cousin, Kate McIntosh."

Lorna smiled and adjusted the baby in her arms so she could shake Kate's outstretched hand. "I've heard so much about you. I used to live across the street from Emily and she talked about you all the time."

"Oh," Kate said, realizing that this was the woman who had married the sheriff last winter. "Emily went to your wedding," Kate remembered.

"Yes. She and Elizabeth helped me out a lot."

"And your husband's the sheriff."

"Who's working today," she added. "He hated to miss the party, but he couldn't help it."

"You have a beautiful baby. How old is he?"

"Four months." Lorna smiled again. "He just started sleeping through the night."

"I hope mine is as good as this little one here," Elizabeth said, touching the baby's soft head with her fingertip. "Lorna's let me baby-sit so I could practice being a mom."

Kate had the unsettling fear that all of this baby-making might be contagious. Beauville appeared to be a hotbed of fertility. She was rescued from panic when Jake tapped her on the shoulder.

"They're lighting the candles now," he said, "so we'd better move over to the dessert table."

"Daddy?"

Kate glanced past Elizabeth to see a young dark-haired boy tugging on Dustin's calloused hand. His son. Of course. He was a miniature version of his father, though small for his age.

"What is it, Dan?" Dustin's tone was patient, as if he was used to answering the boy.

"Grandma Gert said I could help."

"With what?"

"The candles," he said, sounding almost timid. Kate would have expected any Jones child to be hell on wheels. The entire family had had a wild streak the size of the Rio Grande. "She said I could help blow them out if she didn't have enough air."

Jake reached over and tousled the boy's hair. "Well, you'd better come on. She's my grandma, too, and Kate's. So we'd better get over there pronto.''

Dustin hesitated, frowning a little. It didn't diminish those looks, Kate saw, watching from a few feet away. Elizabeth, standing next to her, held out her hand to the child. ''Danny, can you take my hand? I could use some help.''

Danny looked up at his father.

''Go ahead,'' Dustin said. ''But walk slow. Mrs. Johnson has to take it easy.''

''I know,'' he said, sounding more like his father with that Jones confidence. Kate moved out of the way so the boy could accompany Elizabeth, flanked carefully by her husband. Kate joined the group just as Dustin moved to follow his son and Kate found herself in the awkward position of walking with him toward the front of the room.

She couldn't think of a thing to say. A woman who had most likely written hundreds of thousands of words of dialogue in the past four years couldn't come up with her own script. What do you say to an old lover? Kate couldn't imagine, could only hear her own words of nine years ago, *get out*. Funny, she wished she could say that again, so he would turn around and leave the building and that would solve everything. And what did that say about her own emotional maturity if her reaction to this man was still the same? Not much, she decided. Kate attempted to paste a smile on her face as various townspeople greeted her and said they were glad she was here for ''the big day,'' but she was conscious of Dustin walking so close to her.

Pathetic, she told herself. It's been nine years and being close to him still makes my heart race. Her mother would have a fit when she saw him, which was the only vaguely humorous thing in this whole encounter.

Unfortunately, Martha was too busy rearranging the dessert table to notice the man she had once described as ''the wild, no-good Jones boy'' who would date her daughter ''over my dead and lifeless body.'' Then her attention was taken by Elizabeth and Jake, and Gert's delight over their presence at the party was clear to see. Kate watched the small boy shyly approach her grandmother, but Gert put one arm around the boy's thin shoulders and hugged him close to her.

''You remembered, did you?''

He smiled a little, as if afraid to be too happy. ''Yep. I've never seen so many candles before.''

''Neither have I,'' her grandmother said. ''Do you think I can blow them all out?''

''I'll bet you can,'' Kate replied, stepping closer. She would not let Dustin's presence here ruin such a special occasion. ''If you have enough help.''

Gert smiled. ''Kate, have you met my buddy Danny?''

''I sure have. He looks ready to help, and—''

she caught her mother's frantic wave by the kitchen door right before someone turned off the lights ''—here it comes now.''

Someone began to sing ''Happy Birthday'' and everyone joined in as the three-layer cake was wheeled across the room and placed in front of Gert, who looked as if she was enjoying the celebration. Kate blinked back tears and tried to sing as she watched her grandmother's expression of delight. Dustin's deep baritone rang out, reminding her that he'd liked to sing along to the radio as they drove around the county, looking at ranches and land and talking about their dreams.

Well, she'd dreamed of loving someone who wouldn't get someone else pregnant. When that didn't work out she'd dreamed of getting out of town. Getting out of Texas.

''Now?'' Danny asked, as soon as the singing stopped and the crowd waited expectantly.

''Now,'' Gert declared, and Kate edged closer to help if she was needed. Jake, on the other side of Gert, gave Kate the thumbs-up signal. ''One, two, *three!*''

It took a few tries, but the four of them managed to get the candles extinguished.

''Did you make a wish, Gert?'' someone called out from the crowd. Carl Jackson, Kate noticed, because he winked at her mother after he asked the question.

"Sure did," Gert replied, dipping her index finger into the butter cream frosting and taking a taste. "But don't ask me what I wished for, because I'm not allowed to tell, am I, Danny?"

"Nope."

"Take a lick."

The boy dared a glance at his father, who must have nodded his permission, because Kate watched him dip a tentative finger into one side of the cake and take the tip off of a pink rose and stick it in his mouth. Yes, Kate thought, watching him. Charming the women, just like his father. Daring to take what he wanted and damn the consequences.

"*Kate,*" her mother hissed, as if she had grown impatient saying her name. "Pay attention. I need you to help cut the cake."

"Sure," she said, picking up one of the knives readied for the task. "Any special directions?"

Her mother frowned. "Yes. Cut the pieces small and keep your mind off that cowboy."

"I'll try to cut the pieces small," Kate promised. "And I don't have any idea what cowboy you're talking about." Dustin had moved to the other side of the table where he could supervise his son. She watched as he bent down and said something to Gert that made her chuckle.

"Ha," Martha said, placing a stack of small

rose-decorated paper plates in front of her. "You and Gert. Cut from the same cloth."

"I know."

"You'd better pay attention to what you're doing or you'll cut your fingers off with that knife," her mother said.

"Don't worry," Kate said, slicing the top layer of the cake into neat squares. "I know what I'm doing."

"Yes," her mother sighed, scooping cake slices onto plates with a sterling server. "You always thought you did."

Kate bit her tongue to keep from saying something she would regret. Her mother could turn a self-assured television writer into a cranky teenager with only a few sentences. Kate smiled to herself. Maybe that's how she'd inherited her flair for dramatic dialogue.

"Give that piece to your grandmother," her mother said, pointing to the section of cake with the most frosting. "She still has a sweet tooth."

"All right."

"And make sure Elizabeth gets some cake and doesn't have to wait. I imagine Jake wants to get her home and off her feet."

"Okay." She looked for Jake and, when she caught his eye, pointed to the cake. He nodded and came around the back of the table.

"You need help with that?" He started to take the knife from her hand.

"No, Mom wanted to make sure that Elizabeth had cake before you left."

"You should take her home soon," Martha advised. "She should be resting."

"That's what I told her too, Aunt Martha, but she's got a mind of her own."

"She's lovely," her mother said, nodding approvingly toward the pregnant woman sitting on a metal chair near Gert. She handed Jake a piece of cake. "Here, make sure she eats something. And don't forget there's lemonade and iced tea, too, in case she's thirsty."

Her cousin winked at Kate and took the plate that was almost as big as the piece of cake it held. "Yes, ma'am. I'll take good care of her."

"Such a nice couple," Martha murmured. "I don't know why you can't find a nice man like that in New York."

"Neither do I," Kate said, which was her standard reply every time her mother stated this particular complaint.

"You work too hard."

"Yes."

"Well, now you're on vacation. You can get some rest."

"And keep my mind off cowboys?" She couldn't help teasing.

"Good Lord, I hope so."

Kate had to laugh, but she watched Jake deliver cake to his wife, noticed Lorna cradling her baby while an elderly woman talked to her, saw Dustin take his son in hand so other well-wishers could talk to Gert, and she felt another stab of envy. She was home, so why all of a sudden did she feel like a stranger in her own town?

HE'D BE DAMNED IF he was going to stare at Kate McIntosh, but then again, she sure looked good. Too thin and too pale, as if living in the city wasn't healthy. Tense, too. The way she gripped that cake knife meant trouble for anyone who got in her way. Her mother was probably aggravating the hell out of her. Some things didn't change.

He heard his son giggle. And some things did. Like the fact that he was a father now, responsible for a child. He had to get the boy away from Gert before he ate so much frosting he'd be sick. No one could say this kid had the Joneses' iron stomach.

"Come on, Danny." He bent down to Gert, who sure looked as if she was enjoying her party. "You look pleased with yourself. Are you sure you don't have a bottle of Jack Daniel's in that old purse of yours?"

The old lady laughed. "Don't go broadcasting my secrets, Dustin. I'm just feeling real good, that's all. I survived almost a whole century. No one else in town can say that, can they? Poor Mike Monterro would have celebrated his ninetieth this month, too, if he'd lived that long.'' She sighed. ''So I guess I'd better be grateful about living so long.'' She gave Danny a kiss and thanked him for helping with the candles, then looked at Dustin. ''What do you think of my granddaughter?''

''She's very beautiful.'' No lie, even dressed in black and looking like a ghost, Kate was as gorgeous as she ever was.

''Yep. She's home for two weeks, you know.''

''Yeah. I know.'' Gert had informed him at least twice a day for the past month. He'd had time to figure out that ignoring Kate would be the easiest way to deal with her.

''She'll be coming out to the ranch.'' The old lady studied him as if waiting for a reaction. So Dustin didn't say anything, just waited for Gert to continue. ''You can show her what you've been doing.''

''I'm not real sure she'd—''

''Be interested?'' Gert finished for him, a mischievous glint in those pale blue eyes of hers. ''I think she would be.''

Dustin shrugged. Gert could think whatever she wanted, but it was time to drag Danny away from the cake. ''Come on, son. We've got chores to do.''

"It's Saturday afternoon," Gert protested. "You've got the rest of the day off."

"And, unless you need me to take you home, I'm going to spend a couple of hours putting a two-year-old quarter horse through his paces."

"Can I stay?" Danny looked up at him. "Please?"

"I'll watch him," Gert promised. "And Kate and Martha will bring us back to the ranch later."

"Sorry, buddy," Dustin told his son. "But I need your help this afternoon." He wasn't about to leave the boy with people he barely knew, not that he doubted Gert's good intentions.

"Excuse me." Martha McIntosh appeared behind Gert's chair. "The photographer is here for the pictures, Mother. He said you might make the front page."

"How about that." Gert grinned at Danny, who giggled. "I'm gonna be a star." She waved at the photographer, a thin young man who wore a serious expression. "Over here, young man. Do I know you? What's your name?"

He shook his head. "I just moved here, ma'am."

"Well, that's all right," she told him and tugged Danny back into her embrace. "Take a picture of me and my friend here."

"Is he your great-grandson, ma'am?" He focused, then counted to three. "Smile."

They did, and then Dustin tried once again to get Danny away from Gert and out of the grange hall.

"Come on, Danny. Let's let the folks get the real picture," he said, over Gert's objections. He eased the boy away as he saw Jake and Kate heading toward them.

"What about the cake? Grandma Gert said I could have a big piece. A corner piece."

"You haven't had enough frosting?"

Kate, holding two plates, handed one to Danny. "Here you go," she said, producing a white plastic fork to go with it.

He looked down at the cake, cut from the coveted corner, and then up at the dark-haired woman who had handed it to him. "How'd you know?"

"It was just a lucky guess."

"What do you say, Dan?" Dustin urged, wanting his son to make a good impression, and hating himself for wanting to impress this woman.

"Thank you. A *lot*."

"You're welcome." The smile she gave his son surprised him with its warmth. The visiting princess, dispensing favors to the little people. He wished the glamour girl would head back east, as far away from him and the boy as possible.

CHAPTER FOUR

"I MISSED SEEING Emily this afternoon. I need to call her tonight and see if she's okay." Kate dumped a stack of dirty paper plates into the plastic garbage bag and continued to clear the banquet tables. The ninetieth birthday party was over, the guests long gone, and three ladies from Gert's church were cleaning up the kitchen. All Kate had left to do was take out the garbage and help her mother wipe down the tabletops.

"When's that baby due?" Martha looked up from wrapping the leftover cake in plastic.

"Anytime now."

"Same as Elizabeth. It sure was a hot afternoon to be nine months' pregnant."

"Yes, it was. Jake's wife looked as if she needed a cool shower and a nap," Kate said, remembering how easily Dustin had helped Elizabeth from her chair. She wondered if he'd helped Lisa when she was pregnant. And if he'd married her. "Jake wanted to stay and help clean up, but I told him to go home and see that Elizabeth had some rest,'' she added.

''We'll have them out to dinner one night this week, unless she has the baby.'' Martha finished packing the leftovers into a cardboard box. ''There. All done. Now all we have to do is find your grandmother.''

''Last time I looked she was in the kitchen drying dishes.''

''I told her to do nothing but sit down and rest.''

Kate hid a smile and wiped off the last table. ''She doesn't take orders very well.''

''Neither one of you does.''

''It runs in the family.''

''Well, you didn't get it from me. You and Gert are an awful lot alike.''

''Is that such a bad thing?'' Her mother started to lift the cardboard box, but Kate stopped her. ''I'll take that.''

''Be careful,'' she warned. ''Hold it from the bottom.''

''I'll put it in the car while you get Gran. And I'll drive right up to the front door, so wait for me.'' Gert loved big luxurious cars, said they made her feel like a movie star.

''Oh, my,'' she said, ten minutes later as she settled herself on the front seat of the rented silver Lincoln. ''I feel like Elizabeth Taylor. All I need is one of those big diamond rings.''

''Oh, Mother,'' Martha said, chuckling from the back seat. ''If you liked a big car so much, why didn't you ever buy one?''

''Your father never would buy anything but a Chevrolet, Martha. You know how he was.'' She peered out the window. ''Are these tinted?''

''Yes,'' Kate replied.

''Power windows?''

''Absolutely.''

''Just like Dustin's truck,'' Gert murmured. ''I like riding in that, too.''

''He's supposed to be working on the ranch,'' Martha pointed out. ''Not out joyriding.''

''I asked him to take me to town, Martha. I had some errands and—''

''I would have taken you,'' her daughter insisted. ''I ask you all the time, 'Do you want to go to town, Mother?' don't I?''

''How is your car, Mom?'' Kate attempted to divert the conversation. ''Did you get those new tires you were—''

''I had private business,'' Gert insisted, ignoring her granddaughter's sigh. ''Important business. In the library. And I wanted to see those villa places you're always yapping about.''

''You went to see them?'' Martha sounded almost delirious with relief. ''Aren't they going to be lovely?''

Gert turned around and frowned. ''It's a hole in

the ground right now, Martha. With cement. There wasn't anything 'lovely' about it at all.''

''I showed you the picture.''

Gert waved to Kate. ''Drive us out there, honey. We'll take another gander at the place and see what it looks like. Your mother's real anxious to get us a couple of rooms there.''

''Well, maybe we should do that another day,'' Kate hedged. ''You must be tired from the party. How about if we go to the Steak Barn for dinner? Do they still have those small filet mignons with the mushrooms and the baked—''

''I'd rather eat at home,'' her grandmother replied.

At the same time Martha said, ''That would be nice, dear.''

Kate wondered which decision would get her into the least trouble. She wanted to laugh, but didn't dare. The familiar squabbling meant she was home again.

''It's your birthday, so you decide,'' Kate said, glancing toward her grandmother as she drove down Main Street. ''We'll go past the drive-in and then turn around and take you home. How about if we pick up a pizza for dinner and take it back to the ranch? We'll go to the Steak Barn another night.''

''They do have an early bird special on Tuesdays,'' her mother said.

"Good. Pizza it is," Kate said.

"Better make that two pizzas," Gert said. "The boys and I can have the leftovers for lunch tomorrow."

"The boys?" Kate echoed.

"Dustin and Danny."

"Oh." So Gran fed the hired help now.

"He said he knew you when you were in high school."

"Yes. A little." She ignored the snort from the back seat. "How long has Carl Jackson been working on the retirement home project, Mother?"

"Not retirement homes, Kate," her mother corrected. "Senior villas. 'Independent living' is the phrase that Carl prefers to use."

"I'm living independently right now," Gert said.

"Mom, I can't believe you'd want to sell the house and move into a small place like that," Kate said. She'd pictured getting married in that house. Imagined her children visiting their grandmother in the enormous yellow kitchen.

"Honey, can you turn the air-conditioning down? I'm one big goose bump."

"Mother never feels the heat," Martha said.

Kate obediently turned the fan to "low," though the cold air blasting from the vents had been heavenly. She'd removed her jacket three hours ago and, even in a pink tank, had still been uncomfortably warm. "I guess it's going to take me a while to get used to the temperature again."

"It's not like this in New York?"

"Sometimes," she said, stepping on the gas as they left the main part of town and headed north. "Maybe not this hot."

"We have a nice breeze in the evening out on the ranch."

She eyed the air-conditioning dial and wished she could turn it to "high." "Your birthday party was wonderful, Gran." She raised her voice. "Mom, you did such a good job putting the party together."

"It was fun, wasn't it?" she murmured, sounding pleased with the compliment. "I have the guest book, so we can look at all the names later. And there were so many cards!"

"I think I'll put them in a scrapbook," Gert said. "That way I can keep 'em nice."

"Is this it?" Kate slowed down as they approached what used to be the drive-in. On the left side of the road was a large construction site and an enormous foundation.

"Yes," her mother said, leaning forward to point to the cement structure. "Isn't that going to be something?"

"It's going to be something," Kate remarked. "I'm not sure what, though." Kate turned into the makeshift parking area, but didn't turn off the engine. Surely they wouldn't want to sit here for more than a minute or two.

So much for the drive-in. The only recognizable fixture was the distant screen, its metal posts shining in the late afternoon sun. Her memories of this place were of sunset, waiting for the sky to darken enough so the movies could be shown. And then a broad black sky would surround them and the picture on the screen would practically pulse with color and then she and that young man she'd thought she was in love with would tumble into the back seat and pretend to eat popcorn until…

"—old enough to know my own mind," Gert was saying, having turned around to face her daughter in the back seat. "Besides, I've got plans of my own," she said.

"What kind of plans?" Martha asked. "I hope you mean you've decided to sell the ranch after all."

"Sell the ranch?" Kate echoed. "Why would you want to do that?"

"My plans are my own business," Gert said. "You'll both know them soon enough, but I think it's time I did something new. Something kind of exciting."

"My ninety-year-old mother wants excitement." Martha leaned against the back seat and closed her eyes. "Oh, Lord," she muttered. "Give me strength."

And give me a frozen margarita, Kate thought, turning the car around to head to the Lazy K. Add a pair of cotton shorts, a T-shirt and a view of the southwest grazing land and she'd be content.

"It's good to have you home," Gert declared, reaching over to pat her granddaughter's arm. "New York is too darn far away."

"Yes," Kate agreed, heading toward town. "Much too far." She hadn't been home for six months and in that time, both of the women in her family seemed bent on making changes. Her grandmother wanted excitement and her mother wanted the local real estate developer. Everyone else was having babies—she'd seen no less than seven pregnant women at the birthday party—and the drive-in was going to house retired seniors who'd be too busy making quilts and playing cards to remember watching movies at the Good Night Drive-In.

"WE NEED BEER." Gert shut the refrigerator and looked at her beautiful granddaughter. Kate had changed into a set of clothes she kept on the ranch, in the little bedroom that was always hers, and Gert thought she looked lovelier in those faded denim shorts than she'd looked in that black suit. She didn't like Kate wearing black. It reminded her of too many funerals. "Don't wear black when I die."

"What?" Kate opened one of the pizza boxes and plucked a piece of pepperoni off the top and plopped it in her mouth.

"No black. It's too depressing."

Kate laughed. "I'm going to be depressed when you die, Gran."

"Wear something pretty," Gert said. "None of those city gal clothes."

"Fine. No black suits." She saw Kate glance at Martha, who was too busy reading the paper to listen to what was going on. Martha would no doubt have an opinion, and three women with opinions in the same kitchen was downright dangerous. "Who wants pizza?" She reached into the cupboard and brought out three plates.

"I do, but I want a beer, too."

"Do you *have* any beer?"

"No. But I'll bet my foreman does. Go over to the bunkhouse and see if he'll loan me some."

Martha looked up from the paper. "Mother, since when did you start drinking beer?"

"I don't tell you everything," Gert said. "Just because I'm ninety doesn't mean I can't have secrets."

"Secrets, Gran?" Kate grinned at her. "Are you going to share?"

"Not yet. Go see Dustin, will you? And ask him and the boy back for pizza, too. There's plenty here to go 'round."

Kate hesitated, clearly displeased with the idea, which made Gert struggle to keep from chuckling.

"I'll go out and buy some," Kate offered, reaching for her purse.

"Nonsense. By the time you get back the pizza will be cold," Gert insisted, enjoying herself. Oh, she remembered a few years back when Martha was worried about an eighteen-year-old Kate. When the girl was sneaking out to meet some young cowboy and upsetting her parents. Her poor father, Ian, had had his hands full that last summer.

"We don't need beer," Martha said, putting the paper down. "I'll have a piece of that pepperoni pizza, Kate. Mother, why don't you sit down and get off your feet? I'll fix us a nice pitcher of lemonade."

"Never mind," Kate said, replacing her purse on the counter. "I'll see if I can find Dustin."

"Good. I've had enough lemonade for one day."

Kate kissed her grandmother on the cheek as she headed past her toward the door. "You should have what you want on your birthday."

"Well, for starters, you can settle down and make me a great-grandmother," she replied, giving Martha a wink. "That's what I'd like for my birthday."

"When I find a man, you'll be the first to know," Kate promised. Gert watched her granddaughter leave the kitchen, the screen door banging shut behind her.

"She says there's no one special in New York," Martha said, coming over to take Gert's arm. "Sit down, Mother. You're going to give me fits."

"There are good men here in town." Western men. Texas men. Men who knew about the land. "She sneaked out with Dustin Jones that summer, didn't she?"

Martha hesitated. "I never knew for sure. Then Ian died and Kate went off to college. There were rumors."

"And you thought it was him she was seeing?" How very, very interesting...and convenient.

"For a while, until he got some waitress in Marysville pregnant."

"Hmm," was all Gert could say to that, but she frowned.

"I didn't approve of Kate getting involved with a Jones," Martha said, settling Gert in the chair. "And I'm not sure I'd approve now, so don't go matchmaking."

"We could keep her here," Gert pointed out. "Right here in Beauville." Now she had her daughter's attention. "If we play our cards right. Maybe she'd like to move back home one of these days, take over your house in town when you move to the fancy villa place."

"Kate's life is in New York. She makes good

money, she has a good job and she likes her life just the way it is.'' Martha folded up the paper and set it aside. ''Let me get you a piece of pizza. You didn't eat anything but cake this afternoon.''

''That'd be good, Martha. Thanks.''

''And you're not fooling anyone with that beer nonsense,'' her daughter said, walking past her to the counter. ''I know you don't drink that stuff.''

''I'm going to start,'' she declared. Kate would do as she asked, hunt down that handsome young man and seek a favor for her poor old thirsty granny. He might smile down at her and Kate would be all businesslike, with that cool expression of hers.

These young people could be so foolish.

''BEER?'' DUSTIN LED the horse closer to the fence where Kate stood. She looked better now, he noticed, in clothes that didn't look as if she was trying to impress anyone. Her face was flushed, as if she'd been running. Maybe that's how she kept so slim in the city. He told himself he didn't care how she looked, wouldn't bother looking at her if she was stark naked and begging for his attention. ''Have you worked up a thirst this afternoon?''

''Beer,'' she repeated, looking exasperated. ''My grandmother seems to have a craving and asked me to ask you if you had any she could borrow.''

He laughed, and the horse raised his head and took a few steps backward. "Whoa there," he told him, but he looked over Kate's shoulder to make sure Danny was there. The boy never seemed to tire of pushing metal trucks around a hole he'd dug near the old water trough, and sure enough, he was still hunched over a yellow bulldozer. "I have a few bottles in the fridge. Do you know where I— we live?"

"No." And he could tell she didn't want to.

"Danny and I are in the largest bunkhouse."

"Not the foreman's house?"

"Too far away." Her eyes were still that odd shade of blue, with dark fringed lashes and eyebrows tilted like bird wings. "Gert needs someone to live close to the house."

"I see."

Dustin pointed to the bunkhouse, the one with the blue curtains in the windows that faced a front porch. "You can help yourself to the beer. I'm not quite done here."

"Thanks." She started to turn away, then stopped and looked over her shoulder. "Oh, I almost forgot. Gram wanted to know if you and…your son would like to join us for pizza. And beer." She smiled, just a little.

"Not tonight," he said. "But tell her thanks anyway."

"I will." She strode away from him, toward

the bunkhouse, and Dustin watched her step onto the front porch and open the door. Dustin wanted nothing more than to remind her that they'd made love. More than once. He wasn't a stranger she could walk away from as if they'd never spoken more than a few words.

He should have known he'd run into her. Obviously. Dustin fiddled with the horse's halter and pretended not to watch Kate leave the bunkhouse, two bottles of beer in her hand, and those long legs hurrying down the porch steps. He watched her round the corner of the bunkhouse and head toward her grandmother's.

"What did the lady want?" Dustin looked over the fence into his son's dark eyes.

"To borrow something."

"What?"

"Something to drink for Grandma Gert."

The boy smiled up at him. "She's pretty."

"Yes." The horse bumped him with its head. "I'll finish up here and then we'll go find us something to eat, okay?"

"Okay." Danny climbed on the fence and hung his thin arms over the top rail. "I forgot about supper."

"Me, too."

"What about Grandma Gert?"

He backed up the horse a few feet and began to let out the rope. "What about her?"

"Is she having supper?"

"Yep. With her family."

"*We're* her family, too," the boy insisted. "She told me."

"There's a lot of different kinds of family," Dustin said, but couldn't think of anything else to add to that. So he led the horse into the middle of the corral and urged him into a trot as he let out the rope.

Yeah, lots of different kinds of family, all right. The kind that beat the crap out of you for nothing and the other kind, the birthday party kind. *We're making our own kind of family* was what he should have told the boy, but truth was he wasn't sure he believed that himself.

CHAPTER FIVE

ONLY FOR HER grandmother would Kate have confronted the cowboy and asked for a favor. Tomorrow she would buy plenty of beer, replace Dustin's, and make sure her unpredictable grandmother would have all the drinks she wanted. For the rest of her time home, she should certainly be able to avoid the man, or at least act as if the sight of him didn't affect her.

And why should it? She was a different person, a woman with a life far from Beauville, Texas, and cheating cowboys.

"I don't know why you hired that particular young man," Martha said, when Kate returned to the kitchen with the bottles of beer.

"Why did you, Gran?" Kate flipped the cap from the bottle and tossed it into the garbage can by the ancient refrigerator. "I thought you were looking for another married couple."

"Or thinking again about a move into town," Martha said. "Which makes a heck of a lot more sense than living way out—"

"I'll move when I'm good and ready, Martha," Gert interrupted. "And it's not that easy to find help. Dustin's only been here a few weeks, but we're getting along just fine." She turned to Kate. "Honey, I don't need a glass. I'll drink it right from the bottle. It's more fun that way."

"You should have a cleaning woman, someone to help you here in the house all the time," Kate said, looking around the cluttered kitchen. She would clean while she was here, give the place a good scrubbing, wash the checked curtains, clean the windows. "I'm sure Dustin does his job outside, but you shouldn't be alone in here all day."

"The boy visits."

Martha rolled her eyes. "A little boy isn't the same as a housekeeper, Mother. You know that. And those Jones boys aren't trustworthy. Isn't the older brother in jail?"

"Jail?" Kate almost dropped her pizza in her lap. Gert ignored both questions and continued on as if it wasn't important or newsworthy.

"Dustin worked for Jake at the Dead Horse before he came here and Jake had nothing but good things to say about him."

"Why did he leave?" She plopped a piece of pizza on her grandmother's plate, then lifted a piece toward her mother.

"Thank you, dear," Martha said, reaching for her glass of iced tea. "That sure smells good."

Gert pulled her plate closer. "Mmm, thanks. He needed a place for the boy, he said. With Jake running his own spread and Bobby Calhoun on his own, the Dead Horse has gotten kinda wild."

"Bobby was always a character. He's still on the ranch, then?"

"Oh, my goodness, yes," Gert agreed. "Martha, do you remember when he was a little guy?"

"I sure do. Wildest kid in first grade."

Kate figured she'd earned a little prying. "What about Dustin's wife? Where is she?"

"I have no idea," Gram said. "I don't ask him much about his personal life, but he tries real hard with that boy of his. I don't think they've lived together very long."

"Why?"

She shrugged. "He's not real comfortable being a father, I guess. Sometimes the man looks like he doesn't know what to do or say to the boy. And little Danny seems in awe of his father, like he's on his best behavior all the time."

"Maybe he just got custody of the boy," Martha said, finishing the slice of pizza with one last bite. "I wonder who his mother is."

Kate knew. Lisa Gallagher. Lisa had been everything Kate had not been, including free to spend as much time as she wanted with Dustin and the rest of the wild Jones family. A year older than Kate, she'd been a waitress at a bar outside of town that summer. Which was why she'd calculated that Danny would be at least eight.

"Dustin's son is very small for his age," she said, not realizing she'd spoken aloud until her grandmother answered.

"He's a little thin, I guess."

He looks more like seven, she thought, thinking of the child actors she'd seen on the set of *Loves of Our Lives.*

"He's a nice boy," Gert declared, but Kate didn't know if she meant Dustin or his son, and decided not to ask. She'd had enough of Dustin Jones for one lifetime.

"Have you opened all your cards?" she asked, hoping to change the subject of the conversation. Her mother reached down and lifted a large wicker basket filled with pastel envelopes.

"Looks like you have your work cut out for you, Mother," she said.

"My, my, this will be fun," Gert said, taking another sip of beer. "Reading all of those might take me a week or two."

"And there are presents to open," Kate said. "They're in the trunk of the car. I'll bring them in as soon as we're done eating."

"My, what a day." Gert beamed at her grand-daughter. "Having you home is the best present of all."

Kate blinked back sudden tears and leaned over to hug her grandmother. "I'm glad to be here."

"And we're glad to have you back," her mother added. "There isn't anything we've looked forward to more than that."

"Me, too," Kate managed to answer. "I'm always glad to be home." She left the older women and went out to the Lincoln under the guise of getting the birthday gifts. She really needed to breathe the thick, heated air and look up at the sky for a few moments of peace. New York seemed very far away.

"I WANT TO GIVE IT to her *now,*" the boy insisted, "cuz today's her birthday."

"It can wait 'til tomorrow," Dustin said. "She's got company."

"So?"

"So…" Dustin repeated, wondering how to explain without hurting the boy's feelings. Gert was with her family now. "It's not polite to interrupt when Gert has company, that's why."

"She won't mind," Danny said, pulling his sneakers on over his clean feet. He'd just gotten out of the tub and, instead of putting pajamas on, he'd dressed in clean clothes and figured he was going visiting. "Maybe they're gone and she's all alone."

No such luck, Dustin knew. He was able to see

the driveway of the main house from his second-story bedroom window. Kate's Lincoln was still parked there. How long was she going to stay in town? Long enough to talk Gert into a retirement home? Long enough to sell the ranch and kick him and the boy out? He'd tried this afternoon to ask Jake if he knew anything about his grandmother's future plans, but they'd been interrupted before he could get to it. Still, Gert had told him to buy more breeding stock, had given the green light to his ideas for improving the range lands, had agreed to tearing down some of the buildings that would blow down in the next storm. Gert had even hinted that she'd be willing to sell some shares of the Lazy K to the right man.

"Dad," the boy said, tugging on his sleeve as if to remind him that he was standing there. "She's gonna like it, right?"

"Sure she is, but—"

"Good." Danny, dressed in clean clothes that were too small for him, picked up the tissue-wrapped gift and gave his father one of his rare smiles. "This is the best part, you know."

"Best part of what?" They wouldn't stay long, wouldn't even move from inside the back door. They could be in and out in five minutes and then Danny would go to bed happy.

"Birthdays."

"And the best part is what, the presents?"

"Yep," the boy said, pushing the screen door open. "Can I have a party when I'm nine?"

"Sure."

Danny turned back toward his father. "Really? You mean it?"

"I'll do my best," Dustin promised, though he didn't know where the boy would be come fall. And he wasn't even sure when his birthday was, exactly. He'd have to find out without Danny catching on that he didn't know when the boy was born. Damn Lisa for this whole mess, he thought for the hundredth time. She'd no right to mess up the boy the way she had and leave other people to pick up the pieces, but that was Lisa. A more self-ish, self-centered woman hadn't been born.

"Are you coming with me?"

Dustin hesitated. "You want me to?"

"Yes," the boy answered, his eyes big. "It's getting dark."

"Well, then I'm coming with you," he said, following the boy out the door and into the dusk. It was his favorite time of day, when chores were done and the wind had died down and everything seemed to be settled into place for the night. Kate and Martha should have gone by now, leaving Gert to go to bed. The old woman's lights were off before nine most nights and here it was almost that time now.

"I'm not really scared," Danny whispered,

waiting for Dustin on the porch. "You know that, right?"

"Yeah." He hid a smile. "I know that. Sometimes a guy just likes a little company at night."

"Yeah," the boy echoed. "Sometimes a guy does." They walked together in silence. "You think she'll like it, right?"

"Right."

"It smells."

"It's supposed to."

"Oh, yeah, I forgot." He sniffed the package. "Flowers, huh?"

"Roses."

"Okay. Roses, roses," he whispered to himself, trying to memorize the name of the scent, Dustin supposed. He escorted the boy to the back door of the sprawling ranch house and knocked against the peeling frame of the door. The whole place needed work. From sanding and painting the house and outbuildings, to repairing the cracked windows on the second story, to putting a new roof on the barn, the Lazy K needed a lot of work to lose its neglected appearance. If it were his...

It wasn't the first time Dustin had caught himself thinking that way, knowing that the amount of money he'd managed to save over the past few years while working at the Dead Horse wouldn't be enough for a down payment on the outbuildings, never mind the house and land. Still, if Gert was willing to sell shares, then maybe anything was possible.

"Come on in," he heard Gert call, and Danny was three steps ahead of him into the kitchen, the present clutched in his small hand and the birthday card scrunched into his jeans pocket, no doubt.

"Pizza," Danny declared, sniffing the air before hurrying over to where Gert sat at the table. "Happy Birthday," he said, and handed her the gift.

"My, my," the old woman murmured, reaching out to envelop the child against her. "This is too pretty to open."

"I wrapped it myself," he told her, with a shy look at Dustin. "My daddy helped a little."

"Not much," Dustin confessed, staying by the door. Kate wasn't there, but her mother was eyeing him as if he'd come to steal the silver. "I'm not very good at wrapping."

"Come sit down," Gert said. "Pull out a chair. Are you hungry?"

"No, ma'am, we ate already."

Martha rose and began to clear the table of the dirty dishes. "We have plenty of pizza left. And there's lots of cake, too." She surprised him by smiling at the boy. "I'll bet I could interest you in a piece of cake." Danny looked toward him for permission.

"Sure, go ahead," Dustin said, relaxing now that there was no sign of Kate.

"Coffee?" Martha McIntosh asked. "I was just going to make a pot. Decaf, though," she added.

"Thank you, but don't go to any—"

Gert waved her hand at him. "No one's going to any trouble, Dustin. My daughter's afraid I drank too much beer, so she's bound and determined to pour coffee in me." She winked at Dustin. "Isn't that right, Martha?"

"My mom drank too much beer," Danny said. "The policeman said—"

"Danny," Dustin interrupted, giving the boy a look he hoped would stop him from saying anything further.

"Well, she did," the boy said, lifting his chin as if daring Dustin to argue with the truth. "*Lots* of times."

"Let's see what's in this pretty package," Gert said, diverting the child from any more revelations. "How did you know I like pink?" He shrugged. Gert lifted the package to her nose. "Ooh-wee, this smells good."

"Roses," the boy announced.

"Roses? Well, how nice. I'd better open it up." She untied the bow and the tissue paper fell apart to reveal three bars of pink soap. Until Danny had spotted those in a Marysville gift shop, Dustin had had no idea that soap could be so expensive. Still, it wasn't much of a gift, not after what Gert had done for them. But Danny had insisted—the rose soaps or nothing.

"Do you like it?" Danny leaned over and helped move the tissue away so Gert could see the soaps, individually tied with pink satin ribbons.

"My, my, how beautiful. And these are too pretty to use," she declared. "But I think I will anyway, first thing tomorrow morning when I take my shower." She gave him a big hug and kissed his cheek. "Thank you so much, Danny."

"You're welcome."

"And you, too, Dustin," Gert said. "Thank you."

He opened his mouth to tell her it was nothing, but the kitchen door opened and he had to move out of the way or get hit with a load of shopping bags.

"Here," he said, reaching to take them out of Kate's arms. He should have known she would still be around somewhere. He couldn't be that lucky. "Let me take those."

"I've got them," she insisted, refusing to relax her grip on the bags she held in front of her like a shield. "If I let go of one I might let go of all three of them."

He backed off, but he didn't like doing it.

"Sit down, Dustin," Gert said. "You don't need

to hover by the door like that. We've plenty of room around the table.''

''Here, Daddy,'' the boy said, pointing to two empty chairs beside each other around the old oval table. ''You sit here and I'll sit here.''

He'd look like a fool if he refused, but he watched Kate navigate toward her grandmother and set the bags at her feet.

''There.'' She smiled down at Danny. ''I'll bet you came over to have more cake.''

''And to give me a present,'' Gert said, holding one of the soaps up. ''Smell. Isn't that nice?''

''Mmm,'' she said. ''Rose?''

''Yep,'' his smitten son declared, staring up at Kate with an eager-to-please expression. Dustin pulled out a chair at the table, when he really wanted to grab the boy and run for the bunkhouse. *Careful, boy,* he wanted to say. *She's the kind of woman who'll smile at you one day and break your heart the next.* ''Oh,'' he said, reaching into his pocket to pull out a crumpled envelope. ''I forgot this.''

''Oh, my,'' Gert said, taking the envelope. ''I just love getting birthday cards.''

''You must have a lot,'' the boy said, climbing on a chair and leaning forward to watch Gert.

''Coffee's just about ready,'' Martha McIntosh announced. ''Kate, do you want some too?''

Kate began unpacking one of the shopping bags. "Yes, thanks."

Dustin walked over to the table and took a seat. Trapped, that's what he was. A man surrounded by three generations of women determined to celebrate a birthday for as long as possible. He watched Kate pile gifts at Gert's feet, while Danny and Gert exclaimed over the mounting pile of presents.

"You're gonna open 'em now, right?" Danny asked.

"I sure am. And you can help me. You know where I keep the scissors," Gert said, and Danny scrambled off the chair and hurried across the room. He dug the scissors out of a drawer by the telephone and hurried back to Gert. "Thank you," she said, and cut a fistful of purple ribbons tied into a curly knot on top of a white box. "What do you suppose this is?"

Dustin glanced toward Kate, who looked as intrigued as Danny did. Her hair was lighter, though not as long as it was in high school. Her pink top and blue shorts showed off a figure that had only improved over the years. She looked as if she worked out in one of those fancy New York City gyms. He wondered if she had a lover, if they jogged together in Central Park and drank coffee in those restaurants with tables that lined the sidewalks.

"What do you take in it?"

Dustin turned as Martha set a cup of coffee in front of him.

"Just black, ma'am. Thank you." He hated himself for sounding like the hired help, but that's what he was. And that's the way Kate's mother eyed him. Did the woman know he'd made love to her daughter for one short summer so many years ago? Probably not, or she wouldn't have invited him to stay for coffee.

Cake appeared for everyone, plus a glass of milk for Danny, who watched as each present was unwrapped and exclaimed over. And the women were careful to include the boy in the impromptu party. How did women—some women—understand all of this, anyway? How did they know that a little boy had probably never been to a birthday gathering like this one? He sat back in his chair and sipped his coffee, despite that it burned his tongue. He ate cake—two pieces, even—and tried not to look at Kate too often.

She was still beautiful, of course. It was natural to be attracted to her, as he would be to any beautiful woman who smiled at Danny and made the boy feel part of things. He couldn't remember the last time he'd been with a woman, couldn't imagine anyone in Beauville he'd want in his bed. In his life.

And now here was Kate, the only woman he'd

ever loved. He'd been young and foolish, but he'd been in love just the same. And seeing her again could still tie his tongue in knots.

"It's time for bed, Danny," Dustin said, once the gifts were opened and the boy had stuffed all the wrapping paper in a garbage sack. Gert, frugal as ever, insisted on keeping the ribbons and bows, so Danny stuffed them into a deep drawer filled with string and assorted other things the woman figured she might need some day.

"Aww," the boy groaned. "Really?"

"Yep." Dustin scraped his chair back from the table and picked up his empty coffee cup to set in the sink. It was long past time to leave this house full of women and take the boy home to bed.

CHAPTER SIX

"Mother, are you sure you don't want to come back to town with us tonight?"

"I'm sure." Gert felt a little stiff after sitting at the kitchen table for so long, but she tried not to let on. Any complaint or sign of weakness would bring Martha down on her with that relentless worrying of hers. She shuffled into the sitting room, which used to be the dining room during the days when there were people to feed every day and night, and settled herself in her favorite overstuffed chair. "I like my own bed, Martha. You know I do."

"I know." Martha exchanged a look with Kate, who only smiled and sat down on the old maroon sofa.

"Your kitchen is all cleaned up, Gran," she said. "But I'll come out tomorrow and see what else you need to have done around here."

"It's your vacation, honey. You don't need to be working out here." But she knew Kate would come out anyway. The girl loved to clean, always had, but Gert had other plans for her granddaughter. If you wanted to write a book and your only granddaughter was a television writer, well, how lucky could an old lady be?

"I want to," she insisted. "You know I like to be out here. It's a chance to get the city out of my system."

"But your friends—"

"Will see plenty of me. I'm going to call Emily first thing tomorrow and see how she's doing. Make a cleaning list, Grandma, and I'll work my way through it."

"Cleaning. Now that's a good idea." Martha plopped on the couch and patted her daughter's knee. "Your grandmother has never been much for throwing things away and I'll bet there are some closets upstairs that could use a good going through."

"Closets," Gert muttered. "I don't care much about what's in those old closets. Tell me about the show, Kate. Is that nasty redheaded nurse going to kill someone else this week?"

Kate laughed. "I guess you've been watching the show. Lillian is a pretty frightening villain, isn't she?"

"You need a cowboy or two on that soap opera of yours, Katie." Her granddaughter hadn't fooled anyone with that I-hardly-know-Dustin-Jones attitude. Why, the young man could hardly take his eyes off her the entire time they were all in the kitchen eating cake. Gert watched Kate fidget with a crocheted pillow. "Have you ever thought of that? *Loves of Our Lives* could use some Texan men, to show those silly women in Apple Valley what real men are like."

"I'll see what I can do," Kate promised. "The head writer might be leaving, so there could be some changes. It's going to be a nerve-wracking summer on the show."

Changes. Gert wanted to tell her beloved Kate that changes were part of things, part of life. Of course, a woman could always dig in her heels and refuse to budge, or she could change right along with everything else. "How do you like my new ranch hands?"

"Hands?" Martha repeated. "You hired someone else?"

"The boy," Gert sighed. Her daughter didn't have much of a sense of humor, all things considered. Edwin sure had been funny, though, in his own way. She sure missed him, missed him teasing her about things. "Little Danny. Isn't he something?"

"Where do you think his mother is?" Kate asked, and Gert suspected there was more to her question than she was willing to let on.

"Dustin didn't say and I didn't ask. I think Dustin said Danny was going into third grade here in the fall,'' Gert mused, wishing she knew what was going on in that girl's head. ''Why?''

''Just wondering.''

''He sure likes cake.'' Martha looked at her watch. ''We should let you get to bed, Mother. You've had quite a day.''

''A good day,'' Gert reminded her, but truth to tell, she was tired. But she had a few more things to discuss with the girls before they left. ''Did I tell you I'm writing a book?''

''About what?'' Kate asked, sounding interested. Almost as interested as she'd been in Dustin's boy.

''About my life. Beauville. Texas. Everyone keeps telling me that I must have a lot of stories to tell.''

''Oh, Lord,'' Martha moaned. ''Whatever for?''

''I'd like to be rich before I die,'' her mother said. ''And I sure would like to meet Katie Couric.''

''What does Katie Couric have to do with the price of beans?''

''She's the cute little gal on TV.''

''I know who she is, Mother. I want to know what she has to do with your writing a book.''

Kate began to laugh. ''Gran, do you want to be on television?''

Gert nodded. ''I sure do.''

"If you'd come to New York you could be an extra on the show."

"I'm not fancy enough for that, Katie. I want to be like those old women who were on TV a few days—or was it weeks—ago. They'd made themselves a bunch of money, just talking about their lives and giving advice."

"It's a good idea," her granddaughter declared. "I would think your stories would be very interesting."

"You can't even type." Martha hesitated. "Can you?"

"Enough. Maybe I'll get me a computer."

"A computer." Her lips pursed with disapproval.

"That's what I said, Martha. A computer. One of them little ones like Kate carries around. So I could put it on the kitchen table."

"I brought my laptop with me," Kate said. "I can teach you how to use it."

"Don't encourage her. The attic is already filled with scrapbooks and letters and heaven only knows what else. I suppose some things could be donated to the county historical society someday," Martha said, still unenthusiastic about book writing and television appearances.

"*Someday* meaning after I'm dead and buried?" Gert didn't like the idea of strangers looking through her personal letters, and there were a few secrets here and there that folks in town wouldn't like made public. Come to think of it, though, things like that might spice up the book a little bit. Make it more interesting than dust storms and recipes.

"I'm not sure writing a book guarantees you'll be on TV," Kate said, but she looked like she was enjoying the conversation. Gert bet the girl didn't do a lot of smiling in New York City. Too much stress, that's what everyone said about living in the city. The girl needed more clean air and good hearty food. "We'll have to go through those things upstairs. For ideas."

"I don't think that's such a good idea," Martha said, rising from the couch. "What's in the past should stay in the past."

"Why, Martha, are you so goldarned upset?"

"Mom?"

"I've had enough of this talk. And I don't think anyone should be writing anything about family secrets." Martha didn't look at either one of them. Instead she stalked out of the room.

"Gran didn't say anything about family secrets," Kate called after her. Gert could have told her that wouldn't work. When Martha was in one of her fusses, there was no talking her out of it. Sure enough, Martha returned to the living room and kissed Gert goodbye, but she didn't look happy.

"I wish you'd change your mind," Martha said.

"About writing a book?"

"About coming home with us."

"I'm staying here," Gert declared, "until I sell the place or the hearse comes to take me away."

"Gran," Kate said, making a face at her. "I'll be back in the morning, so have a list ready for me. That is, unless the hearse beats me out here."

Gert chuckled. "Go on, both of you. Thank you again for a lovely day." She took Kate's hand and whispered, "You won't forget to bring your computer tomorrow?"

"No. Go to bed."

"I will," she promised, wishing Martha wasn't leaving in such a snit. What secrets would her daughter want to keep private, anyway? Martha Knepper McIntosh had never done anything wrong in her life.

Unlike a lot of other folks around here.

"She really shouldn't stay out here alone anymore, should she?" Kate turned the car around and headed away from the ranch house. She drove slowly, reluctant to leave her grandmother on her own.

"No." Her mother sighed. "I've tried so hard to get her to move into town with me, but you know how stubborn she is. And she makes me feel ridiculous for worrying about her after we argue about it.''

''She loves that place.''

''Kate, honey, it hasn't always been a bed of roses out there for Gran.''

''Because?''

''Gran's first husband wasn't anything to shake a stick at.''

''Meaning?''

''Meaning I don't know how she did it. My father—Mother's second husband—ran the grocery store. We lived in town until my father retired.''

''And that's when they moved back to the ranch?''

''Yes. Your grandmother always ran the place, even when I was a little girl. We all spent weekends out there. She always was a really hard worker.''

''She's a very strong person,'' Kate said, wishing she had just one-tenth of that strength. Here she was, a twenty-seven-year-old woman in the prime of her life, and she felt ridiculously exhausted at the end of each day. ''Why are you upset about her writing her memoirs, Mom? Do we really *have* family secrets?''

''I guess I don't want everyone knowing our business,'' she said, but Kate wondered if there was more to it than that.

"But Gran's life is so unique, and she's lived so long."

"Long enough to know that you shouldn't go stirring up the past and making folks remember things."

"Remember things like what?"

Silence greeted that answer, so Kate tried again. "Was her first husband a criminal or something?"

"I am not going to discuss this with you, Kate."

Bingo. The first husband, Hal Johnson, must have done something very wrong. And Martha didn't want it rehashed, though he'd been dead long before Martha was born. Why would Martha be embarrassed by anything that Hal had done? It didn't make sense, but maybe Gran would explain it all.

"Okay," Kate said, then changed the subject. "Gran seems to be getting around pretty well, don't you think? And her mind is just as sharp as it ever was."

"I go out there every morning and every evening," Martha said, her voice breaking as if she was trying not to cry. "Or sometimes I come out and spend the afternoon. It would be so much easier if she would move into town. I worry so."

"What can I do to help? I know a week isn't much but—"

"Would you stay with your grandmother out at the ranch for a few days?

"Of course," Kate replied, glancing toward her mother. "Is that all?"

"It's a lot," she said. "Not that I don't want you at the house with me, but if you were there I wouldn't worry so much. And your grandmother listens to you. If *you* tell her she needs to move off of the ranch, she might just do it."

"I don't want to force her to leave the Lazy K, Mom." In fact, she couldn't picture her grandmother anywhere else but puttering around the old ranch house and wearing one of her faded print cotton dresses.

"None of us may have a choice much longer, Kate," her mother warned. "One fall, one false step…it scares me to think of all the things that could happen to her and no one would be there to help her."

"Dustin told me he doesn't live in the foreman's house because it's too far away from Gran. The bunkhouse is only a short walk from the main house."

"I didn't know that."

"I think he looks out for her," she said, picturing him hovering over her at the party. He was just as handsome as he ever was, she thought. More so, even. And the boy looked just like him. Each time she looked at him she remembered the pain she'd felt when she'd heard about Lisa Gallagher and her pregnancy. She shook off the memory. "Grandma loves having that little boy around."

"He seems nice enough. I imagine he reminds her of your uncle Hank at that age."

"No one ever really talks about Hank. What was he like?" Her mother's half brother had died several years before Martha married Ian McIntosh.

"Hank liked a good time," was all Martha would say. Before much longer they were driving past the crowded Steak Barn, then through town and onto Knight Street. Two blocks took them to "A Street," toward the two-story Victorian that had been Kate's home from the day she was born. Pale yellow with black shutters, it sat with other grand homes in the section of town referred to as "The Park," since its four blocks were a dead end, a self-contained area within the city.

The McIntosh house faced the park, with a view of grass, benches and a small play area for the local toddlers in the far northeast corner, across the street from what used to be the town's elementary school and now housed the Good Day Preschool.

"It's still so quiet here," Kate said, pulling the car into the driveway and parking in front of the garage. "Not like New York at all."

"Even Saturday nights aren't too wild in Beauville," Martha said, opening the car door. "My bed is sure going to feel good tonight."

"You must have worked so hard on the party. It was great."

"Thanks, honey. I'm lucky. How many people get to give their mother a ninetieth birthday party?" She smiled at Kate before stepping out of the car. "If you'll open the trunk I'll get the food out that needs to be refrigerated."

"I'll do it," Kate said. "Go on in and get the lights on." Her mother didn't argue, and instead went up the steps to the front porch. Soon the lights came on both inside and out, illuminating the tall windows and their lace curtains. A storybook house, Kate had always thought, filled with lovely polished silver and velvet-covered couches and gleaming cherry furniture. Her home had always smelled of furniture polish, not an unpleasant scent, but Kate had preferred the smell of hay and horses on her grandmother's ranch.

She didn't go inside right away. Instead she listened to the silence and became accustomed to a street devoid of taxis and traffic. Peaceful, Kate knew, unlike her life in the city. *Loves of Our Lives* was in turmoil, with a new director and executive producer. The writers had been told to come up with something spectacular for the November sweeps.

She thought of Gran's suggestion to bring in some Texas cowboys. Yes, the show needed a new hero.

Who didn't?

CHAPTER SEVEN

"I'D BE GLAD TO come with you." Kate watched her mother fuss over her hair in the hall mirror. They'd spent a hurried breakfast together and now her mother was rushing off to church.

"Honey, I would rather you spent the time with Gran. She'll be expecting you, you know. And aren't you supposed to stop in and see Emily?"

"Yes. But I could wait an hour or so."

"I'm off," her mother said, ignoring the offer. She picked up her purse and tucked a tissue inside.

"I'll pick something up for dinner," Kate offered. Her mother wore a fashionable navy linen dress that disguised her plump figure and made her seem younger than sixty-four years old. "I've never seen you wear that color before. You look nice."

"Well, thank you," she said, smiling. "I try. And don't worry about dinner. I'll meet you out at the ranch later on."

"Do you want me to pick you up?"

"I'll get a ride," she said, sounding more mysterious than a retired town clerk should sound.

"Okay." She watched her mother hurry out the front door as if she couldn't wait to get away. Usually when Kate was home she followed her everywhere. Kate would bet a week's salary that this had something to do with Carl Jackson, the romancing land developer. She couldn't picture her mother involved with any man, but the pudgy businessman who'd shaken her hand yesterday didn't look like someone her mother would fall for. And she couldn't envision her mother with anyone other than her sweet-tempered father, the quiet store owner with the patience of a saint. What on earth was the matter with the woman?

"So, WHAT DID I MISS at the birthday party?" Emily, her round face puffy from pregnancy, gave Kate a wicked grin. "Any romantic reunions? Unrequited longing? Lust? What?"

"Your hormone levels must be a mess," Kate told her, laughing as she sat across from Emily in her friend's tiny kitchen. George had taken the children to visit his mother for a while so Emily could get some rest. "Your imagination is just getting worse."

"Ha," she said, shifting in her chair so she could rest her legs on the seat of the chair next to hers. "You saw Dustin, right? And it's been eight—nine—years. And he's still as handsome as sin, isn't he?''

"Yes.''

"As handsome as those New York actors you boss around?''

"Those New York actors are either married or gay,'' Kate said. "Maybe Dustin's married. He has a boy.''

"Not married,'' Emily said. "George said.'' And if George said it, then it was fact. The man knew everything that went on in three counties. "So he's all yours for the taking.''

"Oh, Em. I don't want him.'' She was no longer stupid, she hoped. Or gullible. She now knew that when a man said, "No commitments, no strings,'' he meant exactly what he said.

"I don't know about that. Some things don't change that much,'' Emily said, patting her belly. "Except for my stomach, which keeps getting bigger.''

"How are you feeling?'' she asked, grateful for the change in subject.

"Fine, unfortunately. I had false labor pains yesterday, which is why we missed the party. I knew it wasn't the real thing, but George made me go to bed and rest.''

"You didn't miss much. A cake with candles blazing, my mother making eyes at Carl Jackson, Dustin's little boy getting his picture taken with my grandmother, Elizabeth and Jake looking happy and ready to be parents, Lorna Sheridan with a cute little baby." She took a sip of coffee. "I understand you all know each other."

"Lorna and Elizabeth are great," Emily said. "And eager recipients of all of my maternal advice. And I have a lot of advice."

"Do you have any for me?"

"Yes. Come home and make babies, too. Think of the fun we could have."

"Any other advice?"

"Make those teenagers on the show behave. That little blond gal—Becky?—needs to be grounded, or locked in her room." Emily looked over at the shopping bag Kate had brought with her. "Did you bring food?"

"Better than food," Kate declared, bending down to lift a gift-wrapped box out of the bag. "Saks."

"Be still my heart. And tell me it's something that doesn't have a waist."

"Would I do that to you? Open it." Every summer she brought her best friend something outrageously New York and chic, something meant to make Emily laugh. But this time Kate had opted for something less flamboyant. She watched as her friend ripped off the paper and lifted the lid of the dress box to reveal a buttercup yellow linen sundress.

"Oh, Kate, it's beautiful."

"Calf-length, machine washable, with buttons up the front. It's for after you have the baby." She helped move the wrappings away and shoved the paper into the shopping bag. Poor Emily could barely move. "And it doesn't have a waist, I promise. Waists aren't in this year."

"Thank goodness." She held it up and grinned. "I absolutely love it, Kate. You know redheads love yellow."

"If it doesn't fit I can exchange it when I get back, so hurry up and have the baby so you can try it on."

"I told George I'd take a long walk today, to get things going. Want to come?" She carefully folded the dress and tucked it back into the box.

"I can't. I'm heading out to the ranch."

Emily giggled. "Of course you are."

"To help my grandmother, Em, not to ogle the hired help."

"There are rumors she's going to sell him the place, you know."

"Rumors," Kate repeated. "That's all they are, because she hasn't said anything to me about selling." And selling was something her grandmother would never do. "The only thing she's told me is that she's writing a book."

"A book about what?"

Kate rose and, making herself at home at Emily's as she always had, refilled their coffee cups. "Her life, the story of the town. I'm not really sure, but she wants to meet Katie Couric and be on television."

Emily laughed. "If anyone can do it, it's Grandma Gert."

"My mother is having a fit. She thinks Gran is going to spill the family secrets."

"You mean she knows what you and Dustin were doing in the drive-in that summer?" Her belly went up and down as she laughed. "Now *that* would make interesting reading."

"I really hope you give birth to triplets."

"Unrequited lust must be making you a teeny bit vindictive," Emily said. "You'd better hurry up and get out to the ranch before I make you my birthing coach."

"Birthing coach?" she echoed. "Are you having contractions?"

"I will," Em promised, "if you keep making me laugh like this." She patted her belly and spoke as if talking to the child inside. "Don't mind Auntie Kate. She's never been able to resist a cowboy."

"I can resist," Kate promised. "I'm not going to be around long enough to get into trouble."

"We'll see," her friend said, smiling as if she knew exactly how flustered Kate felt whenever Dustin Jones was in the vicinity.

THE BOY GREETED her when Kate drove up in the yard. He clutched a dirty metal truck and gave her one of his shy smiles as she climbed out of the Lincoln. Oh, yes, she thought. His father all over again, and Kate willed herself to resist the kid's charm—which wasn't going to be easy, because he was staring up at her as if she was a goddess.

"Hi." It was surprisingly nice to be a goddess, even when it was this particular kid making her feel that way.

"Hi," Danny answered, falling into step beside her as she headed toward the kitchen door.

"How are you this morning?" she asked, wondering why she had an escort. She wasn't exactly sure what to say to him. She didn't really want to talk to the boy.

"Good."

"It's a nice day to play with your truck," Kate said, hesitating in front of the kitchen door. She wondered if he waited to be invited inside. She surprised herself by inviting him. "Did you want to come in?"

"Okay." He hurried to hold the door open for her, and Kate struggled to keep a straight face. He was so serious about being a gentleman, even though he was covered in a layer of Texas dust and had a cowlick sticking straight up from the back of his head. The truck came right into the kitchen with him.

"Grandma Gert," he called. "Guess who's here!"

Gran looked up from reading the newspaper and pretended to be surprised. "Well, my goodness! Kate and Danny have come to say good morning."

"I brought lunch, too," Kate said, crossing the kitchen to give her a hug. "Don't get up. Stay right there and I'll make a fresh pot of coffee for us." She turned to Danny. He may as well make himself useful. "Would you like to carry in the groceries? They're in the back of the car."

"Sure." He set the truck by the door and hurried off, the door banging shut behind him.

"I suppose you brought that fancy coffee again."

"I sure did." She leaned against the scratched Formica counter and surveyed the kitchen. Pine cupboards lined two walls, the refrigerator sat at the end of the south wall. She'd bet it could use a good scrubbing, since Gran was known for saving food long past its prime.

"You've got that look in your eyes, Katie. That cleaning look." Gert frowned at her. "I thought we would work on the book instead."

"We'll talk about it while I clean. How about that?" She rinsed out the coffeepot and filled it with cold water. "Do you want an early lunch or just coffee right now?"

"Coffee and cake sounds good." She shoved

the papers aside and stood. "I'll fix the cake. There's so much left over we could be eating it 'til Labor Day."

It was useless to argue with her. Useless to try to spoil her. Kate went to the door and held it open for Danny, who had somehow managed to carry four plastic bags in one trip.

"That's a lot of stuff," he said, dropping it on the old linoleum. Thank goodness she hadn't bought eggs. "You're gonna clean a whole lot, huh?"

"Yes, I sure am."

"Ladies like to do that, huh?"

"Some do," she said, picking up two of the bags and setting them on the counter. She found the electric grinder she'd purchased three years ago in the same cluttered cabinet where she'd left it, then opened the bag of coffee beans and proceeded to finish making coffee.

"Here, Danny," she heard Gran say. "I saved the comics for you." She turned to see the little boy seat himself at the table as if he did so every day. And maybe he did. Gran reached over to smooth his hair, then set a plastic plate filled with cake slices on the table. "Where's your father this morning?"

"Cleanin' the barn, I think."

"Oh, dear," her grandmother said.

"What's the matter?"

"Dustin should be taking the day off. It's the only time he gets off, except for Saturday afternoons."

Danny shrugged. "We're gonna go to town later."

"Does he know where you are?"

The boy shrugged again and Gert answered for him. "Danny's allowed to play between his house and my house, Kate. His daddy will know where to find him."

A ninety-year-old woman and a little boy certainly seemed to have everything under control.

"I froze cinnamon rolls," Gran announced. "You could heat 'em up for your coffee, put 'em in that microwave oven you gave me, if you're tired of birthday cake."

Her mouth watered at the thought. "I guess cleaning can wait."

"Grandma Gert makes good stuff," the boy declared before he returned to the comics spread out in front of him.

"Yes, I know." She wondered how much time the boy spent at the house. He certainly seemed comfortable, which bothered her a little.

"Is your fancy coffee ready yet? It sure smells good."

"Almost," she said, glancing out the window at the barn. Someone had begun painting it white,

which she hadn't noticed last night. "You're painting the barn?"

"Dustin's idea," Gran said. "We're sprucing
the place up."

"That's nice."

"And about time, too. This ranch is a hard place
to keep up," Gran said. "Needs a young man."

"You've done fine so far," Kate reminded her.

"Ha! Take a good look around, honey, and
you'll see all sorts of things I've had to let go."
She shook her head. "I hate letting the ranch get
in this condition. Sometimes I look around and figure your mother is right, and it's time to let someone else take over."

"But—"

"Pour me some of that coffee, Katie," her
grandmother said, changing the subject as if it was
too painful for her. "My mouth is watering."

Later, after the three of them had eaten their fill
of birthday cake and cinnamon rolls dripping with
butter, Kate refilled her coffee cup and began lining up cleaning supplies on the counter.

"You don't have to do this," Gran said, stifling
a yawn.

"You don't have any choice," Kate said, giving
her a smile as she unwrapped a new sponge. "Go
take a nap, or watch television."

"Can I stay, too?" Danny brought his empty
juice glass to the sink.

"I think we'd better let Grandma Gert take a rest now," Kate told him, wondering just exactly how much time the child spent here. Was Dustin using Gran as a baby-sitting service? That was another thing she would have to look out for.

"We were going to talk about the book," Gert said, clearing the table and coming over to set the dirty dishes in the sink. "I've been thinking how to start it, earlier than when I was born."

"Before 1910?"

"My father told me stories," she said.

"Stories?" Danny picked up his truck and tucked it under his arm. "What kind of stories?"

"Oh, about his father and mother, and their parents," Gert said. "Does your daddy tell you stories?"

"No." The boy frowned. "We don't have any family."

Kate and Gert exchanged a look over the boy's head, then Gert patted his shoulder. "I'll tell you a story next time you come over to visit," she promised.

"Okay." With that, he started out the door, but hesitated before he left. "Thank you for the breakfast, um, lunch," he called.

"You're welcome," Kate said, watching him walk across the dusty yard. His serious expression reminded her of his father. *We don't have any family.* Was Dustin estranged from his brothers? She could see why, especially when it came to the one who was in jail. But what of Danny's mother's family?

"There's more to that story," Gran said, shaking her head. "Those two seem all alone in the world."

"I wonder why."

"Dustin doesn't talk much," her grandmother said. "But I guess you know that."

"He never did like to talk about his family," she agreed.

"So you were good friends?"

"For a while," she admitted, avoiding Gran's gaze. "Kid stuff."

"Kid stuff," Gert repeated. "Is that the same as 'puppy love?'"

"I guess." If puppy love meant making love in the back seat of a car twenty or thirty times.

"He's a handsome man," her grandmother said. "Reminds me of your grandfather at that age, tall and strong. You haven't met anyone like that in New York City, I'll bet."

"No." And Kate didn't know why, except that the few relationships she'd had were surprisingly disappointing in the passion department. And yet none of those men—an accountant, an actor and one brilliant associate producer—had broken her heart.

Gran left the table and disappeared into the parlor for a moment. When she returned she held an armload of papers. "I've made some notes."

"You've started already?"

"Oh, yes, dear. At my age it's too risky to put anything off 'til tomorrow." She seated herself at the kitchen table and pointed to the chair across from her. "All this cleaning can wait, dear. Should I start with when I was born or should I start with my grandfather's life?"

"Well, you can do it either way," she said, sitting down and eyeing the large stack of papers. Gran's handwriting, fine and elegant, covered the pages. There were documents, too, yellowed papers with official seals peeking out of the untidy stack. "We can call it a 'rough draft' and then rewrite it any way you think is best. What's important is to get it all down."

"Get it all down," Gran repeated, "in a rough draft." She nodded. "I like that 'rough draft' business. It sounds very professional. Did you bring your computer?"

"It's in the car."

"Well, go get it, Kate, and we'll get started. I'm not going to live forever, you know."

CHAPTER EIGHT

"ASK DUSTIN IF HE could carry those trunks down for us," Gert said, leaning back in her favorite overstuffed armchair. "He won't mind."

"It's his day off," Kate reminded her. "Danny said they were going to town."

"They haven't left yet." Gert could see everything from this chair, including the view from the front windows that showed everyone coming and going along the ranch road. She'd kept a careful eye out for the young man's truck and so far she knew he hadn't gone anywhere at all.

"I can get them," Kate assured her, stacking another pile of papers into a neat bundle. They'd been organizing Gert's papers for a couple of hours, but there was a lot more to do and Gert knew darn well that Kate couldn't move those heavy trunks downstairs all by herself. "I can leave the trunks where they are and just bring down what's in them."

"It'll take too long. And those things could fall apart in your hands," she warned.

"I can figure it out," the girl assured her.

"Suit yourself," Gert said, trying not to smile at the stubborn streak that Kate inherited from her side of the family. How else could anyone stay ranching in Texas for a hundred and fifty years if they didn't have a hard head and a wagon load of determination? "But I'd better come with you, then, to help."

Kate looked horrified, as expected. "Gran, stay right here. I'll manage."

"Nope." She struggled out of her chair. Her darn legs were always stiff after sitting down for a couple of hours, but it didn't last long. "I'll be fine once I get myself going again."

"Never mind," her granddaughter said, hurrying over to the chair to help Gert sit back down again. "I'll get Dustin."

"Well," she drawled, "if you're sure..."

"I'll be back in a few minutes," Kate assured her. "Just stay put."

Oh, she'd stay put, all right. For now. She'd sent her beautiful granddaughter off to find a cowboy. A good man, that Dustin. A hard worker, too. Didn't shirk from dirty work, either. And knew a lot about ranching. Taking care of the boy the way he did showed he was the kind of man a woman wanted around, the sort of man who took his responsibilities seriously.

And Kate needed a man in her life. And Gert

needed a man to take over this ranch. She used to think she'd leave it to Kate and Jake. It was a big enough spread for the both of them and they were smart enough to figure out how to work it out, not that either one of them needed the place. But Kate seemed content to live in that darn city and Jake already had his own place, a nice piece of land given to him by his boss, God rest his soul. R. J. Calhoun had been quite a man.

So she was free to do what she wanted with the Lazy K. She could "get creative," her lawyer had said the last time he was out here for coffee and cinnamon buns. He'd wiped his fingers and licked the frosting from his lips and then given her some advice she thought she just might take after all.

There was a lot to think about these days, but Gert surveyed her home and figured she had a little more time to figure out what was best. Dustin would make a good partner and he was the kind of man her Edwin would have liked.

Then again, Edwin liked just about everybody—except Hank, of course. Hank had always been difficult.

His sister, Martha, was nothing like him; she'd always aimed to do the right thing. And her granddaughter was her mother's child all the way. It was a treat to have Kate home, but it wouldn't be for long. And Dustin was here indefinitely. The man would make a good partner—for the ranch and for a woman, all right. If she could only get Kate to realize it before it was too late.

"My, my," she said aloud, used to talking to herself. "This could get interesting."

"I HATE TO BOTHER you, but—" Kate hesitated, standing in the wide doorway of the barn. The odor of sweet hay assaulted her as the breeze blew through the open doors, and Kate wished she had time to saddle one of the horses and take a long ride along the southern fence line. Later, she promised herself. When Gran took her afternoon rest, she would defy the heat for just a short while.

"But?"

"We—Gert needs your help moving some trunks from the attic and she wondered if you'd mind—"

"I don't mind," he said, those dark eyes looking her over as if he didn't like what he saw. He leaned the hay rake in the corner and pulled off his thick work gloves. "That's what she pays me for."

"She said it was your day off."

He shrugged, as if days off didn't matter. As if he had all the time in the world, which Kate found faintly annoying. No one should look as good as this man, all dust-covered denim and tanned skin. He took off his Stetson and banged the dust off it before replacing it on his head.

"Where's Danny?"

"He should be around the back of the barn. He's got a digging operation going."

"Oh." She fell into step beside him. "He showed me his truck." Odd that they should be talking about the child whose conception had broken her teenage heart.

"It's his favorite toy," Dustin said. "It was the only thing he had when he moved—" He stopped, as if he hadn't meant to say as much as he had.

"When he moved in with you?"

He nodded. "Yeah. A few months ago."

"Where's his mother?"

"Beats the hell out of me."

She hadn't expected that particular answer. Dustin reached the corner of the barn and called to the boy, telling him he'd be over at Gert's for a few minutes. Danny waved, his smile widening as he spotted Kate, but he didn't seem interested in following them this time. She supposed he'd eaten enough cinnamon rolls and pieces of cake to be content for an hour or two.

"Will he be all right out here alone?"

"He knows to stay right there," he said, but he glanced back at the boy as if to make sure Danny was occupied with his trucks. "He's a good kid."

"Gran likes him."

"She's good to him," he said. "He needs—" and then he stopped whatever it was he was going to say.

"Needs what?" she prompted, wishing he wouldn't walk so fast. She'd forgotten that about him.

"A grandmother, I guess," was his reluctant response. "He gets lonely around here, just hanging out with me."

"He doesn't look unhappy," she said, glancing back over her shoulder at the small boy playing in the mud hole. "In fact, he looks like he's doing exactly what a boy his age should do, don't you think?"

Dustin turned, and his frown deepened before he headed toward the house again. "Yeah. Sure." But he didn't sound convinced.

"You're painting the barn."

"Yeah."

"Why?"

"It needs it."

"What else do you do around here? Gran doesn't keep much stock anymore."

"We're running some cattle now. And we're training some of the younger horses, the ones with potential, to sell."

"Whose idea was that?"

"Mine." He stopped and looked down at her. "You got a problem with that?"

"Maybe."

"And this is your business because…?"

"Because she's my grandmother."

"And she's going to be my partner," he said, those dark eyes holding her gaze. Oh, handsome as sin, that was Dustin, especially when he was holding his temper—or trying to.

"Partner?" she echoed. "Since when?"

"Since she suggested it." He'd stopped, crossed his arms over his chest and planted his booted feet firmly on the ground. Almost as if he was daring her to try to knock him down.

"You've bought into this place?"

"The cattle operation, yes. The horses, yes. The land? Not yet."

"She'd never sell any part of the Lazy K."

"Maybe," he said, one corner of his mouth tilting into the faintest suggestion of a smile. "Maybe not. You don't want this place, so why are you getting mad?"

"I'm not mad and I've never said I don't want this ranch." She fought the urge to give his chest a shove, just on the off chance that he would topple backward into the dirt.

One eyebrow rose and he still wore that mocking expression. "So that's why you moved to New York and only come back once a year. You really love ranching, I guess."

It was twice a year, but even that sounded pathetic, so Kate kept her mouth shut as Dustin continued. "And when you come back to Texas to stroll around in your designer jeans and your expensive snakeskin boots you manage to put in fifteen hour days getting the place squared away?''

"Do I sense some animosity?''

He smiled then, a full charming smile that made her blink as she looked up into his face. "No, sweetheart. I don't have time for animosity. I've got a ranch to run.''

"Yes,'' she said, hoping she sounded sickeningly sweet. "That's what you're getting paid for, isn't it.''

"Yes, ma'am,'' he said, all exaggerated politeness. "Now get your sweet little ass out of my way.''

Kate stepped aside. Dustin Jones wasn't anywhere near as nice as he had been nine years ago. "You've changed,'' she muttered.

"Yeah.''

"I suppose we both have.''

"Nine years is a long time,'' he said, as they reached the house and he opened the kitchen door for her. "A lot changes.''

"For instance?''

"Well, for one thing, we just spent five minutes together and kept our clothes on.''

Kate let out a surprised laugh. "You're right,'' she said, hoping the heat she felt on her face didn't show. "I'd forgotten—''

"No, you haven't,'' he said, following her into the kitchen. "You're blushing.''

"It's the heat," she said, fanning her face with her hand as if there were a remote chance that would cool her skin. "I'll fix us something cold to drink. Water, iced tea, coffee?"

"Ice water's fine," he said, stepping through the kitchen to stand in the doorway of the parlor. "Geez, Gert, what are you doing?"

"Working on my book. Kate's going to teach me how to use her computer and I'm going to get rich."

"Sounds like a plan," he agreed. "Where are those trunks you want moved?"

"In the attic. Once you're on the second floor, you'll see a door opposite the bathroom. That's the attic. You think you can carry them yourself?"

"If I can't I'll come back down and get Kate," he assured her, and Kate heard his footsteps on the stairs as she set iced drinks on the kitchen table.

"He's a good man," Gran said, looking pointedly at her granddaughter. "A woman could do a lot worse, and believe me, I know what I'm talking about."

"Your first husband, you mean?"

"He was a drinker. Never grew up. I think the war had a lot to do with it. Or that's the excuse I've given him all these years." She picked up a black-and-white photograph and handed it to Kate. "Our wedding day. Don't we look young, Mr. and Mrs. Hal Johnson?"

Kate studied the photo, especially her grand-mother's unlined face. Her hair was pulled back under a wide-brimmed hat, her dress was floaty and ankle-length. "How old were you?"

"Just seventeen. My parents were furious, but there wasn't anything they could do."

"Why? Did you elope?"

"We did," Gert agreed, "but I was two months' pregnant at the time. Anything less than marriage would have caused a great scandal, and my parents didn't approve of scandals."

"I never knew you had to get married," Kate said, studying Hal Johnson's square face. His ex-pression was defiant and proud as he held his wife's arm.

"You think your generation invented sex?"

"Of course not, though we did put it on televi-sion," Kate admitted, chuckling. "Are you putting that in your book, too?"

"I haven't decided yet. I suppose I should."

"That's up to you." And perhaps why her mother was against this "story of my life" project. "Does Mom know?"

Gert shrugged. "I haven't a clue, Katie. She didn't think much of Hank, not that I blamed her. He was a hard boy to like sometimes, so wild and full of the dickens."

Dustin appeared on the stairs, an old brown trunk in his arms. "Where do you want this?"

"Set it down anywhere," Gert said, indicating a floor covered in papers.

"Maybe under the window?" Kate suggested, wondering how much that trunk weighed. Dustin carried it easily, but then again he was used to hay bales.

"Who were you talking about?" He set the trunk down and fiddled with the padlock until it fell open.

"Mom's half brother," Kate said. "Hank Johnson."

Dustin lifted the lid of the trunk. "Jake's father?"

"And my son," Gert said. "Though he wasn't much to be proud of. He had too much of his father in him, I suppose. I divorced Hal in 1930—write that down, will you, Kate?—which was a big scandal in those days."

"I'll bet." Dustin sneezed. "You must have kept the Beauville gossips busy."

"Bless you," the old woman said. "And yes, the old folks were scandalized. My mother swore she'd never get over the shame of it all."

"Do you want the other trunks down here, too? I think there are three more." He put his hands on his narrow hips, the typical pose of a man waiting for instructions. He stood there patiently, his shoulders impossibly wide, his jeans snug on his long legs. His look of innocence didn't fool Kate. He was the same person who had once ripped off the buttons on her best blouse.

"As long as you're here…" Gert said, leaning over to poke at the contents of the trunk. "I think these are some of the ranch account books. Looks like my father's writing. Go with him, Kate. See if you can find any more photo albums. After the divorce I put a lot of things up in the attic."

Wonderful. She would be in a dimly lit, stuffy attic, alone with a man who'd reminded her that they'd had a, um, physical relationship at one time. A *long* time ago, she told herself, feeling awkward and uncomfortable, amazingly like the way she'd felt the first time she'd gone out with him.

She stepped outside of the refreshment building at the drive-in, her popcorn and soda pop purchased after waiting in a long line of silly junior high kids, only to discover in the growing darkness that her friends had left her. Emily wasn't with them tonight—she was working late at the grocery store and then George was picking her up—so she wasn't there to give her a ride home.

"Hey," Dusty Jones said, from the open window of a banged-up Buick sedan. He was certainly handsome, with a reputation for wildness, though he'd never seemed anything but quiet in the English class they'd shared during her junior year, or the history class when they were seniors. She had never talked to him outside of school before.

The Jones boys were the kind that fathers wouldn't permit to hang around their daughters, but right now Dustin looked pretty safe to Kate, safer than standing all alone in the empty space where Patti Lou's station wagon had been parked.

"Hey," *she answered, trying to sound sophisticated yet knowing her only option now was to call her father for a ride.*

"Your friends left ten minutes ago," *Dusty said.* "They were in a big hurry."

"Great," *Kate said, disgusted with herself for hanging out with a group of cheerleaders. Emily had tried to warn her, but Kate really wanted to see this movie and couldn't bear the thought of another Friday night at home watching television with her parents.*

"Get in," *Dustin said, and she watched as he leaned over and opened the passenger door.* "Before the bugs get you."

She did, of course, with her popcorn and drink balanced carefully so she wouldn't spill on the seat of his car. He took the drink from her fingers and put it in the cup holder by the dashboard. "There," *he said.* "You might as well stay and watch the movie."

"What about your date?"

He shrugged. "I guess you're it."

"Oh." *Now that was stranger than Patti Lou driving off and leaving her stuck. Every girl Kate knew thought he was the most handsome boy in the class, though he kept to himself pretty much and dated some of the wilder girls in the county. Why would he want to be nice to her, the brainy geek with small breasts?*

"Or," he said, looking at her with something she swore was disappointment. "I could drive you home."

And miss out on something exciting to tell Emily tomorrow? No way. She wanted to see this movie. And she didn't want to go home.

She held out the box of popcorn toward him. "Want some?"

"What?" Dustin turned around and looked down at her as she climbed the last of the stairs.

"I didn't say anything."

"I thought you did." He gave her an odd look and then turned around and headed toward another trunk. "Maybe you were just panting."

"I wasn't panting. I walk three miles a day."

"Groaning, then."

She ignored him. The attic looked almost exactly the same as she remembered it from fifteen or twenty years ago. A treasure trove of family paraphernalia, it was an antique-lover's dream. Chairs, tables, boxes and odd containers were jumbled together against the outer walls, though the piles weren't as high farther away from the door. Gran must have dumped things she didn't want to throw away just inside the door. A few dusty paths wound through the mess, and a streak of painted brown floor showed where Dustin had dragged the trunk to where he could lift it.

"I guess it doesn't matter which one," he said, bending toward another dust-covered trunk. "I wonder how long this stuff has been up here."

"I don't think they threw anything out, do you?"

"You come from a long line of pack rats."

"It does run in the family," she confessed, thinking of her closet in the Apple Street house. "If my mother really does move into those retirement villas, I'm in deep trouble. What about you?"

"Our family didn't have much of anything to begin with, never mind anything worth saving for thirty or forty years." He started dragging the trunk toward the door, so Kate moved some boxes aside to give him more room. She backed into something hard and heavy that fell sideways, toward Dustin's shoulder.

They both grabbed the ironing board at the same time, which sent the trunk thudding to the floor. Kate's fingers ended up underneath Dustin's as they prevented the board from falling. His hand was very warm, she noticed, wondering how to move away without dropping the old wooden board on his head. And when she looked up at him, his gaze was on her mouth, and then her eyes.

He looked as surprised as she felt, Kate realized, unable to move. He was very close. Too close, or maybe not close enough, she thought. The muscles in his jaw tightened, as if he was trying to control his temper. And then he said, "Let go. I've got it."

He shifted his hand, breaking contact. And he looked away, stabilized the ironing board against the wall, and then he bent over to grab the handle of the trunk again.

"Katie?"

"Yes?" She'd forgotten how dark his eyes were, forgotten the dimple in his chin and the way his voice dipped lower when he spoke to her.

"You have to get out of the way."

"Sure." Kate climbed onto an old stool and let him haul the trunk toward the attic door.

She hated feeling like this. She was a successful television writer. She'd graduated from NYU, wrangled an internship with *Loves of Our Lives,* and made herself indispensable when her boss needed advice from "a younger generation." She'd worked her way up from assistant to the assistant producer to one of the staff writers on a daytime soap that was consistently ranked in fourth place in the ratings. They'd even been bumped up to third for one two-week period, during the culmination of a story line that Kate had helped develop. She lived alone in a trendy apartment, knew her way around New York well enough to give the taxi drivers directions, had friends on three continents and attended the daytime Emmy awards four years in a row. She went to parties with her friends from the show and got her facials at Elizabeth Arden.

She didn't need sex with Dustin Jones, too.

CHAPTER NINE

HE DIDN'T HAVE time for this. Didn't have extra hours for emptying an attic and digging through old papers. Gert was one hell of a fine old woman, and she and her granddaughter could spend their days messing around with Texas history, but he had a ranch to run. He had a ranch to *build*. Just the thought of making something for himself and Danny made him want to work twenty-four hours a day.

"What do you think?" Gert was asking, looking across the room at him while he took one step backward, closer to the kitchen and freedom. "Should I start with the town's beginnings or should I start from the present—me at ninety—and work back?"

"Flashbacks," Kate mused, sitting cross-legged on the floor while she emptied a trunk. "That could be interesting."

"Well," Dustin said, moving another step closer to the kitchen. "I guess you could do it either way, Gert. I don't think it matters a whole lot." He was a rancher, not a writer, for God's sake. And he didn't want to be within touching distance of Kate McIntosh. He'd gone down that road once and it had cost him.

"It matters," the old woman said. "Kate says I have to 'hook the reader.'"

"Oh." He resettled his hat on his head. "I'd better check on Danny."

"He's coming toward the back door now," Gert said. "I can see him from this chair." Dustin turned and, sure enough, the boy was just about to knock on the door. "That's why I like this chair the way it is," Gert added. "I can see just about everything that goes on, from who's coming up the road to who's coming to the door. It's a pretty good view of the world when your feet hurt."

Kate looked up. "Do your feet hurt?"

"Honey, everyone's feet hurt once in a while. Dustin?" She looked at him and Dustin could swear her eyes twinkled. The old lady was enjoying this. "Your feet hurt?"

"Yes, ma'am," he said. "Sometimes they do."

"I like a good foot rub," Gert declared. "My second husband was sure good at that." She raised her voice. "Come on in, Danny!"

The boy didn't need to be told twice. Dustin watched the kid hurry toward them. He'd left the truck outside the way Dustin had told him, which was good. He was catching on to all sorts of things:

manners, conversation, chewing with his mouth closed and remembering to flush. His mother hadn't spent much time teaching him the basics; she couldn't raise a kid and drink herself into a stupor at the same time.

"Did you wipe your feet?"

"Yep." Danny smiled up at him, one of those rare smiles that made Dustin wonder how the boy had survived living with Lisa and her assorted boyfriends. "I sure did. There was mud and everything." He looked past his father to Gert. "Wow, you've made a mess."

"We're working on my book," Gert told him. "I'm telling my stories to Kate and she's going to type them into her computer for me."

"Cool."

"Well," Dustin said, putting his hand on the boy's shoulder to keep him from entering the room, "if there's nothing else to carry, we should get going."

"You could help sort." Gert pointed to an unopened trunk. "We're dividing things by decades."

"Decades?" Danny frowned. "I don't know much about 'decades.'"

"That means every ten years," Kate said, giving the child the kind of smile that Dustin had taken for granted nine years ago. "Like 1970s, 1980s…"

"1960s?" he asked. "We learned that in school."

"I didn't like the sixties much," Gert said. "I can't say that was my favorite time, except for Martha's wedding. Now *that* was a nice day."

"That was in 1969, right?" Kate rifled through the stack of papers on her lap. "I think I have some of those ranch records here. I could tell you the price of beef in August 1969."

"Doesn't matter," her grandmother said. "No one wants to know about business. They'll want the human interest stuff. That's what they'll want to talk about on the *Today* show. I'm going to have to write about your uncle Hank, and my first husband, and what it was like to grow up without cars and toilets and CNN." She shook her head and looked over to Dustin. "My grandfathers were some of the first men to ranch this territory, you know."

Now there was something interesting. In spite of all the things he had to do, Dustin found himself curious. "You're related to R. J. Calhoun somehow, aren't you?"

"Oh," Gert said, those blue eyes twinkling at him. "The Calhouns. Now there's a story for you."

"Wait," Kate said, leaning over to grab her laptop computer. "Let me type while you talk."

Dustin released the boy, who tiptoed through the

piles of papers and sat at Gert's feet. Dustin leaned
in the doorway, content to stay on the opposite side
of the room from Kate. She looked too good, even
if she was a little too thin and too pale. He liked
his women robust, blond and holding a beer. Of
course, since he'd become a father there hadn't
been any women at all, robust or otherwise. The
Last Chance Saloon was off-limits, as were late
nights and female companionship. Maybe that's
why Kate unnerved him the way she did. Just
touching her hands sent him into thoughts of bed-
ding her. Several times. In a split second of mad-
ness, he'd wanted to lift her onto one of those old
chairs, spread her legs and take her right then and
there.

He had to get a grip.

"I've got work to do," he muttered.

"I thought you got the barn all cleaned up,
Dad," the boy said. "You said you were done."

"Yeah," he said, realizing that fathers didn't
have any privacy. "But there's always something
to do around here, and I have plenty of barn left
to paint whenever I run out of chores."

"It's too hot," Gert said. "Kate fixed you a nice
glass of ice water. It's there on the table behind
you." Dustin had no choice but to turn around and
pick up the glass. He took a few swallows of water
and cleared the dust from his throat while he tried
to think up a way to get out of this house and away

from Kate. He wished like hell she would go back to New York and leave him alone.

He hadn't thought of her much these past years, except once in a while. Like when he passed the Good Night Drive-In on his way to Marysville. Once or twice he'd awakened next to a woman whose name he couldn't remember and he wondered—just a few times—what it would have been like to wake up next to Kate. She'd been eighteen; there had been no beds in their summer romance.

"Dustin?"

He jerked back to attention. "What?"

"I said you shouldn't be working in this heat."

"Not a problem, Gert. Really." He smiled at her. "I know what I'm doing. Thanks for the water. Danny? Come on, it's time we were on our way."

"He can stay," Gert said. "Come back for dinner. We're eating at four."

"Thanks, Gert, but we're all set." He ignored the disappointed expression on the boy's face as Danny stood up and crossed the room. "We'll see you tomorrow morning, unless you need me before that."

And that, he figured, leaving the house, was that. All he had to do was keep his mind off work and his body away from Kate's. Two weeks was all.

Not much could happen in two weeks.

"WOULD YOU LIKE a beer, Carl?" Gert opened the refrigerator and pulled out a bottle. "We've got an extra."

"It's Sunday, Mother," Martha said, hurrying over to return the beer to the refrigerator and shut the door. "And it's not your beer, remember?"

"I borrowed a couple from my foreman," her mother explained, looking entirely too pleased with herself, "for my birthday."

"Thank you, Mrs. Knepper, but I'll take a rain check on the beer. Your foreman, is that one of the Jones brothers?"

"Dustin," Martha said.

"Those boys sure had their share of trouble," Carl said, looking every inch the successful Texas gentleman in his beige suit. Martha especially liked the turquoise and silver bolero at his collar. "That party was quite a celebration. There should be some good pictures in the newspaper tomorrow."

"I hope they got my good side," Gert said, winking at him as she walked past them into the parlor. Or what used to be the parlor. The room was filled with trunks, papers, boxes and some opened maps. It looked as if her mother had dumped the contents of her closet into the middle of the room.

"Mother, what are you doing?"

"Research," was the reply, "for my book."

"You're writing a book?" Carl looked intrigued.

Martha was real sorry she'd let Carl bring her here. She'd thought they might take a drive to Marysville after lunch, but Carl wouldn't hear of her missing a minute more of her daughter's visit home. She suspected he might be a little starstruck over Kate's job since he'd just started talking about making television commercials for the villas. "How about some iced tea, Carl?"

"Excellent, Martha, excellent," he said, rubbing his hands together as if he couldn't wait. That's what she liked about him. Enthusiasm. A willingness to do interesting things.

"Coming right up," she said. "Mother, what about you?"

"I'm having coffee right now. Kate brewed us a fresh pot."

"And where is Kate?"

"Back up in the attic," her mother said, "looking for old yearbooks."

"Yearbooks," Martha echoed. "Whatever for?"

"Because she thought she'd like to see what people looked like, so she could help me write about them better."

"I don't think you should write about them at all," she declared, getting out the good glasses from above the stove. They looked a little dusty, so she gave them a good rinse before filling them with ice cubes. She really should ignore her mother and come down and clean out these cupboards one of these days. "Why stir up trouble?"

"Trouble?" Carl shook his head and made himself comfortable in a kitchen chair. "It's history, Martha. And who better to tell it than the oldest woman in town?"

"I'd like to think I have more to recommend me than my ninety years, Carl," Gert sniffed. "Like my steel-trap memory and my scintillating story-telling ability."

"Well, yes, but—"

"I'm going to call it *My Beauville—A Woman Remembers.*"

"Hmm," Carl said. "Sounds literary."

"Is that good or bad?"

"Well, I guess it could be either, but—"

"Ridiculous," was all Martha could think to say. "No one's going to want to read about Beauville. We're boring."

"No, we're not," her mother said. "We've had range wars and droughts, war heroes and love stories, buried treasure and mysterious deaths—all the things that make good reading."

"Scandals, too," Carl said. "We've had our share of scandals. Remember when that body was found out by the river? And the time the sheriff's deputy got shot and no one ever found out who did it? Old Bishop went to his grave not telling anyone the true story.''

"He was messing around on his wife," Martha said. "I think she shot him and he was too embarrassed to tell. Besides, she only took his big toe off.''

"I think she was aiming higher." Gert chuckled.

"Mother, please," Martha begged, handing Carl his drink.

"I should put that story in," the old woman muttered. She fished around the seat cushion and pulled out a pen. "I think that was in the 1970s." She scribbled something on a legal pad, ripped off the page and handed it to Carl. "Put that on the pile next to your feet, Carl. Last time I looked that pile was the seventies.''

"Sure." He did as he was told and took a sip of his iced tea. "I must say, Mrs. Knepper, you have quite a collection of historical information arranged here. Are you getting ready to move?''

"The Lazy K isn't for sale," Gert declared. "Dustin and I are going back in the cattle business.''

"The cattle business," Martha groaned. "Good Lord.''

"I think it's nice your mother still keeps active," the man said. "Writing books and raising cattle at her age is remarkable.''

She'd show him remarkable, Martha thought, if

she could get him alone and out of that nicely pressed suit. Nine years without sex was starting to make her cranky. She was getting more lines around her face and she worried that the insides of her body had dried up and disappeared from disuse.

Menopause hadn't fazed her, but loneliness and boredom were about to do her in.

"TAKE SOME OF THAT over to Jake's," Gert said, pointing to the oven-fried chicken breasts left in the pan. "I imagine Elizabeth isn't doing much cooking these days, poor thing."

"All right. I'll do it on my way home." Kate set one aside on a plate and covered it with plastic wrap. "I'm leaving you one for lunch tomorrow, or in case you get hungry later."

"I don't eat much," Gran confessed. "Gives your mother fits, but that's the way it is."

"Is she serious about Carl, do you think?" She put the rest of the chicken on one of Gran's scarred plastic dinner plates and wrapped it tightly with plastic wrap. Her mother had accepted a ride home from the real estate king instead of staying for dinner, which suited everyone. Gert wanted to talk about her book and Kate hoped to avoid any more scenes of her mother making eyes at Carl Jackson. What on earth was wrong with the woman?

"Hard to tell, but I wouldn't be surprised."

Gran turned on the hot water and squirted dish detergent into the sink. "Your father's been gone nine years now. Maybe she's looking for a new husband. A woman gets lonely."

"She'd be better off getting a dog."

"Now, Kate," her grandmother said in that warning tone Kate had heard many times before. "You can't expect your mother to live alone in that fancy house for the rest of her life."

"Yes, I can," she said, but she laughed at herself. "I depend on her—and you—to stay the same. It's comforting to know that the two people I love most in the world are right here—you here on the ranch making cinnamon rolls and Mom fussing over the dust on the mahogany banister. I can't picture anything else."

"That's plain ridiculous. Round up the silverware and toss it in here." She squeezed the water out of a sponge and wiped off a section of the counter closest to her, then spread a clean flour sack towel over it. "Things change."

Kate did as she was told and stacked the remaining dishes next to the sink. "People don't."

Gran gave her a sharp look and then turned her attention back to dishwashing. "Sometimes they do and sometimes they don't. That's what keeps life interesting. What about you? Is there a man there in New York who makes your heart beat fast when you look at him?"

"Not right now."

"It's time you started looking, you know," Gran said. "You're not getting any younger and it's time you settled down and started having a family."

"Yes, ma'am," Kate said, knowing full well her job and lifestyle wouldn't include a husband and babies any time soon. "I'll do my best."

"You should marry a Western man," Gran mused. "They don't come any finer." She frowned to herself and rinsed the silverware under the running water. "Most of 'em, anyway."

CHAPTER TEN

SHE'D FORGOTTEN about the yearbooks—those black-and-white photographs of the class of '55, the autographs, the recounting of dances and football games. Martha thumbed through the musty-smelling pages of the *Beauville Bonanza*—what a silly name for a Texas yearbook—and searched for the photos of herself with her best friend, Nancy. They'd been inseparable since first grade, had stayed friends until Nancy's death in 1982. She thought about her nephew. Poor Jake. He'd been all alone then, out there on the Dead Horse with old R.J. depending on him. Martha wanted to take the teenager home with her, but R.J. wouldn't hear of it. Nancy had been his housekeeper for years; together they'd raised Jake.

The following year R.J.'s son and daughter-in-law had been killed in a car wreck, their son Bobby left an orphan. And Jake had been there for the old man, helping to raise a wild kid as best as he knew how.

Until, of course, he'd gotten married and moved

onto his own place. At least R.J. had done the right thing by leaving Jake that ranch. A man needed something of his own, her Ian always said whenever Gert made noises about them moving out to the Lazy K. Ian enjoyed his store, liked selling hardware and all that kind of thing. Martha had kept the books and they'd done real well, especially after Kate was older and Martha had taken that job at the town hall. She'd always been glad she'd lived in town.

"Mom?"

Martha looked up to see Kate standing in the bedroom doorway. "Hi. I didn't hear you come in."

"I tried to be quiet, in case you were asleep."

"Oh, I stay up later now that I don't have to get up for work in the morning." She shut the yearbook and set it aside on the nightstand. She'd been sitting on the edge of her bed and had been so engrossed in the yearbook she hadn't even put on her nightgown yet. "I guess your grandmother stopped writing?"

"Yes." Kate smiled and sat down on the bed beside her. "She let me straighten the piles. And I even swept the kitchen floor before she sent me home. I left the computer with her, though, so she knows I'll be back tomorrow." She reached over for the *Bonanza*. "Is this your class?"

"Yes." She waited while Kate thumbed through the book and found her picture.

"You were so pretty. You don't look like Gran, though."

"My father said I was the image of his mother." She gently took the book out of Kate's hands and held it on her lap. "Enough of all that," she said. "You've been digging around this stuff all day. What are your plans for tomorrow?"

"Emily and I were going to try to have lunch together if she could get a sitter. I told Gran I'd be out in the afternoon to do some work on the book and then I thought we could all go to the Steak Barn for dinner."

"It's closed on Mondays."

"Oh. Well, we'll go on Tuesday night instead."

"This is supposed to be your vacation," Martha sighed. "I can't believe your grandmother is making you help her write a book just because she wants to be on television."

"I don't mind. It's fascinating, actually." Her beautiful daughter smiled her father's smile and Martha blinked back tears. She missed Ian so much. "It's giving me ideas for the show," Kate added.

"Speaking of the show, my goodness, Kate, every time I turn it on someone's always pulling someone else into bed."

Kate laughed. "That's what the viewers want to see. Romance."

"Romance," Martha repeated, thinking of her own situation. "Well, I guess we could all use a little more of that."

"Are we talking about Mr. Jackson?"

"No, we are not." She stood up and went over to her dresser to find a nightgown. "He's just a friend." For now, though he'd kissed her good-night tonight.

"Emily said he's quite the town bachelor."

"Emily's mother-in-law keeps inviting him over for dinner."

"Does he go?"

"I don't ask," she said, picking out a chaste lavender gown. "It's none of my business." But she knew anyway, of course. Carl had gone once, thinking he was going to a dinner party. Party of two was more like it, but Irene had always been a little sneaky like that. Like not giving anyone the correct recipe for her lemon bars that year they'd tried a Christmas cookie swap.

When she turned around, Kate had the yearbook again. The girl had a one-track mind, just like her grandmother.

"Your best friend married your brother? That must have been wonderful."

"It should have been, but Hank wasn't an ideal husband." There. She'd spoken the truth without saying anything. It was a skill she'd honed over the years. Even Ian, bless him, never suspected a thing.

"Why not?"

"He drank. Like his father, Mother's first husband. Handsome, charming, all Texas good ol' boy, but with a streak…"

"A streak of what?" Kate prompted, an absolutely fascinated look on her face. For heaven's sake.

"A dark side," Martha said. "Like those people on your soap opera. Nice on one side, yet not so nice on the other. I guess alcohol can do that to a person."

"I guess. So Nancy married your charming, handsome alcoholic older brother. And then what?"

"Older *half* brother." Martha made a move toward the door. The bathroom was just across the hall and as good a place as any to hide from her daughter's questions. "They didn't live happily ever after," she said.

"What happened?"

"The usual things that happen when a husband spends more time in bars than at home. Kate, I'd like to get dressed for bed now."

"Oh." But she held on to the yearbook. "Do you mind if I look through this?"

"Of course not, but it smells," she pointed out. "You should air it out for a few days."

"I'll take it to show Emily tomorrow. It might take her mind off being ten months' pregnant." She kissed her mother good-night before leaving the room. "See you in the morning."

"Good night, Kate," Martha said, wishing Gert had never started this book-writing business. What was past should stay in the past.

And some secrets should stay buried. For everyone's sake.

"WE SHOULD BE LOOKING at our own yearbooks if we really want to laugh," Emily said. She lay stretched out on her living room couch while Kate served her tea and graham crackers. She set the 1955 yearbook on the table and reached for the crackers. "This is the only thing I can eat lately," she confessed, hiding the box under the couch. "If the kids find them, they'll be finished in five minutes."

"I think I can wait a few more years before looking at our pictures in the yearbook," Kate said, moving her chair closer. "I didn't really keep in touch with anyone but you and George. Are you sure you're feeling okay?"

"I'm fine. I'm sorry about lunch, though. I was looking forward to—Elly, honey, don't put that in your mouth."

Kate reached over and pried a sandal from the three-year-old's chubby fingers. "Elly, come sit with Auntie Kate?" She lifted the little girl onto her lap and gave her a hug before replacing the sandal on her fat bare foot.

"Mommy's gonna have a baby," the girl stated.

"Yes, she sure is." Kate thought Emily looked awfully pale and uncomfortable. "What can I do to help you, Em?"

"Pull the baby out with your bare hands."

"Why don't I take the kids out to the ranch for a while instead?"

"Masochist," Emily muttered, but she looked relieved. "You mean I could have a nap?"

"Sure. What are single friends for?"

"What about Gert? She might not want three little kids around." Emily struggled to a sitting position.

"Four kids, counting Dustin's son."

"How old is he?"

"Eight or nine, I guess. Maybe he and John could play trucks or something. I think there's a mud puddle behind the barn."

"If I have this baby while you're gone, you'll have to keep the kids for three days," Emily warned. "My mother-in-law may decide she could use a break, too."

"Martha will know where to find her. Stay

where you are," Kate said. "The kids and I will be fine."

"They have to wear seat belts in the car, and Elly has to sit in a booster seat."

"No problem," she promised, scooping the toddler into her arms as she stood. "They'll have a ball and I'll bring 'em home dirty so you don't feel too guilty about my baby-sitting."

"Guilty?" Emily chuckled, then winced as she tried to get comfortable. "Not a chance. Once in a while you career gals need a dose of how the other half lives."

The next adult she saw turned out to be Dustin, who came around the ranch house as she stepped out of the car. Danny was next to him, a small shadow of his father whose mouth fell open when he saw a carload of children.

"You kidnapped the Bennett kids," Dustin said. "*Now* what are you going to do with them?"

Kate unbuckled Elly's car seat and lifted her out of the car. "I'm going to show them horses and cows and anything else you have around here. Emily needed a nap."

He looked a little stunned as Jennie and John tumbled out of the car and grinned at Danny.

"Hi," John said, his face split into a wide grin. He was an outgoing child, like his father. "I know you."

"Danny," he said, leaving his father's side as

John reached back into the car and retrieved a couple of Tonka bulldozers.

"I told John that you liked trucks," Kate said, hoping Danny would take over and show off his play area.

"Yep." But Danny didn't budge. Kate exchanged an amused look with Dustin, who looked almost as surprised as his son that they had company.

"Come on, boys," Dustin said. "I'll show you the ranch."

"What about us?" Jennie took her little sister's hand. "Can we see, too?"

"Sure," the cowboy said, moving closer. "We can all go together."

Well, this was different, Kate mused. He was actually being nice. She didn't know why she was surprised, since he had been kind when she'd been in love with him. Kind, gentle and very, very sexy.

Kate sighed and wondered if she should start dating that lighting technician the show had just hired. Maybe she needed to get out more, spend less time working. The problem was obvious, though. She'd never seen anyone like Dustin Jones in New York.

He knew the ranch inside and out—knew enough to understand where and how to make changes, and what to put on hold. He'd taken a couple of the older outbuildings down, he told her, before they blew down in the next bad storm and caused injury to people or animals. He was painting the barn because Gert said a well-kept barn made a ranch look prosperous. The Bennett children had visited ranches before, of course, but horses and cows were a pretty good show no matter how many times they'd been seen before.

"This is so cool," John said, when they reached Danny's digging hole. He eyed the large area of dirt tracks and drying mud. "What are you making?"

"A lake. And a river. And a fort."

"I brought my dozers," the younger boy said, dropping them in the dirt. "Can I play?"

"Yeah." Danny smiled, still shy but recognizing a kindred spirit. "Sure." He looked over at Dustin. "We'll stay here."

"Nowhere else, right?"

The boy nodded, and Dustin turned to John. "It's very important, John, when you're on a ranch, to stay where you say you're going to stay." He pointed to the bunkhouse. "That's where Danny and I live, so you boys can go in there if you want." And then he turned and showed John the main house. "Mrs. Knepper—Kate's grandmother—lives there and there's a path to her kitchen door."

"That's where I'll be," Kate interjected, "with your sisters."

"I know her," Jennie said. "She's the oldest lady in town."

"That's right."

"Nowhere else," Dustin said. "The barn and the outbuildings and the corrals are off-limits unless I'm there with you." He smiled down at the younger boy. "Your mom would be real mad at me if anything happened to you and I don't want her yellin' at me, okay?"

John laughed. "Okay."

Dustin turned back to the girls. "Do you want to see the new calves?"

And that was that, Kate realized. The boys stayed in their construction zone while Dustin led the girls past several small barns toward a fence line that held his new stock. He showed them the calves and let them name the newest one. There was a breeze, though it was getting near the hottest part of the day.

"I'd better get the girls inside to see Gran. She'll be wondering where I am."

"I think she saw you," he said. "She doesn't miss much."

"We'll go get lemonade and birthday cake," Kate told the girls. But she looked up at Dustin. "Are you going to join us?"

"I have work to do." But he held her gaze and for one odd and crazy moment she thought he was going to bend down and kiss her. She knew he wanted to and she wondered if she would protest if and when he did it.

Of course not. She felt the familiar flutters in the pit of her stomach when he looked at her like that, as if he wished they were alone and horizontal. She'd seen that look before. And when she took the girls' hands in hers and walked them to see Gran, she wondered if she'd had a similar yearning expression on her own face.

DUSTIN CHECKED ON the boys, then went into the barn to work on the tractor. He'd told Gert he was sure he could get it started again. He was pretty damn good at fixing machinery, knew grasslands from years of studying and reading, and could train a horse to do just about anything a man required it to do. But when it came to women—when it came to *this* woman—he was so damn frustrated that he might as well make it easy on himself and just ride off into the sunset...alone.

Kate McIntosh was driving him crazy and she'd only been around for, what? A couple of days? Danny talked about how pretty and nice she was, Gert rattled on with ''Kate said'' this and ''Kate did'' that. The woman was about as useless as teats on a bull, with her fancy little computer and designer clothes and big eyes looking around the ranch as if she would know how to do it better.

He'd better remember that she'd left him. She'd

never explained, never said goodbye. And he'd gotten stubborn. And proud. Too proud to go to her and tell her he loved her, that he cared more than he'd said. And after her dad died, she'd left for college and never looked back, not at Beauville and not at the man who wasn't good enough for her.

He'd never been good enough for her, which rankled. He was a hell of a lot better a man than she'd given him a chance to be. Oh, he'd heard about her fancy career in New York. Read the article in the newspaper a couple of years back that even had a picture of her and one of the characters on the show, a toothy actor with a big head of blond hair who was supposed to be a big star.

Dustin made a concerted effort to keep his mind on the tractor engine and off Kate. It bothered him that he still cared, still felt like an awkward kid when she was around.

But if she ever looked at him like that again, he was going to kiss her. *Really* kiss her.

And damn the consequences.

"SURE IS NICE HAVING children around," Gert declared, leaning back in her chair. "I like the noise." She watched Elly to make sure she didn't fall off the kitchen chair, but she needn't have worried. The little girl knew how to kneel on a chair and lean over a table to eat birthday cake. Being the youngest in the Bennett family must have taught her a great deal early on. Jennie was lady-like and kept a watchful eye on her younger sister while trying not to stare at Kate, who must look pretty darn glamorous to a five-year-old. Martha had been serious like that, too.

"I hope Emily gets some rest," Kate said, looking for all the world like an anxious mother.

"Do you plan to have kids?" Gert knew it wasn't politically correct to ask young women that question, but she thought she could ask her grand-daughter just about anything. But then Dustin Jones came to mind and she thought, well, just about anything.

"Of course."

"Well, what are you waiting for?"

"The right man." She licked frosting off her fingers and moved the knife off the table.

"I'm glad you're not one of those women who goes to, you know," she said, lowering her voice, "one of those banks."

Kate grinned. "I'd rather have a baby the old-fashioned way."

"My mom's having a baby," Jennie said. "Any day now, she said, and she hopes it's a boy so we'll be even. You know, two boys and two girls." She looked at Kate. "You think my mom's okay?"

"How about if I call her in a little while and check?" Kate refilled the girl's glass with milk.

"I'd call her now but she said she wanted to take a nap."

"Oh."

"I don't like naps," Elly declared, frowning at Gert across the table. "Just babies do."

Gert nodded. "I hope you'll bring your new baby sister or brother out here to visit me." She looked at Kate. "It's not like you're going to bring me any babies to hold in the near future. What kind of man are you looking for, anyway?"

Kate shrugged, looking for all the world like one of those television stars she wrote stories for. Such a beautiful girl, who would have beautiful babies. "The right one."

"You're not going to find him in New York City," Gert grumbled. "There're plenty of fine men right here in town. Right here on this ranch, actually. There's one walking around out there— probably swearing over that old John Deere— who'd make a fine husband and a fine father."

"I wonder who that could be." Kate winked at Jennie, who giggled.

"This place needs kids, needs a family," Gert sighed, knowing full well Kate wasn't going to pay any attention to her advice.

"I'm going to take the kids home in a while, then I'll come back to work on the book. Mom's going to come back with me and we'll bring dinner. Is there anything special you'd like?"

*I'd like to give you the ranch. I'd like you to
come home and take over, with your husband—a
nice Texas boy. I'd like to watch a baby or two
come into this world and call the Lazy K home.*

"There's still pizza left over from Saturday,"
Gert said instead, reaching over to help Elly wipe
her face with a "Happy Birthday" napkin. "We
could have that. Or you could make one of your
meat loaves."

"Meat loaf it is," Kate said.

"And we'll invite Dustin and Danny," Gert
said.

Heck, no one had ever called her a quitter.

CHAPTER ELEVEN

"YOU'RE NOT WATCHING the show today?"

"We're taped three weeks ahead during the summer, Gran." The all-too-brief summer break would end with frenzied attempts to complete story lines for the November sweeps, the all-important ratings war. And as soon as she returned, the meetings would begin and the next nine months of the show would be determined. The sponsor wanted something "different and trendy," while the viewers resisted the new paranormal story line and wrote asking for more romance. Kate found herself wishing she spent more time on her own life instead of the lives of the fictional characters of *Loves of Our Lives*. It simply wasn't as much fun as it used to be, when she was young and enthusiastic and more than willing to work eighteen hours a day. There had to be something more in her life, she knew, but what? And where?

Kate looked out the window and saw Danny and John heading their way. "Here come the boys.

They're going to want their share of cake and milk, or maybe sandwiches.''

"Such good children. We'll give them all lunch before you take them home," Gran said, looking as content as could be in her easy chair, a stack of old newspaper clippings on her lap. The girls sat nearby on the couch, a pile of Kate's childhood books stacked in between them. Elly was almost horizontal, her eyelids half-closed as her sister pretended to read a story aloud. "I should call Elizabeth, too, and see how she's holding up."

"I can't believe she hasn't had that baby yet and made you a great-grandmother." Kate scribbled the ingredients for meat loaf on a piece of scrap paper. She could bake potatoes and pick up a fruit salad from the deli section of the supermarket. Gran would want green beans. "Maybe we should ask them for dinner, too."

"Call them," Gert said. "See what's going on out there. We can have ourselves a little party."

"Sure." It was better than Dustin as the only adult male at the dinner table. She really should grow up, Kate mused. She should get over her hopeless attraction to denim-clad men in cowboy boots. She should get over the undeniable sexual pull she felt every time she was within ten feet of Dustin Jones.

"Honey, do you see yourself living here someday?"

"Maybe," Kate said, looking out the window again. "After I've saved enough money."

"Having extra money is a good thing, don't get me wrong, but it won't buy happiness, never will," she declared. "This is a good place to raise children. Edwin and I did just fine. We didn't have much, but we managed."

"Your family was rich." She'd heard her grandmother's stories of growing up in the middle of a proud and prosperous ranching family, one of the oldest in the county if not the state, but Gert had been quiet about her first marriage. "What happened?"

"I was disinherited after I eloped with Hal," she said. "It was quite a scandal at the time. And my father wasn't the easiest man to get along with. He never got over my marrying that man, but my mother helped me out from time to time without my father knowing. Even after Hal died of influenza one winter, my father wouldn't let me in the house."

"That's terrible, Gran. What did you do?"

The woman smiled. "Oh, you'll know soon enough, when I get to that chapter."

"By the way," Kate said. "I thought I'd teach you how to use the computer. Don't frown at me like that. You can learn how to turn it on and turn it off and open your own file."

"I'd rather talk while you type. It's faster that

way and, after all, I'm ninety years old and not getting any younger." She set the clippings aside and struggled to her feet. "I'll help you with lunch, and then later we'll go back to storytelling. Katie Couric isn't getting any younger either."

"Okay." She turned back to the window. Dustin had joined the boys and had stopped walking to listen to something John had to say. Danny still had that shy grin on his face, an expression that tugged at her heart. The boy was too quiet, though, with secrets behind that shy smile and those dark eyes. "I found out Danny hasn't always lived with his father."

"No. I think Dustin is real new to fatherhood, but he does it well." She stood beside Kate at the window and looked out. "He's a fine-looking man," she said. "A girl could do worse."

"If a girl was looking," Kate amended.

"You're looking," her grandmother declared. "At *him*."

Yes, she was. And looking was safe enough.

Safer than touching. Or standing too close. Or, heaven forbid, kissing. She might as well be eighteen again, because she felt as awkward and curious as she had nine years ago. "You'd better start watching what you say. He's heading here with the boys."

"Good," her grandmother said. "We'll ask

them for supper and you can show him what a good cook you are.''

"I'm not auditioning for him, Gran.''

"It's a start.'' The old woman ignored her. "Make a fresh pot of coffee, Kate. And let's see what the man wants.''

THE MAN WANTED KATE, of course. Simple biology, Gert figured. Mix the two of them together often enough and something would happen—such as Kate staying in Texas, and Dustin taking over the ranch permanently. Kate would be a good mother to that little boy. Heaven only knew where that "Lisa" woman was. Gert had asked a few questions, put two and two together. A few years ago a Lisa Jones had rented a garage apartment from the cousin of one of the ladies from church. She'd owed some rent, and the cousin had once commented that Lisa was "bad news all around.''

Well, it didn't take a college graduate to understand that little Danny hadn't lived the kind of life anyone would want for a child. Somehow he'd ended up with Dustin, which certainly was the right place for the boy. Just like the ranch was the right place for Kate. She shouldn't waste her life on those slick city men, with their expensive suits and cologne. Gert even heard that men in the city got manicures, just like women. She'd never heard anything quite so silly in all her life.

She and Kate fed the little boys—to her disappointment Dustin hadn't joined them—and now Kate was off to town again, the Bennett children and Danny tucked into her car. Dustin would come for supper—Gert would see to it he couldn't refuse—and all Gert would have to do was prevent Martha and her opinions from ruining a budding romance. Jake and Elizabeth could be the perfect example of happiness. Gert knew her granddaughter; she wanted children and she loved the ranch. All Kate needed was a little push in the right direction.

"DON'T PUSH," JAKE hollered. "Pant."

Elizabeth glared at him. "I'm having minor—I repeat, *minor*—contractions, Jake. I am not pushing or panting or getting ready to deliver this baby on your grandmother's kitchen table, so please sit down and eat your meat loaf. It could be a while before you get another home-cooked meal this good."

"Thank goodness you're not in pain," Martha said. "Should we be timing them?"

"Not yet," Elizabeth said, picking up her fork and looking for all the world as if she intended to finish her supper. "I'm sure my husband will tell me when I'm ready." She laughed. She was about to have a baby and she was laughing. Kate was impressed.

"Can I get you anything?" Kate lifted the iced tea pitcher. "Something cold to drink?"

"We have beer," Gert added. "If you feel the need."

Elizabeth smiled. "I think I'll stick with the tea. Please don't look so worried. This could be false labor, you know. I've heard it happens."

"Whatever it is," Jake said, looking very pale, "we're going to the hospital to check it out."

"After dessert," his wife said. "And only if we need to."

Dustin and Jake exchanged worried looks, and Kate didn't feel so confident either. The remark about delivering the baby on Gran's kitchen table suddenly wasn't so funny. Elizabeth had a mind of her own, but there was no sense taking any risks.

"Dessert coming right up," Kate announced, standing to clear the table. Dustin rose to help, even though there was still food on his plate. Martha's eyebrows rose as the cowboy lifted her empty plate from in front of her.

"Excuse me," he said, then looked across the table at Kate and gave her one of his quick, rare smiles.

"Why, thank you," Martha said, flustered. "I can help, too."

"Stay there, Mom," Kate told her. "The coffee's ready and I'll serve the last of the birthday cake."

"There's still cake?" Gert frowned. "You'd think we'd have eaten it all by now."

"This is the last night," Kate promised. "Tomorrow we'll have apple pie at the Steak Barn."

"I love cake," Danny said. "'Specially this kind."

"You can have my piece, too," Gert told him. "I think I'm just about caked out."

"Ooh," Elizabeth inhaled, as her worried husband leaned closer.

"Another one?" She nodded, and Jake grew even more pale. He looked over to Dustin, who returned to the table with coffee mugs.

"We'd better go," was all he said, and Dustin nodded, banging the mugs on the table as he set them down.

"I'll drive you," he told Jake.

"Danny can stay here with me," Gert piped up, which made the little boy smile again.

"Take my car," Kate said. "She might be more comfortable in the Lincoln than in a truck."

Elizabeth allowed herself to be helped to her feet as soon as the contraction was over. "I'm sorry to miss dessert," she said, "but I wouldn't mind having this baby finally arrive. Kate? Come with us?"

"What?" Her first panicked thought was how on earth was she going to deliver a baby in the back seat of the Lincoln? She set the dessert plates on the table before she dropped them on the floor. "Are you sure?"

"I think I could use some female companionship right now." In other words, she didn't want to be alone with two frowning ranchers.

"Sure," Kate said, wiping her shaking hands on the sides of her shorts. "Should I bring anything?" Towels, she thought quickly. Boiling water. Rubber gloves. Bandages?

"Fill a thermos," Dustin said.

"With what?"

"Coffee. For the waiting room."

"I'll do that," Martha offered. Since no ranch kitchen held less than five thermoses, Martha easily prepared coffee while Kate ran to the bathroom and grabbed an armload of clean towels, just in case. Jake carried a protesting Elizabeth to the car and tucked her into the back set, then sat beside her and took her hand. Kate and Dustin hurried into the front seat and, once Martha had tossed the thermos into her daughter's lap, Dustin started the Lincoln and sped toward town.

"Should we call the doctor?" Kate moved the stack of towels aside and lifted her cell phone from her purse.

"Good idea," Jake said, but it was Elizabeth who told her the number she'd memorized. Kate dialed and left a message with the answering service.

"Three minutes apart," Elizabeth said anxiously. "Maybe this is going to happen faster than I thought."

Jake swore, and Dustin's fingers tightened on the steering wheel as the car went even faster along the straight empty road. Kate clutched the thermos and wished she'd taken CPR classes.

"I've seen it on your show," Elizabeth said in a breathless voice to Kate. "Babies are born in strange places all the time, right, Kate?"

"All the time," she agreed, thinking her cousin's wife had lost her mind. That was television. Carefully scripted, rehearsed scenes with plastic dolls for babies or, occasionally, a nice healthy infant for the close-ups. She glanced over at Dustin, who looked at her as if she really had lost all sense. "But contractions three minutes apart still gives us time to get you to the hospital." She hoped she sounded as if she knew what she was talking about. "I'll check with Emily," she said, punching the number into the cell phone. "Hi, George? It's Kate and—what?" She listened for a moment, then said, "Okay, good luck," before turning the phone off.

"What?" asked Elizabeth.

"Emily's in labor, too," she said. "George said she was taking a shower."

"A shower?" Jake repeated, incredulous.

"This is her fourth time," Elizabeth exclaimed, still sounding calm. "She's a pro."

"I guess we'll see everyone at the hospital," Kate said, turning around to see how Elizabeth was doing. She lay in Jake's arms, her legs stretched out on the seat, and looked for all the world as if she was enjoying herself. Jake, on the other hand, was a picture of a man about to fall apart. Grim and nervous, he clenched his jaw.

"Is this as fast as this thing can go?" he asked, frowning at the back of Dustin's head.

"Yeah," Dustin answered. "Without flying into a ditch."

"I don't want to give birth to my first child in a ditch," Elizabeth said. "Calm down, Jake. We're going to get through this."

"First and last child," he muttered.

"Uh-oh."

"What?"

"I think my water broke."

Kate tossed a couple of towels to Jake, who helped his wife spread them underneath her.

Dustin slowed down as they drove through Beauville and then sped up again as they flew past the former drive-in north to Marysville. "It won't be long now," he promised.

"Thank goodness," Elizabeth said.

"It's getting worse?"

"No, I don't think the contractions are coming

any faster,'' Elizabeth said. ''But Jake's about to pass out.''

''I am not,'' he said, but Kate wondered. She wasn't feeling so good herself. She looked at her watch at least twenty times on the drive to Marysville, though she was certain Dustin drove it in record time. He pulled up in front of the hospital's emergency room doors and before Dustin could open his door, two paramedics appeared to help Elizabeth from the car.

''Go park,'' one of them told Dustin. ''We'll take it from here.''

''Thank God,'' she heard him mutter under his breath as he put the car in ''drive'' and headed toward the visitors' parking lot.

''You did a great job getting us here,'' she told him, once he'd found a spot and parked. Once the engine was turned off it became very quiet and Kate was aware that the last time they had been in a car together they had taken off most of their clothes and made love.

''I haven't driven that fast since I was seventeen,'' he said, leaning back against the seat. He closed his eyes. ''I was sure hoping she wouldn't have that baby in the car.''

''That only happens on television,'' she assured him.

''Well, you would know.'' He didn't open his eyes as she leaned over and turned the key in the ignition, then pushed the button to lower her window. Almost sundown, the air had cooled slightly, just enough to be comfortable for a few moments.

"Is that supposed to be a slur on my job?" She turned the key to the off position, but before she could lean back Dustin took hold of her wrist to stop her.

"No," he said, looking down at her while he held her arm with gentle, calloused fingers. "I'm sure you got what you wanted."

"You make that sound like a bad thing."

He shook his head. "Nah." He released her, but Kate didn't move far. Instead she waited for him to explain. He just looked at the hospital and said, "I've never seen Jake so nervous."

"Weren't you nervous when your son was born?"

He turned to her and frowned, and she knew she'd somehow trespassed on forbidden territory. "What?"

She tried to sound casual, but she hoped that he would explain about Lisa and Danny and that summer. "When Danny was born. You and, uh, Lisa must have been pretty nervous yourselves."

He stared down at her.

"Danny," he repeated, as if he couldn't understand her. "You're talking about *Danny?*"

"It was a shock," she admitted, willing to get this out in the open. "I admit it. And I was glad to get out of town, especially after my father died.'' Dustin didn't say anything. ''I saw you at the funeral,'' Kate said, remembering a time in her life that she'd rather not think about for too long.

He still didn't say anything.

''I guess I shouldn't have brought this up,'' she said, deciding she'd rather be delivering a baby than having this conversation. She shouldn't still care if he'd had sex with another woman and made her feel like the biggest fool in the world.

But Dustin surprised her. ''We used to spend a lot of time sitting in my old Buick.''

''Maybe we should go in,'' she said, thinking that sitting in a car—any car—with him again was certainly having a sensual effect that was extremely disconcerting. She thought she'd be over that by now, a mature woman of twenty-seven with a career, pension plan, matching furniture and a fistful of mutual funds.

''Not yet,'' he said.

He'd always had the most beautiful mouth. Kate gulped as he reached over and lifted her chin with his index finger. A familiar gesture, and her reaction was to lean closer as his mouth descended. It was the briefest brushing of lips, a mere whisper of what their kisses used to be. Then he kissed her again for a longer time, a kiss that promised hours of kissing and touching and lots, lots more. Kate wanted to sink into his arms, but she kept herself from reaching up to him, kept from moving any closer toward this man who could have her stripped naked in ninety seconds, tops.

Some things didn't change.

DUSTIN DIDN'T STOP her from leaving the car. He followed slowly, moving across the parking lot at his own pace.

So all along she thought Lisa Gallagher had had his baby. She'd left town because she thought he'd slept with Lisa and gotten her pregnant. And all along he had been sure—deep in his heart where it hurt the most—that Kate had left him because she'd finally realized the kid from the wrong side of town wasn't good enough for her.

CHAPTER TWELVE

"THIS ISN'T GOING to work, Mother." Martha rinsed the last of the dinner plates and stacked it in the drainer with the rest of the drying dishes. She'd dry them a little later, while the pans that held the meat loaves soaked.

"What isn't?" Gert looked up from the papers she'd spread all over the kitchen table. Once again, her mother was involved in this silly book business. You'd think a ninety-year-old lady would be content to crochet afghans, not spend her time airing the town's dirty laundry.

"Your matchmaking." She looked into the living room to make sure the boy couldn't hear. He was engrossed in a television show, having explained to "Grandma Gert" earlier that he and his Dad didn't have a television set in the bunkhouse and he sure missed "watchin' all the shows." He seemed like a nice enough child, though a little too quiet. But a quiet child was a refreshing change from some of the little hooligans Martha saw with their mothers in town.

"What are you talking about, Martha? I'm just a nice old lady happy to have the young folks around."

"Don't give me that," her daughter said, tossing the dish towel onto the counter. She sat down at the table and looked at her watch. "You're pushing Kate and that cowboy together, and don't you think I don't know it."

"She could use a man in her life."

Who couldn't? Martha wanted to reply, but she didn't discuss such things with her mother, never had. "Not that man," she said, lowering her voice to a whisper. She didn't want that little boy to hear. "I had to chase him off when they were teenagers. Those Jones boys were never any good."

"Dustin is a good man. And, Martha, you sound like an old witch."

Now that hurt. She didn't want to be called old, witch or not. "I just want the best for Kate."

"In New York?" Gert snorted. "She belongs here, and don't you tell me you don't miss her."

"Oh, I miss her, all right," she admitted. "And I'd do just about anything to see her married and happy and living close to me here in Texas, but everyone has to live their own lives, Mother. We just have to accept that Kate's life is in New York, working on that TV show."

"Speak for yourself, Martha," her mother said,

looking decidedly grumpy. "I don't have to accept any such thing."

Now would be a good time to change the subject, Martha decided. "I wonder how Elizabeth is doing. Poor Jake. He looked terrified that she would have that baby on the way to the hospital."

"I'm sure they made it," Gert declared. "First babies take their time."

"I remember." She'd been in labor with Kate for nineteen hours. Ian, her sweet, quiet, well-mannered Ian, had come close to assaulting the physician to make him do something. The pregnancy itself had seemed like a miracle after wanting a baby so many years. And then "labor" had been exactly that, before the days of so-called "natural" childbirth and all that breathing and panting the young women were so fond of. How proud her husband had been of that wrinkled red infant. "Maybe I should plan on sleeping here tonight."

"The boy, too," Gert agreed. "But Kate will call us, or Dustin will. We'll have news soon enough."

"I suppose," she said, turning around an old newspaper so she could read the headlines. "You're really enthused about this book, aren't you?"

"As the oldest living resident of Beauville, I

think it's important that I write my memoirs," she said.

"Nonsense," Martha replied. "You just like having Kate at your beck and call. And you like the idea of using her computer."

Gert chuckled and smacked the back of Martha's hand with a yellowed envelope. "You're a funny girl, Mattie," she said, using a pet name she hadn't used in years. Martha blinked back tears, silly tears she couldn't explain to herself. "You and Hank were as different as night and day that way."

"Hank had a mean streak." She avoided her mother's eyes and instead pretended to be interested in a yellowed copy of the Dallas paper.

"He must be dead," Gert declared, her voice devoid of emotion. "The last time I talked to him was March 5, 1965. He was falling down drunk and I told him to sober up before he killed someone."

"And what did he say to that?" Martha asked, though she'd heard the story before.

"He said some very unpleasant things," her mother replied. "He was worse than his father that way."

"What do you think happened to him?"

"In my book, I wrote that I think he died in a car accident somewhere. I pray to the good Lord that he didn't take anyone with him." She sighed. "Poor Jake."

"Poor Jake? He was spared, in my opinion. Nancy loved her job at the Dead Horse and R.J. was a better father than Hank could ever have been." Martha took a deep breath and waited for her mother to argue with that opinion, but Gert didn't seem to want to talk about her firstborn any longer.

"Here," she said, pushing the pile of newspaper clippings toward Martha. "Why don't you look through there and see if you can find anything about Beauville and World War I? My mother must have saved those for a reason."

"I suppose," she said, turning them around so she could read the headlines. Nineteen seventeen was safe enough; there was nothing in that year that could stir up trouble.

"IT'S GOING TO BE a while," Jake announced as he entered the hospital's second-floor waiting room. "Elizabeth wants me to send you two home."

"Yeah?" Dustin eyed his friend and former boss. Jake was looking a little gray around the edges. "We've only been here for half an hour." And ten minutes of that had been spent in Kate's car.

"Yeah," Jake said. "This could be a long night."

"We'll stay for a while longer," Dustin said,

wishing Kate wasn't standing so close to him. How in hell was he supposed to carry on a conversation when all he wanted to do was kiss her again? "I'll give Gert a call and fill her in."

"Wish Elizabeth good luck for us," Kate said, giving Jake a hug. "Can we get you anything? Coffee? Something cold?"

He shook his head and released her. "Thanks, hon, but we're all set. The nurses are taking good care of everything and Beth's real comfortable—except for the contractions. They're still three minutes apart, so the doctor said nothing is going to happen right away."

A lot had happened already, Dustin figured, remembering a very willing woman in the front seat of the Lincoln. Kissing her hadn't been in his plans—not even close—but she'd leaned over to turn the key and suddenly she was so close…and it was so easy to touch her, kiss her, taste her.

And so damn dangerous.

Dustin shoved his hands in his pockets and watched Jake hurry out of the waiting room and head back to his wife. They were alone in the small room; its walls were decorated with framed southwestern prints and worn blue-cushioned chairs sat at the edges of a blue-and-green rug.

"I'll call home," Kate said. "If you want to go home to Danny, just take the car. My mother can always pick me up later."

"The boy will be fine with Gert," Dustin said. "For a while longer, anyway." He watched her pull the cell phone out of her purse. "You can't use that in here," he said, pointing to a small sign by the door.

"I'll take it outside."

"I'll go with you." Dustin didn't question why he didn't want to let her out of his sight, but that's the way it was. He should be running from this woman he used to know, a city woman now with a life he could only imagine, and with men and love affairs of which he was immediately and irrationally jealous. He'd always hoped he'd see her again, but for some reason he'd pictured rescuing her—coming upon her while she stood on the side of the road with a flat tire or a broken fan belt, smoke pouring out from under the hood of her car.

And he would, of course, help her. She would be grateful. And he would, as the song played constantly on the radio this spring, ask, "How do you like me now?"

But he hadn't counted on being angry, either. Angry with her for believing the worst of him, for not even asking him if what she'd heard about Lisa was true.

And he was angry with himself, too, for having told her "no strings" and then fallen in love with her. Served him right, too, for being such a cocky bastard.

"Dustin?" He looked over to see her by the door of the room. She looked beautiful and uncertain and a little bit shy, as if she wasn't sure of him. Good. No reason why both of them shouldn't be uncomfortable.

"Coming," he said, wishing he could haul her out of this hospital and to the airport, where she would board a plane to New York and never return. He didn't need Kate McIntosh messing up his life now, not when he was trying to make a life for himself and the boy. He should be running like hell back to the ranch, back to his empty double bed with the cheap sheets and the faded blankets. Back to hard work and dreams of someday owning a piece of the Lazy K.

If he kept his mind on work, he would be fine. If he started remembering nights with Kate, he would get more than a little sidetracked.

He followed Kate down the hall, oblivious to the smell of medicine and the glances of the nurses. Instead he noticed that Kate still had the nicest little body he'd ever had the privilege of getting his hands on. She wore a simple T-shirt and a pair of black shorts, but he'd bet they cost more than a week's pay. She was the elegant type now, and maybe she always had been. When they stepped outside to the portico and she leaned against the wall, Dustin stood a respectable distance away. He watched her dial the phone, talk to Gert and then to her mother while he stood there, hands in his pockets to keep from touching her.

"Just a sec," Kate said, and held out the phone to him. "Gert wants to know if Danny can sleep at the house." He took it from her, brushing her fingers with his own.

"Gert? That would be fine," he told his boss. "Just let him fall asleep on the couch and I'll get him when I come home. Thanks." He handed the phone back to Kate, who spoke for another minute or so, trying to talk Martha out of coming to the hospital, and then tucked the phone away in her purse.

"My mother wants to be here," she said. "She's always been close to Jake."

"She's his aunt, right?"

"Yes, but her best friend is—was—his mother. I think she thinks his mother would want her to look out for him."

Dustin couldn't picture anyone worrying about Jake Johnson. The man was virtually unflappable, and those years on the Dead Horse with Bobby proved that Jake could deal with just about anything. Except childbirth, he thought, remembering the panicked expression in Jake's eyes when they'd arrived at the hospital. The man had looked as if he was going to drop to the pavement in a dead faint. "I worked at the Dead Horse when Elizabeth and her niece came to visit,'' he said. ''I've never seen a man fall so hard so fast.''

''So you met the niece from Paris?''

Dustin smiled. ''Amy Lou. She caused quite a commotion at the ranch last summer. She and Bobby Calhoun were supposed to get married on the Fourth of July, but Amy went to cooking school in France and Elizabeth ended up marrying a cowboy instead.''

''She and Jake are lucky.'' Kate moved to the door. ''I guess we should go back in and see if there's any news.''

''Lucky?'' He shook his head and followed her, holding the door open so she could pass through. ''Not lucky. Smart. They were smart enough to know what they wanted—marriage, family, a place of their own. And they got all three.''

She hesitated. ''And what about you? Didn't you have all that, too?''

''No,'' he said, heading toward the stairs. ''But I have a boy to raise and, if I work hard and cattle prices don't drop, I'll have some money to invest in the Lazy K. Two out of three ain't bad.''

SHE SPENT TIME jotting ideas in the small spiral notebook she kept in her purse. *Harry's baby would be stolen, and its mother would disappear. Christian would discover that he was sterile and he couldn't have fathered Harley's twins. A hos-*

*pital scene where, while waiting for her mother to
come out of a coma, Isabel would fall in love with
a handsome stranger in the waiting room. He
would turn out to be a serial killer, a mental patient or a Texas cowboy about to discover oil on
his property. Or he was the reincarnation of the
man Isabel used to be in love with and—*

"Kate?" She looked up to see Dustin holding
out a cup of coffee. "I thought we could use
some," he said, handing her the cup.

"Where did you find more coffee?"

"The cafeteria was still open. I checked in with
Jake, but he said there's still no baby. You look
beat."

"Baby-sitting the Bennett kids will do that to a
person." She moved the papers off her lap and
opened the lid on the coffee. "I should check again
and see if Emily's here, too."

"I'll ask this time," he said, and left the room
as quietly as he'd entered it. Kate watched him,
wondering if there was a woman in town who
loved him. Wondering if Lisa, wherever she was,
had deserved him. Surely she hadn't, though Kate
didn't know why she was so sure of that. Her
grandmother trusted him, Jake liked and respected
him, his son worshipped him and she herself was,
as she had been nine years before, attracted to him
to the point of forgetting that she was the kind of

woman who usually had more sense than to make love to a man in the back seat of a car.

She was also the kind of woman who sure wouldn't mind doing it again.

CHAPTER THIRTEEN

"IT'S A GIRL," Jake announced. He entered the waiting room and accepted Kate's hug and Dustin's handshake and congratulations. "We're calling her Nancy, after my mother."

Kate blinked back tears. "That's so wonderful, Jake. My mother will be so thrilled."

"Her middle name is Comstock, Beth's middle name," he added, smiling broadly. "She weighs seven pounds, nine ounces and she's twenty-one inches long. Do either of you know what time it is in Paris?"

Dustin chuckled. "Seven or eight hours ahead of us, I think. Does this mean Amy Lou is going to return to Beauville?"

Kate hoped the niece would visit so she could meet her. Her mother alluded to Amy Lou as "the crazy niece who cooks." "She'll want to know she has a new cousin."

Jake nodded. "Beth is the only family the girl has, so she's been worried that something might happen. I'm supposed to call her because Elizabeth has gone to sleep.''

''She's all right?''

''Yeah. Just worn out.'' He looked at his watch. ''Not bad. We were only here for four hours. I passed George Bennett in the hall. It turns out Emily barely made it to the hospital also. I guess the poor guy thought he'd be delivering his baby himself.''

''Is she okay?''

''Yes, and George told me to tell you he'd be—'' He turned as Emily's husband stuck his head in.

''It's a girl,'' he said, beaming. ''Healthy and screaming her lungs out. Em's fine and says she'll see you tomorrow for lunch.''

''That's a joke, right?'' There was no way to know, not with Emily.

''Yep,'' her husband, a beefy ex-high school football player, said. ''Go home. You all look exhausted.''

''Congratulations,'' Dustin told him, walking over to shake his hand. ''Four kids. I don't know how you do it.''

''We're crazy, that's all,'' he said, still grinning. ''You know what it's like raising kids.''

''Yeah,'' Dustin said. ''They keep you busy.''

''Hey, Kate,'' George called, on his way out the

door. "Thanks again for taking the kids to the ranch today."

"Any time," she answered, wishing for a moment that she lived in town and could spend more than a few hours a year with her best friend. Jake turned to follow him.

"I'd better get back, just in case Beth wakes up and needs something. Do you want to see little Nancy?"

"How do we do that?"

"Follow me," Jake said, his voice ringing with pride. "She's in the nursery so Beth can sleep." Kate grabbed the empty thermos and her purse, then hurried to catch up with him as they headed down the hall. Sure enough, the baby Jake pointed to was being held by a nurse. "That's her."

"She's beautiful," Kate said, completely awed by the appearance of this new person into the family.

"Are you sure you don't want a ride home? You look like you could use some sleep," Dustin said.

"I'm fine. One of the nurses said there was a cot I could use, so I'll sleep later." He grinned. "I'm too excited to close my eyes. I'll see you two tomorrow. Thanks for everything."

Kate wrenched her gaze from the baby and turned to her cousin. He looked tired, but triumphant. "Should I call Mom and Gran or will you?"

"I'll call them right now," Jake promised, "if you think they're still awake."

"Mom will be. She's staying at the ranch to-night."

"Sure."

"And Jake? Congratulations," Kate said, tear-ing up. "That little girl is very lucky to have you for a father."

"A father," he repeated. "I'm going to be the kind of father I wish I'd had."

"Yeah," Dustin said. "I know what you mean."

"COME ON," DUSTIN SAID, tugging Kate away from the glass. Eight little babies, in various moods, lay in their bassinets or in a nurse's arms. And they seemed to have the oddest effect on Miss New York City standing beside him. She made smiley faces and waved and even talked baby talk when George lifted his new daughter to show her off. The newest Bennett was already plump and pink, with a strange shock of red hair sticking up from the top of her head. They'd caught another brief glimpse of little Nancy—a tiny round face peering out of a pink blanket—as she was taken into her mother's room.

"Just a minute," Kate said, pointing for George to come over to the door. "What's her name?"

she mouthed, before the nurse opened the door to let her speak.

George shrugged. "Emily's still thinking. She said she was too tired to make a decision."

"Oh. Well, tell her I'll stop in tomorrow and find out."

"Sure. Hey, make that cowboy take you home," he called before the nurse shut the nursery door.

"There," Dustin said, figuring he needed to take her arm and remove her physically from the building. "You've had your orders."

"Okay," she said, but with great reluctance.

"I didn't know you liked babies so much."

"Why wouldn't I like babies?"

He shrugged, figuring he should have kept his mouth shut, and headed for the stairs. "I don't know. You have the fancy career and all." He didn't feel like talking about babies and he sure didn't feel like waiting for an elevator to go down one floor. He wanted to get out into the fresh air and away from those excited fathers. Fatherhood was tough enough with an eight-year-old; he didn't know how Jake and George could be so excited about starting from scratch.

"What about you?" she asked, keeping up with him as they hurried down the stairs to the lobby.

"What about me?" He crossed the antiseptic-smelling area in quick strides and pushed the door open for Kate to go through first.

"Do you want more children?"

"Hell, no." He hadn't really wanted the one he had, but he couldn't say that. Danny was a decent boy, but it wasn't easy trying to build a home for him. And a future. Life had been a lot easier when he'd been alone, during the years he'd left Beauville and worked on other ranches. He'd returned to the Dead Horse a few years back and stayed away from his brother's troubles for as long as he could. And then he'd done what he had to do for the sake of the boy. Danny was family, after all. "I'm not figuring on getting married real soon."

"Does Danny see his mother at all?"

"Not if he's lucky." He was too tired to worry about what Kate thought, he realized. He'd been up since four, trying to get a lot of the heavier work done before the heat of the day. He didn't like to work the horses in this heat unless it was the crack of dawn.

"She's that bad?"

"Yeah," he said, knowing that Kate, with her perfect parents and perfect childhood would never be able to understand. "That bad." She had that look on her face as if she wanted to ask a lot of questions, so Dustin braced himself to withstand the onslaught.

"Want me to drive?" She held out her hand for the keys. "You look beat."

"I'm not that tired," he said. "We'll stop at the

truck stop and get breakfast before we head home. It's after two already and I just realized how hungry I am."

"We used to do that after the movies." And then she blushed, remembering, as he did, exactly how they had worked up an appetite.

"Yeah. There were a lot of things we used to do." He unlocked the doors, held the passenger door open for her and went around to the driver's side of the car. She still had a great set of legs. And a great rear end, too. And since he'd never been accused of being brilliant, here he was fantasizing about making love to this woman. Again.

He'd started up the car and was halfway out of the parking lot before she spoke again.

"Remember the time the sheriff almost caught us?" Kate asked, turning toward him with a wry smile on her face. "We hadn't known the movie was over and everyone else had left."

"He figured I was up to no good, all right."

"I talked him out of arresting you and not telling my dad."

"Your father would have come after me," Dustin said.

"No, he wouldn't," she said. "I think he liked you. It was my mother we would have had to worry about."

"She's still someone I don't want to tangle with," he admitted, and Kate smiled at him.

"I know what you mean. She's probably worried about us being together right now, in the middle of the night, without Jake and Elizabeth to chaperone."

"I have an idea," he said, stepping on the gas. "We'll get breakfast, if you can wait another twenty or thirty minutes."

"Sure, but why—"

"For old time's sake," he said. "And because I'm starving." And also because he didn't know when or how he would have the chance to be alone with her again. He didn't want to think about making love to her, but there was something about Kate that made him think of nothing else. Maybe it was time to get it out of his system once and for all. And from all indications, Kate would agree.

"WE'RE TRESPASSING," Kate whispered, holding the bag filled with fast-food breakfast items on her lap. The coffee, sitting in the cup holders, smelled delicious. She was suddenly ravenous, she realized as she peered out the window at the Good Night Villas construction site.

"You don't have to whisper," he said, guiding the car past the building toward the back of the property. "There's no one around."

That was true. She felt a little more at ease when Dustin found the spot off to the side in back, where the original parking area hadn't been disturbed, and shut off the car engine and lights. He switched the interior light on so Kate could distribute the food, but turned it off again when they had their breakfast sandwiches on their laps.

"This is very strange," Kate said, after she'd eaten half of an egg- and cheese-filled croissant.

"Why?"

"You and me. Here. With our clothes on."

"You can take your shirt off," he offered, "if it would make you feel better."

"No, thanks." She hoped he was only joking. "We'll just stay dressed and act like adults," Kate said, though the temptation to toss the uneaten food back into the bag and climb into the back seat was certainly unsettling. "What would you have done if it was me who had gotten pregnant that summer instead of Lisa?"

Dustin choked on his English muffin egg sandwich, so Kate handed him a napkin and waited for him to catch his breath. "For cripe's sake, Kate," was all he could say, "what made you bring that up?"

"We're sitting here at the scene of the crime, so to speak. It's nine years later, and I want to know."

"I would have married you, of course, if your parents didn't kill me first."

"Really?"

He frowned at her. "Well, of course. What kind of a question is that?"

She shrugged and took a sip of the coffee, which was pretty terrible stuff. "I've always wondered."

"Yeah? What else have you wondered?"

"Why you had sex with her at the same time you were having sex with me." There. She leaned back against the car door and watched him, wondering if he would give her the answer to the question that had bothered her for years. "I know that was a long time ago," she added, not wanting him to think this was something she dwelt upon on a regular basis. "But this seems a good time and place to ask."

"Yeah?" He set his coffee cup on the dashboard. "Nine years later seems like a good time to ask? Did you ever think of asking me any of this before you kicked me out of your life?"

She remembered that night all too well. She'd been hurt and embarrassed and miserable because she had fallen in love with him. He'd warned her beforehand. He'd said, "No strings, sweetheart." And she'd foolishly believed she could make love to him without her heart getting broken. "No. I was too angry."

"*You* were angry?" He stared at her, his gaze intense upon her face. She wanted to look away, but she didn't. "Look, Kate, you asked me a question. I answered it. I didn't grow up rich and pampered in a big house on Apple Street facing the park. I had a pretty crappy home life, Katie, but if

you were the one who'd gotten pregnant that summer I would have married you and done whatever
I could to make you happy. Does *that* answer your
question?''

''I guess it does.'' She wished she could see
Dustin's face, but the interior of the car was fairly
dark except for the dim glow of the construction
site spotlights coming in through the back window.
She reached her hand out to touch his arm.

He tugged her toward him. ''There's something
about sitting in a car with you—''

''Do you think it's an automobile fetish?''

''Definitely,'' Dustin whispered. Their lips were
almost touching, and then came the kind of kiss
she remembered—and had tried to forget. Her
arms looped around his neck and the half-eaten
breakfast sandwich slid off Kate's lap and onto the
seat. He tasted of coffee when her tongue touched
his when her lips parted to allow him entrance. She
moved closer, not noticing that her knee squished
an uneaten square of fried potatoes or her coffee
was perilously close to tipping out of the cup
holder. All Kate knew was she was kissing Dustin
again, at the Good Night Drive-In, and all was
right with her world.

His hands held her waist, then inched up under
her blouse to smooth her skin. Oh, yes, Kate
thought, murmuring a little sound of approval as
his fingers touched her. He was still the best kisser

she'd ever known, with the most tantalizing long fingers and a way of moving his tongue that made her want to wrap her arms around his neck and hang on. And she did.

Kate didn't know if she was eighteen or twenty-seven, if it was sunrise or sunset, if she was in Manhattan or Beauville. None of that mattered anyway. His hand was on her breast and his tongue tangled with hers and everything was as it should be. Familiar and yet so amazing and different, kissing Dustin brought back memories of hot sex and even hotter Texas nights.

"Damn bucket seats," he muttered, after easing his mouth from hers.

"I should have rented a van."

They tried to catch their breath, but it wasn't easy. Kate could feel the heat emanating from his body and knew her own was equally warm, willing and able. Her brain and common sense disappeared when he lifted her and easily positioned himself in the passenger seat, with Kate on his lap.

Straddling him was a heavenly position, Kate decided. Not ladylike or remotely subtle, but an easy angle from which to lower her head and kiss him. She felt his arousal through layers of cotton and resisted wriggling against him. Kissing was enough for now, and his fingers fumbling with the buttons of her blouse more than enough stimulation to make brain activity impossible.

Leaning into his body would guarantee that she was lost, so Kate held herself back. But clearly Dustin had other ideas. Once her blouse opened, he moved his hands to her waist and tugged, bringing the heat of her against the hardness of him and setting them both on fire. Clearly, Kate thought in a haze, there would be no turning back. And, with the delicious sensations radiating from her body, why would she want to?

Dustin's hands moved to the waistband of her shorts and found her zipper as Kate attempted to unbutton his shirt. She used to be better at this, she remembered, but—

"You're trespassing," came a loud male voice, and a beam of light shone on Kate's face, making her open her eyes and then close them again before she went blind. Dustin released her, then turned toward the intruder. The windows were open, so the flashlight came closer. "This is the deputy sheriff. You two, break it up. You're under arrest."

"THEN WHAT HAPPENED?" Emily tucked her baby against her breast and rearranged the blankets so that nothing was exposed. She was due to leave the hospital this afternoon, but had convinced the nurses she needed a few more hours rest before going home to care for four children. "Was it Carter? He picks up all the extra hours he can since he got engaged. I think he's saving up for a house.''

"Yes. And Dustin knew him. He went to school with Dustin's older brother.''

Emily chuckled. "It's still a small town. Lucky for you.''

"Not exactly. I guess Darrell, the brother, had—has—quite a reputation in the county. It took a while to convince the man that we weren't there to steal construction supplies or deal drugs. He finally caught on that we were two stupid adults making out in a rental car, but it took forever before he let us go.''

"And then what?'' Emily leaned forward, her eyes sparkling. "Tell me you had sex with him.''

"I did not have sex with him.'' But she certainly would have, if the Beauville sheriff's deputy hadn't interrupted. "I'm not sure things would have gone that far.''

"Hah,'' her friend said. "Your face gets red every time you talk about him.''

"It's because of our past together.''

"It's because you're on vacation and he's around and you're around and—'' she waved her free hand to indicate the cheery hospital room—"one thing leads to another and then you're in here having your fourth baby.''

"Speak for yourself,'' Kate said, but her gaze

was on the little girl who was intent on nursing. "She really is beautiful."

"Then have a few of your own," Emily said. "Grab that cowboy and take him back to the drive-in tonight. Or here's a novel idea—why don't you ask him out?"

"On a date?"

"Don't they do that in New York?"

"They do, but—"

"No 'buts,'" Emily insisted. "I want you to stay here in Beauville with me and Elizabeth and Lorna. Our kids can grow up together and raise hell while we complain and drink frozen margaritas and give birthday parties."

"I'd need a husband first."

Emily grinned. "Now why do I think that wouldn't be any trouble?"

"He was never in love with me," Kate said, knowing Emily would know who she was referring to. "So there's no reason to think he'd fall in love with me now."

"No?"

"No," Kate declared. This was the problem with being a romantic. She was a writer with a wild imagination, and he was a rancher trying to relive the good old days. These kinds of sexual journeys into the past never worked.

And she'd better keep reminding herself that if she got hurt again, she had only herself to blame.

CHAPTER FOURTEEN

SHE'D HOPED TO keep the drive-in incident quiet, but Kate realized she should have known that her mother would hear of it.

"I knew he'd get you in trouble," Martha declared, shaking her head outside of Emily's hospital room. It hadn't taken her mother long to track her down this morning. Martha was on her way out the door of the ranch when Kate finally woke up. It had been a long, sleepless night. "Those Jones boys are no good. He almost got you put in jail for trespassing!"

"It wasn't exactly—" Kate tried, moving her mother toward the nursery window so the sight of the babies might distract her.

"Carl thought it was somewhat humorous," her mother continued, having declined Kate's offer of a ride to Marysville this morning because the real estate mogul had offered first. "The sheriff's office called him at two this morning to check out your story. It's a good thing Carl knew who you are."

"I'm sorry they had to wake him," Kate said,

taking her mother's elbow and moving her toward the babies in the window. "Have you seen Elizabeth? Doesn't she look wonderful?"

"Yes, of course she does, but Kate, how on earth could you start up a relationship with that man?"

"It's not a relationship. It was just…" Kate hesitated. "I don't know what it was," she fibbed, knowing it was lust, pure and simple. On both sides. And it had felt great, before the deputy sheriff's intrusion.

"It's embarrassing, that's what it is," her mother informed her. "I know those kind of men, and they're no good."

"Mom, what on earth are you talking about? Dustin's a perfectly nice man, who happens to work for Gran. I've known him for years. Oh, look, here we are in front of the babies. Aren't they sweet?"

"You won't find little Nancy in there," Martha said, barely glancing toward the infants. "Your grandmother is still holding her in Elizabeth's room. Did you get pictures?"

"I sure did. Where's Carl? I'll apologize to him in person."

"He's visiting a friend of his father's who had surgery. I'm going to meet him at noon and we're going to have lunch on the way back to town. How is Emily?"

"Fine, of course. She's going home later."

"I'll stop in and say hello. Oh, is that the Bennett baby?" She pointed to the glass, where George was bundling up an infant to cradle in his arms. "Such a good father, that man," Martha said. "You should be so lucky to find a man like that, instead of fooling around with actors and cowboys."

"You know, Emily and George did their share of making out at the Good Night Drive-In, too," Kate pointed out. "Jennie may even have been conceived there, Mother."

"Oh, stop your teasing," Martha said, waving to George, who grinned at them and held up his new daughter.

"Teasing? I'm serious. And there's nothing wrong with cowboys," Kate replied, remembering Dustin's hands on her skin. Those very skillful hands had been heading toward her breasts when James Carter decided to earn his moonlighting money.

"Are we going out to dinner tonight?" Kate added.

"Oh. Yes." Her mother didn't look as excited as Kate thought she'd be about filet mignon and peach shortcake with freshly whipped cream tinged with cinnamon, a tradition when Kate was home on vacation. "I almost forgot that was tonight."

Her mother was more interested in what Carl

Jackson was doing tonight, Kate supposed. This behavior wasn't typical of her pleasant, overprotective, domestic and contented mother. For a split second Kate wondered if Carl had shown Martha his construction site one late night, but then she thought better of it. Martha McIntosh, age sixty-four, would never be caught dead in a compromising position.

For the thousandth time, Kate thought about kissing Dustin last night. Her mother was missing a lot of fun.

THERE WERE SOME things a man wanted to dwell upon and some things that didn't bear thinking about twice, Dustin decided. He'd spent the morning riding fence, checking water supplies and listening to Danny chatter on and on about Grandma Gert and Aunt Martha. Since when had the boy made Kate's cranky mother an honorary relative? No, he didn't want to think about the disapproving glances Kate's mother gave him whenever he walked into a room. And that he wished he could stop thinking about the way Kate felt in his arms last night, all trembling and warm and very, very willing.

Like the past nine years had never happened. Put the two of them together and it was just so damn hard to remember that they hadn't seen each other since they were teenagers.

Kate wasn't at the ranch now. He'd seen her take Gert in her car, most likely heading to the hospital to see that baby, and he'd seen Martha leave with Jackson, who was sure to tell about last night.

This would be a good day to lie low, Dustin figured. He'd work on remembering that he was a father now, with a ranch to run and money to make. He shouldn't be lusting after an ex-girlfriend as if he had no more sense than a longhorn bull.

"Daddy?" Danny's voice broke into his thoughts, and Dustin glanced toward the boy who was hanging on to the door of the pickup as if he was afraid of being tossed out the window.

"What?"

"Where's my mom?"

"I don't know," which was the honest truth, but Dustin didn't add "and I don't give a damn," which also was the truth.

"Am I gonna live here with you all the time?"

"Yeah," Dustin promised. "Remember how I told you we have to talk to the judge and make everything legal? Well, we're set to do that in a few weeks."

"Lee-gal," the boy repeated, liking the sound of the word. "Everything legal."

"Yeah. That's right." And Lisa would never be able to get her hands on the boy again. Lisa Gallagher Jones sure as hell didn't deserve any rights to her son.

"Are you gonna get a wife?"

Dustin chuckled and stopped the truck at a metal gate. He hopped out and pushed the gate open before returning to the truck. The boy was too small to open and close gates, but one of these days he'd be big enough to help out.

"Why do you think I need a wife?" he couldn't help asking as he drove through the gate and parked again.

The boy shrugged. "To make dinner and cake and stuff like that."

"We have Grandma Gert for that." God, it was hot today. He wiped his forehead and thought once again about Kate and last night. He'd have given a lot to take her home to bed, to have spent the night making love to a warm and willing woman who had the sweetest way of parting her lips—

"Daddy," Danny said. "What about the gate?"

"Yeah," he said, realizing he almost forgot to close the damn thing. He climbed out of the truck and pushed the heavy metal gate shut, making sure it was latched securely, before striding back to the Ford. If she was any other woman he'd take her out for dinner or into Marysville to see a movie, then for drinks and some snuggle-up dancing at the Last Chance. But she wasn't just any woman. Now she was Kate, big city lady, with fancy clothes and an even fancier attitude.

Dustin stopped short of the truck and looked at what he had to offer a woman like that: a dusty three-year-old truck, some shares in a struggling cattle venture, a bed in the bunkhouse and a little boy recovering from a broken heart. It wasn't much, he knew. And no amount of great sex would convince Kate McIntosh even to consider staying in Beauville past next week.

"WELL, THAT'S A REAL nice picture," Gert said, admiring herself on the front page of the "What's Happening" section of the *Beauville Times*. "That Danny's such a cute little fella."

Martha muttered something Gert couldn't hear, then raised her voice. "He looks as if he's one of the family, for heaven's sakes. And look, there's Kate standing there like she's his mother."

"I told you they were perfect for each other." Gert didn't mind needling her daughter now and then, just to hear her squawk.

"He's a nice enough child," Martha admitted, having spent Monday evening teaching him card games and feeding him cake. Gert had seen her make sure the boy was comfortably settled on the couch, with a light on so he wouldn't wake up in a strange place and be afraid.

"You need grandchildren," Gert declared.

"Shh," Martha warned, settling herself onto the couch. "She's coming down the stairs now."

"Kate?" Gert peered over her pile of scrapbooks to see if Kate had found the photo albums. Sure enough, her granddaughter had an armload of them. "I'm glad I thought of putting pictures in my book," she said.

"Yeah, I think the pictures will really—"

"Are we going over to see Jake's baby again tomorrow?" Gert interrupted. She liked babies, and she figured Kate's exposure to the little sweethearts might just keep her in Texas.

"Sure. They'll be home from the hospital." Kate set the photo albums on the floor at Gert's feet. "We'll bring them some casseroles."

"About this book," Martha began, frowning before she sneezed. "Who have you told about this, Mother?"

"Just the family. And that man friend of yours." Gert reached for the top album. What she wanted was a picture of herself with her horse. For the cover.

"Did you by any chance tell Doris Hansen?"

"The librarian? Why yes, when I did my research a few weeks ago. She seemed interested."

"Well, it's all over town that you're writing a book and several people came up to me at bridge this afternoon and asked me about it."

"What'd they want to know?" She was up to

the 1940s now and still going strong. Kate had only been home a few days and already she'd taught her grandmother how to run that mysterious computer. It wasn't so hard after all, Gert decided, as long as you didn't hit too many keys at once and didn't spill anything on it. Once you got the thing turned on it pretty much told you what to do, though she forgot how to turn it off and had to follow Kate's written directions each time.

"I'm not sure," Martha answered. "I think folks are a little suspicious of the whole thing."

Kate looked amused. "Do people in Beauville have that many secrets?"

"Well," Gran said, "Doris Hansen's great-grandfather was said to have escaped a murder charge in California by jumping on a train. When he woke up, he was in Beauville."

"Mother," Martha said, pushing the photo albums aside as if they were dead cats. "I don't know why you think you have to resurrect the past."

"We've had our share of problems, too," Gert declared. "Your brother—wherever he is—caused his share of heartache."

"Amen to that," Martha breathed.

"And his father wasn't much better," Gert added. "I've written that part already. Now I'm at the time when the boys were going off to war."

"It's very good so far," her writer granddaughter said. "Gran has a terrific memory for details."

"All I'm saying is that no one wants their dirty laundry aired in public, Kate. What's private should stay that way."

"Mom, I'm beginning to think you have a deep dark secret you don't want anyone to find out."

Gert raised her eyebrows at that. The guilty expression on Martha's face proved Katie right. "Is that so, Martha? And can I use it in the book?"

Her daughter stood up and picked up her purse. "I'm not going to listen to this kind of talk," she said. "Besides, I thought we were going out to dinner tonight."

"It's only three o'clock, Martha," Gert felt obliged to point out. "You want to eat at three o'clock?"

"I'm going to get my hair done," her daughter said. "I'm thinking of a blond rinse. And I'm tired of talking about secrets." With that, she swept out of the room. A few seconds later the back door slammed and, sure enough, when Gert leaned back in her chair and peered out the front window, she saw Martha's car making dust as she headed out to the highway.

"My goodness," Gert declared, chuckling at her granddaughter. "Your mother's a little edgy lately, don't you think?"

"Maybe she's spending too much time with Mr. Jackson."

"Or not enough," Gert pointed out. Seemed like Martha might need some male companionship. The woman had to get lonely; after all, Ian had been gone for nine years. "Your father was a fine man, but it just might be time for your mother to marry again."

"Marry? She's talking about moving into those retirement villas, not getting married." Kate didn't look too pleased.

"I'm sure you both miss your father," Gert said. "That heart attack took him so fast, I've never seen anything like it."

"I couldn't wait to leave and go to college," Kate admitted. "The house was so empty without him."

"Maybe Martha's feeling the same way now." She managed to lift herself out of the chair and wandered over to the kitchen window. "Dustin's back. His truck is parked by the horse barn. You haven't been riding yet, have you?"

"No."

"I still keep a few horses," Gert said. "They could use some exercise, if someone wanted to go out there and saddle them up."

"I'll ride tomorrow morning," she said, "when it's not too hot. I'm going to get the rest of my things from town and spend the rest of my vacation here. That way I can get some work done.''

"What kind of work?" She watched for signs of the man or the boy. Sometimes Dustin stopped in to tell her what was going on. She liked that, when he'd come over and talk to her about cattle and feed and how the water was holding up. The boy would drink lemonade or milky, sugared coffee and it would be like the old days, when she ran this place and the foreman—Sandy, that was his name—would check in and see what she thought needed doing.

She liked a man who knew how to communicate. Gert turned toward her granddaughter, a young woman who didn't have the sense to know she had a place in the world and a good man to claim. Kate was pretty and smart, independent, too—a good thing in a woman, Gert knew, because it kept you from depending on other people to make you happy—but she should be running the Lazy K. She should be having babies and making love to a hard-working man who would work along with her and make something of their lives together.

"Kate," Gert said, and her granddaughter looked up from the photo albums, "the barn needs painting real bad."

"Dustin said he was working on it."

"The man doesn't have time," Gert said, sighing to show how worked up she was about it.

"And I just get so depressed looking at that barn now and seeing how run-down it looks."

Kate untangled her legs and walked over to look out the window, too. "Well," she said, "I have ten more days. You must have a ladder around here somewhere."

"Dustin can do the high spots. If you could work on the barn and then maybe the outbuildings it would sure be a big help." And it would put Kate outside with the cowboy, who sure as shootin' wouldn't be able to stay away from her.

"Sure."

"We'll stop and get more paint and brushes tonight in town," she said. Painting could lead to other things, of course. Gert hid her smile of satisfaction and then decided to try one more thing. "Why don't you make a fresh pot of coffee? I could use a cup myself, and Dustin might stop by."

"Dustin? Why?"

"Well, to tell me how things are going," Gert explained. "He usually comes by around three-thirty." And he would come if she hung a red rag in the window. That was their private signal, one that meant Gert wanted to talk. She rummaged through her linen drawer—Kate must have re-arranged it—while Kate fussed with the coffee grinding machine she liked so much. It only took a second to tuck the edge of the red bandanna into the window latch.

CHAPTER FIFTEEN

"YOU'RE GOING TO finish painting the barn," Dustin repeated, as if he'd never heard anything so crazy in his life. Kate set a mug of coffee in front of him and ignored that she was only inches away from him. If they were alone she'd sit on his lap and start kissing him again, so it was a good thing Gran and Danny were in the room. In fact, she noticed, the chaperones were destroying a perfectly good cup of coffee by adding large amounts of cream and sugar.

"Yes." Kate brought her own cup of coffee to the table and sat down across from Dustin. "It was Gran's idea. She's doing most of her own typing now." And she'd cleaned out the refrigerator, scrubbed the cupboards and washed the kitchen floor until the old linoleum turned a shade lighter. "And she'd like some of the outbuildings painted."

He frowned and turned to her grandmother, who was busy dishing out cookies to Danny.

"They're only store-bought," Gran explained,

plopping several chocolate chip cookies onto Danny's napkin. "But I like 'em anyway."

"Yeah," the boy said. "Me, too."

"Gert," Dustin said, trying to get her attention. "I'll get the barn done myself, but Kate—"

"Is perfectly capable of holding a paintbrush," Kate finished for him. "I've done it before."

"Not in this kind of heat you haven't."

"I'll wear a hat." She would show him. Maybe she wasn't baking cinnamon rolls or having babies or training horses, but she could dip a brush into a bucket of paint and slap it on the side of a barn.

"You'll start at dawn then," the man said. "You can't work much past nine, not in these temperatures."

"What time is dawn?" she asked, though she thought she should know, having been out with him until three-thirty or so the other morning.

"Five." Dustin took another sip of coffee. "I'll meet you on the west side of the horse barn tomorrow morning."

"You're going to paint, too?"

"No. I'll just get you started, get a ladder, things like that." That's when he looked at her and smiled. "I'll bet ten bucks you're not an early riser, are you?"

"I can manage," she promised. "Don't worry about me."

"Kate's a good worker," Gert declared, passing

Dustin a plate full of cookies. "'Course she doesn't belong in New York, but that's her business. She'd be better off comin' home and takin' over the Lazy K."

"Gran—"

Dustin turned that cool gaze her way again. "So why don't you?" He really was handsome, better looking than nine years ago.

"I—" she began, then stopped when she realized she didn't have an answer. Her home was here, in Texas, but her job—her career—was in New York. But was she really happy working seventy-hour weeks and dealing with the insanity of an hour-long television show that ran five days a week?

"See?" Gert chuckled. "My granddaughter is speechless. That doesn't happen very often."

"I'm a television writer. I don't know anything about running a ranch," Kate said, leaving the table on the pretense of getting the coffeepot. She would refill cups that didn't need refilling and try to change the subject back to painting barns. "We'll get more paint tonight when we're in town."

"I've got plenty," Dustin said. "Enough to get you started, anyway."

"You know more than you think you know," her grandmother insisted, not content with discussing paint. "You hire the right people and you start learning from those who know more than you do, people you trust.'' Gran smiled and handed Danny another cookie. ''Besides, ranching's in your blood. You come from five generations of Texans, Katie. How many people can say that?''

''What's 'in your blood' mean?'' the boy asked.

''It means you're born liking things your daddy likes,'' Gert replied. ''And you've got a good daddy. Maybe you'll grow up to be a rancher, too.''

Kate glanced toward Dustin, who was looking at her as if he wanted to get into a car and drive away someplace private and without deputy sheriffs with flashlights and attitudes. Well, there was a lot of land here on the Lazy K. If he wanted to be alone with her, all he had to do was open a car door and ask.

''I've got some cows to check on,'' the man said, serious as he could be though his dark eyes held a gleam that could only be described as X-rated. ''Do you want to take a ride with me?''

Bingo.

''Go on,'' her grandmother said. ''Danny and I will play a game of cards, won't we, boy?''

''Sure.'' He didn't even check with his father first, Kate noticed. The little kid really liked having Gert for a grandmother.

''Okay,'' Kate said, wondering if she should

sound so eager. It probably wasn't ladylike. "Let me get a hat."

"There's an extra in the truck." He stood and took his empty coffee cup to the sink. "We won't be gone more than an hour or two."

"I need to be back by five-thirty."

"There's no hurry," Gert said. "I'll call your mother and tell her we'll meet later, say about seven. Go on." She made a gesture as if shooing them out of the kitchen. "Go make my granddaughter into a rancher," she told Dustin. "I could use some more help around here."

"You got me," Danny piped up. "I help."

"Yes, you sure do, honey, and—" her voice was drowned out by the squeak of the back door opening. Dustin put his hand on Kate's back and gently pushed her outside into the hot afternoon sun.

"I'd say we're going to be gone quite a while," the man declared.

"Look, Dustin, I—"

"Let's make your grandmother happy," he said. "And I wouldn't mind some cheering up myself."

"Is this about last night?"

"Forget about that," the man said, and Kate turned around to look up at him. "Let's go for a ride."

Forget about last night? Forget the way the cowboy's hands felt on her skin and what heated relief it was to sink against him and start making love?

Not likely.

HE TOLD HIMSELF he wanted to talk about the ranch, wanted to know where he stood should Gert move to town or—God forbid—die and leave the ranch to Jake and Kate. Jake would keep him on as foreman; he couldn't see the Johnsons moving off their own place and setting up housekeeping at the Lazy K. In a perfect world Kate would stay in New York and he would stay on as foreman, with free rein to improve the place, turn a profit and continue to run a few head of cattle himself.

In a perfect world, Kate would be naked and willing in his bed tonight, too.

She looked about twelve years old sitting beside him wearing a faded green baseball cap sporting the logo of Beauville Feed & Grain. He headed the truck north, with no particular destination in mind, except there was a pretty stand of cottonwoods by the creek up there. He decided there was only one way to deal with Kate McIntosh, and that was by making love to her. It was safe enough, he told himself. He was older and wiser. The boy who had promised "no strings" and gotten tangled up in love was now a grown man. A serious man with responsibilities and all sorts of experience. A man more than capable of protecting his heart against visiting city women.

But the rest of him wanted her. After all, here was Kate—long legs, gold-streaked hair, hazel eyes that with one look could make him hard. Could make him long for privacy and a long dark night to have her all to himself.

A hot bright afternoon would be the next best thing.

"Where are we going?"

He glanced toward her. "Do you care?" He dared her to protest, dared her to object.

"I suppose not." She stifled a yawn.

"Short night."

"Yes." She chuckled. "I think we'd better stay out of drive-ins from now on."

"Do you think that would solve this?"

"I don't think anything will, until I go back to New York."

"Out of sight, out of mind," he muttered, annoyed with the reminder of her other life. They rode in silence, as Dustin wondered if he'd made another mistake. He should have left her to paint the barn, should have spent his day far from any living creatures except for cattle.

But he wanted her. He hadn't slept much last night, knowing she was within walking distance.

He'd vowed to get her out of his system and then get on with his life, whatever it was he ended up doing. Fatherhood was going okay, even if he didn't have much experience at it. The boy seemed content enough with three meals a day and his own bed to sleep in.

Dustin parked the truck in the meager amount of shade a couple of scraggly trees provided. The brook was a mud puddle, and a couple of heifers eyed them from the other side of the sloping bank.

"Now what?" She turned to face him and he thought he saw her smile as if to tease. He didn't feel like smiling back.

"You're angry," she said. "Why?"

He could have told her then, he supposed. Explained he was angry that she'd believed some stupid rumors. Because she'd tossed him aside and all this time he'd thought it was because a wild Jones boy wasn't good enough for the honor student in the fancy home. She hadn't cared enough to ask him for the truth, hadn't loved him enough to suspect that there could have been an explanation, hadn't given him a chance to explain that he couldn't think of making love to someone else when Kate was in his life and in the back seat of his car.

"Sweetheart," he drawled. "Why would I be angry?" He was, though. It was old and went deep and he didn't like himself for holding on to it. He could tell her the truth any time he chose, but he didn't want to. Not yet. Let her think what she wanted—she had for all these years, so what difference did it make now?

Dustin took a deep breath and looked out the window. The heifers looked back at him as if they too waited for the next move. He turned to face her. "You kiss like a woman who hasn't been with anyone for a long time."

"And you're an expert on women, of course," came the reply. She looked at him as if she was trying to solve a puzzle. He didn't think she'd have much luck.

"Of course."

"You act like a man who hasn't been with a woman in a long time," she answered.

"And you would recognize the signs?" He didn't want to think of the other men she'd slept with. She was his—or she would be soon, if his instincts were right—and that was all that mattered.

"Let's stop this," Kate said. "I don't want to fight with you anymore."

"No," he agreed, taking his hands from the steering wheel. His fingers were stiff. He turned off the ignition and looked at her again. She took off the cap and ran her fingers through her hair as casually as if they were in the middle of a crowd.

"We can leave anytime," she said. "And we can stay away from each other for the rest of my vacation. It wouldn't be so hard to do."

"It would be impossible," Dustin said. "Gert is doing her best to throw us together."

"I can talk to her, get her to stop," Kate said.

"We came here to finish what we started last night," he reminded her, though the coward in him wanted her to fly back to New York this afternoon.

"Yes," she said, those hazel eyes studying him. "Do you think making love will help?"

"Couldn't hurt," he answered, as if discussing sex with her was effortless. His insides were re-arranging into knots.

"Oh, yes, it could," came her soft reply. Dustin wondered if she was finally being honest with him.

He reached for her, took her left hand and brought it to his mouth. He kissed her warm palm briefly. "I won't hurt you, Katie," he promised.

She was silent a moment.

"No strings?" Her question echoed his cocky declaration of years before. Her fingers swept his jaw and tempted him to kiss her.

"No strings," he agreed, though he knew as he spoke that he lied. He held her hand against his face for the length of a heartbeat and then, with his free hand, urged her closer. Her arms went to his shoulders, his hands cupped her face. The first kiss was light and sweet, a cautious brush of lips that tested his patience and teased his willpower.

He had neither. The next kiss, heated and intense, meant business. He wondered how he'd survived so long without kissing her, without moving his hands to the back of her head to hold her mouth against his. Kate moved closer, kneeling to meet him as she had so many other times before so that their lips would be level, so that she could slant her mouth and part her lips and take his tongue inside her mouth to tangle and mate with his.

He'd give all the cattle in Texas if he could keep kissing Kate McIntosh. It had been too long, a lifetime too long, since the last time he'd held her. Dustin managed to slide his hands to her back, skim her waist and dip under her T-shirt. Her skin was hot, reminding him of some pretty damn steamy nights in the drive-in. Reminding him of what it was like to be inside of her.

"Kate," he managed, lifting his mouth a scant inch from hers. His hands swept high under her shirt and touched the satiny fabric of her bra. "I don't want to do this on the front seat of the truck."

"No?" Her hands dropped to his chest and fumbled with the buttons of his denim work shirt.

"Not enough room," he managed to explain.

"I should have brought the Lincoln." She kissed the dimple in his chin. "Bigger back seat."

"Next time," he promised. The gods owed him this. Owed him time with the only woman he had ever fallen in love with. He wasn't in love with her now, of course—he was too smart for self-torture—but his physical reaction to her was the same as it had always been: pure unadulterated lust, the best of all feelings.

"Then where?"

"On the grass."

"Uh-uh," the lady said. "Rattlesnakes."

"The truck bed?"

She slipped the last button through its hole and skimmed her hands along his bare chest. "Too hard."

"I have a sleeping bag behind the seat." His hands moved higher, to cup her breasts, satin material covering what he wanted most to touch. It took only seconds to release the clasp so that those breasts spilled into his hands. Another practiced move and her shirt, along with her bra, ended up tossed over the gearshift.

"Works for me." Her bare breasts brushed his chest, her skin so hot and soft he thought he would explode right then and there. His hands rounded her shoulders, held her against him. "Still mad at me?"

"Yeah." His mouth found her neck, her collarbone, the little pulse there beating rapidly beneath his lips.

"I'm not too thrilled with you either," she murmured. Her hand found the waistband of his jeans and tugged on the snap.

"Wait," he managed to say, though the word

didn't come easy. He took a deep breath as he rested his forehead against hers. "If we don't slow down we will be doing it in the truck." It would be a bungled, hasty affair and not at all the stuff that fantasies were made of.

"Yes."

He lifted his hands and released her, but her eyes were closed and she didn't move right away. Dustin turned and fumbled behind the seat for the sleeping bag. "Come," he told her, and she opened her eyes and looked at him.

"We're crazy," was all she said.

"Yeah," he agreed, opening the door. "I know."

CHAPTER SIXTEEN

OF COURSE THIS WAS crazy, Kate decided, as Dustin disappeared from view. She was naked from the waist up in Dustin's truck. She was about to climb into the back of the truck and make love on a sleeping bag. It was the middle of the afternoon. A June afternoon in Texas. If the excitement didn't kill them, the heat surely would.

She was twenty-seven, not eighteen. But her age didn't have anything to do with falling in love. And falling in love she was, all over again. Or maybe she had never stopped. She'd been home for a handful of days and here she was, half-naked and aroused, waiting for Dustin to make a bed. Waiting for Dustin to make love to her.

Some things never changed.

"Kate?" He opened the truck door. His chest, browned and muscled, filled part of the opening. Dustin held out his hand and smiled at her. "I'm ready if you are." His gaze dropped to her bare breasts and then back to her face. "You're more beautiful than I remembered," he said.

Her heart flipped over when he looked at her like that. Her heart remembered a lot of things, she realized, as she took his hand. She grabbed her shirt and climbed out of the truck and took a breath of thick, heavy air. "Are you sure no one will come by?"

"I'm the only one who works this place, remember?"

"But it's not as if it was dark—"

He sat her on the open tailgate and stood in front of her. "No one is going to bother us, Katie, but if you want to leave, just say so."

She sat naked from the waist up and eyed Dustin's wide, bare chest. "I don't think I'm going anywhere."

"Well, that's a relief." He stepped forward, easily moving Kate's knees apart so he could stand closer to her. He took her crumpled blouse from her hand and once again tossed it aside. "You'd break my heart."

"I doubt that," she said, as he moved closer and ran his index finger down her breast.

"Why?" He didn't look at her, but bent to kiss her neck. His lips descended lower, to tease her peaked nipple with his tongue. Kate thought she might fall over, so she reached for him, held his shoulders, ran her fingers along his neck while he explored each breast and sent tingling warmth along her already sensitive skin.

She had no answer for him, of course. She couldn't think, especially when his hands found the waistband of her shorts and unzipped them. His fingers slipped underneath the elastic of her bikini underwear with tantalizing slowness, teasing her, and then returned to her waist.

Kate was lifted and set down in the middle of a fluffy blue sleeping bag, a place that looked like a virtual paradise compared to the front seat of the truck. It smelled of hay and horse, a combination she'd missed in New York. "You sleep here often?"

"Sometimes," he said, eyeing her as he climbed up and stretched out alongside her. "Alone."

She had no time to feel awkward, because Dustin reached over and lifted her on top of him. "There," he said with great satisfaction. "That's better."

She lay along the length of him, her breasts flat against his chest, her hair falling along his cheeks. She tucked it behind her ears so she could kiss him. He was hard against her thigh; she shifted so he pressed against the part of her that throbbed with anticipation.

"You're going to kill me," he said, playing with a strand of hair that dangled near his mouth.

"The sun might do that for me."

He shifted so they were on their sides, facing each other. "Better?"

"Mmm," she said, but not because she no longer felt the heat on her bare back, but because his hands were busy removing the rest of her clothing. She shifted to make it easier, wanting to feel the source of all that heat against her skin. Wanting him inside of her again, the way it used to be. They had never made love in the daylight before. She had never seen his body in other than shadows, in the light of the movie screen, and he had never seen hers.

His hands skimmed her bare thighs, the dip of her waist and back again, as if he wanted to give her time to get used to his touch. He tilted her slowly onto her back and then, with great speed, removed his clothing and returned to her.

Skin to skin was better, Kate concluded. Much better and infinitely more satisfying. She was wet and ready, though he took his time before entering her. Another difference, but not an unwelcome one. His hands were more knowing of a woman's body, his instincts honed. She took him in her arms and into her body and knew that somehow this was right and real and exactly what she wanted.

He filled her, inch by tantalizing inch, and smiled down into her eyes. "It's been a long time," he whispered, moving inside of her.

Too long, she would have replied, but he took her mouth and her breath and every vestige of control she clung to. He fit inside of her perfectly, as she remembered. And made love to her, as she remembered. And her body hadn't forgotten what it was like to tighten and climax around him. Her arms knew to hold him when he came deep inside of her, and her eyes sought his when it was over.

"I'm glad you're home," was all he said, before he kissed her again.

HE WAS IN DEEP TROUBLE.

No doubt about it, this Texan was out of his league. Dustin looked at himself in the cloudy mirror above the bathroom sink and saw a man who was hopelessly and foolishly and once again in love.

Nothing good could come of it. He rubbed shaving cream on his face and lifted his razor to the side of his face. He could end it all now and slit his throat, but Dustin Jones was no coward.

"Daddy?" The boy peered into the bathroom and a look of relief crossed his little face. The kid always looked like that whenever he saw his guardian, like he was surprised that Dustin was doing something normal. Like he was surprised that Dustin was around at all.

"What?" He continued to shave, rinsing the razor in the sink.

"Can I go to Grandma Gert's house tonight?"

"Why?"

The boy shrugged his skinny shoulders, trying to copy Dustin's familiar gesture. "'Cuz."

"Because why?"

Danny shrugged again, then scooted past Dustin to perch on the toilet seat lid.

"Sorry, pal. You'll have to do better than that." He continued to shave. "Besides, no one's home. The ladies have gone out to dinner."

"They have?"

"Yeah." Dustin splashed, making some shaving foam land on Danny's knee. He giggled and scooped it up with his finger, then leaned over and placed it on the back of Dustin's knee.

Dustin turned and pretended to growl with outrage, but the boy's eyes grew wide with fear and he scrambled to tuck himself into the small space behind the toilet.

Dustin tried to reassure him while he quickly cleaned up. He coaxed the boy from his hiding spot and settled him at the kitchen table.

"So I wouldn't get hit," Danny explained when Dustin asked him about his reaction. He still appeared wide-eyed, but was happy for chocolate milk and one of the cookies Gert had given him to take home. "It's a good place," he explained to his new father. "Mommy couldn't get me there."

Dustin managed to hold back his rage at this latest revelation. "Mommy" wasn't ever going to get her hands on this child again, not as long as

Dustin was there to protect the kid. He wished he could put the woman in jail, but a lawyer had already told him that was a waste of time. There'd been few charges against her, and the child abuse couldn't be proved. At least the boy was safe from his parents' destructive influence now. The court had put Lisa in a drug rehab center; Darrell was in prison and would be for another ten years. *Concentrate on the child,* the man had advised. *Make a home for him, so the judge will see he's being taken care of.*

"Does Kate have kids?"

"No." This afternoon he'd concentrated on making love to Kate. Not on work and not on the boy, but on Kate. He allowed himself to wonder what it would be like if she stayed on the ranch, if she took over from her grandmother. If she loved him back.

Oh, yeah. He'd fallen in love with her all over again, from the minute she'd walked into the grange hall in that fancy outfit and high-heeled shoes. Dustin grimaced, but the boy didn't see. He was busy picking chocolate chips out of the cookie and lining them up on the table. For some reason that was big entertainment.

"Why not?"

"Why not what?" He opened the refrigerator and took out some eggs and bacon. Surely there was nothing wrong with eating breakfast for supper.

"Why doesn't Kate have kids? Doesn't she like kids?"

"I'm sure she does," Dustin replied. She seemed happy enough to baby-sit the Bennett kids yesterday. And she was kind to Danny, even though she thought he was the reason she and Dustin had broken up.

"Does she like *me?*" Now the chocolate chips were shoved into a pile, readied to be eaten all at once, Dustin supposed.

"Sure she does."

He should tell her the truth, but would it make any difference? It may have been nine years ago, but the truth wasn't going to change anything now. Let the woman think what she wanted. She would be gone in nine days and he doubted she would stay if he asked her. He didn't have much to offer a woman who already had everything.

But in his heart he knew Kate belonged here, belonged here with him and the boy.

Too bad Kate was the only one who didn't seem to realize it.

"I REALIZE YOU DON'T approve, Martha, but I have to think of my career." Gert shuffled through the stacks of papers spread over the kitchen table.

"Now where did I put those pictures of my mother and father?"

"Your career," Martha repeated, praying for patience. If her mother was really delusional, she was going to need all the patience God could send her way. "You haven't written the book yet, Mother. Maybe you should wait until you've finished it before you give interviews to—"

"I'm ninety," Gert snapped, fussing through a stack of old photographs. "How much longer do you think I should wait?"

Until hell freezes over and the cows come home, Martha wanted to say. Until it snows in July and Texans quit drinking beer. She looked at her watch and realized she had little time to spend arguing with her mother over a newspaper interview. She'd come out to the ranch to see Kate, but the girl had gone off somewhere with Dustin and the boy again. "When's Kate coming back?"

"I didn't ask."

Martha tried another tactic. "You know, Mother, it's a wonderful idea to write the family history, but don't you think telling stories about the folks around here might be considered an...invasion of privacy?"

Gert snorted. "History's history. No one can change it, no matter how much they want to."

Well, that was true. Martha thought of things she'd change and things she wouldn't. Mostly she'd do things a lot smarter if she could do them over again. It was too bad she wouldn't get the chance.

She eyed the piles of papers on the table. With any luck, Gert would lose interest before it was done. "I'll be out tomorrow. Did you write down a grocery list?"

"Kate did." Gert waved in the direction of the refrigerator, so Martha walked across the kitchen and found the list underneath a magnet shaped like Texas. "You have a date tonight, Mattie?"

"As a matter of fact, I do," she admitted. "Carl is taking me to Marysville for the Friday night seafood special at Lou Lou's."

"I'm glad you're getting out."

"It's nice to have a man around," Martha said, which had to be the understatement of the summer. She had plans for tonight that had more excitement than the Super Shrimp Platter. She looked out the window in time to see Dustin's truck, in a cloud of dust, arrive out back. "Here's Kate. Do you think she's serious about him?"

"I hope so," Gert said, joining her at the window. "I'd like to think she's as smart as I think she is."

"That young man is trouble," Martha muttered. "I just know it."

"Kate can take care of herself," Gert declared. "The women in our family are good at that."

"Yes," she agreed, but grudgingly. "Just be careful what you say to that reporter today. You don't want folks getting all riled up."

"I'll be fine. I'm gonna give 'em enough to whet their appetite, that's all."

"Fine," Martha said, knowing full well her mother would say whatever she wanted to say. She glanced at her watch again. She was getting her hair done at two, her nails at three and she still had to change the sheets on her bed and clean the bathroom before she headed to the beauty parlor. Tonight was the night to add a little romance into her own life.

For the rest of this Friday she would pretend that her mother wasn't going to air the town's dirty linen and that her daughter wasn't having an affair with the hired help. Besides, the construction of the Good Night Villas had progressed nicely, which meant there were some secrets in town that would remain buried.

SURELY SHE COULD keep her jeans on tonight, Kate decided, looking at herself in the full-length mirror in the upstairs bedroom she'd claimed as her own this vacation. The red heels could be a little much, but the sleeveless red top with its pearl snaps and demure fringe was perfect for dancing.

Perfect for driving her cowboy crazy, which was the real point, she knew, despite her good intentions. She wanted to look so damn good that the man would take her home early and make love to her all night.

Which would be a dumb thing to do.

Kate kicked off the heels and eyed her sandals. If she wore a long-sleeved denim shirt over a white tank, she would look sporty. If she went with red, she would look like she was asking for sex.

And of course she was, but she didn't have to be obvious about it. They hadn't made love since the time in the truck on Tuesday. So obviously she did have to be obvious, or else she'd be forced to conclude that Dustin had gotten her out of his system.

She hated to think that. Like she hated to think she was falling in love with him again. Like she hated to think the man would *know* she was falling in love with him again. Really, she wasn't sure which was worse.

Kate put the red heels back on and prepared to torture the man. It was the least she could do when, for the past three days, he'd acted as if they'd never made love. A woman had her pride.

CHAPTER SEVENTEEN

THE LAST CHANCE SALOON would never be the
same. Dustin figured from the admiring looks that
were coming Kate's way that he'd be lucky if he
didn't get into a fight before the night was over.
Protecting the lady's honor could get difficult.
Wearing that outfit—snug blue jeans, fancy red
shoes and a top that fit her curves a little too well—
Kate attracted a lot of attention. Oh, there were
other pretty women showing more skin and wearing tighter clothing, but none were as beautiful as
Kate.

And there were none that could cause his heart
to settle in his throat every time he looked at her.
Dustin guided his date through the crowd at the
bar and managed to find a small table in the back
corner. Friday night in Beauville was almost as big
a party night as Saturday night in Beauville.

"You wore that outfit on purpose, right? To torture me?" He pulled out a wooden chair for her
and caught a whiff of her perfume as she sat down.

"Of course."

"That's what I thought. Why?" He took the chair closest to her and angled himself so that no one could approach them easily. Kate had the nerve to smile at him.

"To get your undivided attention."

"You have it." His gaze dropped to the snaps on her blouse. "Those aren't going to come undone while you're dancing, right?"

"I hope not."

Dustin wasn't so sure she wore a bra underneath that red shirt. He frowned. "Don't dance with anyone but me."

"I never intended to."

He looked around, glared at a couple of young cowboys and turned back to Kate. "Maybe this wasn't such a good idea."

"You can't get out of it now," she said. "I asked you to go dancing and you said yes."

He would have said yes to anything she asked. He'd watched her paint the barn, he'd taken her along in his truck when he'd gone to town, he'd been careful never to be alone with her, but a man could only take so much torture before he broke down and agreed to dance. Agreed to take the woman he loved into his arms and hold her while the band played something slow. "Buckle bumping" music, Bobby Calhoun had called it.

"I'm not much of a dancer," Dustin warned, wondering how long they would have to stay at the Last Chance before he could take her home to bed. Danny was staying with Gert, so the bunk-house would be empty. If they didn't turn on any lights neither Gert nor Danny would have to know they were there.

"I'll take my chances." Kate didn't look at all concerned. She also didn't look as if she had thought much beyond simply going dancing with him, though she'd admitted to wearing that outfit to make him crazy.

"I'll go get us a drink," he said, torn between staying at the table to keep predatory cowboys away from her and getting some distance so he wouldn't make a fool of himself by hauling her out of the bar and into his truck within the next ten minutes. "What do you want?"

"Beer is fine." She tapped her fingers in time to the band's rendition of Clint Black's latest hit and looked out at the dance floor.

"I'll be right back," he said, hesitating before he left the table. "Don't go anywhere."

"I won't," she promised. Once again she smiled, and Dustin knew he couldn't possibly let her go back to New York without a fight.

"I mean it," he said, this time he held her gaze until she realized he wasn't talking about leaving the table. The smile disappeared from her face. "Don't go, Katie."

"My job—"

"Could be running a ranch," he finished for her. *With me,* he wanted to add. He placed his palms flat on the table and leaned toward her. He wanted her to be able to hear despite the music. "Do you love it? Your job, I mean?"

She hedged. "Am I supposed to?"

"If you choose New York instead of Texas, yes." He waited a moment for her to answer. Then, figuring he'd given her something to think about, he turned and headed toward the bar.

Tonight he would tell her the truth. He would ask her to stay, to give him a chance to prove to her that she belonged here in Texas, that she belonged here with him. But would she want the boy? Would she want to trade New York glamour for Texas dust?

Dustin bought a couple of beers, greeted some friends, avoided flirting smiles of one of the Wynette twins—he never could tell those girls apart—and headed back to Kate. Would she marry him if he asked her?

He almost dropped one of the beer bottles. Marriage hadn't been in his plans, but loving Kate for the rest of his life looked like a sure thing. Now that he'd lost his heart, he was in too deep to turn back, whether Kate agreed to a wedding or not.

KATE WANTED TO DANCE. Right now she didn't want to think about returning to New York. She hadn't wanted to answer the harried phone calls from her boss and the e-mails from the producer about changes to the mystery baby story line. She'd grown tired of mystery baby story lines, demanding producers and a sponsor who wanted high ratings and no excuses. For now Kate wanted to paint the barn and listen to Gran's stories and mend fence and be worshipped by a little boy and made love to by the only man she'd ever been in love with. She didn't want to think about the future and she didn't want to think about *Loves of Our Lives* or who would be fired after the November ratings sweeps.

Uncharacteristic, true, but then wasn't a woman entitled to a vacation? Especially when a handsome cowboy took her in his arms and two-stepped across the scarred wooden dance floor?

"Nice," she murmured. Dustin's neck smelled wonderful, like spice and leather. He held her tighter, which raised her temperature a few degrees. Dancing was wonderful, but going home should be even better.

"How much longer?" he asked, his hands firmly holding her waist as they rocked to "The Dance."

"Until what?"

"Until we're alone." The music ended, but Dustin didn't release her. They weren't the only ones still embracing on the dance floor; it was close to midnight, so more than a handful of couples had romance on their minds.

"How long does it take to get back to the Lazy K?"

"Too long," he muttered, "but I'll drive as fast as I can."

"Good idea," she said, as he released her and, grabbing her hand, tugged her toward the door.

"Let's go," he said, and Kate hurried to keep up. She liked a man who knew what he wanted. As long as he didn't ask her to stay in Texas again, it would be a wonderful evening.

MARTHA DIDN'T EXPECT him to spend the night. Actually, she thought, carefully slipping out of her double bed so she wouldn't wake her date, she hadn't thought much beyond the lovemaking.

It had been fine and dandy, just not as exciting as she'd hoped. And went on a little too long, too, if the truth be told. She wasn't one to complain. She'd just thought it would be a bit more romantic. Like the movies.

But she wasn't the virginal bride on her honeymoon and Carl wasn't a dashing husband. He was a good friend and a fun companion, and that was the most anyone could expect at sixty-four.

Martha took a shower with the bathroom door locked. It made her a little nervous having Carl in the house at seven in the morning. And his car was still parked out front. She'd wanted some excitement, she reminded herself as she donned a full-length bathrobe and tiptoed into her bedroom for something to wear. But she hadn't intended to be a source of neighborhood gossip. Next time—if there was a next time—she'd make sure he parked his car in the garage while she parked hers in the driveway. Or maybe they'd just use her car, which would be easier. Or go to his apartment—which, come to think of it, she didn't want to do at all. She didn't think she wanted to wake up in a strange bed, in a strange room. She needed her bathroom, her makeup, her magnifying mirror.

"Martha?"

She froze, her clothing clutched to her chest. "Yes?"

"Good morning." Carl fumbled with the covers and sat up. He smiled at her and patted her side of the bed. "Come back to bed, sweetie?"

"I just took a shower," she said, knowing darn well what was in store if she got back in that bed. She'd rather have a good cup of coffee. "I have to dry my hair and—"

"Later. There's something here that can't wait."

"Oh, I'll bet it can," she insisted. "Hold that thought and I'll be back in a few minutes." She locked herself in the bathroom again in order to dress, blow-dry her hair into waves and put on her makeup. With any luck she could get downstairs and put the coffee on before Carl became any more amorous. Really, she wasn't sure men were worth all this trouble.

"Martha?"

"I'll be right back," she promised, once she was out of the bathroom again. "I'll put the coffee on and get the paper."

"We can read it in bed together," he said, looking pleased. Martha smiled at him. She supposed the man got lonely, too. And it *was* nice to have company at breakfast. She wasn't about to take her clothes off and climb into bed in broad daylight, though.

A woman had to set some ground rules.

DUSTIN WOULD HAVE liked to spend the night with her. Would have preferred to wake up and find Kate asleep in his bed instead of the boy.

Danny was spread out on his back, his bony arms and legs sprawled in all directions. He needed a haircut and there was chocolate on his chin. He and Grandma Gert must have eaten cookies all evening. Well, that was okay. At least he hoped it was. He'd heard that grandparents liked to do things like that, and Gert was the closest thing to a grandmother the boy would ever have.

Dustin slid out of bed, the bed that had a few hours earlier held him and Kate. They'd never made love in a bed before, so he was lucky he hadn't had a heart attack from sheer happiness. By the time it was over he'd lost the power to speak, so discussing Danny's parentage hadn't been a topic of conversation, though he knew he had to tell her the truth soon. He'd only been capable of a couple of soft groans as he'd tucked Kate's naked body against his and covered them with a sheet.

They'd had time for a short nap before heading over to Gert's and pretending they'd just closed down the Last Chance. He'd gathered up Danny, asleep on Gert's couch, and left Gert working on her book and Kate looking a little dazed. He knew how she felt.

Dustin threw on his work clothes and headed out to do chores. Later on he'd clean up and see if Kate was free for breakfast. It was long past time for some serious conversation.

It was long past time to tell her he loved her.

"MOTHER, I CAN'T BELIEVE you did this!"

Gert finished fixing the coffeemaker and turned it on before giving her daughter her attention. It was a little early in the morning for one of Martha's indignations. "Good morning to you, too, Martha. The coffee will be ready in a few minutes."

"I'm not here about coffee," she said, placing a copy of the Beauville paper on the kitchen table. It was folded so that Gert could see a photo of herself as a young girl on the front page. "I'm here about *this*."

"I was a looker, wasn't I," Gert murmured. "Did this come out this morning?"

"Yes, unfortunately."

"Martha, what are you so worked up about?" Gert adjusted her glasses and studied the article. The young man had done a good job, except he'd described her as "wrinkled." She wasn't sure he needed to use that word. She preferred "mature." She'd have to inform him of that next time, when the book came out or when she sold the movie rights. She'd heard about movie deals on that television show, *Entertainment Tonight*. What she needed was one of those theatrical agents. Kate would know.

Martha took the paper out of her hands and read, "'Gert's family owned several ranches in this area during the eighteen hundreds, including land north of town where the Good Night Villas are under construction, which was originally the ranch of cattleman Horace Stewart, Mrs. Knepper's great-grandfather.'"

"That's not exactly something to get worked up over," Gert declared. "Horace Stewart was a fine man. Told stories about the winter of the Big Drift, back in 1865, that would curl your toes."

Kate, in a T-shirt and shorts, entered the room

and yawned. "What's going on? I could hear you upstairs."

"Your mother is in a snit about something," Gert said.

"Hi, Mom." She padded over and kissed them both, then headed toward the coffeepot.

"I just turned it on," Gert said. "You'll have to give it a minute."

"Okay."

Gert turned her attention back to her daughter, whose hair looked mussed. It wasn't like Martha to have mussed hair. "What did you do to your hair this morning?"

"Never mind my hair," she said, looking a little embarrassed. She started reading again, "'Mrs. Knepper tells tales of cattle rustling, wagon trains, range wars and family feuds. I hope when she finishes writing her story, she'll tell us if the missing shipment of gold is really buried on her great-grandfather's ranch, as outlaw Dead-Eye Dan claimed it was before the noose finished his life of crime forever.'"

Gert grinned. "That'll make 'em all go out and buy copies of the book, won't it?"

"You never mentioned missing gold, Gran." Kate handed her a cup of coffee, so Gert sat down and dumped some cream and sugar in it. She didn't know why Martha was making a big deal out of this.

"My grandfather used to tell that story, not that anyone believed him, but I thought it would make good reading—Martha, whatever is the matter with you?" Her daughter had gone pale and sank into a chair. "Better put your head down between your legs."

"Mother?"

"I'll be all right," she said, her voice a little muffled in her cotton skirt. "Give me a minute."

"Too much excitement," Gert declared. "I don't think dating that Jackson man is a good idea."

"—not his fault," Martha muttered.

Gert winked at Kate. "Are you having one of them menopausal fits again?"

"That was over ten years ago." Martha raised her head and looked like she was going to cry, so Gert quit teasing and drank some coffee instead while Kate handed her mother a cold washcloth.

"Thank you," Martha sniffed. "Honestly, I don't know what I'm going to do with you."

"Both of us or just Gran?"

"Both of you, I suppose," Martha said, leaning back in her chair. "You're sleeping with that cowboy and your grandmother is destroying my life."

"You're sleeping with him?" Gert turned to Kate. "Well, thank goodness. I thought you'd never come to your senses. I'll have to call my lawyer Monday."

"Why?"

"Yes," Martha asked. "Why?"

Gert decided that neither one of them needed to know the details. "Never mind that," she said. "How could I possibly be destroying your life, Mattie?"

"Everyone's going to start hunting for gold at the drive-in now."

"Oh, Carl won't mind. He'll figure it's good publicity," Gert said. She saw Dustin approach the screen door and waved him inside.

"Of course," Kate agreed, patting her mother's shoulder. "And he has security guards there, remember? I'm sure he won't be angry about it."

Her gray-haired daughter, the perfect child who had never done a thing wrong in her entire life, took a deep breath and said, "There's a dead body at the drive-in and I don't want anyone to find it."

Gert choked on her coffee. "Carl's *dead?*"

"Have you called the sheriff—what's his name, Gran?"

"Sheridan," Dustin said, entering the kitchen. "Jess Sheridan."

"How did it happen?" Kate asked. "Did the poor man have a heart attack or something?"

Martha took a deep breath. "Carl is very much alive, thank you. We were having breakfast together—" She paused, blushed and then continued. "We were having breakfast together when I read the article about your grandmother. After I threw up, I got in the car and came out here.''

"Martha." Gert had never seen her daughter so upset. "Who's dead at the drive-in?"

"I can't tell you that." She put her head down on the kitchen table and started to cry.

Gert leaned close to her. "You can't or you won't?"

Martha only cried harder. Kate turned to Dustin and offered him coffee, but he declined.

"I didn't mean to interrupt a family discussion," he said.

"We could use some advice." Gert pointed to an empty chair. "Sit down. As soon as she stops crying we're going to need a man's opinion." And maybe someone good with a shovel. And if Dustin was sleeping with her granddaughter and going to become a member of the family, he might as well know all the family secrets sooner rather than later.

CHAPTER EIGHTEEN

DUSTIN FIGURED HE wasn't going to get the chance to talk to Kate this morning. Her mother was still crying, her grandmother continued to demand answers and got none, while Kate handed her mother tissues and drank coffee as if her sanity depended on it.

Dustin decided to pour himself a cup and wished he hadn't picked this time to see if Kate was awake and ready for serious conversation. He didn't figure Martha for a murderer, couldn't figure out why she'd know about a body in the drive-in and certainly didn't want to contemplate the reason why the woman had been having breakfast so early on a Saturday morning with Carl Jackson.

Clearly there was a lot going on here that he didn't understand, so Dustin gestured to Kate the next time she glanced his way.

"We'll be right back," he told Gert, and took Kate's hand.

"Don't go far," the old lady replied. "She'll

have to stop crying soon and then we'll get some answers.''

''Right.'' He hauled Kate outside and around the corner of the house, in the shade of the overhang. First he kissed her, and was glad to note that she kissed him back.

''Good morning,'' she said, smiling up at him.

''I missed you.''

''I know.'' Her smile faded. ''I wanted to wake up with you and instead—do you think my mother is having a nervous breakdown?''

''Does she cry like that a lot?''

''Never. Not since Daddy died.'' She lowered her voice, though Dustin was certain neither Gert nor Martha could hear. ''But this talk about a dead body really seems strange. If she knew there was someone dead there, why would she want to buy one of the villas and move in?''

''Maybe she just discovered it.''

''My mother? Discovering dead bodies?'' Kate shook her head. ''Bargains, yes. Bodies, no.''

''Kate, honey, how did all this start?''

''Mom was upset because Gran told the reporter about some buried treasure rumored to be hidden at the drive-in. Supposedly Gran's great-grandfather lived on a ranch there at the time and told her the story. She thought it would make her book more interesting.''

It had certainly made his morning more interesting, though he would have preferred waking up naked and next to Kate. That would have been interesting enough. "All I heard was the part about not wanting anyone to find 'the body.'"

"We should call the sheriff."

"Not so fast," Dustin warned. "If your mother isn't, uh, in her right mind, you don't want to make things worse."

"Maybe we should call a lawyer, or a doctor."

"Your mother can't cry forever," he said, hoping he was right. "Give her a chance to explain before you call for reinforcements."

She sighed. "You're right." Kate stood on tiptoe and kissed him lightly. "Where's Danny?"

"Still sleeping. Gert wore him out last night. I think they watched movies 'til midnight."

"Figures. She likes the company."

"Me, too." They smiled at each other for a long moment.

"I was going to go see Emily today and take her some groceries. I'm not sure if I can do that now. But if I go, do you think Danny would like to ride along?"

"I think he'd like that a lot. He has a crush on you, you know."

"I've noticed. He's a nice kid, Dustin," she told him.

"Yeah," he said, before kissing her again. "I know."

"I'd better get back," she said, pulling away. "Do you think maybe Mom was involved in a hit-and-run accident last night?"

"I can't see your mother doing anything illegal," he assured her, but over the top of Kate's head he saw the sheriff's car pull up in the drive. "Kate?"

"What?"

"Maybe you'd better go tell your mother that the sheriff is coming."

"Oh, my God," she breathed, peering around him. "He's going to arrest her."

"I doubt it," Dustin said, setting her away from him and turning her toward the kitchen door. "Go. I'll see what he wants."

He made sure she went inside before heading toward Jess Sheridan, who had just stepped out of his car. "Jess? Hey."

"Hey, Dustin," the man said, settling his hat on his head. "It's going to be another hot one."

"Yeah, it sure is." He shook the man's hand and waited for the reason he was here, knowing Sheridan would get around to it in his own time.

"I could have called," Jess said, "but I was out this direction anyway." He looked around. "Where's the boy?"

"Still asleep."

"Good. I wanted to tell you that Lisa is out of jail, as of yesterday. She supposedly completed a drug treatment program and got time off for good behavior.''

Dustin felt like someone had punched him in the gut. ''Where is she?''

''I don't know. That's why I thought you should know.''

''Thanks.''

''You've got custody, right?''

''Yeah, so far. We go to court again in September.''

Jess nodded and opened the car door. ''Good. Take care of the boy and call me if there's any problem.''

''Thanks.'' He watched the sheriff put the car in reverse and turn around before heading back to the road. Jess Sheridan hadn't brought good news, but at least he hadn't arrested Dustin's future mother-in-law.

''IT WAS JUST A NIGHTMARE.'' Martha sniffed and tossed a large handful of tissues into the trash. ''I guess I just had a bad dream.''

''You expect us to believe that?'' Kate crossed her arms over her chest and thought once again about calling a doctor, preferably one who carried sedatives around with him. ''After crying for half an hour about a body at the drive-in and how gold hunters might find it?''

''It was quite a nightmare, I must say,'' her

mother declared. She reached into her purse and found her lipstick. "Excuse me. I'm going to go freshen up."

Kate watched as her mother left the room and headed around the corner for the bathroom. "What do you think, Gran?"

"I think we're lucky the sheriff didn't come into the house," her grandmother said. "There's no telling what Martha might have told him."

Kate reheated her coffee in the microwave and then sat down at the kitchen table. "What do you think she was talking about?"

"I'm not sure," her grandmother said, but she avoided Kate's gaze and instead went over to the window. "Looks like Dustin's working on the roof. That man is always working."

Kate wondered if he had his shirt off. If he was thinking of last night. Or planning how they would be together tonight. "Maybe I should take Mom home. She isn't in any condition to drive."

"I'm going to sell him the ranch, Kate." Gert left the window and shuffled over to the table and sat down. "If you don't want the Lazy K, that's what I'm going to do."

"Gran—"

"Don't say anything now," her grandmother told her. "You have another week here to think about what you want to do, but I can't run this place much longer. It needs a man and it looks like it's got one, so I might as well make it official."

Kate took a deep breath. She'd never thought the ranch would leave the family. "I don't think Dustin can afford to buy a ranch, Gran. And where will you live? Certainly not in the Good Night Villas with Mom?"

"I'll make Dustin a good deal. Lord knows neither you nor Jake needs money. Jake has his own place free and clear and you have your fancy career. Your mother is fixed just fine for money, with or without the Lazy K so it's not like we're gonna go broke."

"No," Kate said, feeling as if she was going to lose something she didn't know she wanted so much. "I guess not."

"It's yours, though," her grandmother said, "if you want to stay."

"What is?" Martha said, entering the room. "Are you trying to bribe Kate with this ranch again, Mother?"

"I'm not discussing my business with a crazy woman, Martha," Gert declared. "Are you feeling better?"

"I am," she said. Kate saw that her mother had combed her hair and put on lipstick. Her eyes were still red and puffy, but at least she wasn't crying anymore.

"So, who's in the drive-in?"

"Don't start, Mother."

Kate frowned at her grandmother, then took her mother's arm. "Let me drive you home. I'd planned on visiting with Emily for a while this morning."

"I'm perfectly capable of taking myself home. Besides, I'm playing bridge with the girls this afternoon." She avoided looking at either one of them and fussed with her blouse, making sure it was tucked neatly into her skirt.

"Do you want to come out here for dinner tonight?"

"No, thank you, dear," Martha said. She dropped her lipstick into her purse and snapped it shut. "I think I'll go to bed early tonight. I could use the rest."

"Hmph," Gert said, looking worried. "I should say so."

Kate walked her mother to her car, but Martha didn't say a word until she got behind the wheel. "I'm sorry I frightened you."

"Are you sure you're okay?"

"Of course," she said, but to Kate she looked ten years older than she had yesterday. "I just need some time to rest. That article in the paper just…upset me, that's all."

"Gran's book has upset you from the beginning," Kate said, leaning down so she could look through the open car window. Her mother's fingers gripped the steering wheel, but she didn't say anything. Instead she fussed with her keys and started the car, so Kate had no choice but to back away and let her mother leave the ranch.

It was one of those mornings she should have stayed in bed—with Dustin. Dead bodies, gold hunters, sheriffs, hysterical mothers and career decisions would have been ignored, at least until after she'd rolled on top of his naked body and had her way with him.

SHE WOULD NOT MAKE that mistake again, Martha decided. At first she'd thought that newspaper article was the last straw, that there was nothing to do but to come clean and confess everything.

And then she'd seen her mother's face. How could she tell her ninety-year-old mother the truth? Gert couldn't live forever. Let her find out in heaven, when some nice angels would gather around her and explain everything. That would certainly be much easier than hearing it this way.

And the mess that would follow couldn't be helped. There were a few people around town who would remember and understand, but there were lots more who would judge without knowing what it was really like to have a best friend.

A best friend was someone you would do anything for.

"YOUR LIFE IS SO much more exciting than mine," Emily declared, tucking her baby to her breast.

"I guess that depends on how you define 'exciting.'" Kate suffered another unfamiliar twinge of envy as she watched Emily feed her baby. "I thought I was coming home for a peaceful vacation with my family."

"And instead?" Emily's face took on that expression of blissful contentment as the baby began to nurse. "An affair with your grandmother's foreman, a mysterious dead body and a grandmother trying to get famous."

"Exactly. I should be writing all of this down for the show. My boss would love the 'mysterious dead body' part."

"I personally prefer the romance," her friend said. "I'm glad you brought Danny with you. John could use some male company."

"I'll take him back to the ranch with me for the afternoon, okay?"

"You have to ask?" Emily laughed. "My mother's taking the girls with her to Marysville, so that will work out great. I hate to ask this, but when do you have to go back to New York?"

"Next Saturday. I could make my boss happy and leave the day after tomorrow, but I won't."

"You can't leave now," Emily said, "not until you decide what to do about your mother, never mind the ranch and Dustin. And you promised to go out to lunch with Elizabeth and Lorna, too, remember?''

She remembered. And looked forward to it, too, though she didn't really think she'd fit in.

"If I stayed," Kate said, thinking out loud, "I'd live with my grandmother out on the ranch. With Dustin so close, I'm not sure if that's a good idea or not. If he started dating someone else, it would be messy. And if I started dating someone else, it would be even messier.''

"You're not ready to admit that he's the one man for you, huh?" Emily shook her head. "I can't believe it.''

"He slept with someone else and made a baby while he was going out with me," Kate reminded her. "He might not make the best husband.''

"That's history. He's a responsible father now. People change. And people grow up. Look, you could buy your mother's house and live here in town.''

"By myself in a house with four bedrooms? The place is huge.''

"It's the nicest house in town. Forget the past. Marry Dustin and fill it up with kids.''

"He hasn't asked." She watched Emily lift the tiny baby to her shoulder to burp her. "And what would I do here in Beauville?''

"Run the ranch. You've always loved that place.

I assume you have some money saved so you could afford to get it going again?''

''Yes,'' she said, thinking of her hefty savings account. She'd never been a big spender, having learned frugal ways from Gert, and writing for daytime television was a lucrative career. ''When I was eighteen that was all I wanted, Dustin Jones and the Lazy K. Makes me wish I hadn't grown up,'' she admitted, watching Emily comfort her fussing baby. ''Can I hold her?''

''If you don't mind if she spits up on your clothes.'' Emily leaned over and tucked the baby, bundled in soft cotton, into Kate's arms.

''I don't mind.'' She kept her voice quiet, as the baby's eyelids closed. Her little lips pursed, as if she wondered where her lunch disappeared to. ''You make all of this look so easy, Em.''

''It's hard work—don't let anyone tell you different,'' Emily drawled. ''But first, Kate, you have to decide what you want. If it's that big career, then run—don't walk—to the airport before you start breaking hearts.''

''And if it's Dustin and the ranch?''

''The two go together?''

''I think so.''

''Then tell him you're thinking about staying and see what happens.''

''You make it sound so easy.'' She could hold this baby all day long, Kate decided. It was too bad she had a barn to paint and her grandmother's latest chapters to read, a mystery to solve and a mother to comfort—plus a man to love and his son to care for.

"It is easy," Emily insisted, struggling off the couch. "You sit there and rock the baby while I go clean up, then we'll plan your future."

"Okay," Kate agreed, inhaling the sweet scent of baby as she lifted her closer. "You win. I want one of these."

"Don't tell me," Emily said. "Tell that cowboy of yours."

"He's not 'my cowboy.'"

Emily laughed. "Sure he is. You're the only person in town who doesn't know it."

There was a lot she didn't know, Kate mused, rocking slowly so the baby would sleep. She didn't know if Dustin loved her, didn't know whether or not she should take over the ranch, and certainly didn't know whose body was buried at the former Good Night Drive-In.

But she did know she was in love. That was something to think about.

CHAPTER NINETEEN

GERT DIDN'T UNDERSTAND what all the fuss was about, but it boded well for the success of her book. Seemed like everyone in town wanted to know what she was writing about or if she knew the location of the gold—as if she'd tell if she did—and did Gert need any more stories or photos because so-and-so was going through her mother's things and there was quite a bit of information there. The Jeffersons were upset, since they didn't want anyone knowing their great-great-grandfather had come to town when he jumped off a train, having escaped a murder conviction in California. And Irene Gardiner wanted to make sure that no one found out her mother was illegitimate. The phone rang a lot more than it ever had, not that she had to answer it. Kate did that for her.

Kate did a lot of things that helped Gert spend more time writing. She made coffee and cleaned. She cooked and shopped and proofread each chapter of the manuscript.

"You're a good girl," Gert told her. "I don't

know what I would do without you." It was a pretty big hint, but Gert didn't care. When a person was as old as she was, she was allowed to say anything.

So she said things like, "You'd have to go a long way to find a man as good as Dustin Jones" and "I hope I see your children before I die." Sentiments like that were bound to make the girl think twice about leaving for New York.

The boy came around, too. He and Gert drank coffee milk and ate cookies. Gert promised to make cinnamon rolls as soon as her book was done because she had no time for baking now. She was in the 1960s already, so it wouldn't be long before the book was done. She hadn't much cared for the sixties—except for Martha's wedding in 1969—so she didn't intend to dwell on much of it. There were some things worth skipping over, some things just too painful to write about.

"Gran?" Kate stood in the entrance to the living room. "Do you want to take a break for lunch?"

"No, thanks, dear. You and Danny go ahead without me." She wanted to finish this section before she stopped for a sandwich and a nap. Besides, Kate needed to get used to being with the boy. She would make a good mother, that girl would. Gert could see them from where she sat. Danny never strayed far from Kate's side, which was good. Dustin would be in soon, too, since he'd taken to eating lunch in the main house.

Kate was getting real good at fixing lunches, and painting outbuildings. And Gert had heard her talking to Dustin about cattle prices and land management. Danny started talking about getting his own horse and Emily's little boy had been over to play three times in three days. Jake and Elizabeth were bringing the new baby over to visit tomorrow.

Yes, Gert thought, going back to her memories of the 1960s. Everyone was acting like one big happy family. Everyone but Martha, who refused to talk about her mother's book except to beg her to stop working on it.

"ARE YOU SURE YOU don't mind?" Dustin hesitated at the kitchen door. "I'm not going to be back from Marysville until evening. There's no knowing how long these stock auctions will last."

"It's okay," Kate said, though she wasn't sure what she would do with an eight-year-old boy for the entire day. Danny was quiet enough, but there seemed to be a lot going on behind those serious brown eyes. She'd give a lot to know what the boy was thinking, especially when she caught him staring at her.

"Tomorrow's Friday," Dustin said. He lifted her chin with his index finger. "We have a date?"

"We'd better," she said. "We haven't been alone in a long time."

"Between grandmothers and kids, it's not easy," the man agreed, then brushed a kiss across her mouth.

"Maybe we should sneak off to the hayloft tonight." There hadn't been much chance to be alone with him. Gert was typing and Danny was gathering his trucks together to play with by the back door, which meant Kate could at least get a few kisses.

"I can't ask Gert to baby-sit Danny so her foreman can have sex with her granddaughter."

"I guess not." Kate sighed. "But you have to admit it's tempting."

"Tomorrow night," he promised. "Let's go out to dinner, just the two of us. We haven't had much time to be alone this week," he said, voicing her thoughts.

"I'd like that."

"Okay." The next kiss lasted much longer, until Kate's knees turned weak and she wondered how on earth she could wait until tomorrow night before being alone with him. The only reason they stopped was because they heard Danny singing as he came around the corner of the house.

"Gotta go." Dustin released her, then called goodbye to his son. "Be good," he reminded the child.

"You're coming back, right?" the boy asked.

"Yeah. After I buy some cattle, and maybe a horse or two."

"I can't come?"

"It's too long a day, pal," Dustin said, giving the kid a hug around his skinny shoulders. "And you have to be a little older before you can go. I think you'll have a better time here with Kate and Grandma Gert."

"Kate could go with us," Danny said, obviously unwilling to let his father out of his sight.

"I can't," Kate answered. "I promised Gran I'd make fried chicken for dinner tonight. And I bought all the stuff to make homemade ice cream." She almost laughed at the expression on Danny's face. Fried chicken and ice cream made up for missing an auction, if Danny even knew what an auction was.

"Well," the boy drawled, unconsciously mimicking his father. "I guess that's okay then."

Kate looked up at Dustin. "See ya."

"Yeah." He glanced at her lips and then frowned. "How many hours until tomorrow night?"

"Too many. Bye." Falling in love was ridiculous, she knew, but it was also the best thing that had happened to her in a long time. She watched him leave, watched Danny dump a load of metal vehicles by the back door, and thought she'd never been happier. And that meant, according to her one experience with falling in love, that something was about to go dreadfully wrong.

Or maybe, she thought, going back into the kitchen, she'd been writing soap opera story lines for too long. Maybe she didn't recognize something normal and uncomplicated when it landed in her lap.

GERT SAW THE WOMAN first. She'd dozed off in the chair, but she woke when she heard the car. Even an old woman could hear a car with no muffler when it chugged up the road. So she wasn't too surprised when the woman who got out of the driver's side of the car looked pretty scraggly. Gert didn't think she'd ever seen her before.

"Kate?" Gert didn't like the looks of this. Too many years living alone gave her a suspicious nature, especially when a beat-up station wagon with a tough-looking young woman entered the ranch yard. *"Kate."*

"What?" She poked her head in the living room. "What's wrong?"

"Someone's here and I don't like the look of her."

"Her?"

Gert pointed to the window. The young woman took a final drag of her cigarette and tossed it to the ground before walking toward the front door.

"You don't know her?"

"No, but that doesn't mean anything. I forget faces once in a while." Gert hauled herself to her feet. "Where's Danny?"

"Out back with his trucks. I gave him a bucket of water and he's dug a hole—"

"You answer the door then," Gert said. "I'm going to check on the boy. Keep the screen door locked, though. Don't open it and let her in. You just never know these days."

Kate was at the door when the knock came, and she opened it and peered through the screen at a woman her age who looked as if she could use a shower. "Hello?"

"Hi." Pale and very thin, the woman wore her dark hair past her shoulders. A blue T-shirt hung to her hips, and her blue jeans were faded and worn. "Does Dusty Jones work here?"

"He's not here right now. Can I give him a message?" The woman looked familiar, but Kate couldn't come up with a name to fit the face.

"But he works here, right? That's what they told me at the Dead Horse." She looked around the yard as if she expected Dustin to come around the corner of the house.

"He works here," Kate agreed. "But he's not here right now." She tried again. "Can I give him a message?"

Once again Kate was ignored. "You're Kate

McIntosh. I know you." She smiled, but it wasn't the kind of smile that made Kate relax. "I'm Lisa Gallagher." She chuckled. "Well, I *was* Lisa Gallagher and then I was Lisa Jones."

"Sure," Kate said slowly, but she didn't open the screen door and invite Lisa inside. "I remember you from high school."

"I came for Danny," the woman said. "I had a little trouble, but I got out of rehab and here I am," she announced, as if she expected Kate to be happy to see her. "So tell my kid that his mom is here."

Kate hesitated. *Rehab?* Danny's words rang in her head. *My mom drank a lot of beer. We don't have a family.* The child rarely mentioned his mother, and Dustin hadn't said anything good about her either. She didn't think he'd want Danny to see her unless he gave his permission.

"I don't think so," Kate said, attempting a pleasant smile. "He's with his father."

"His father?" Her confused expression cleared. "Oh, you mean Dusty."

"Yes. They went to Marysville." Let Lisa head somewhere else to make trouble, because Kate just knew this woman was up to no good.

"I saw Dusty in town. Alone." Lisa moved closer to the door and raised her voice. "So where's my kid?"

"He's not here." Kate thought about shutting the inner door in her face, but worried that Lisa would head around back and find her son. She hoped Gert brought the boy inside and locked the back door behind her.

Her eyes narrowed. "You lying bitch. You have my son and I want him. Dusty has no right to keep him from me." She tried to push the door, but Kate had made sure the screen door was locked.

"That's it," Kate said. "Get out of here." She shut the inner door, locked it, and hurried through the house to the back door. Gran had Danny by the hand in the kitchen, so Kate rushed across the room to make sure the door was locked.

"Is my mom here?" Danny's eyes were huge in his little face.

Kate sighed. The woman pounded on the back door and yelled Danny's name. "Yes. I guess she's upset. She wants to see you, but—"

The child nodded and threw himself into Kate's arms. "Don't let her take me away," he cried. "I want to stay here."

"I called the sheriff's office," Gert said. "They're going to send someone over as soon as they can."

Meanwhile the screaming continued at the back door. Lisa was threatening to sue everyone and make sure Dustin never saw Danny again. Kate knelt on the floor and gave Danny a hug. "No one's going to let her take you away from your daddy," she promised.

"She's mean," he whispered. "And she was in jail 'cuz she hurt me. And she took drugs. And my *real* daddy's in jail 'cuz he took drugs, too, and he hid it in our house and then the police came."

"Real daddy?" Kate looked at Gert, who shrugged. "I thought Dustin was your daddy."

The child shook his head. "I *pretend* Uncle Dustin is my daddy," he whispered, then wrapped his arms around Kate's neck in a viselike grip as Lisa's shouting grew louder. "He lets me."

"Well, I told your…daddy that I would take good care of you, so we're all going to go upstairs," Kate told the two of them. She would think about this "Uncle Dustin" revelation later. "There's no reason why we have to listen to this. Danny, you run up there and watch for the sheriff's car, okay? I'll help Grandma Gert."

"Okay." He hugged her and then did as he was told.

"I have my grandfather's hunting rifle," Gert muttered, opening the utility closet. "I can't remember where I locked up the bullets, but I'll bet just the sight of it would scare the living daylights out of that woman." She rummaged through the closet and pulled out a rifle that had seen better days.

"Gran, I don't think—"

"Kate, mind your business," Gert said. "The

young woman outside needs to learn some manners.''

"I'm going to call the sheriff again.'' She picked up the phone and hit the redial button. "Don't shoot anyone, please?''

"I remember now,'' Gert said, going to the cupboard above the stove. "I locked the bullets up with the liquor.'' Kate had never seen her grandmother move so fast.

"Gran, I don't think—oh, hello, this is Kate McIntosh out at the Lazy K. Yes, she called a few minutes ago…yes, she's still here. Lisa Gallagher, I mean, Lisa Jones. She's causing a real scene and we're not sure what to do.''

"Speak for yourself,'' Gert muttered, loading the rifle with stiff fingers.

"Great. Thank you.'' She hung up and eyed her grandmother, who was now heading toward the back door. "Put the rifle down, Gran. Someone's on the way. Besides, I think Lisa's gone.''

Gert peeked out the kitchen window. "I don't see her. Check and see if the car's still out front.''

It was. Kate saw Lisa sitting on the steps, her head on her knees and her shoulders shaking. She didn't know why she felt sorry for the woman, but Kate opened the front door and went over to her. She didn't dare look up at the front bedroom window, because she knew she'd see her grandmother's rifle. Kate didn't know whether to laugh or cry.

"Lisa?"

She didn't lift her head. "Go away," she mumbled, or at least that's what Kate thought she said.

"You don't have custody of Danny, do you," Kate said, sitting beside her on the wide step.

"No. I'm a lousy mother."

Candid, too. "So why are you here?"

"I just wanted to tell him I was sorry for everything. I'm going to California," she said, raising her head to look at Kate. "A friend there's gonna give me a job in his bar." She sniffed and wiped her face with the edge of her shirt. "I'm sorry I lost my temper. I do that sometimes and it gets me in trouble."

"My grandmother called the sheriff, Lisa. You scared us."

"I just wanted to see my kid."

"He's afraid of you, especially after all that yelling." Kate thought for a moment. "Would you like to write him a note? I'll see that he gets it."

"That'd probably be better, I guess."

"I'll be right back." Kate went inside and grabbed a legal pad and a pen from Gert's desk, then hurried back outside. She handed them to Lisa and then returned to the house to assure Danny and Gert that everything was okay. Danny was under her bed and didn't want to come out, so Kate left him there while she convinced Gert to unload the rifle.

Three minutes later she went back outside to find Lisa waiting by her car and the notepad and pen on the front steps.

"Thanks," Lisa said, pulling her hair back into a ponytail and securing it with a leather strip. "Tell Danny I won't be back."

"I will."

"Dusty will be really pissed when he finds out I was here. Can you explain it to him?" She opened the car door and slid in behind the wheel.

"Sure. If you explain something to me." Lisa nodded. "You weren't pregnant with Dustin's baby nine summers ago, were you?"

Lisa's eyebrows rose. "Not me. I had the hots for Darrell, his older brother. We got married." She grimaced. "What a mistake that was. When we weren't trying to drink ourselves to death, we were doing coke."

"And what about Danny?"

"When we got arrested, that's when Dusty found out what was going on and took Danny. He's not a bad kid, but when you're a junkie, having a kid around is a real pain in the ass." With that, she turned the key in the ignition and Kate backed away and let her leave.

When Kate looked back at the house, sure enough, Gert still had the rifle in the window. Sheriff Jess Sheridan, arriving five minutes later, turned out to be the only person who could get Gert to put down the gun once and for all.

"WHAT DO YOU WANT to do?"

"I dunno."

Kate lay on her stomach beside Danny underneath the iron bed that used to belong to her mother. The boy stretched out beside her, his chin resting on his folded arms. She wished she knew the magic words that would comfort him. He'd been under the bed for an hour, even after being reassured that his mother had gone away for good. "Want to go for a walk?"

"Nope."

She slid the plate of cookies closer to him. "Help yourself." The boy hesitated, then reached out to take one.

"I'm glad I cleaned under here," Kate said, hoping to make him smile. "Otherwise you'd be eating dust bunnies."

He didn't smile, but at least he still had his appetite. "When's my dad coming home?"

"Tonight. After supper, I would think." She'd thought about having the sheriff find him at the auction, but maybe this way was better, with Danny having a chance to calm down and the three of them going on with their afternoon as they'd planned.

"You still making ice cream?"

"*We're* still making ice cream," she said.

"When?"

"When we get out from under the bed."

Danny sighed and closed his eyes. "Not yet, okay?"

"Okay." Kate was more than willing to wait until the little boy wasn't afraid anymore. And oddly enough, lying on the floor under the bed, a curtain of white chenille fringe surrounding them, made a good place to think.

So Dustin had been lying to her all along. Well, maybe he'd never come right out and said it, but he certainly hadn't explained that he was the child's uncle. He'd let her think he got Lisa pregnant. But why? Because that was an easy way to break up with her so many years ago? An easy way to get rid of the gawky girl who thought he was her first love?

Kate looked over at Danny, who had fallen asleep with a half-eaten cookie in his hand. She wanted to smooth the hair from his face, but was afraid she'd disturb him. He was a sweet boy who needed a mother. Maybe that's what Dustin wanted this time, a mother for the boy and—as a bonus— his own ranch. Not bad for a man who never had much of anything of his own.

She wanted to be angry, but she felt more like crying. *Loves of Our Lives* was simple compared to the goings-on in Beauville. She'd return her boss's phone calls later on. She'd book herself a seat on the first flight to New York Saturday and from now on she'd never look back. Gran would finish her book; Mom could have her mysterious nervous breakdowns, her real estate developer and her new apartment; Jake would have more babies; Emily would have her tubes tied; and life would go on.

Kate didn't think she'd be taking many more vacations in Texas.

CHAPTER TWENTY

DUSTIN ARRIVED BACK at the ranch feeling pretty good about the heifers he'd bought. Gert was going to like the price, too.

"Hello?" he called at the back door, but there was no answer and the door was locked. Good thing the animals weren't going to be delivered until Saturday, or he'd be herding cows all by himself tonight.

There was a note tacked on the bunkhouse, informing Dustin that the women and Danny had taken food over to Jake and Elizabeth's ranch and would be back later, before dark. He would clean up and get some paperwork done before they returned.

He was pleased with the way the afternoon went. Danny was going to get a large pony named Boomer, outgrown by his previous owner. Kate was going to get a marriage proposal. And poor Martha McIntosh was going to get a cowboy for a son-in-law, if Dustin was lucky.

And he felt pretty damn lucky.

"YOU'RE LUCKY SHE didn't hurt you," Gran said, still fuming over Lisa's invasion of the home place. She waved goodbye to Danny, who had paused at the door of the bunkhouse as Dustin held the door open for him to go inside.

"I told you, I felt sorry for her," Kate said, turning the car around. The headlights swept across the windows she knew were part of Dustin's bedroom. She wouldn't be spending any more time in that room.

"Better she should have seen my gun."

"Gran, for heaven's sake. You've got to get rid of that thing. At least get it out of the closet and put it in the attic."

"I keep the bullets locked up," she muttered. "But all right, you can put the rifle away. I guess you'll know where it is when you need it."

It would have been a good time to tell her she wasn't staying, but Kate figured her grandmother could wait another day to be disappointed. She hadn't come up with the right way to tell her yet, either. Hopefully, after a long night thinking about this, she would think of the least painful way to leave.

"Jake's baby is beautiful," Kate said, hoping to change the subject. "She looks just like Elizabeth."

"She does," Gran agreed. "She's a good little

thing. Snuggled in my arms like she belonged there.''

"How does it feel to be a great-grandmother?"

"I'm glad I lived long enough to see it," she said. "Jake will be a good father."

"Yes." Her cousin was as devoted a husband and father as she'd ever seen. Jake had always been the steady one, the man everyone depended on in a crisis. The last man in the family.

"I didn't know Dustin was that little boy's uncle," Gran said, shaking her head. "But I knew something wasn't quite right."

"Why?" She parked the car and opened the door to illuminate the interior, then gathered up the empty casserole dishes.

"He'd never had a chocolate milk shake."

"What?"

"Never mind. It was just something that struck me as odd at the time. And he said those strange things about his family, remember?"

"Yes." And Dustin hadn't explained. Not a word. He'd let her go on thinking he'd made Lisa pregnant, let her go on assuming that he had married and divorced the woman, that he had a son. He hadn't been honest. Again. And she supposed that's what hurt the most. He'd let her into his bed but not into his life.

It was exactly what happened nine years ago.

"Kate?"

"Oh, sorry," she said, and hurried over to help Gran out of the car. "I guess I'm tired."

"I guess we both are," Gran said, "but your cowboy is heading our way, so you'd better perk up. He's going to want to know what happened here today."

"Danny must have told him."

"You're going to give him the letter?"

Kate nodded and helped her grandmother cross the gravel drive and negotiate the path to the kitchen door. "He can decide what to do with it."

"He's not going to like any of this," Gran warned.

"I don't either," Kate said and braced herself.

"Danny told me Lisa was here," Dustin said, following them into the kitchen. "I can't stay long," he added, with a glance toward Kate, "but I wanted to thank both of you for taking care of him this afternoon. I'm really sorry she scared you. She has a mean temper when she gets going."

"We wouldn't let anything happen to that boy. And we were fine, didn't even need the sheriff," Gert said, patting his arm. "I'm off to bed. Come over in the morning and tell me all about our new cattle. I assume you bought some?"

"I sure did," Dustin said, standing close to Kate. She moved away from him. "Good night, Gert."

"Good night, Dustin. That boy of yours did just

fine," she said, before she left the room and headed for her bedroom.

"What a mess," he said, turning to Kate. "I'm really sorry you had to deal with it."

"Lisa wrote a letter to Danny." Kate moved away and reached on top of the refrigerator for the legal pad. "Here. I suggested she write to him instead of trying to talk to him, so I hope you don't mind."

He took the pad and glanced at the brief note. "Fair enough. Danny said she's going away?"

"Yes." She took a deep breath. "We both are."

His eyes narrowed. "You want to explain that?"

"Not necessarily. I don't think you've wanted to explain things to me either. Not about Danny's father and mother. Not about who he really was, or who you really are. So I guess we're even." She managed to keep her voice from trembling.

"Just like that," he said. "You're going back to New York?"

"Yes. I'm flying out first thing Saturday." She looked away, hoping that he wouldn't see how much she was hurt. "Gran will sell you the ranch, I'm sure."

"Yeah." She could hear the anger in his voice. "When you decide to leave, you don't waste a hell of a lot of time, do you?"

She didn't know how to answer, but then again, she didn't think he expected her to say anything.

"I should have learned the first time," he muttered and walked out the door.

"Me, too," Kate said, and this time she let herself cry.

"THIS IS ALL WRONG." Gert rearranged her papers again, then poured herself another cup of coffee to take back to her chair. "I don't like this a bit, young lady." She didn't understand young people. How foolish could they be? Didn't they know how quickly time passed?

"I'm sorry, Gran." Kate finished washing the breakfast dishes and dried her hands. "But I have to leave."

"Nonsense. You and that young man can patch things up." Kate didn't fool her grandmother. The girl wasn't leaving because of her fancy job. Why, she'd only returned a couple of the dozen or so phone calls she'd gotten from New York. And she'd stopped watching the show on TV after the first couple of days.

"I don't think so."

"Where's the boy this morning?"

"George Bennett picked him up. He's taking the boys fishing for the day. I guess John's gotten tired of having a new sister."

"Sounds nice," Gert said. "Means Dustin's free to talk some sense into you." She leaned forward to look out the window. "Oh, dear. Here comes your mother with that Jackson fella. I sure hope she isn't having one of her fits.''

''Me, too.'' Kate stepped into the living room and eyed the piles of paper. ''What decade are you in? I'm going into Marysville today to buy you your own laptop and printer so you can take your time finishing the book.''

''Aw, hon, that's real nice, but—'' She looked out the window again. ''They're raisin' a lot of dust, and the sheriff is right behind them. Do you think it's one of them high-speed chases like they have in California?''

Kate hurried over to the window. ''Is that *Jake*'s truck?''

''It's a regular parade,'' Gert declared, hauling herself out of her chair. There was no reason getting upset until there was something to get upset over. ''I'd better make a fresh pot of coffee. Looks like we're getting company.''

Before she fixed the coffeepot, she hung the red rag in the back window to summon her foreman. She might need some help and Kate might need a man. A woman never knew when one would come in handy.

''REMEMBER HOW I told you there was a dead body in the drive-in?'' Martha wrung her hands and looked at everyone gathered around her mother's kitchen table, except for Dustin Jones, who leaned against a wall and looked like he'd rather be anywhere else but inside this house. That nice sheriff thanked Kate for his coffee and acted like he was here on a social call, but Martha knew different. She'd be arrested by noon and all hell would break loose. Her picture would make the front page of the next issue of the *Beauville Times* and it would be all grainy and make her look twenty years older and thirty pounds heavier.

"Mom," Kate said, reaching out to take one of her hands, "are you sure you—"

"I'm sure," Martha said, giving Kate's fingers a little squeeze before she took her hand away. "Carl's offered to dig it—him—up. If I want him to. But he has to do it soon or miss his window of opportunity."

"Dig *who* up, Martha?" her mother asked. Martha couldn't look at her mother. This really wasn't going to be a very good morning.

"Excuse me," that nice Sheriff Sheridan interjected. He gave her a kind smile. "Why don't we make this an unofficial conversation? You could say something like, 'what if?' and we could all assume you were just asking for information and not making an actual confession."

Carl nodded. "That's a good idea, Martha. Start over again."

"Okay." She took a deep breath and looked at the sheriff. "What if I—I mean, *someone*—helped someone else bury a dead person so no one would know he'd been killed?''

Jess Sheridan looked thoughtful. ''I guess that would depend on the circumstances.''

''Mother, what about calling a lawyer?''

Martha shook her head. ''*What if* someone had a best friend—'' She glanced at her nephew, who stared at her as if he'd never seen her before. ''A best friend,'' she repeated, ''whose husband couldn't hold his liquor.'' She heard her mother's quick intake of breath but didn't dare look in her direction. ''And he beat her. A lot. And when he found out she was pregnant he threatened to kill her.''

Kate handed her a tissue, so Martha wiped her eyes. She hadn't wanted to cry, but the whole thing was really getting to be too upsetting.

''Oh, Lord,'' she heard Gert mutter.

''*What if,* uh, this person hit her husband with a frying pan, one of those cast-iron pans?'' Everyone nodded. They knew cast iron. ''Accidentally, of course,'' she added.

''Of course,'' Kate agreed.

''As in self-defense,'' the sheriff said.

''Yes, that's it.'' She blew her nose. ''Then, *what if* that person called her very best friend and asked for help and they didn't know what to do because they were pretty young and one was pregnant and they were both very scared and neither one wanted the baby to be born in jail—'' Here, at this part, she couldn't help looking at Jake, hoping he would understand.

"Go on, Aunt Martha," he told her. "It'll be all right."

"Mrs. McIntosh," Jess said, his voice low and very casual, "let me ask you this. If someone was going to get rid of someone's friend's husband's body, where would someone put it?"

"Maybe in an old well on someone's great-great-grandfather's ranch that became a drive-in."

"And where is the best friend now, the one that was pregnant?"

"She died in 1982."

"And the alcoholic abusive husband who was killed accidentally in self-defense, what year was that?"

Martha opened her mouth to speak, but it was Gert who answered. "I would imagine that was March of '65, Sheriff. And the only one who might have missed him was his mother."

"And his son?" Jake had gone very, very pale.

Martha's heart ached for him, but she didn't know what else to say to make him feel better. "No," Martha said. "His son was better off without him."

Gert eyed the sheriff. "Well, I guess you've heard quite a story today."

"Is this going in your book, Gert?" He stood

and slid his chair into place, then put on his Stetson.

"No. Is it going in yours?"

Martha held her breath when he looked at her.

"Well, let me put it this way. If someone found a body, I'd have to investigate. It probably would be real hard to figure out what happened though, considering how that, uh, incident occurred in 1965." He cleared his throat and turned to Gert. "If someone wanted to leave well enough alone, maybe fill in that well, then that'd be the end of it. All I heard here this morning was some unofficial conversation."

"Thank you," Martha said. If Gert and Jake understood, she would probably be able to sleep tonight—unless Carl insisted on staying over again. "I thought you'd arrest me."

He smiled and headed toward the door, but stopped to pat her on the shoulder. "No, ma'am. Not unless you insist."

"IS THERE ANYTHING else you'd like to tell us, Martha?" Gert certainly hoped there wasn't. She'd always known, deep in her heart, that her only son, Hank, had come to a bad end. And she could admit that it was a relief to find out he hadn't taken anyone else with him. She'd always been afraid he'd died driving drunk, with innocent victims dead on the road because of it.

"Well," Martha said, fidgeting with her hands again.

"Mother?" Kate had gone pale. "You mean there's *more?*"

"Your grandmother started it," Martha protested, "with all this talk of history and town secrets and buried treasure. What was I supposed to do? Wait for Hank to get dug up?"

"Please," Jake said, briefly closing his eyes. "My mother never said much about my father, but—"

"He wasn't your father," Martha said.

Jake frowned. "If he wasn't my father, then who was?"

"You really don't know?"

"Aunt Martha, if I knew I wouldn't be sitting here asking."

"Ah," Gert sighed. "Of course."

Kate looked at her. "Of course what?"

Gert smiled at her grandson, who technically wasn't her grandson at all. "You can't guess?"

Jake shook his head. "Not R.J."

"Yes," Martha said. "He and your mother were very much in love. He would have married her, but she didn't think it was proper for a man as wealthy as R. J. Calhoun to marry his housekeeper. She was old-fashioned that way."

"And he left you his mother's ranch," Gert said. "Now it all makes sense."

Carl cleared his throat. "May I say something?"

Since he hadn't spoken since he'd arrived, Gert figured it was only fair he get a word in now.

"Go ahead," she told him.

"It's about the well, and the, uh, body," he said, with a quick glance at Gert. "What do you all want me to do? I halted construction this morning—told the men I had to get another permit—but I'm gonna have to start up again sooner or later and I have to know what to do about that well."

Gert noticed that Dustin was trying to sidle toward the back door. She wasn't going to let him stand by and let Kate leave without a fight, especially not now. "Dustin?"

"Yes, ma'am?"

"We're all going to the Good Night Drive-In. You and Kate are going to take me in the Lincoln."

Neither one of them protested, which was a darn good thing, too, because Gert had had enough aggravation for one morning.

"GET OUT," KATE SAID. "Now."

Dustin made no move to get out of the car. He rested one wrist on the steering wheel and acted as if he had all the time in the world to sit there and look at her. "That sounds familiar. *Get out.* That's what you told me that night I came to pick you up to go to the movies. *Get out,* you said. Just like that.''

''You could have told me the rumors about you and Lisa weren't true.'' She looked out the side window and prayed that her grandmother would return soon. Jake, Gran and Mom were huddled in the distance, where Kate assumed the well was— where Uncle Hank was. Gert had ordered her and Dustin to stay put and keep anyone from snooping around.

Not that there would be anyone snooping around, not at noon in the summer, in the middle of an empty construction site.

''If I'd had any idea what you were talking about,'' Dustin said, which made Kate turn to look at him again.

''You *had* to know,'' she said.

He shrugged. ''I didn't even live at home that summer. I worked out at the Dead Horse six days a week, from dawn 'til dinnertime. I only came into town to see you.'' He paused. ''You never even asked me if it was true, Kate. You just believed that I'd gotten someone pregnant instead of believing that I loved you too much to do something like that.''

''You never said you loved me. You said 'no strings,' and 'we'll just have fun.'''

''I lied.''

She held his gaze with her own. "You seem to be good at it."

"I was going to tell you about Danny," he said, having the decency to look guilty. "I guess at first I thought you didn't deserve the truth. And later on there never seemed to be the right time to go into the whole story." He smiled. "Making love got in the way."

She wished he hadn't reminded her of that. "I loved you, too, a long time ago."

"And now?" He reached over and took her hand.

"No."

"Now who's lying?"

Kate shook her head. "It's not going to work, Dustin. You know it's not."

"You're running away again, Katie," he said, planting a kiss in her palm. "You ran away from me. Why?"

"I loved you. You didn't love me. Simple."

"And you ran away from town after your dad died."

She turned away and wished he would release her hand. She should go check on her mother and her grandmother. And she bet Jake could use a hug right now. What on earth could they be talking about for such a long time?

"Kate?"

"What?"

"Stay and love me." He tugged her across the wide seat of the Lincoln and against that hard wide chest. "I've been waiting for you to come back for nine years."

"Liar," she whispered, but she smiled against his chest.

"It's true." Dustin lifted her away from him and looked down into her eyes. "I want to marry you, even though your grandmother thinks she's going to be famous and your mother helped bury a dead body and my son likes you more than he does me—"

"That's not true. He worships the ground you walk on."

"Yeah?"

She nodded. "He told me that his other daddy hit him all the time, but you just make a frowny face."

"And that's a good thing?"

"Definitely. And my grandmother is actually writing a very good book."

"I'll believe it when I see it," he said, and with one easy motion lifted her over the seat and into the back. He climbed over the leather upholstery to join her as she scrambled to sit up.

"What are you doing? There are people around. They'll be back any—"

He kissed her then, his hands holding her face to his, until she melted against him. Habit, she thought. Making love in cars was a very dangerous habit.

"Marry me," he said, lifting his mouth a fraction of an inch. "We'll conceive our first child in the back seat of any vehicle you choose."

"Second child," she reminded him. "Danny's the first."

"That's a 'yes?'"

"Uh-huh," she said, wrapping her arms around his neck. "You get me, the ranch, my mother and my grandmother. What do I get?"

The damn cowboy grinned. "Take your jeans off and I'll show you."

Kate looked out the window. "Too late. Here they come. Hurry up, get back in the front seat."

He grabbed her wrist as she started to straddle the front seat. "Are you going to marry me or not?"

"Kate!" Martha's voice carried across the wind. "What on earth are you doing?"

"Discussing my honeymoon," she shouted, and saw her mother's mouth fall open. Gran waved and Jake gave her a "thumb's up" sign.

Gran came over to the car. "You two stay there and work things out. Martha and I will get a ride home with Jake." She winked. "Take your time. I've got a lot of writing to do this afternoon and Martha's going to help me with the 1980s."

"Okay." Kate tumbled into the back seat again.

"Now," she said, moving toward her new fiancé, "you were going to show me something?"

He chuckled, his mouth against hers, as they tumbled backward. Kate landed on top of him, which was a very satisfactory place to be.

"Do you think it's right to leave them here like this?" Kate heard her mother complain. Jake chuckled.

"Martha," Gert snapped, "leave the children alone. We need a couple of cold beers and a box of tissues and a good long talk, so keep walking and mind your own business."

Dustin tilted his head to whisper in Kate's ear, "Isn't that the pot calling the kettle black?"

Kate laughed when she kissed him. It was so good to be home.

EPILOGUE

"TELL YOUR MOM I have big news," Martha announced, pleased that little Danny had answered the phone so promptly. That boy was growing up. She'd bet he'd shot up two inches this past year and a half since his father married Kate.

"Really, Grammy? *What* big news?"

"Grown-up stuff, Danny. Where's your mother?" Martha liked it that he called her "Grammy." She thought she'd mind at first, but she'd discovered she really liked the sound of that word. And with Kate seven-and-a-half months' pregnant, it was a good thing she'd gotten used to being a grandmother so quickly.

"Here," the boy said, and Martha heard the rustling of papers and her daughter's voice in the background.

"Mother? Hi. What's going on? I thought we were going to meet later on in—"

"We still are," Martha assured her. "If you're feeling up to it."

"I wouldn't miss it, you know that. What's this big news?"

"Jake and Elizabeth are expecting again," she announced. "Isn't that wonderful? Your babies will grow up together." Martha chatted a little bit more, pleased to have been the first one to tell Kate the news, but she didn't stay on the phone long. She'd been satisfied to hear her daughter's voice and know that she and the baby were doing all right.

You couldn't be too careful these days, Martha thought, looking out the window of her corner apartment. It was a nice place. Carl had seen to it that she had one of the larger units with a view of the back acreage. He'd sulked a little bit when she'd refused to marry him—he'd sure wanted to move in to the house on Apple Street—but he'd accepted her decision to sell the house to Emily. She and George and their growing family could use the space.

Martha had grown tired of cleaning all those rooms. Her spacious one-bedroom villa, with its panoramic views and ivory wall-to-wall carpet suited her just fine. Living alone suited her just fine, too, but sometimes she let Carl spend the night. Just for fun.

She glanced at her watch. Mother would be waiting for her. And Mother didn't like to be kept waiting these days.

"How many days?" Danny asked, watching Kate take another batch of sugar cookies out of the oven.

"Until Christmas? Nineteen," she replied, accustomed to the question Danny asked daily. "In nineteen days we'll open presents Christmas morning, with Grandma Gert and Grammy, right here in our house."

"Our house," he whispered, smiling up at her with such joy that Kate immediately choked up. She felt that way often these days, as the baby grew bigger and the boy more affectionate and her husband more protective. She managed to slide each cookie off the tray and onto a cooling rack before Dustin came downstairs and entered the kitchen.

"Are we ready?" He tousled Danny's hair and gave Kate a hug. "Mmm," he said. "You smell like vanilla."

"Mom's makin' sugar cookies," Danny said, "for the party at school. We're gonna decorate them tomorrow."

Dustin's arms tightened around her and he rested his chin on the top of her head. "You okay?"

"Never better," she managed to say, though her husband looked down and his gaze softened at the tears she was trying so hard to hide. "We're going to be late."

"Gert will wait for us," Dustin said.

"I'm not so sure. She's a big star now." Kate shifted sideways so she could snuggle closer to her husband. She couldn't imagine living anywhere but on the ranch. She never missed her life in New York; instead, she submitted story concepts, via e-mail, to her boss. Two had been accepted this fall, meaning she and Dustin would be able to start on the new horse barn, and Danny's college account had begun. But she was happy letting Gran take the stage as the writer in the family. "Gran loves the attention."

"As long as she doesn't get too big for Beauville," he said.

"Please don't say the words 'too big' around a very pregnant woman," Kate told him, and hugged her husband even tighter. "Or I'll never get in the back seat of a car with you again."

THE MEMBERS OF THE newly formed Beauville Book Club gathered together for the December meeting in the Good Night Villas' library. It was actually the southwest meeting room, but the members of the book club liked to refer to it as the library on the days they met.

Gert fiddled with her notes.

So far she'd taken all this hoopla in stride, selling her book to a Texas publishing house, moving to the Villas and even signing a television deal with The History Channel.

But speaking in front of all these gabbing women, women who couldn't sit still for more than fifteen minutes without having an opinion, was something else all together. So Gert gripped her notes and walked over to the window that overlooked the west end of the Villas' property.

After the well had been filled in, she and Martha had covered the top with some pretty flowers. Gert liked being close to Hank this way. At least she knew he was safe and she felt better knowing where he was buried.

Gert liked looking after him.

Irene Bennett called the meeting to order as Kate, Dustin and Danny slipped into seats in the back. Jake and Elizabeth, bless them, were in the second row. They must have gotten a sitter for little Nancy, which was a good idea. Gert didn't know if she could talk loud enough to compete with that happy little girl of theirs.

Martha waved to her, gesturing that it was time for her mother to go to the podium. She'd finished stacking the copies of *A Woman Remembers* on a nearby folding table. Irene was pretty long-winded, though, so Gert didn't rush. No one could make a ninety-one-year-old woman hurry across a room, no matter how loud the applause.

"Thank you," she told her audience. "I'm real pleased to have my books here. And I'm real pleased to see my family." She took a deep breath and read from the notes she'd tucked inside a copy of her book.

"From the Comanche raids of 1850, to the Civil War and later, when the railroad came, my family was here. Here fighting to survive and prosper, to raise their children and build a town. Somehow they managed to survive, despite all the hardships thrown their way." Gert paused and looked for the faces of her own family. *My, my, this might be fun after all,* she thought. She opened her book and turned to page one. Holding one gnarled finger on the page, she cleared her throat and then began to read, "I blame it all on Texas..."

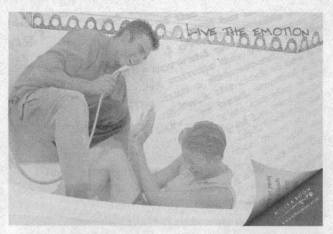

Blaze™

...scorching hot sexy reads

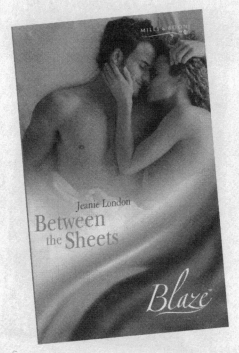

Jeanie London
Between the Sheets

Blaze™

2 brand-new titles each month

*Available on subscription with 2 brand-new
Sensual Romance*™ *novels every month
from the Reader Service*™

Historical
romance™

...rich, vivid and passionate

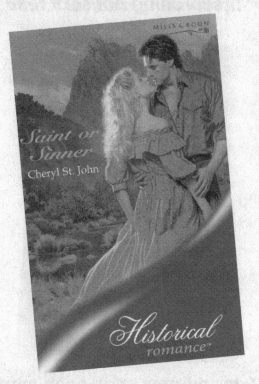

4 brand-new titles each month

Available on subscription every month from the Reader Service™

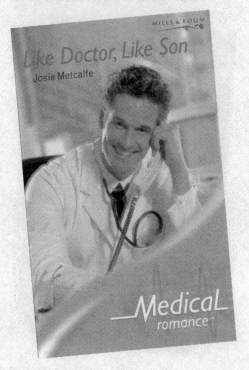

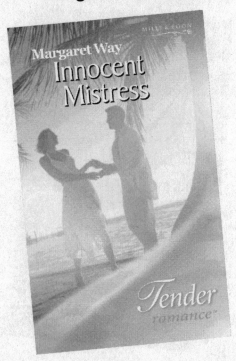

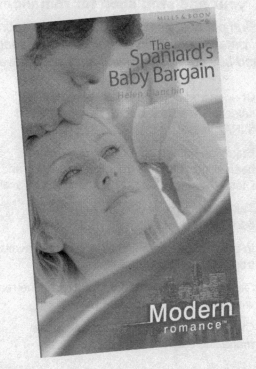